The Curious Casebook of Inspector Hanshichi

This book has been selected by the Japanese Literature Publishing Project (JLPP), which is run by the Japanese Literature Publishing and Promotion Center (J-Lit Center) on behalf of the Agency for Cultural Affairs of Japan.

THE CURIOUS CASEBOOK OF INSPECTOR HANSHICHI

Detective Stories of Old Edo

Okamoto Kidō

Ian MacDonald, translator

University of Hawai'i Press HAWAI Honolulu

Original title: *Hanshichi torimonochō,*
by Kidō Okamoto
Published in Japanese by Kobunsha, Tokyo

English translation © 2007 Ian MacDonald
Printed in the United States of America
12 11 10 09 08 07   6 5 4 3 2 1

Library of Congress Cataloging-in-Publication Data
Okamoto, Kidō, 1872–1949.
[Hanshichi torimonocho. English. Selections]
The curious casebook of Inspector Hanshichi : detective stories
of old Edo / Okamoto Kidō ; Ian MacDonald, translator.
p. cm.
Includes bibliographical references and index.
ISBN-13: 978-0-8248-3053-3 (hardcover : alk. paper)
ISBN-13: 978-0-8248-3100-4 (pbk. : alk. paper)
I. MacDonald, Ian. II. Title.
PL813.K3H36213 2007
895.6'344—dc22   2006028182

University of Hawai'i Press books are printed on acid-
free paper and meet the guidelines for permanence
and durability of the Council on Library Resources.

Designed by April Leidig-Higgins

Printed by The Maple-Vail Book
Manufacturing Group

In memory of my father,
William McCullough MacDonald,
who loved a good detective story

Contents

Acknowledgments

First and foremost I wish to thank the Japanese Agency for Cultural Affairs, without whose generous financial support, through the Japanese Literature Publishing Project, I could not have undertaken this translation. Equal thanks must be accorded the dedicated staff of both the Japanese Literature Publishing and Promotion Center and the Japanese Association for Cultural Exchange, without whose skillful stewardship the completed translation would not have been published. In particular, I would like to acknowledge the invaluable assistance of Moriyasu Machiko, who proofread the first draft and pointed out numerous errors, and of Hoshino Kiyo, who expertly managed the logistical and contractual arrangements. In addition, John Bester — as accomplished a translator as I could ever hope to be — extensively edited the final draft; his knowledgeable and insightful comments helped me to improve the translation significantly.

I also wish to acknowledge the support of my dissertation adviser in the Department of Asian Languages at Stanford University, Jim Reichert, who guided my Ph.D. research in Edo literature — which inspired me to translate *Hanshichi* — and then graciously allowed me to take a year off to work on it.

On a personal note, I wish to thank my friends David Gundry, Peter Maradudin, Jennifer Miller, Chris Scott, and Daniel Sullivan, who collectively read all of the stories and offered many helpful suggestions. The ultimate debt of gratitude goes to my wife, Sujatha Meegama, who was forced to endure countless tedious soliloquies about the trials and tribulations of translation but nevertheless proffered helpful and encouraging feedback, always lending an enthusiastic ear to my readings of Hanshichi's adventures.

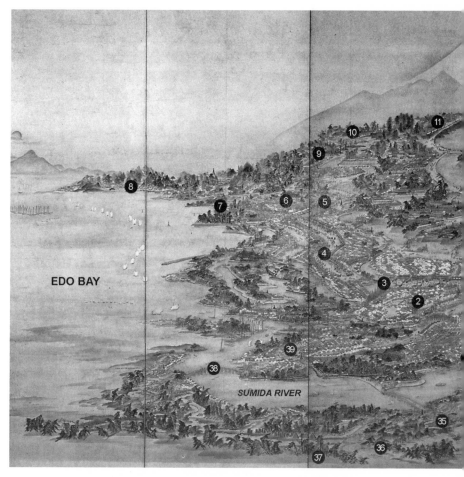

EDO BAY

SUMIDA RIVER

Map of Old Edo

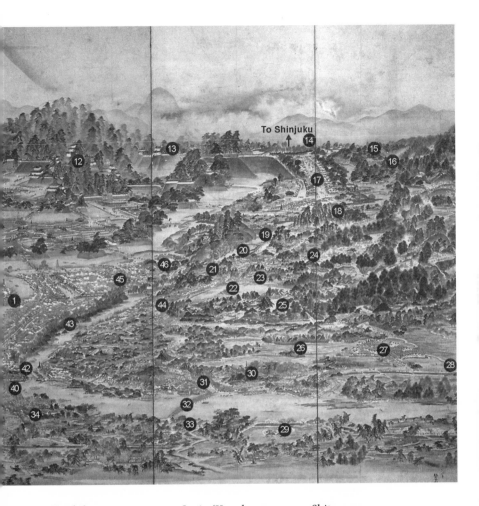

To Shinjuku

Introduction

The *Curious Casebook of Inspector Hanshichi (Hanshichi torimonochō)* must certainly be one of the last great, and beloved, works of early-twentieth-century popular Japanese fiction to find its way into English translation. This fact, however, in no way reflects any neglect of the work in Japan, where today, nine decades after the first stories in the series were published, it remains in print — in multiple editions, both hardcover and paperback, no less. *Hanshichi* is that rare example of Japanese detective fiction that provides both a view of life in feudal Japan from the perspective of the period between the First and Second World Wars and an insight into the development of the fledging Japanese crime novel.

Although it is a product of the early period of Japanese modernism — when writers such as Akutagawa, Tanizaki, and Kawabata began experimenting with psychological realism — *Hanshichi* does not seek to challenge literary conventions. Instead it aims to entertain and thrill its readers with well-crafted prose, realistic dialogue, and compelling plots, enabling them to escape into a world both strange and familiar. Strange, in that the customs of mid-nineteenth century Japan must have seemed antiquated, even quaint, to readers of the late 1910s and early 1920s. Familiar, in that *Hanshichi* was not an imitation of Western fiction — as was much crime writing of the time — but boasted characters and settings uniquely Japanese. In short, it is a work widely read in Japan that is crucial to our understanding of the Japanese during their nation's ascendancy to the ranks of world powers, and of their aspirations toward a literature that steps outside the shadow of the West to stand on its own.

The Restoration

In November 1867, Tokugawa Yoshinobu, the last shogun, reluctantly ceded sovereignty to the young emperor Mutsuhito (later to be known by his reign name, Meiji), bringing to an end nearly three hundred years of Tokugawa dominion over Japan. In April of the following year, pro-imperial armies marched into Edo, the shogun's capital, and defeated the last holdouts of the ancien régime. This relatively bloodless, if not entirely peaceful, transfer of power known as the "Restoration" *(ishin)* replaced the autocratic shogunate with a constitutional monarchy that, over the next thirty years, instituted a series of democratic reforms. To make the transfer of power complete, the new government took the symbolic step of renaming Edo "Tokyo"—the "eastern capital"—in July 1868 and, two months later, changing the era name from Keiō to Meiji, meaning "enlightened rule." Finally, in the spring of 1869, the emperor abandoned his palace in Kyoto, the imperial seat for over a thousand years, and moved to Tokyo to take up residence in the castle of the deposed shogun.

As these events were unfolding, a samurai by the name of Okamoto Keinosuke fled Edo to nearby Yokohama, hiding out in the foreign concession there for some time. The eldest son of a minor samurai family from northern Japan, Keinosuke, like many samurai from outside Japan's political and geographic center, had been a member of the pro-Tokugawa faction (or *sabakuha*) during the waning days of the shogunate. As a shogunal loyalist, his fortunes were upset by the Restoration; but in the end he proved to be luckier than the vast majority of samurai under the new Meiji government: he managed to secure a job at the British legation in Tokyo, remaining faithfully employed there until his death in 1902.

Keisuke had a son, Keiji, who under the Japanese lunar calendar was born on the fifteenth day of the tenth month of 1872. Seven weeks later, Japan officially adopted the Western solar calendar, jumping ahead one month to January 1, 1873. Due to the traditional practice of counting children as aged one at birth and adding another year to their age each New Year's Day, the infant Keiji turned two on the day the new calendar was adopted. Much later, writing under the pen name Okamoto Kidō, Keiji assigned no small significance to the timing of his birth. The change in the calendar was symbolic of the many social and political changes taking place as Kidō was growing up,[1] even becoming a minor theme in his later work: Kidō's fictional hero, Inspector Hanshichi — an old man in the 1890s when the narration of the series is set — represents many Japanese at the turn of the century who had not entirely adjusted to the changes of two to three decades earlier. Hanshichi (who in the stories shares the same birthday as Kidō, October 15) still thinks of the seasons and the weather in terms of the old lunar calendar, wherein New Year's fell sometime in late winter (as does the Chinese New Year today). Unable to adjust completely, he feels himself somewhat out of tune with the modern world. Likewise, many traditional customs and practices persisted in Japan amid the onslaught of modernity. Western democracy and industry were embraced as more "advanced" and "enlightened" than Japanese institutions, but the feudal order proved surprisingly durable.

Kidō's coming-of-age in the early years of Meiji also sheds light on his efforts to adapt Western artistic forms to Japanese tastes. The trajectory of his career illustrates the difficulties many Japanese experienced in adapting to the new social order, as well as the opportunities it afforded. His father arranged to have Kidō tutored by members of the British legation, and by all accounts he acquired an excellent command of English. In his youth the family seems to have been comfortably off, so much so that the talented boy met with no resistance when he announced his intention of pursuing a career as a kabuki playwright. But all that changed when Kidō was sixteen and his family was bankrupted by his father's guarantee of a loan for a friend whose business collapsed. During the three years it took for his family to disentangle itself from the ensuing legal morass and restore its assets,

Kidō was forced to forgo a university education. He was instead apprenticed to a newspaper at the tender age of eighteen. In this, he was typical of the literati of his generation, many of them former samurai who earned their living by the pen rather than the sword. As a journalist, Kidō pursued a career that had not even existed prior to 1868, one that enabled him to witness at first hand the changes that were literally transforming the fabric of the old city around him and, as a correspondent during the Sino-Japanese war of 1894–1895, to observe Japan's increasing role in the outside world.

The early years of Kidō's literary career were spent working full-time editing newspaper copy and writing theater reviews. His spare hours were devoted to penning historical fiction adapted from Western literature and plays that were occasionally published but never performed. His first breakthrough came with his 1909 play *Shuzenji monogatari* (Tale of Shuzenji), a historical drama set in the early thirteenth century about an imagined romance between the deposed shogun Minamoto Yoriie and the daughter of a mask carver. First staged in 1911 at the Meijiza Theater, with the great Sadanji playing the lead, *Shuzenji* today remains Kidō's best-known work apart from the *Hanshichi* series and is still occasionally performed. Propelled by this success, Kidō became active in writing, producing, and even performing in dozens of plays annually throughout the 1910s, enabling him to give up journalism once and for all. By the late 1920s he had even garnered an international reputation as *Shuzenji* and other of his works were translated into English and various European languages.

And yet, for a man who by his own account had set his heart on becoming a kabuki playwright at the age of fifteen, it is ironic that Kidō should be remembered principally as the author of a series of short popular fiction rather than for his dramatic oeuvre. He attempted to merge the two in 1926 by adapting three *Hanshichi* stories for the stage (translated here as "The Death of Kampei," "The Dancer's Curse," and "The Room over the Bathhouse"), with Onoe Kikugorō VI (1885 – 1949) playing the starring role. Yet he seems to have done so more in response to popular demand (and perhaps financial incentive) than out of a genuine desire to see his famous detective spring to life from the printed page. In this regard, he perhaps felt much the same about his creation as Sir Arthur Conan Doyle did about Sherlock Holmes: when word got out in 1897 that Conan Doyle was writing a play featuring his legendary sleuth, he reportedly told his mother, "I have grave doubts about Holmes on the stage at all — it's drawing attention to my weaker work which has unduly obscured my better."[2] Like Conan Doyle, Kidō never repeated his experiment of dramatizing *Hanshichi*. Instead, he continued writing new *Hanshichi* episodes for magazine serialization while reserving his dramatic gifts for the tales of historical intrigue that were his true love.

The Serialization of Hanshichi, 1917 – 1937

In 1916, when Kidō began writing the first stories in the *Hanshichi* series at age forty-four, he had already secured his reputation as one of Japan's preeminent literary figures by virtue of his activities as a war correspondent in China, drama critic, author of short historical fiction, and playwright. Between June of that year and the following March, he completed the first seven stories that would be serialized monthly in the popular magazine *Bungei kurabu* (Literature club) starting in January 1917. The serialization, shortly followed by a book containing the first six stories, met with immediate acclaim, and Kidō resumed work on the series later the same year. By April 1918 he had brought the total number of stories to thirteen, eleven of which appear in the volume translated here.[3] Over the next two decades — until just two years before his death in February 1939 — Kidō would go on to write a total of sixty-nine stories featuring his master sleuth, Hanshichi, a police detective in mid-nineteenth-century Edo. Although Kidō is also recognized as a major figure in the so-called *Shin-kabuki* (New kabuki) theater movement, who is credited

— in collaboration with the actor Ichikawa Sadanji II (1880 – 1940) and other playwrights — with introducing modern, Western-influenced conventions into this best-loved of Japan's traditional dramatic forms, his most enduring literary legacy by far has proven to be Inspector Hanshichi, an icon of Japan's feudal past. While particular emphasis is always placed on the longevity of the *Hanshichi* series, it should be noted that most of the episodes were written in relatively brief spurts that, all told, account for less than half of its total twenty-year run. The period beginning with the publication of *Ofumi no tamashii* (translated here as "The Ghost of Ofumi") in January 1917 and lasting until 1920 — when *Hanshichi* appeared exclusively in *Literature Club* — saw the production of roughly half the stories. In the early to mid-1920s, a handful of the sleuth's adventures popped up in the pages of several other weekly and monthly periodicals. Then, in 1926, Kidō put *Hanshichi* on hiatus for the better part of a decade.[4] In his memoirs, he wrote: "The *[Hanshichi]* stories have piled up in large numbers without my quite realizing it. . . . Given that the author himself has already lost interest in them, I can't imagine that they are of interest any longer to readers."[5] Like Conan Doyle before him, however, Kidō was mistaken. In 1934 he resumed serialization of *Hanshichi*, this time in *Kōdan kurabu* (Storytelling club), which published all but one of the final twenty-three episodes[6] before Kidō's ill health finally put an end to the series in February 1937.

By any measure, Kidō's output was rapid and prolific — all the more so considering that he was simultaneously besieged with commissions for plays and other short fiction, not to mention plagued by frequent bouts of illness and various chronic medical complaints, exacerbated by overwork, that left him bedridden for weeks and often months at a time (these included anemia, rheumatism, stomach ulcers, flu, ear and sinus infections, and toothache so severe he eventually had all his upper teeth removed). While on the one hand Kidō's poor health undoubtedly curtailed his literary activities, on the other the time he spent recuperating from these afflictions — often at resort spas in scenic locales such as Hakone, the Izu peninsula, and central and northern Japan — evidently left him feeling refreshed, and sometimes even furnished him with new ideas for historical settings to use in future writing projects. It was on his trip to the hot spring town of Shuzenji in Izu, for example, that he conceived *Tale of Shuzenji*. During another of his extended illnesses, Kidō is said to have read *Edo meisho zue* (The illustrated famous sites of Edo) — a twenty-volume bestseller published between 1829 and 1836, depicting in words and pictures virtually every aspect of daily life in the shogun's capital — a work Kidō credited in part for having inspired him to create the world of Inspector Hanshichi.

A Tale of Two Cities

Hanshichi is set in two cities, Edo and Tokyo, occupying the same geographic space at different historical moments. The implicit contrast between past and present, accompanied by a palpable sense of nostalgia for what has been lost in the process of modernization and industrialization, is one of the series' defining features.

Some may conclude that Kidō's use of a traditional Japanese setting represents a rejection of the West and a retreat into a familiar, safer time; but it might as validly be argued that Edo itself would have seemed more "foreign" to Kidō's younger readers and was in fact more, not less, dangerous than the present. Kidō does not paint a rosy picture of Edo as belonging to some idealized golden age: his stories are about crimes and the often sad and tragic lives of the people affected by them. He does not stint on depicting the social ills of that era and those who preyed on the weak: unscrupulous slave traders, lecherous monks, shady con men, murderous *rōnin* (masterless samurai), greedy merchants, compulsive gamblers, to name but a few. Also described are the anonymous threats posed by fires, earthquakes, epidemics, social unrest, and financial instability, not to mention foreign "barbarians," faced by the denizens of Edo. In short, Kidō took a calculated risk in writing stories that swam against the rising tide of modernization. He did not set them in Edo so as to appeal more to his readers. On the contrary, he turned to the detective genre as a way of bringing the past to life.

When *Hanshichi* was launched in 1917, very few of Kidō's readers would have had firsthand knowledge of Edo in the 1840s to 1860s, the period when the adventures are set. As the series progressed and more and more of the old city vanished (most notably after the Great Earthquake of 1923), decreasing numbers of his readers could have recalled what Tokyo had been like in the time before Japan's overseas wars with China and Russia in 1894 and 1904, respectively. And by the time *Hanshichi* concluded in 1937, with the nation on the brink of world war, the majority of *Hanshichi* fans would have been born well after the death of the fictional sleuth.

Like the modern city that replaced it, Edo had consisted of two halves: the "high city" (*yamanote*) in the western foothills and the "low city" (*shitamachi*) in the flatlands near the bay and around the mouth of the Sumida River flowing into it from the north.

The high city consisted of the shogun's castle, set within extensive grounds and surrounded by inner (*uchibori*) and outer moats (*sotobori*). Between these moats lay the mansions of the *hatamoto*, the shogun's highest-ranking direct vassals, comprising the neighborhoods of Jimbōchō and Banchō (home today to Yasukuni Shrine) to the north and northwest, respectively, and Kasumigaseki, Nagatachō, and Kōjimachi to the south and southwest. The northern portion of the outer moat was formed by a man-made waterway known as the Edo River above where it flowed into the moat near Banchō from the north, and as the Kanda River from there until it emptied into the Sumida just above Ryōgoku Bridge. Beyond the outer moat lay more samurai residences in (starting from the north and moving counterclockwise) the areas of Hongō, Koishikawa, Ushigome, Ichigaya, Yotsuya, Akasaka, and Shiba. More government buildings and warehouses lay along the waterfront, and samurai residences also occupied the prime real estate along the banks of the Sumida.

The low city comprised only the narrow strip of land (much of it reclaimed from the bay) between the waterfront and the castle's outer moat, which was crisscrossed by a network of canals that spiraled outward from the castle toward the bay. Moving from south to north, it was home to the tightly packed plebian neighborhoods of Kyōbashi, Nihonbashi, Kanda, and Shitaya.

Over time, the low city slowly sprawled along its north–south axis toward Shiba in the south and Asakusa in the north, as open land was filled in and the upper classes abandoned their low-city residences in favor of the more fashionable and less flood- and fire-prone western suburbs. It also spilled eastward across the Sumida into the extensive marshlands of Honjo and Fukagawa. The heart of the old city was Nihonbashi, the "Bridge of Japan," spanning the busiest of Edo's canals, which served as the mercantile hub of the city and was home to large emporiums and wholesalers. But the bustling entertainment quarters of the city lay farther north, most notably around the three great public plazas known as *hirokōji,* or "broad alleyways." These were located in Ryōgoku, at the western approach to the bridge of the same name over the Sumida; in Asakusa, outside the Kaminarimon, or "Thunder Gate," of Sensōji Temple; and in Shitaya, south of Shinobazu Pond (of these three, only the last retains the *hirokōji* designation today, though it is now called Ueno Hirokōji). Just north of Asakusa lay the licensed quarter of the Yoshiwara, a small island of debauchery amid the green paddy fields of Iriya, destined, too, one day to be swallowed up by the expanding city.

The basic unit of the old low city was the *chō,* usually translated as "block," but in most cases a single main street lined by rows of one-story tenement houses *(nagaya)* to which access could be controlled at night by way of a gate at its entrance. It was commonly said that the low city was composed of "808 neighborhoods" *(happyaku hachi chō),* a term coined in the mid-1600s. In fact, it is estimated that by 1843 there were actually more than 1,700 *chō*. In terms of population, it is estimated that nearly 600,000 commoners lived in Edo at that time, occupying just 20 percent of the available land. Together the samurai and clergy numbered about the same, or perhaps even more, yet controlled the remaining 80 percent of the city. Kidō's hero Hanshichi was the consummate child of Edo, or *edokko*, born in 1823 just a stone's throw from the arched wooden bridge of Nihonbashi, the center from which all distances throughout Japan were measured. His father, we are told, had been employed in the most quintessential of all Edo trades, cotton wholesaling, a sober occupation that the young, fun-loving Hanshichi eschewed. But fortunately, the wayward young man fell under the stern but steady guidance of Kichigorō, a detective who chose him as both his son-in-law and his successor in law enforcement, a career that afforded some measure of upward social mobility if not the promise of great wealth. After Kichigorō's untimely death, Hanshichi took over his residence in Mikawachō in Kanda, a street bordering the plebian and samurai neighborhoods in the north of the city near the foot of Kudan Hill. From there, Hanshichi was well positioned to roam throughout the city on cases, his most frequent haunts being Shitaya, an area north of the Kanda River and south of Ueno's Shinobazu Pond, where his sister lived on a street below the Myōjin Shrine; Nihonbashi and Kyōbashi to the south (in the heart of today's Ginza); and Hatchōbori, east of Kyōbashi, home to his boss, Chief Inspector Makihara, and other top officials. At the end of a long and storied career, Hanshichi, like many men of good status and modest means, retired to Akasaka in the southwestern suburbs beyond Edo castle. It is there that he is living a comfortable existence—a widower, alone but for an old housekeeper, and supported by his grown son, a dealer of imported goods in Yokohama—when he first encounters the young narrator of the series.

By contrast, Kidō himself hailed from the high-city neighborhood of Kōjimachi west of the castle. It is here that the first story of the series, "The Ghost of Ofumi," opens in the 1880s, with the narrator, a boy of ten, paying a visit to an "uncle's" house in Banchō, located on a gloomy street bordered by former samurai estates left vacant in the tumultuous aftermath of the Meiji Restoration. The adventure the uncle recounts is set in 1864, when Hanshichi, aged forty-one, was in the prime of his career. The sleuth, however, does not make an appearance until halfway through the story, when he swoops down in true deus ex machina fashion to play Sherlock Holmes to the uncle's Watson. He quickly salvages the uncle's foundering investigation of a suspected ghost that has been haunting the wife and child of a high-ranking samurai, demonstrating his tact in negotiating all three realms of Edo society — samurai, townspeople, and clergy — in the process.

After this introductory adventure, the *Hanshichi* series settles into what would become a fairly predictable pattern: each installment consists of a brief prelude in which the young narrator visits old Hanshichi at his home in Akasaka (often on some special occasion such as a festival), whereupon the latter launches into a story of one of his past exploits; this is followed by a conclusion in which old Hanshichi sums things up and makes a brief pronouncement on how times have changed.

As with his kabuki plays, Kidō was motivated as much by a desire to educate his readers as to entertain them. He does this by infusing his stories with information about feudal institutions, customs, festivals, geography, and historical events. Moreover, his detailed knowledge of Edo's layout was no mere fabrication — it was gleaned from detailed maps *(kiriezu),* such as the one old Hanshichi is depicted pouring over at the beginning of "The Haunted Sash Pond," that were commonly available from the mid-1600s onward and labeled every street, building, and piece of land in Edo along with the name of its owner. The stories translated here run the gamut of geographic locales in the old city (one, "The Mountain Party," is even set in the post town of Odawara on the bustling Tōkaidō road) and feature an eclectic parade of colorful characters from all walks of life: samurai, Buddhist priests, rich merchants, courtesans, acrobats, traveling salesmen, music teachers and dance instructors, teahouse waitresses, blind masseurs, sword makers, fishmongers, gamblers and petty criminals, not to mention the omnipresent and nondescript clerks, servants, and apprentices. Kidō's keen observation of human nature is augmented with knowledgeable allusions to popular literature and kabuki. Above all, he never fails to tinge his stories with a wry sense of humor.

Hanshichi's Edo is populated not only by flesh-and-blood men and women but also by ghosts, spirits, and monsters of various descriptions, whose existence, while never actually proven, is frequently hinted at. They take the form of human specters, fox spirits, shape-changing cats, and other mischief makers such as the goblin-like *tengu* and watery *kappa* that lurk in rivers and on desolate moors, liminal spaces where the relative safety afforded by the city and the presence of other human beings gives way to the unfathomable and forbidding natural world. As the opening sentence of the very first adventure suggests, the Edo period was a time when the supernatural exerted a strong grip on the Japanese imagination. It was used to explain any strange and troubling event, and was as readily accepted by most samurai as by the less well-educated townspeople. Even Hanshichi, the wise and worldly expert on human nature, is never willing completely to rule out the supernatural as a plausible explanation. In recounting his adventures, he defers to his young interlocutor on all matters of modern science and empiricism, modestly professing that such things are beyond his ken. Above all, it is the mystery of the unknown and unknowable prevailing in Edo times, Kidō seems to suggest, that is the greatest victim of Japan's modernization.

Hanshichi's Namesakes

Later in life, Kidō was frequently asked by readers to explain how he had come up with the idea for the *Hanshichi* series. In various memoirs, essays, and published interviews he addressed some of the basic facts, always maintaining that *Hanshichi* first emerged out of a chance encounter he had had during his days as a fledgling journalist with an old man who, over the course of several meetings, recounted to him many stories about the past and, in particular, the adventures of a "friend" who had been a detective in pre-Meiji times. Other information has been provided by various disciples who, in the traditional Japanese manner, gathered at Kidō's feet to glean insights into the master's craft.

In regard to the matter of the name "Hanshichi," for example, Kishii Ryōei, one of these disciples, testifies that Kidō went to great pains to select a moniker for his sleuth that would have staying power, evidence that from the very beginning the author envisioned a long run for *Hanshichi*. Kishii recounts how Kidō agonized over a dozen possible names, trying to choose one that had a sufficiently "romantic ring" to it but was also short and practical, given that he would have to write it "hundreds of times" over the course of the series.[7] Kidō's final choice was a success on both counts, especially the second: it is hard to imagine a name in Japanese that is easier to write, for whereas typical Japanese male names of the Edo period (such as Jūzaburō or Hachiemon) consisted of three or even four fairly complex Chinese characters, "Hanshichi" is composed of just two — the first meaning "half" and the second "seven" — which together can be written with a mere seven strokes of the brush.

As for the first criterion, Imai Kingo — one of the foremost *Hanshichi* scholars in Japan today — points out that upon hearing the name, no educated theatergoer of the time could fail to be reminded of the story of Akeneya Hanshichi, son of a wealthy saké merchant, and the geisha Minoya Sankatsu, two star-crossed lovers whose real-life love suicide *(shinjū)* at a temple cemetery in 1695 scandalized all of Osaka. The tragic tale was immediately made into a *jōruri* puppet play entitled *Akane no iroage* (Akane's love reawakened); many kabuki versions of the story followed over the course of the eighteenth century. The most famous of these, *Hade sugata onna maiginu* (The captivating beauty's dancing robe) became a staple of the kabuki repertoire in the nineteenth century. The original *jōruri* version of the play is said to have broken all box-office records at the time, enjoying an unprecedented run of nearly six months and firmly establishing the love-suicide romance as a major dramatic genre (a longevity that Kidō, as a playwright, no doubt aspired to emulate).[8]

Another famous literary association evoked by Hanshichi's name — and one perhaps more relevant to the notion of detective fiction — comes in connection with the shogun's persecution of a scholar of Western learning *(rangakusha)* named Takano Chōei, who in 1838 published a book critical of government policies. Arrested and imprisoned for sedition the following year, Takano escaped in 1845 during one of Edo's frequent conflagrations and went on the lam for five years. He was ultimately tracked down by the authorities, one of his pursuers being a policeman named Maruya Hanshichi, and took his own life in Aoyama rather than allow himself to be captured. Takano's act of dissent was a prelude to the gradual downfall of the Tokugawa regime that began a few years later when the arrival of Commodore Perry's four "Black Ships" in July 1853 sparked tensions between the moderately pro-Western shogunate and virulently anti-Western southern and northern daimyo. In 1886 Kawatake Mokuami wrote a kabuki play dramatizing Takano's escape and subsequent capture by Maruya Hanshichi entitled *Yume monogatari Rosei no sugatae* (A portrait of Lusheng's dream story). Staged at the Meijiza Theater when Kidō was fourteen years old, it was no doubt one of many performances the aspiring young playwright saw that led him to set his heart on a career in the theater. It is telling that, according to a theater review of *A Portrait of Lusheng's Dream Story,* the real Maruya Hanshichi was at that time living in retirement in Akasaka, the same area of Tokyo that Kidō later chose as the home of "old Hanshichi" in his stories.

There can be little doubt that Kidō brought all of these associations to bear in shaping the character of his sleuth, who em-

bodies the various complex attributes of the Edo townsman—
romantic and pleasure-seeking on one hand and bound by duty
and obedience to authority on the other. These competing in-
stincts, known as *ninjō* (emotion) and *giri* (duty), in one way
or another inform the plots of almost all kabuki plays. While
the amorous image of Akaneya Hanshichi in the seventeenth-
century *Akane's Love Reawakened* might at first seem at odds
with the sober Inspector Hanshichi, romantic entanglements,
tragic love, and the conflicting demands of *giri* and *ninjō* are
in fact frequent themes in the sleuth's adventures—as seen in
the love suicide featured in "The Haunted Sash Pond," to cite
but one example. The abstemious Hanshichi himself might be
said to have a bit of the roué in him, for he admits in "The Stone
Lantern" to having spent a wild and dissolute youth.

The Influence of *Sherlock Holmes*

As in his plays—which blended fiction and fact from Japanese
history with modern dramatic techniques—Kidō ventured into
uncharted territory in creating the *Hanshichi* series. Western detective fiction *(tantei shōsetsu)* was by that time no longer new to
Japan, having a history that dated back to the late 1880s, when the
Japanese reading public was introduced to the genre through the
many translations and adaptations of Western detective novels,
mostly French, made by Kuroiwa Ruikō and others (amazingly,
Ruikō was responsible for some forty of sixty such translations
published from 1888 to 1890). According to Yoshida Kazuo, the
very first translation of a Western detective novel into Japanese
was actually a work by a Dutch author, Jan Christenmeijer, published in 1820.[9] On the other hand, non-Western precedents for
Japanese crime writing have been found as far back as 1649, with
a translation of a Song-dynasty collection of Chinese criminal cases by Gui Wanrong entitled *Tangyin bishi* (in Japanese,
Tōin hiji monogatari, or Cases heard beneath the Chinese bush
cherry). Its success inspired Ihara Saikaku in 1689 to write his

own collection of stories set in Japan entitled *Honchō ōin hiji* (Cases heard beneath the Japanese cherry tree).

The democratic reforms of the Meiji era (1868–1912) had given rise to a new and relatively free press (though censorship was commonplace on issues relating to politics and "public morality"), the like of which had been unknown in Edo times, when any mention of contemporary events in published material was strictly prohibited. This, coupled with the usual panoply of urban ills caused by rapid industrialization and population growth, contributed to a demand for sensational accounts of crimes that became, as in Europe and America, a staple of Japanese newspapers of the time. Extremely popular in this period were lurid serialized stories about "poison women" *(dokufu)* — murderesses and femmes fatales wrapped into one — of which Kanagaki Robun's 1879 work *Takahashi Oden yasha monogatari* (Tale of the she-devil Takahashi Oden) is the most famous.

Yet crime fiction itself was still seen as an exclusively modern genre derived from Western fiction. *Hanshichi* forever changed this perception, becoming the first truly homegrown example of Japanese historical detective fiction and establishing an entirely new genre. In a 1927 essay published in *Literature Club*, entitled *Hanshichi torimonochō no omoide* (Reminiscences of *Hanshichi torimonochō*), Kidō identified his series' closest precursor as being the courtroom dramas recounted by oral storytellers known as *Ōoka seidan* (Accounts of Judge Ōoka), which were inspired by the exploits of Ōoka Tadasuke (1677–1751), a real-life Solomonic figure who had been the shogun's chief magistrate. In such accounts, as in *dokufu* stories, the perpetrator of the crime(s) is known from the outset, and his or her ultimate capture and punishment are never in question. Kidō acknowledged that these were not true "detective tales" *(tantei monogatari)* in the modern sense, adding that he preferred to focus on the process of tracking down criminals rather than on the legal machinery for trying and condemning them. This approach allowed him to emphasize individual personalities rather than the apparatus of the state. As a result, the world of *Hanshichi* is painted in shades of gray rather than the broad black-and-white strokes of Edo morality tales that followed the time-honored pattern of "encouraging virtue and punishing vice" *(kanzen chōaku)*. The series is not simply about capturing criminals and righting injustice, but about resolving conflict and negotiating a complex web of social relationships to bring about harmonious resolutions—even if this sometimes involves letting someone who is criminally or morally culpable go free or, more likely, allowing them to commit suicide rather than face capture.

For Hanshichi's character, Kidō the playwright also drew on theatrical representations of the Edo *okappiki,* or "cop," a minor character in the kabuki domestic dramas known as *sewamono,* whose reputation rested more on ready brute force than Sherlockian ingenuity. Kidō's achievement was to imbue this stock figure from the stage with a subtler, more three-dimensional persona. But he also made no secret of the fact that his hero was modeled on Conan Doyle's master sleuth Sherlock Holmes who, in 1887, exactly three decades before Hanshichi's first appearance, had been launched on his own long-running and sometimes sporadic serialized adventures (totaling fifty-nine episodes). In the aforementioned essay, Kidō recounted having begun to write *Hanshichi* after reading all three volumes of Holmes' exploits, *The Adventures of Sherlock Holmes* (1891), *The Memoirs of Sherlock Holmes* (1892), and *The Return of Sherlock Holmes* (1903). While these works were available in Japanese translation (*The Adventures* was published in Japanese in 1892), Kidō evidently read them in English, as implied by his pointed mention of having purchased them at Maruzen, a well-known dealer of foreign books in central Tokyo.

Kidō explained that, although he was attracted to the idea of creating a character modeled on Holmes, he chose to set his detective series in the historical past so as to avoid falling into the trap of imitating Conan Doyle's work too closely, a charge to which he knew he would be susceptible given the popularity of Holmes' adventures. Kidō was convinced that by bringing his considerable knowledge of Edo culture and customs to bear on his stories, he would sufficiently transform Conan Doyle's work so as to create something entirely new and better suited to Japanese literary tastes.

But imitate Conan Doyle Kidō certainly did. To forestall his critics, he forthrightly acknowledged the influence of his predecessor at the end of Hanshichi's very first adventure, "The Ghost of Ofumi." In the story's final paragraph, he proudly proclaims, in the voice of his young narrator, Hanshichi's own Dr. Watson: "I realize that this piece of detective work was mere child's play for Hanshichi. There are many more adventures of his that would astound and amaze people, for he was an unsung Sherlock Holmes of the Edo era." And yet even this statement bears more than a passing resemblance to the following line that issues from the mouth of a character in Conan Doyle's "The 'Gloria Scott'" (in *The Memoirs*): "I don't know how you manage this, Mr. Holmes, but it seems to me that all the detectives of fact and of fancy would be children in your hands." Indeed, a close stylistic comparison of Conan Doyle's and Kidō's writing reveals that, far from being an isolated case, other stories in the *Hanshichi* series (at least the early ones translated here) contain similarly Sherlockian language. "The Room over the Bathhouse," for example, begins with the narrator paying a visit at Hanshichi's house to wish him a happy New Year, echoing the opening line of "The Adventure of the Blue Carbuncle" (in *The Adventures*): "I had called upon my friend Sherlock Holmes upon the second morning after Christmas, with the intention of wishing him the compliments of the season." Kidō undoubtedly intended such borrowings as a deliberate nod to Hanshichi's Victorian counterpart, allusions that the more knowledgeable among his readers would have appreciated.

When it comes to the plots of Kidō's stories, however, there are fewer correlations to Holmes' adventures than one might imagine. The abduction of a young boy and the circumstances of his return in "The Mansion of Morning Glories," for example, share some similar features with "The Adventure of the Priory School" (in *The Return of Sherlock Holmes*). In "The Dancer's Curse" the discovery in a darkened room of a corpse, its face hideously contorted and a venomous snake entwined around its neck, was undoubtedly inspired by a nearly identical scene in "The Adventure of the Speckled Band" (in *The Adventures*), but the two stories have nothing else in common. Much more similar in design are Kidō's "The Samurai's Maidservant" and Conan Doyle's "The Adventure of the Copper Beeches" (also in *The Adventures*), both of which feature a young lady who unwittingly takes part in a plot to impersonate someone else. In addition, the former also contains the unmistakable imprint of Conan Doyle's "The Greek Interpreter" (in *The Memoirs*), the story of a Greek linguist who is abducted, taken in a shuttered carriage to some remote location, forced to participate in the interrogation of a fellow countryman, paid handsomely for his services, and deposited far from home with a warning to tell no one about what has transpired.

Kidō's stories are sufficiently different in their specific attributes, however, that one is forced to admit he has created something entirely unique, and one might even say superior to Conan Doyle's work. Whereas many of the London sleuth's adventures tend toward cases of — as Holmes himself often says — the most "outré" variety, involving international intrigue, sinister crime syndicates, and schemes of diabolical cunning, Hanshichi's cases treat relatively quotidian events that depict human vices and foibles in a much more realistic and plausible fashion. Holmes' adventures — which are for the most part contemporaneous with the time of Watson's narrative, or set in the recent past — emphasize the modernity of life in fin de siècle London, making newfangled inventions such as intercity express rail service, bicycles, and the transatlantic telegraph integral to their plots. Kidō's stories, by contrast, look backward with a complex historical perspective consisting of a frame within a frame: one being the time of Kidō and his readers, the late 1910s to 1930s; the other that of the narration, or the early 1890s.

Perhaps the most enduring attribute shared by Hanshichi and Holmes is the devoted following both series have inspired among their reading publics. Neither has gone out of print since their initial publication, and both series have been adapted repeatedly for film and television. Sherlock Holmes set the gold standard against which all later fictional detectives have come to be measured. He was much more than just a popular fictional character. A paragon of science and reason, symbolizing all that was good about the British Empire, Holmes was the answer to the evil that lurked in its dark recesses — a true national hero. When Conan Doyle, tired of his creation and disappointed at the relative lack of attention being paid his other literary endeavors, twice tried to rid himself of Holmes (first in 1893, apparently sending him plunging over Reichenbach Fall), twenty thousand irate readers immediately cancelled their subscriptions to London's *Strand Magazine,* which carried the series, and men and women took to the streets wearing black armbands and veils. Eight years later Doyle succumbed to pressure and resurrected the sleuth.

If similar anecdotes about readers' reactions to the fits and starts of Kidō's series exist, they unfortunately have not so far been told, for in general *Hanshichi* has yet to be subjected to the same level of scholarly scrutiny in Japan as Holmes has by "Sherlockians" in Great Britain and around the world. Perhaps the best gauge of the public response to *Hanshichi* is Kidō's 1936 essay in *Sunday Mainichi* entitled *Hanshichi shōkai-jō* (Introducing Hanshichi), written to answer readers' frequent queries about Hanshichi's true identity. In it Kidō dramatizes his first encounter with the energetic and loquacious "old man" who purportedly supplied the material for some of the sleuth's adventures. The meeting takes place on a Sunday afternoon in April 1891 at the Okada restaurant in Asakusa, where the two men strike up a conversation and then take a stroll together across the Sumida River toward Mukōjima, stopping along the way to have tea and sweets before returning to Asakusa in the evening to dine at an eel restaurant. The young Kidō's fascination with this well-preserved walking time capsule, with his old-fashioned Edo accent, is akin to that of an ornithologist stumbling upon an exotic bird long thought to have been extinct. One is tempted to think the story apocryphal, and yet the scene is nearly identical to the opening of "Hiroshige and the River Otter," written many years earlier, which suggests that Kidō regarded it as a formative moment. Ultimately, Kidō prevaricates about whether or not the old man — who purportedly died a few years later while Kidō was in China as a war correspondent — was actually "Hanshichi," or only an acquaintance of the detective. Nevertheless, his tantalizing account undoubtedly satisfied most of Hanshichi's fans.

Kidō's memorable and oft-quoted phrase describing Hanshichi as "an unsung Sherlock Holmes of the Edo era" was not only prophetic but also clearly aimed to appeal to the patriotic sentiments of Japanese readers raised on a steady diet of foreign translations and contemporary fiction heavily influenced by Western literature. As with Sherlock Holmes, the Japanese public seems to have been eager to believe that this hero of a bygone age was made of real flesh and bone and had been living among them until relatively recently. Yet if British and Japanese readers were fooled into believing in the reality of their fictional heroes, it should not be surprising given the journalistic narrative style both authors adopted in situating Holmes and Hanshichi realistically in time and place and providing an "eyewitness" in the form of an amanuensis for their great exploits.

The Origins of the *Torimonochō*

Strangely enough, the title of Kidō's series, *Hanshichi torimonochō*, also possibly owes a debt to Sherlock Holmes' adventures. An Edo term no longer in use in Kidō's day, *torimonochō* is a combination of the words *torimono*, meaning "an arrest" or "one who commits a crime," and *chō*, a notebook or log. While its very antiquatedness could not have failed to conjure up images of feudal law enforcement in the minds of Kidō's readers, the word's exact meaning was evidently obscure enough that his editor at *Literature Club* felt compelled to append an explanatory subtitle: "Great Detective Stories from the Edo Period" *(Edo jidai no tantei meiwa).*

For his part, Kidō, foreseeing the need to educate his readers, defined the term at the beginning of Hanshichi's second adventure, "The Stone Lantern":

> "What's a *torimonochō,* you ask?" said Hanshichi by way of introduction. "Well, after hearing a report from one of us detectives, the chief inspector or assistant magistrate in charge of the case would relay the information to the City Magistrate's Office, where a secretary wrote it all down in a ledger. That's what we called a *torimonochō* — a casebook."

Yet the origins of this unusual word and its true definition have aroused some debate among Hanshichi aficionados. The renowned Edo scholar Mitamura Engyo, for one, points out that a *torimonochō* was not in fact a detailed police report like those familiar to readers of modern detective fiction, but rather a dispatch log indicating where and when officers had been sent out to apprehend suspects.[10] Kidō may well have been aware of this discrepancy but chose to exercise poetic license in creating his own definition.

Remarkably, according to Imai Kingo, the term is never mentioned again anywhere else in the series. Instead, in a later story, "Three Cheers for Mikawa" (published in January 1919), Kidō made reference to one or more "bound books" *(yokotoji no chō),* unfortunately destroyed in a fire, that Hanshichi's predecessor, Kichigorō, had kept to record his past cases. And in "The Case of the Fox Spirit" (published in 1926), Hanshichi is depicted following his former boss' example in keeping a "notebook" *(hikaechō)* of his own cases. The two Japanese detectives' unofficial case notes seem analogous to what in Sherlock Holmes' adventures are referred to variously as his "records of crime," "case-books," and "commonplace books," volumes that hold notes, newspaper clippings, and documents pertaining to past cases. In "The Musgrave Ritual" Watson writes of these, "it was only in every year or two that [Holmes] would muster energy to docket and arrange them." But it is Watson's own meticulous notebooks that provide the fictional basis for Conan Doyle's narrative, and to these the good doctor is constantly referring and selecting interesting cases to "set before the public." Likewise, Kidō's counterpart to Watson, his young unnamed narrator, states at the end of "The Ghost of Ofumi": "I have managed to fill an entire notebook *(techō)* with these detective stories of Hanshichi's. I have chosen those I find most compelling, and I hereby put them before my readers, though not necessarily in chronological order."

The ambiguity between the *torimonochō* and Hanshichi's "notebook" also has an analogy in the Sherlock Holmes series: what starts out in *The Adventures* and *The Memoirs* as being Watson's "notebooks" eventually merges with Holmes' "case-books" and by the end of the series becomes an encyclopedic, alphabetical compendium running into many dozens of volumes, created jointly by the two men, which Watson describes as the record of "our" cases. While it has been suggested by some Hanshichi scholars that Conan Doyle's "case-books" are the direct precursor of Kidō's *torimonochō,* it should be noted that the former did not appear as a title for Holmes' adventures until 1927, when *The Case-Book of Sherlock Holmes* was published.

Strictly speaking, Hanshichi's adventures are not a true *torimonochō* at all, even according to Kidō's own definition. Rather, they represent oral accounts of the detective's cases transmitted long after the fact by "old Hanshichi" to his young companion, who has transcribed them onto paper. In 1920, three years after Hanshichi's debut, Kidō tried to correct the misnomer by renaming his series *Hanshichi kikigakichō* (The Hanshichi notebooks) — the word *kikigaki* signifying "dictation" — and publishing a collection of the first six stories under this title in 1921.

But by then it was already too late; the label *torimonochō* had stuck, and that is how the series has been known ever since. Despite its uncertain origins and dubious definition, *torimonochō* was taken up by later writers of historical detective fiction who sought to imitate Kidō's success.

Notes

1. The Japanese practice of referring to the author by his pen name, Kidō, rather than by his family name, Okamoto, has been followed here.
2. John Berendt, "Introduction," in *The Adventures and Memoirs of Sherlock Holmes* (New York: Modern Library, 2001).
3. The present work is a translation of fourteen stories published in Japanese, *Hanshichi torimonochō*, vol. one.
4. One story, "Hakuchōkai" (The white butterfly), was serialized in *Nichyō hōchi* (The daily news) in fifteen installments from December 1931 through July 1932.
5. Mark Silver, "Purloined Letters: Cultural Borrowing and Japanese Crime Literature, 1868–1941 (Ph.D. diss., Yale University, 1999), 153.
6. One story, *"Yasha jindō"* (The Yasha shrine), was published in the magazine *Kingu* (King).
7. Imai Kingo, *Hanshichi torimonochō Edo meguri — Hanshichi wa jitsuzai shita* (Tokyo: Chikuma Shobō, 1999), 268.
8. Interestingly, in the later Kabuki version two new twists were added to the plot that involve Sankatsu giving birth to an illegitimate daughter and Hanshichi being falsely accused of murdering a man in a brawl, becoming a fugitive, and being disowned by his father — developments that trigger the couple's inevitable suicide.
9. Kazuo Yoshida, "Japanese Mystery Literature" in *Handbook of Japanese Popular Culture,* ed. Richard Gid Powers and Hidetoshi Kato (New York: Greenwood Press, 1989), 276.
10. Ibid., 64.

Bibliography

Doyle, Sir Arthur Conan. *The Adventures and Memoirs of Sherlock Holmes.* New York: Modern Library, 2001.
Imai Kingo. *Hanshichi torimonochō Edo meguri — Hanshichi wa jitsuzai shita.* Tokyo: Chikuma Shobō, 1999.
Kidō Okamoto. *Hanshichi torimonochō,* vol. one. Tokyo: Kobunsha, 2001.
Nawata Kazuo. *Torimonochō no keifu.* Tokyo: Shinchōsha, 1995.

Nishiyama Matsunosuke. *Edo Culture: Daily Life and Diversions in Urban Japan, 1600–1868.* Honolulu: University of Hawai'i Press, 1997.

Okamoto Kidō. *Kidō zuihitsu—Edo no kotoba.* Tokyo: Kawade Shobō Shinsha, 2003.

Seidensticker, Edward. *Low City, High City: Tokyo from Edo to the Earthquake.* New York: Alfred A. Knopf, 1983.

Silver, Mark. *Purloined Letters: Cultural Borrowing and Japanese Crime Literature, 1868–1941.* Ph.D. diss., Yale University, 1999.

———. "Putting the Court on Trial: Cultural Borrowing and the Translated Crime Novel in Nineteenth-Century Japan." *Journal of Popular Culture* 36.4 (Spring 2003): 853–885.

Yoshida Kazuo. "Japanese Mystery Literature." In *Handbook of Japanese Popular Culture,* ed. Richard Gid Powers and Hidetoshi Kato, 275–299. New York: Greenwood Press, 1989.

The Curious Casebook of
Inspector Hanshichi

The Ghost of Ofumi

OFUMI NO TAMASHII

[1]

My uncle was born at the end of the Edo era[1] and was a great authority on the various bizarre and gruesome legends that were so popular in those days: tales of haunted houses with rooms no one dared enter; tales of the souls of scorned women, still living, tormenting an unfaithful lover; tales of ghosts unable to relinquish an attachment to their former lives. . . . Yet he took great pains to deny there was any truth to these legends, repeating the lesson of his samurai education that "a true warrior does not believe in ghosts." Even after the Meiji Restoration,[2] it seems he retained the same outlook. Whenever we children, inevitably, got onto the subject of ghosts, he would look displeased and have nothing to do with us.

On just one such occasion, this uncle of mine uttered the following remark: "Some things in this world really *are* beyond explanation. Take the case of Ofumi, for example. . . ."

No one had any clue what my uncle was talking about. As if he regretted letting slip something that seemed to undermine his stated convictions, he refused to divulge anything further about these events that were "beyond explanation." I asked my father

---

1. 1603–1868; also known as the Tokugawa period, when shoguns of the powerful Tokugawa clan ruled Japan from their capital in Edo (present-day Tokyo).

2. The return of de facto power by shogun Tokugawa Yoshinobu to Emperor Mutsuhito in 1868, whereupon the imperial court was moved from Kyoto to Tokyo. Mutsuhito ruled under the reign name of Meiji, meaning "enlightened government."

for clarification, but he too would tell me nothing. I divined from the tone of my uncle's remarks, however, that somewhere lurking in the background of this tale was the figure of another uncle, "Uncle K." My child's curiosity aroused, I hastened to pay him a visit. I was twelve years old at the time. "K" was not in fact my real uncle, but my father had known him since before the beginning of the Meiji era,[3] and I had called him "Uncle" for as long as I could remember.

K's responses to my questions, however, did not satisfy me either.

"Well, it's nothing really. Just a silly ghost story. If I tell you, your father and your uncle will be very angry with me."

With the normally loquacious Uncle K choosing to be tight-lipped about this particular matter, my investigation ran up against a brick wall. At school, I was too busy cramming my head with physics, mathematics, and all manner of subjects to think of Ofumi, and gradually the name vanished from my mind like a cloud of smoke.

Two years passed. As I remember, it was late November. Since my return from school, a cold drizzle had been falling, and around sunset it turned into quite a downpour. A neighbor had invited Auntie K to go to a play at the Shintomiza with her,[4] and she would be out from late morning.

"I'll be all on my own tomorrow night, so come by and see me," Uncle K had said the previous day. I'd promised I would, so as soon as I'd had dinner I headed out. Uncle K's house was only about four blocks from ours as the crow flies, but it was located in Banchō, an old part of town where a number of former samurai

3. 1868–1912.

4. Formerly called the Moritaza, one of Edo's three major kabuki theaters, founded in 1660. In 1872 it moved to Shintomichō in central Tokyo, and in 1875 changed its named to the Shintomiza, or Shintomi Theater. Many of Okamoto's own plays were staged there.

houses still stood.[5] Even on clear days, the neighborhood seemed for some reason to be cast in shadow. In the rain, as dusk fell, it was especially gloomy. Uncle K's house lay inside the gate of an old daimyo estate, and long ago it must have been the residence of a senior retainer, steward, or some other high-ranking samurai. At any rate, it was a free-standing house[6] with a small garden attached, surrounded by a roughly woven bamboo fence.

Since coming home from the government office where he worked, Uncle K had eaten dinner and been to the local bathhouse. For about an hour, he sat across from me in front of an oil lamp and we chatted about trivialities. Only the occasional sound of raindrops striking the broad leaves of a fatsia that brushed against the rain shutters reminded one of the darkness outside. As the clock on the pillar struck seven, Uncle K suddenly stopped in the middle of what he was saying and turned his head to listen to the rain.

"It's really coming down, isn't it?"

"I wonder if Auntie K will have any trouble getting home."

"No, I sent a rickshaw to meet her."

With this, Uncle K sipped his tea in silence for a few moments. Then, his tone suddenly rather somber, he said: "Hey, why don't I tell you that story about Ofumi you asked me about once? This is just the kind of night for a ghost story. Or are you too much of a scaredy-cat?"

Truth be told, I *was* a scaredy-cat. All the same, whenever someone had a scary story to tell, I would be all ears, my small body rigid with expectation. Thus, when of his own accord Uncle K unexpectedly brought up the subject of Ofumi that had per-

---

5. A neighborhood in between the inner and outer moats of Edo Castle in the northwest corner of the city. After the Meiji Restoration, many of its large mansions were left abandoned, their samurai occupants having returned to their provincial domains.

6. As opposed to a rowhouse, in which the vast majority of commoners and mid- to low-ranking samurai in Edo would have lived.

plexed me over the years, my eyes immediately lit up. Sitting up straight, I looked him in the eye, as if to say that no matter how scary his ghost story might be, I was immune from fear in such a brightly lit room. My child's attempt to put on a show of bravery evidently amused him. He sat quietly for a few moments with a big grin on his face.

"All right, then, " he said, " I'll tell you the story—but don't go asking me afterward if you can sleep over tonight because you're too scared to walk home!"

With this stern warning, K launched into his account of the case of Ofumi.

"I was exactly twenty years old at the time, so it must have been 1864—the year of the battle of the Hamaguri Gate in Kyoto," he said by way of introduction.[7]

IN THOSE DAYS, a *hatamoto*—a direct vassal of the shogun—by the name of Matsumura Hikotarō maintained a big mansion in this neighborhood on an income of 300 *koku*.[8] Matsumura was highly educated and, being especially well-versed in Western learning,[9] he had risen to become quite a bigwig in the Bureau of Foreign Affairs. Four years earlier, his younger sister, Omichi, had married another *hatamoto* by the name of Obata Iori who

---

7. A battle that took place outside the Hamaguri Gate of Kyoto's imperial palace on August 20, 1864, between pro-shogunal forces and anti-Western, pro-imperial armies from Chōshū Province in southern Japan.

8. A *koku* was a measure of rice weighing approximately 330 pounds (150 kilograms). In 1862 prices, one *koku* was worth 145 *monme* in silver, or about 1.8 *ryō* in gold. It has been estimated that one *ryō* is equivalent to about 41,500 yen in 1999 prices. One *koku* of rice, then, would have cost nearly 75,000 yen in today's terms. Matsumura's income of 300 *koku* (540 *ryō*) today would be worth 22.5 million yen (approximately US$200,000). Though a samurai's income was measured in *koku,* by the nineteenth century, most samurai no longer received their income in rice, but the equivalent in coin.

9. *Rangaku,* or literally "Dutch Learning," that is, the study of Western science and medicine.

lived in Koishikawa on the west bank of the Edo River, and the couple had a daughter named Oharu who was nearly two years old.

Then, one day a strange thing happened. Omichi showed up at her brother's house with Oharu in tow and announced: "I can't remain in my husband's house any longer. Please help me to get a divorce." Matsumura was dumbfounded by this sudden turn of events and tried to question her as to the details, but Omichi just sat there, white as a sheet, and would not say another word.

"You can't just keep quiet! Tell me exactly what happened. Once a woman has married into another family, she doesn't just cut her ties and run off without good reason. How can you come strolling in here suddenly and tell me you need my help getting a divorce without telling me what's happened? If you can convince me that you have just cause, then I'll go speak to your husband. You must talk to me!"

In such a situation, there was really nothing else for Matsumura or anyone else to say, but Omichi stubbornly refused to go into any of the details. Twenty-one years old and the wife of a samurai, she simply kept repeating over and over, like a spoilt child, that she refused to spend another day in *that* house and wanted a divorce. In the end, even her patient brother lost his temper.

"Don't be stupid. How can I go and ask for a divorce if you won't tell me what's happened? Do you imagine Obata would agree? You didn't just get married yesterday, you know. It's been four years already, and you have a daughter. I mean, you don't have to worry about looking after in-laws, and your husband's a kind and honest man. Though of humble status he holds a position of great importance in the government. What grounds could you possibly have for wanting a divorce?"

Scold and reason with her as he might, he got nowhere. But then something occurred to him—seemingly incredible, perhaps, but such things were not unheard of in this world. After all, there *were* several young samurai in service at Obata's house. And the nearby residences were full of second and third sons who led idle, dissolute lives. Wasn't it possible that his sister, who was still very young, had gotten herself into some sort of mess from which she was trying to extricate herself to avoid sullying her good name? As he imagined such a scenario, his interrogation became more intense. "I've an idea," he said, "why it is you won't tell me the whole story. I've a mind to drag you back to Obata's house right now, make you look him in the eye, and then we'll see if you'll talk. Come, let's go!" He grabbed her by the collar and pulled her to her feet.

The look of anger on her brother's face terrified Omichi almost out of her wits. "All right," she cried, tears of remorse streaming down her face. "I'll tell you everything."

As Matsumura listened to her pleading her case, sobbing as she did so, his surprise turned to astonishment.

The incident had taken place seven days earlier. Omichi had just put her daughter Oharu's dolls away after the third-month festival.[10] That night, a pale-faced young woman with tousled hair appeared at Omichi's bedside. The woman was soaking wet from head to toe, as though she'd been drenched in water. She made a deep bow, placing her hands squarely on the tatami floor, her demeanor suggesting a servant in a samurai house. Without a word, or any hint of menace, she simply sat there, kneeling in demure silence—but that alone was unimaginably terrifying. Omichi lay there trembling, unconsciously clutching the edge of the quilt, until suddenly she awoke from her nightmare.

Meanwhile, Oharu, who lay sleeping beside her, seemed to be having a similar nightmare, for suddenly she burst into a storm of tears and shouted, "Ofumi's here! Ofumi's here!" It seemed that the woman with wet clothes was haunting her daughter's dreams as well. "Ofumi," Omichi surmised, must be the woman's name.

Omichi lay awake the rest of the night, too terrified to sleep.

10. The Dolls' Festival *(Hinamatsuri)* held on the third day of the third month.

Having been born and raised in a samurai household, and what was more having married into one, she was too embarrassed to mention her ghostly nightmare to anyone. She kept the events of that night secret from her husband, but the woman with wet clothes and a pale face reappeared at her pillow the following night, and again the night after that. Each time, the young Oharu cried out, "Ofumi's here!" just as before. At last, the timid Omichi could stand it no longer, but neither did she have the courage to tell her husband.

After this had gone on for four nights in a row, Omichi was exhausted from worry and lack of sleep. At last, throwing shame and decorum to the winds, she gave in and told her husband, but Obata merely laughed it off and refused to take her seriously.

The ghostly apparition continued to appear at her bedside. No matter what Omichi said, her husband brushed it aside. Finally, he got angry and said something to the effect of "Are you the wife of samurai, or aren't you?"

"Samurai or not, how can you look on and laugh while your wife is in distress?"

Omichi began to resent her husband's callous attitude. If her suffering continued indefinitely, she was sure that sooner or later she would be hounded to death by the mysterious ghost. No, she told herself, there's nothing left for me now but to take my daughter and flee from this haunted house as soon as possible. The time had passed when she could afford to spare a second thought either for herself or for her husband.

"That's why I can no longer remain in that house. Please understand."

Several times, as Omichi recounted her story to her brother, she had paused, catching her breath and shuddering as though the mere recollection of what had happened still sent shivers down her spine. The look of sheer terror in her eyes suggested that every word she'd spoken was true.

It gave her brother pause. Could such a thing be possible?

No matter how he looked at it, the whole story seemed highly improbable; it was no wonder that Obata had not taken his wife seriously. Matsumura himself was tempted to shout "What nonsense!" at the top of his voice. Yet his sister was clearly so tormented that to fly into a rage and dismiss her concerns out of hand seemed altogether too cruel. Besides, despite what his sister had said, there was a distinct possibility that there was more to the situation than met the eye. In any case, he resolved to visit Obata and confirm the particulars with him.

"I'll have to get more than just your side of the story. I'll go see Obata and hear what he has to say. Leave everything to me."

Leaving his sister at his own house, Matsumura set out immediately for Koishikawa with one servant in tow.

[2]

On the way to Obata's home, Matsumura mulled things over in his mind. His sister was childlike and had never responded well to reason. However, he himself was a man of considerable standing and a samurai to boot. How could he look another samurai in the eye and launch, with a straight face, into a discussion about ghosts? It would be most regrettable if Obata should feel that Matsumura Hikotarō, for all his mature years, revealed himself as a fool. He racked his brain for a good way of broaching the subject, but it seemed so straightforward that, whichever way he looked at it, no solution presented itself.

When he reached Koishikawa, the master of the house happened to be at home, and Matsumura was immediately shown through to a reception room. Once they had exchanged the obligatory pleasantries about the weather, Matsumura struggled to find an opportunity to bring up his business. But even though he'd resigned himself to inevitable ridicule, now that he sat there looking his companion in the eye, he simply could not bring himself to say anything about a ghost. He was still wavering when Obata himself broached the subject.

"Omichi hasn't been to see you today, I suppose?"

"Yes, as a matter of fact, she has," Matsumura replied, but was unable to add anything further.

"Well, I don't know how much she's told you, but you know how foolish women are. Lately she's been saying there's a ghost in the house. Can you believe it?" Obata said, breaking into raucous laughter.

Matsumura had no choice but to laugh along with him. But knowing that he couldn't let the matter rest there, he seized the opportunity and began to talk about Ofumi. When he was through with the story, he wiped the sweat from his brow. By this point, Obata was no longer laughing. He frowned as though deeply troubled and fell silent. If this had been a simple question of a ghost, he could have derided his companion as a coward and a fool, and laughed the whole thing off. But his brother-in-law had been sent over to discuss a divorce, so he had a real problem on his hands. Obata had no choice but to take the haunting seriously.

"All right, let's consider this carefully for a moment," Obata said.

If there really were a ghost in his house — if it were a "haunted mansion," as people say — then surely, he reasoned, some other member of the household would have seen something strange by now. He himself had lived in the house for twenty-eight years and, of course, had never seen anything. Nor had he heard any rumors to that effect. Neither his grandparents, who died when he was a boy, nor his father, who had passed away eight years earlier, nor his mother, who had departed this world six years before, had ever said anything to him about a ghost. The oddest aspect of the situation was the fact that Omichi, an outsider who had married into the family four years earlier, was the only person to have seen the spirit. Even assuming that, for some reason, only she was capable of seeing the ghost, wasn't it odd that it had waited four years to make its first appearance?

Either way, the only other means of resolving the matter was to gather everyone in the household together and question them.

Matsumura readily agreed. "I leave the matter to your discretion," he said.

First, Obata called his steward, Gozaemon. He was a hereditary vassal who had served the family for forty-one years. "I never heard any rumors to that effect during your father's tenure, milord," he said emphatically. "Nor did *my* father ever mention any such story to me."

Next, several young junior retainers were questioned. They were mere hired help, however, and newcomers as well, so of course they knew nothing. After that, the maidservants were called in. They said it was the first they'd heard of it, and sat there trembling in fear. The investigation was leading nowhere.

"In that case, we'll dredge the pond," Obata ordered. The fact that the woman who'd appeared to Omichi had been soaking wet suggested that some clue to the mystery might lie at the bottom of the old pond on the grounds of Obata's estate, which measured some sixty feet across.

The next day a large group of laborers was brought in and the dredging began. Obata and Matsumura were both on hand to supervise, but apart from catching a few carp, their search was fruitless. The mud yielded not a single strand of hair, not even an object such as a comb or a hairpin upon which a spurned lover's curse might have been cast. At Obata's suggestion, they also cleaned the bottom of the well, but its depths produced nothing except, to everyone's great astonishment, a single weatherfish.[11] All their efforts had been in vain.

The investigation had reached an impasse.

This time, it was Matsumura who hit upon the idea of summoning Omichi, over her protestations, back to the mansion in Koishikawa and having her sleep in her usual room with Oharu. Matsumura and Obata hid in the adjoining room and waited late into the night.

---

11. *Dojō*, a freshwater fish considered a delicacy in Edo times. Also known in English as a loach.

It was a warm night and the moon was hidden behind clouds. Omichi's nerves were on edge, and it seemed unlikely that she would be able to sleep soundly. But her young daughter, who had no inkling of what was happening, was soon fast asleep. No sooner had she drifted off, however, than she let out a piercing shriek as though someone had stuck a needle in her eye. Then she began moaning, "Ofumi's here . . . Ofumi's here . . ."

"There, it's the ghost!"

The two samurai who had been lying in wait grabbed their swords and hurriedly threw open the door to the next room. The warm air of a spring night hung heavily about the tightly closed room. By the side of the bed, a paper lantern shed a dim, unwavering light. There was no hint, even, of the telltale draft that signaled the presence of ghosts. Clutching her child tightly to her breast, Omichi lay with her face pressed against the pillow.

Confronted by this irrefutable evidence, Matsumura and Obata turned and looked at one another. How could it be, they wondered, that the young Oharu knew the name of an intruder whom they were unable even to see? That was what troubled them the most. Obata tried questioning Oharu, but no matter how much he coaxed and cajoled the child, who was not old enough to speak properly, he got nowhere. It seemed that Oharu's tiny soul had become possessed by the dead woman's ghost, which was using the girl to bring her name to the attention of the living. The two sword-bearing samurai began to feel distinctly ill at ease.

Obata's chief retainer, Gozaemon, was also troubled. The next day, he paid a visit to a famous fortune-teller in Ichigaya. The fortune-teller told him to go and dig around the roots of the large camellia tree on the west side of the house. They hurriedly set about digging under the tree until it fell over, but the entire exercise produced no result other than to destroy the fortune-teller's credibility.

Saying she was unable to sleep at night, Omichi took to spending the daytime in bed. As one would have expected, Ofumi's ghost did not come to molest her while the sun was up. Everyone was relieved by this, but the idea of a samurai's wife leading such an unorthodox lifestyle — staying up at night and sleeping during the day like some sort of prostitute — was extremely annoying, not to say downright inconvenient. Unless somehow he was able to exorcise this ghost for good, it seemed doubtful whether the peace of Obata's household could be preserved. If news of what was happening leaked out, it would cause a scandal. With Matsumura, of course, the secret was safe. And Obata saw to it that his retainers kept their mouths shut. Still, it appeared that someone had let the cat out of the bag, for outrageous rumors began to reach the ears of people who frequented the house.

"Obata's mansion is haunted. They say a woman's ghost appears at night. . . ."

While other samurai might spread wild rumors about Obata behind his back, when they were in each other's company no one would dare ask him about the ghost to his face. Among his associates, there was only one man sufficiently lacking in the proper sense of decorum — Uncle K, the second son of a *hatamoto* who lived in the same neighborhood as Obata. The minute he heard the rumor, he raced over to Obata's mansion in order to verify it. Obata was on very good terms with K, so he confided everything to him. He even asked K whether he couldn't come up with a plan to find out the truth behind the haunting.

Now during the Edo period the second and third sons of samurai — even samurai of the highest rank who served the shogun — were, generally speaking, idle loafers with no responsibilities. An eldest son, of course, had the duty of succeeding his father as head of the family, but younger sons had virtually no prospects in the world, save for two: either to receive a special appointment from the shogun in recognition of some extraordinary talent or to be adopted into another family. Most simply lived under their elder brothers' roofs, passing the time without any work worthy of a full-fledged samurai. From one perspective, theirs was an extremely enviable lot. From another, it was pitiable.

The inevitable consequence was the creation of an entire class that excelled at idleness and license. Most younger sons were mere playboys. The whole lot of them simply sat around and waited for something to come along to alleviate their boredom. Uncle K, having been born into this unfortunate class, was a prime candidate for a task like the one Obata had consulted him about. Naturally, he accepted it eagerly.

Then he got down to thinking. These were no longer the days of old when a legendary figure such as Kintoki[12] would keep a solemn vigil at the bedside of his lord, Yorimitsu. The first thing he would have to figure out, he realized, was who this woman Ofumi really was, and what connection she had with Obata's family.

"So there is no woman by the name of Ofumi in your family, nor among your servants?"

Obata gave a firm negative to K's question. In his family there certainly was no one of that name. As for his servants, they changed frequently, so of course he could not remember them all, but no one of that name had worked there in recent times. Further questioning revealed that, for as long as anyone could remember, Obata's family had employed two types of women: those sent from villages in Obata's provincial domain, and those hired independently from a referral agency in Edo. The agency was located in Otowa and had done business with Obata's family for generations.

From Omichi's story, it seemed likely that the ghost had been a servant in a samurai family. Uncle K decided that before he

---

12. Sakata no Kintoki, a legendary warrior famed for his fierce loyalty to his master, Minamoto no Yorimitsu (948–1021), a.k.a. Minamoto Raikō, who was known for immortal feats such as slaying the ogre Shutendōji and the monstrous earth-spider.

went trekking off to Obata's feudal domain, he would first make inquiries at the nearby referral agency. It was not at all impossible that, unbeknownst to Obata, there had been a woman named Ofumi who served his family many generations ago.

"Well, do your best," Obata said. "And please, be discreet about it,"

"I understand."

With this promise, the two parted. That was at the end of the third month. It was a clear day, and the cherry trees in Obata's garden were already covered with fresh green leaves.

[3]

Uncle K headed for Otowa and studied the records of servants who had passed through the referral agency. Since Obata's family had been using the agency for generations, it followed that all the names of servants who had come from there would be entered in their books.

Just as Obata had said, there was no record of any Ofumi in recent times. K gradually went further and further back, checking first the past three years, then the past five, and finally the past ten, but found not a single name beginning with "Ofu" — not even an Ofuyu, Ofuku, or Ofusa, much less an Ofumi.

"So maybe she was a woman from the provinces," K thought to himself, still stubbornly gripping the edges of the ledger and poring over it. The agency had lost its old books in a fire thirty years before, so they had no records beyond that. Even if he examined all the old ledgers available, he would run into a dead end when he got to that point. Nonetheless, Uncle K pored patiently over the smudged pages and the faded writing, intent on examining every ledger for those thirty years.

Naturally, the ledgers had not been made especially for the Obata family; each thick, horizontal tome contained records for a number of samurai houses that patronized the agency. Just going through and picking out Obata's name from among all the others was no easy task. Moreover, since the handwriting covered such a long period of time, it was not consistent throughout. Clumsy masculine calligraphy was interspersed with wispy feminine script. In some places, the entries were in a childish hand and written almost entirely in phonetic lettering rather than Chinese characters. Trying to decipher this hodgepodge was enough to make K's head spin and his eyes glaze over.

Uncle K soon began to grow bored and to feel pangs of regret at having impulsively taken on so formidable a task.

"Well, if it isn't the young master from Koishikawa!" came a voice. "What's he up to, I wonder?"

The man with a big grin on his face who had just sat down at the front of the shop looked to be about forty-two or -three. He was lanky and, in a striped kimono with a striped jacket over it, looked the very picture of a respectable merchant. He was somewhat swarthy, and his long, thin face was extremely distinctive, with a prominent nose and expressive eyes that gave him the air of a kabuki actor. His name was Hanshichi of Kanda,[13] and he was a detective. He had a younger sister who was a teacher of Tokiwazu[14] ballads and also lived in Kanda, just below the Myōjin Shrine. Since Uncle K occasionally paid her visits, he was on friendly terms with her brother Hanshichi as well.

Hanshichi was an imposing figure in the world of law enforcement. He was a rarity in his profession, an honest and unpretentious child of Edo about whom no one had ever whispered an unkind word. He never abused his authority to torment the weak under the guise of official business, and he treated everyone with the utmost civility.

"You're as busy as ever, I take it?" Uncle K asked.

---

13. In Edo times, commoners were not permitted to take surnames.

14. A style of narrative music (vocal and instrumental) accompanying dance pieces in the kabuki and puppet theaters.

"Yeah. Just popped in on a bit of official business."

They were exchanging small talk about what was going on in the world when Uncle K had a sudden idea. Surely there couldn't be any harm in revealing Obata's secret to this detective — telling him the whole story and taking advantage of his wisdom and experience?

"I'm sorry to trouble you while you're on a case, but there's a small matter I'd like to consult you about . . . ," he began, glancing left and right over his shoulders. Hanshichi nodded pleasantly.

"Well, I can't imagine what it's about, but why don't we talk it over? Hey, ma'am. We need to use your room upstairs. That's okay, isn't it?"

He led the way up the narrow staircase to the second floor. Upstairs consisted of one six-mat room, in a dark corner of which sat a wicker clothes trunk and a few other things. Uncle K followed Hanshichi inside, sat down, and told him the whole story of the bizarre events at Obata's mansion.

"Well, what do you think? Do you know how we could get to the bottom of this? The way I see it, if we can figure out the ghost's identity, then we could hold a service to pray for her soul, and maybe then everything will be all right."

"Hmm, perhaps . . . ," Hanshichi replied, shaking his head. He thought for a few moments. "Look here, sir. Do you suppose there really is a ghost?"

"Well . . ." Uncle K was at a loss for a reply. "I *think* there is. I mean, I haven't actually seen it . . ."

Hanshichi fell quiet again, smoking his pipe for a while. Then he said: "So the ghost appears to have been a servant in a samurai house, and she's soaking wet, you say? In other words, it sounds a lot like that old ghost story about Okiku who was thrown down a well for breaking one of her master's plates, doesn't it?"

"Yes, I guess so."

"Do they read popular storybooks at Obata's house?" Hanshichi asked suddenly, taking K by surprise.

"The master can't abide them, but it seems they read them in the women's quarters. I hear that someone from the Tajimaya, a local book-lender,[15] has been coming to the house often lately."

"What's the name of the Obatas' family temple?"

"Jōenji, in Shitaya."

"Jōenji. Hmm . . . really?"

"Are you on to something?"

"Is Obata's wife a beautiful woman?"

"She's more attractive than most, I guess. And she's just twenty-one years old."

"I see. Now, sir, what do you think of this idea?" Hanshichi said, smiling. "It won't do if I go sticking my nose into a private matter like this, so just leave everything up to me. I'll have the matter solved for you within two or three days. Of course, this is just between you and me — I won't breathe a word about it to anyone."

Uncle K expressed his confidence in Hanshichi and asked him to take care of everything. Hanshichi gave him his word.

"But there's just one condition," he said. "I'll only be working behind the scenes on this case in an unofficial capacity — it's got to look as though you're the one in charge of the investigation, and you who report to Obata. So if it's not too much trouble, I want you to come with me when I make my inquiries tomorrow."

Uncle K readily agreed; he always had a lot of time on his hands, anyway. Even among Edo's merchant community, Hanshichi had a reputation for being a man who could get things done, and Uncle K was eager to see how he'd handle the case. Looking forward to the following day, K left Hanshichi and headed off for Fukagawa, where a haiku party was being held that evening.

It was late when K returned home. Getting up early the next morning was a trial for him, but somehow he managed to meet Hanshichi at the appointed time and place.

---

15. *Kashihon'ya,* a business that lent out books for a small fee.

"Where are we going first?"

"I thought we'd start with the book-lender."

The two headed for the Tajimaya in Otowa. The head clerk was a frequent visitor at Uncle K's house, too, and they were already well acquainted. Hanshichi questioned the man about the books he'd taken to Obata's house since New Year's. Such information wasn't recorded in detail in the shop ledger, so at first the clerk was at a loss. However, after racking his brain for a moment, he managed to recall the titles of two or three books.

"You didn't by any chance lend them one called *Tales of the Macabre*,[16] did you?" Hanshichi asked.

"Why, yes, I did. It was around the second month, as I recollect."

"Could you show it to us?"

The clerk went and checked his shelves. He soon reappeared with a two-volume set. Hanshichi took it, opened the second volume and began turning the pages. When he came to the fifteenth or sixteenth page, he spread it open and showed it to K. The illustration depicted a woman, apparently the wife of a samurai, seated in a room. Nearby, close to the veranda, stood a young woman, presumably her maidservant, staring down despondently at the ground. There was no mistaking that she was a ghost. By the side of a pond in the garden, irises were in bloom. The servant seemed to have emerged from the pond, for her hair and her clothes were sodden. Her face, depicted in a highly grotesque manner, was obviously intended to strike terror into the hearts of women and children.

A chill went down Uncle K's spine. It was not so much the gruesomeness of the scene that startled him, as the fact that the servant in the picture looked exactly as he'd imagined Ofumi's ghost. Taking the book from Hanshichi, he saw that the cover bore the full title, *Tales of the Macabre: Revised Edition,* and the name of the author, one Tamenaga Hyōchō.

---

16. *Usuzumi-zōshi.* Date of publication unknown.

"Go ahead and borrow it, sir. It's a good read," Hanshichi said, giving him a knowing look. K slipped the two volumes inside his breast pocket and left the shop.

"I've read that book, you know," Hanshichi said once they were out in the street. "As I was listening to your story yesterday, I thought of it immediately."

"So you think the pictures in this book frightened the girl and her mother, giving them nightmares?"

"I don't think that's all there is to it. In any case, I'd like next to pay a visit to the Obatas' temple in Shitaya."

Hanshichi led the way. The two headed up Ando Hill, and, after passing through Hongō, reached Ikenohata in Shitaya, at the edge of Shinobazu Pond. There'd been no wind at all since morning, and the clear sky on that late spring day was like a polished blue jewel. A kite sat perched atop the local fire watchtower as though asleep. Sunshine suggesting the approach of summer glinted off the helmet of a young samurai, apparently on a long journey, hastening his sweaty steed along the road.

Jōenji, the Obatas' family temple, was quite an imposing edifice. The first thing that struck them on passing through its gate was a great profusion of globe flowers in bloom. They asked to see the head priest.

The priest seemed to be around forty, with a pale face showing a dark shadow where he'd shaved. He greeted his two distinguished guests, samurai and government official, with extreme courtesy.

The two men had discussed their plan on the way there, so Uncle K spoke first and told the priest about the recent bizarre events at Obata's residence, recounting how Obata's wife had seen a ghost at her bedside. Then he asked the priest whether there was not some sort of incantation he could recite to exorcise the evil spirit.

The head priest listened attentively.

"Are you here at the behest of his lord- and ladyship?" the priest asked, fingering his rosary nervously. "Or have you gentlemen taken this consultation upon yourselves?"

"That is unimportant. What matters is, are you able to comply with our request?"

Under the piercing gazes that both Hanshichi and Uncle K were directing at him, the priest turned pale and trembled slightly.

"I am a man of humble training, so I cannot guarantee that it will have any efficacy. Nonetheless, I will undertake to pray for the repose of the woman's soul as best I can."

"We would be most grateful."

After a while, the priest announced that it was time to eat, and a meticulously prepared vegetarian meal was promptly brought out. Saké came as well, and though the priest did not touch a drop, the other two men had all they could drink and eat. When it came time to leave, the priest said, "Let me have a palanquin take you home . . ." and surreptitiously handed Hanshichi something wrapped in a piece of paper.[17] Hanshichi thrust it back at him and left.

"Sir, I think we found what we came for. That damn priest was shaking like a leaf," Hanshichi said with a smile. The way the priest had gone white as a sheet, and the lavishness of the feast, were a more eloquent admission of guilt than words could ever be. But there was something that was still bothering Uncle K.

"Even so, I don't understand why the little girl should be calling out Ofumi's name."

"I don't know the answer to that either," Hanshichi replied, still smiling. "But we can dismiss the possibility that the child came out with it unprompted. She must have learned it from somewhere or someone. But, mark my words, that priest is a bad sort. . . . I've heard occasional rumors that he's up to no good, much like that monk long ago at Enmei Temple.[18] That's why he

---

17. Undoubtedly some coins intended as a bribe to buy Hanshichi's silence.

18. A temple where, in 1803, a monk was found to have been carrying on an affair with a maidservant in Edo Castle under the guise of visiting her to recite prayers.

acted as though he was hiding something as soon as we barged in, even before we opened our mouths. I think we've nipped his plans in the bud. He won't go trying anything stupid now. My job is finished here. I'll leave it up to you how best to explain everything to Lord Obata. Well, you'll have to excuse me."

The two parted at Ikenohata.

[4]

On his way home, K dropped in on a friend of his who lived in Hongō. The friend told him that a dance teacher of his acquaintance in Yanagibashi was holding a performance featuring her students, and he was obliged to show his face. "Why don't you join me?" he asked K, who readily accepted. The place was full of attractive young ladies and the festivities lasted until the lanterns were lit for the night. Uncle K returned home in high spirits. As a result, he was unable to make it to Obata's house that day to report on the results of the investigation.

The next day, he went to Obata's residence and found the master at home. Omitting all references to Hanshichi, he spoke as though he had investigated the matter entirely on his own, proudly announcing his findings concerning the storybook and the priest. He saw Obata's expression cloud over as he listened.

Omichi was immediately summoned before her husband. He thrust a copy of *Tales of the Macabre* at her and interrogated her closely. "Isn't this the ghost that you saw in your dream?" he demanded. Omichi paled and was unable to utter a word.

"I know all about that Jōenji priest's corrupt and depraved ways. Are you sure he didn't trick you into doing something reprehensible? Tell me the truth!"

But however forcefully her husband accused her, Omichi tearfully denied that she had behaved improperly in any way. But she *was* guilty of one thing, she said. Begging her husband's forgiveness, she confessed her secret to the two men.

When she went to pay her respects at the temple on New Year's Day, the priest had shown her to a private room. They'd chatted for a while, then he gazed intently at her face for several moments and let out a deep sigh. Finally he muttered, as though to himself, "Alas, what a cruel fate awaits her." With that, he'd bidden her farewell. Then, in the second month, she'd been to the temple again. Once more the priest looked at her face, uttered the same words, and sighed deeply. This bothered her quite a bit, so she'd asked him timidly what he meant.

"Your physiognomy is not at all good," he'd warned her in a pitying tone. "As long as you have a husband, a life-threatening calamity lies in store for you. If at all possible, you should renounce married life. Otherwise, a terrible fate awaits not only you, but your daughter too."

A chill went down her spine. "I don't care about myself," she said, "but isn't there some way that I can help my daughter escape such a misfortune?"

"I'm afraid that mother and daughter are inseparable," the priest replied. "If you do not take steps to head off this disaster, then not even your daughter will be safe."

"You can imagine . . ." Omichi said, choking back sobs, "how I felt . . . at that moment."

["Hearing this story today," Uncle K interjected at this point, "you young people would no doubt dismiss it as a load of rubbish and silly superstition, but in those days everyone — especially women — believed such things."]

The priest's words plunged Omichi into a despair that she could not dispel. Whatever calamity might befall her, she was resigned to renouncing the things of this world. But the mere thought of her darling daughter having to share in her misfortune was terrifying. It tortured her unbearably; without doubt, she had a great affection for her husband, but she loved her daughter even more. Oharu's life was dearer to her than her own. If she was to save her daughter's life, not to mention her own, what choice did she have but to leave the house to which she had grown so accustomed?

Even then, Omichi hesitated time and again. Soon, the second month had slipped away, and the time came for Oharu to celebrate the Dolls' Festival. At Obata's house, the family dolls were taken out and displayed on a set of shelves. When night fell, two paper lanterns atop the display were lit, causing the red and white peach blossoms set on a lower shelf to cast flickering shadows in the night. Omichi stared dismally at the lanterns. Would they be celebrating this way next year, she wondered, and the year after that? Would her daughter be safe forever? Which of the ill-fated pair would meet with misfortune first, the girl or her cursed mother? Sad and terrifying thoughts rose up in poor Omichi's mind, leaving her in no mood that year to get tipsy on the customary "sweet saké" drunk during the festival.

In Obata's house the tradition was to put the dolls away on the fifth day of the month. Omichi was loath to see them go, fearing it might be for the last time. That afternoon, she sat down to read a book she had borrowed from the Tajimaya. Clinging to her mother's knee, Oharu innocently peered at the pictures. The book was the aforementioned *Tales of the Macabre*, containing the story of a servant named Ofumi who is killed by her cruel master. He throws her body into an old pond, beside which some irises are in bloom. The illustration to the scene that Omichi happened to be reading depicted Ofumi's ghost in an especially gruesome manner, as she told her former mistress of the injustice she had suffered. Terrified, little Oharu had pointed at the picture and asked timidly, "Mommy, what's that?"

"That's the ghost of a woman named Ofumi. If you're not a good girl, her ghost will come out of the pond in our garden," Omichi had lightheartedly replied, not meaning to scare the girl. But Oharu had seemed to have received a tremendous shock. She turned white as a sheet, almost as if she were having a seizure, and clung to her mother's knee with all her might.

That night, Oharu cried out in her sleep as though being attacked.

"Ofumi's here!"

This was repeated the following night.

Regretting the terrible thing she'd done, Omichi made haste to return the book immediately. But Oharu cried out Ofumi's name three nights in a row. Sick with worry and guilt, Omichi, too, was unable to sleep properly. Then she became fearful lest this might be a harbinger of the terrible misfortune that was to befall them. She herself began to have visions of Ofumi too.

Omichi at last came to a decision: there was no choice but to follow the advice of her trusted priest and abandon her husband's house. She used her innocent child's calling out of Ofumi's name as a basis for concocting her own ghost story, which she made a pretext for her attempt to return home to her family.

"Stupid woman!" shouted Obata, appalled, as his wife lay prostrate before him, sobbing. Uncle K, however, could not help but recognize the strong maternal instinct that lay beneath this silly's woman's deceit. And thanks to his good offices, Omichi finally received her husband's forgiveness.

"I'd prefer that her older brother, Matsumura, not hear of this," Obata said to K. "Is there some way we can resolve the matter so that nobody in this house or at Matsumura's will suspect the truth?"

Uncle K pondered Obata's dilemma. In the end, they decided, for the sake of appearances, to ask the priest from K's family temple to perform a memorial service for the repose of the mysterious Ofumi's soul. A doctor was called in to treat Oharu, who soon stopped screaming in the middle of the night, and thanks to the power of the Buddha—or so it was plausibly rumored—Ofumi's ghost was never seen again.

Meanwhile, Matsumura Hikotarō, not knowing the truth of the matter, would shake his head in amazement every time he quietly related, to two or three chosen friends, the story of Ofumi, which he always concluded by saying, "Strange things happen in this world that cannot be explained by reason." My father's brother was one of those to whom Matsumura told this tale.

K gained a newfound appreciation for the keen insight that had enabled Hanshichi to discover the truth about Ofumi's ghost in the pages of a storybook. As for the motivation behind the Jōenji priest's terrifying prophecy about Omichi's fate, Hanshichi always refrained from giving a precise explanation. But six months after the events described in this story, Omichi was shocked to hear that the same priest had been hauled before the Office of Temples and Shrines on charges of lascivious conduct with women. So, she had been teetering on the edge of a precipice, and had only been saved thanks to Hanshichi!

"AS I'VE SAID," K concluded, "no one is privy to this secret save Lord and Lady Obata, who are still living, and myself. After the Restoration of 1868, Obata became a government official and has since risen high in the world. You'd best not let anyone else get wind of what I've told you tonight."

By the time he had finished talking, the night rain had eased to a light drizzle, and the fatsia that had earlier stirred against the shutters had subsided into repose.

Uncle K's story made a huge impression on my young mind. But in retrospect, I realize that this piece of detective work was mere child's play for Hanshichi. There are many more adventures of his that would astound and amaze people, for he was an unsung Sherlock Holmes of the Edo era.

It was ten years later, just around the time when the Sino-Japanese War came to an end, that I began seeing Hanshichi frequently. Uncle K had already passed on. Hanshichi purported to be "well over seventy," but he was an astonishingly youthful and vigorous man. He had helped his son-in-law open an import business and was enjoying the leisure of his golden years. By chance, I was able to make his acquaintance and began visiting him at his home in Akasaka. The old man was fond of luxuries

and always served me the choicest tea and most delicious cakes.
Over tea, he would tell me about his younger days.

I have managed to fill an entire notebook with these detective
stories of Hanshichi's. I have chosen those I find most compelling, and I hereby put them before my readers, though not necessarily in chronological order.

The Stone Lantern

ISHI-DŌRŌ

[1]

Old Hanshichi was once kind enough to give me a detailed account of his standing in that long-ago world. Thinking it might prove useful to people today unfamiliar with Edo-period detective fiction, I have decided to pass on to the reader part of what he said.

"What's a *torimonochō*, you ask?" said Hanshichi by way of introduction. "Well, after hearing a report from one of us detectives, the chief inspector or assistant magistrate in charge of the case would relay the information to the City Magistrate's Office,[1] where a secretary wrote it all down in a ledger. That's what we called a *torimonochō* — a casebook.

"The public had a whole bunch of names for men in our line of work: *goyō-kiki, okappiki, tesaki* . . . that sort of thing. *Goyō-kiki* — 'inspector' — was a polite form of address; at least, it's what people used when they wanted to show us respect . . . it's also what we ourselves used when we wanted to intimidate someone. Our official job title was *komono* — 'senior deputy' — but that didn't carry much clout on the street, so we preferred *goyō-kiki* or *meakashi* — 'investigator.' In general, though, we were known as *okappiki* — 'detective.'

"Now the line of command was like this: each assistant magistrate had four or five chief inspectors[2] working under him, and

---

1. *Machibugyō.* There were two City Magistrate's Offices in Edo, divided into north and south.
2. *Yoriki* and *dōshin,* respectively. By the mid-nineteenth century, there were 50 assistant magistrates, and about 200–250 chief inspectors in Edo at any given time. It is estimated that the number of detectives like Hanshichi in Edo was never more than about 380.

under each of them were two or three detectives like me. Below each of *us,* there were four or five junior deputies, though if a detective made a name for himself, he might have seven, eight, or possibly even ten deputies at his command. A detective's monthly take-home pay from the City Magistrate's Office was as little as one *bu*—if you were lucky you might get that and one or two *shu* more.³ Say what you will about prices being cheap back then, even in those days it wasn't enough to live on. Not only that, but the City Magistrate's didn't allocate any funds whatsoever for deputies. So as their bosses, we detectives had to see to it that those five to ten men under our command were provided for. In short, financially speaking, it was a hopeless system to begin with and naturally rife with abuses. The general public tried to steer clear of the whole lot of us. Most detectives ran some sort of business on the side—a bathhouse, say, or a small restaurant—under their wife's name."

According to Hanshichi, officially, the City Magistrate's only recognized detectives, of whom there were relatively few, and took no notice of the many deputies laboring under them. The latter's only job was to do the detective's legwork. In a way, the relationship between the two was like that of a lord and his vassal. Sometimes, detectives even provided meals for their deputies in their own homes. Of course, some deputies were men of great ability. No detective could have made a name for himself without good men working under him.

Hanshichi was not the son of a detective. His father, Hampei, had worked as a clerk for a cotton merchant in Nihonbashi, but had passed away when Hanshichi was just thirteen and his sister Okume five. Their widowed mother, Otami, raised the two children on her own. She had hoped to see her son follow in his

---

3. A *bu* was a gold coin (also known as *ichibukin*) with a value of one-fourth of a *ryō,* or about 10,400 yen in today's currency. A *shu* was valued at one-sixteenth of a *ryō,* or only about 2,600 yen. Therefore, the pay range for detectives was about 10,400–15,600 yen (approximately US$100–150).

father's footsteps some day, but Hanshichi had a self-indulgent nature and was not interested in the strict life of an apprentice.

"I was quite an unfilial son. When I was young I gave my mother no end of grief."

Hanshichi regretted his profligate youth. He said he had developed a taste for pleasure at an early age and ended up running away from home. He was taken under the wing of a detective named Kichigorō in Kanda. Kichigorō had a nasty temper when drunk, but he looked after his underlings and treated them kindly. Hanshichi had been working as a deputy for Kichigorō for a year when he got his first chance to really distinguish himself.

"I'll never forget it. It was the twelfth month of 1841, and I was nearing the end of my nineteenth year . . ."

And so, Hanshichi proceeded to tell me the tale of his first great exploit.

IT WAS A CLOUDY DAY in the twelfth month of 1841. The twelfth year of the Tempō era was drawing to a close. Hanshichi was strolling along the main boulevard in Nihonbashi when a pale young man with a troubled look on his face trudged out of a side street next to the Shirokiya.[4] He was the head clerk at an old haberdashery located down the same street that was owned by a family named Kikumura. Having being born in the area, Hanshichi had known the man ever since he was a child.

"Sei . . . Where are you going?"

Hearing his name, Seijirō bowed his head silently. Increasingly, the gloom of the young man's expression struck Hanshichi as outdoing even the wintry sky over their heads.

"You don't look at all well. Are you feeling under the weather?"

"Uh, no . . . not really."

Seijirō seemed to be struggling to decide whether or not to tell

---

4. The predecessor of today's Tōkyū department store.

Hanshichi something. Finally, he drew closer to the detective and said, almost in a whisper, "As a matter of fact, Okiku has disappeared."

"Okiku . . . What happened?"

"Just past noon yesterday she left for Asakusa with her maid, Otake, to pay her respects to Kannon.[5] Somewhere along the way they got separated, and Otake wandered back home by herself."

"Just past noon yesterday . . ." Hanshichi repeated, frowning. "And she hasn't been home since then? Her mother must be frantic. You've no idea where she might be, you say? How odd."

Naturally, the people at the Kikumuras' shop had split up and searched high and low for Okiku from dusk till dawn, but according to Seijirō they had found no clue to her whereabouts. The clerk looked as though he hadn't had any proper sleep the night before, for the only light in his bleary, bloodshot eyes was a sharp gleam deep in the pupils.

"Seijirō. Stop having me on," Hanshichi said with a laugh, slapping the other man on the shoulder. "You've taken her off and stashed her away somewhere, haven't you!"

"Never!" Seijirō stammered, his pale face reddening slightly. "How can you say such . . . ?"

Hanshichi had always had a vague suspicion that the relationship between the Kikumuras' daughter and Seijirō was not simply one of employer and employee. But Seijirō was too sensible to have talked the girl into running away from home. At the moment, he told Hanshichi, he was on his way to Hongō to visit a distant relative of the Kikumuras on the off-chance that Okiku had gone there. Not that he thought it would do any good. His disheveled sidelocks waved forlornly in the cold winter wind.

"Well, go and have a look. I'll keep my eyes open as well."

"That's very good of you."

---

5. The bodhisattva of compassion (Sanskrit *Avalokitesvara*), a popular image of whom was housed at Sensō Temple in Asakusa.

As soon as Seijirō had gone, Hanshichi headed for the Kikumuras' shop. The haberdashery had a shop front of some thirty-foot width, with a small alleyway running down one side. On the left of the alleyway was an entrance with a lattice door. As Hanshichi already knew, the house was very long from back to front, and at the back there was a living room eight tatami mats in size facing north onto a garden some twenty feet on either side. The master of the house had died some five years back and his wife Otora was in charge of the business now. Okiku, their beautiful eighteen-year-old daughter, was the only keepsake her husband had left her. In addition to Jūzō, the head clerk, they employed two young clerks, Seijirō and Tōkichi, and four errand boys. Otora and her daughter worked in the back of the shop with the maid, Otake, and there were two women who staffed the kitchen. All this Hanshichi remembered in great detail.

Hanshichi met first with the mistress, Otora, then the head clerk, Jūzō, and finally with the assistant, Otake. But each of them just sat there brooding, sighing deeply from time to time. None of them was able to provide any clue as to Okiku's whereabouts.

As he was leaving, Hanshichi asked Otake to step outside with him.

"Listen, Take," he whispered to her, "you're the one who was with Okiku that day, so don't pretend you've no connection with what's happened. You'd better let me know if you have any idea where she is. Got that? If I find you're hiding something, you'll come out the worse for it, believe you me!"

The young Otake turned ashen and trembled.

Hanshichi's threat seemed to have some effect, for when he returned the next morning Otake, who was in front of the lattice door looking cold as she swept the street, ran up to him as though she'd been waiting.

"Inspector! Okiku came home last night."

"Came home? That's good news."

"But she disappeared again right away."

"That's very strange."

"It *is* strange . . . and no one's seen hide or hair of her since then."

"So no one else even knows she came home?"

"Well, there's me . . . and the mistress saw her for sure. But then suddenly she just up and vanished."

Otake seemed even more at a loss than Hanshichi himself.

[2]

"It happened yesterday evening," Otake began, lowering her voice as though recounting a ghost story. "Just as the bell in Kokuchō was tolling six o'clock, I heard the sound of the door here rattling as someone opened it, and when I looked I saw Okiku slipping quietly into the house. The maids were both in the kitchen preparing dinner, so I was the only one around. I blurted out Okiku's name, and she glanced in my direction for just a moment, then headed for the living room at the back of the house. I thought I heard the mistress's voice say, 'Oh, is that you, Okiku?' but the next moment she came out from the back and asked me, 'Is Okiku there with you?' When I said she wasn't, the mistress gave me a strange look and said, 'But I just saw her come this way. Go and look for her.' The two of us searched the entire house but couldn't find Okiku. The clerks were all in the shop and the maids were in the kitchen, but no one had seen Okiku enter or leave the house. We checked to see if she might have gone out through the garden, but the gate was still latched from the inside, which ruled out that possibility. Then we were astonished to find Okiku's clogs sitting on the floor inside the front door — she must have taken them off when she came in. But did that mean she went out again in her bare feet? That's the part that puzzles me the most."

"What was Okiku wearing when you saw her?" Hanshichi asked pensively.

"The same things she had on the day before yesterday — a striped yellow kimono with a purple headscarf."

A striped yellow kimono . . . who would not be reminded of the pitiful sight of Okuma of the Shirakoya in just such an outfit, being paraded through the streets on the back of a horse for all to see?[6] For a while, the look had gone out of style with young women, but lately it seemed to be making something of a comeback, thanks to a popular kabuki play based on Okuma's story. One occasionally saw teenagers dressed in this fashion in imitation of the heroine of the play, "Okoma." In his mind, Hanshichi pictured an attractive young city girl decked out in the familiar high-collared kimono fastened at the waist with a red checkered sash.

"You say Okiku was wearing a headscarf when she left the house?"

"Yes, a purple, silk crepe one."

Hanshichi was a bit disappointed by this answer. He asked Otake whether anything in the house was missing, but she replied that as far as she knew nothing was. In any case, everything had happened so fast. The mistress said she had been seated in the eight-mat living room at the back when someone slid the door to the room open just a fraction. She had looked up casually from what she was doing, to glimpse the figure of her daughter in her yellow kimono and purple scarf. Surprised and delighted, she immediately called out to her, but the door slid silently shut again. After that, her daughter was nowhere to be found. One might be tempted to think that Okiku had already met with an unfortunate end somewhere, and that this had been her spirit wandering back to the house where she was born. But it was certain that Okiku had been observed opening the front door. And

---

6. A true story about a young woman named Okuma, daughter of the owner of the Shirakoya, a lumber business, and her lover, Chūhachi, one of its clerks, who together plotted to kill Okuma's husband. It was later dramatized in the kabuki play *Tsuyu kosode mukashi hachijō* by Kawatake Mokuami, first performed in 1873. Because it was forbidden to depict recent historical events in kabuki plays, names and dates were changed to avoid censorship, even though the audience knew exactly on what the story was based. In this case, Okuma's name was changed to Okoma.

then there were her muddy clogs left inside — further evidence that she was flesh and blood rather than a ghost.

"The day before yesterday," said Hanshichi, "when Okiku went to Asakusa, did she have a tryst with Sei?"

"No . . ."

"Don't lie to me! It's written all over your face, Otake. Okiku and Sei arranged a rendezvous somewhere, didn't they? Say, at a teahouse in Okuyama?"

Unable to hide the truth any longer, Otake confessed everything. Okiku and the young clerk had been romantically involved for some time, and they occasionally met on the sly. Okiku's visit to the temple the day before had been for just that purpose. Seijirō had been waiting for her there, and the two had indeed gone to a teahouse in Okuyama. Told to wait for them, Otake had wandered off and spent an hour amusing herself, strolling around the temple grounds.[7] When she returned to the teahouse, the two were no longer there. According to the woman who worked in the teahouse, the gentleman had left first, followed a short while later by the young lady, who had paid the bill.

"I walked around looking for Okiku for a while," Otake said, "but I couldn't find her. I thought perhaps she'd gone home ahead of me, so I rushed back to the house. But when I got there she still hadn't returned. I discreetly asked Sei about it, but he said he hadn't seen her after leaving the teahouse. I couldn't very well tell the mistress what really had happened, so I said that we'd gotten separated on the way home. Otora has no idea how worried Sei and I have been for the past two days. When Okiku showed up again last night, I practically jumped for joy, but then she suddenly vanished. . . . I can't imagine what on earth has happened to her."

Hanshichi had listened quietly while Otake whispered all this to him in a tremulous voice.

---

7. The temple was at the center of a lively theater and shopping district, with many attractions within the temple precincts themselves.

"Okay, now I understand. Tell your mistress and Sei not to worry. I'm finished here for today."

Returning to Kanda, Hanshichi told his boss, Kichigorō, the whole story.

"That clerk's up to no good," said Kichigorō, shaking his head. Hanshichi, however, disagreed—he could not bring himself to suspect the honest Seijirō.

"I don't care how honest he is," Kichigorō shot back. "If he's the type of guy who messes around with the boss' daughter, there's no telling what else he might do. I want you to go over there tomorrow and put the squeeze on him."

The next morning around ten, Hanshichi went back to the Kikumuras' shop to make further inquiries. He arrived to find a large crowd of people outside. They were whispering among themselves and peering into the shop with a mixture of concern and curiosity. Even one of the neighborhood dogs was milling about with an air of importance, threading his way between the legs of the onlookers. Hanshichi went around to the side and slid open the lattice door. He found the narrow entranceway filled with sandals and wooden clogs. Otake appeared immediately with tears in her eyes.

"Otake, what's happened?"

"The mistress has been murdered!" she replied, bursting into loud sobs.

"Murdered!" Hanshichi exclaimed, shocked. "By whom?"

Otake burst into tears again without replying.

Finally, with much coaxing and cajoling, Hanshichi got the whole story out of her. Her mistress, Otora, had been killed the night before by an unknown assailant. At least that was what the family was saying publicly. The truth of the matter was that the mistress' own daughter, Okiku, had done the deed. Otake had witnessed it with her own eyes. And Otake was not alone—the maids Otoyo and Okatsu, too, had seen everything.

If what she said was true, there was no escaping the fact: Okiku was now wanted for her mother's murder. Hanshichi realized that this had suddenly become an extremely important case. Until now, he'd dismissed it as just another romantic intrigue between a shopkeeper's daughter and an employee, which was nothing unusual. But now, he was taken aback at this sudden turn of events.

"This is a chance for me to prove my mettle," the young detective said to himself, mustering as much courage as he could manage.

Okiku had disappeared three days ago. She had shown up without warning the night before last, only to vanish just as suddenly. Then, just last night she had returned yet again, this time apparently killing her mother before dashing off. Hanshichi was sure there was much more to this case than met the eye.

"What happened to Okiku after that?"

"I don't know," Otake replied, again bursting into tears.

Between sobs, she related her version of events. Okiku had returned home just as it was getting dark, at roughly the same time as the night before. This time, though, Otake was not sure how she had entered the house. From the back room, she suddenly heard the mistress cry out, "Oh, Okiku . . . !" followed by a scream. Alarmed, Otake and the other two maids rushed to the scene just in time to see Okiku's back disappearing swiftly along the veranda. Once again, she was wearing the same striped yellow kimono and purple headscarf.

Rather than chasing after Okiku, the three women turned their attention to Otora. She had been stabbed just below her left breast and lay on the floor, barely breathing. A pool of blood was quickly spreading across the tatami. The women shrieked and stood rooted to the spot. Their voices attracted the attention of the shop clerks, who came rushing to the scene.

"Okiku has . . . Okiku . . ."

Otora seemed to be trying to say something, but her words were barely a whisper, and no one could make out more than this. Then, in the midst of the clamor and confusion, she died.

Someone was sent to inform the local authorities, and an official rushed over to make his inspection. The fatal wound, it turned out, had been very deep and looked to have been inflicted by a sharp implement such as a dagger.

All members of the household were questioned. But each in turn denied any knowledge of the murderer's identity, wary of irreparably harming the shop's reputation by letting the truth slip out. The official's attention, however, was drawn to the fact that the daughter of the house, Okiku, happened to be absent. And when it came to light that she and Seijirō had been having an affair, the clerk was taken into custody on the spot. Otake was terrified that it would be only a matter of time before she, too, was placed under arrest as an accomplice.

"What a mess," Hanshichi said, unable to repress a sigh.

"What will they do to me?" asked Otake, deeply anxious about the extent of her culpability. Then, sobbing hysterically, she cried, "Oh, I wish I were dead!"

"Don't be ridiculous. You're a key witness," Hanshichi said, scolding her. "By the way, I suppose that official brought a detective along with him — do you know who it was?"

"I heard his name was Gentarō."

"Hmm, really? That guy from Setomonochō . . ."

Gentarō was a veteran detective who had a lot of good men working under him.

"I'd sure like to outdo him, just to show the boss what I'm made of," Hanshichi thought to himself, the competitive juices welling up inside him. The only trouble was, for the moment he had no idea where to begin.

"Okiku was wearing a headscarf last night, right?"

"Yes. The same as before — a purple one."

"So from what you just said, she slipped out onto the veranda during all the confusion, and you've no idea where she went after that. . . . Here — could you open the back gate and let me take a look around the garden?" Hanshichi asked.

Otake disappeared inside the house and passed on his request. Soon Jūzō, the head clerk, came out. There were dark shadows under his eyes.

"Very kind of you to help," he said to Hanshichi. "If you could step this way please . . ."

"Sorry to trouble you. I shouldn't be barging in on you at a time like this, but I'd just like to take a quick look around the garden, if you don't mind."

Hanshichi was led inside and through the house to the eight-mat living room. There was still wet blood on the floor. The veranda faced north and looked onto a small garden about thirty meters square, just as he had remembered. The garden was neatly tended and had a wintry look to it — the branches of a pine tree were tied to stakes to support them when it snowed and a banana plant was wrapped in straw to protect it from frost.

"Were the rain shutters along the veranda open?" Hanshichi asked.

"They were all closed except for the one in front of the washbasin outside, which is always left a bit open," explained Jūzō, who had come to show him around. "Of course, that's only in the evening. When we go to bed it's shut all the way."

Saying nothing, Hanshichi looked up at the top branches of the tall pine. There was no indication that the intruder had entered the garden by climbing down the tree. Nor was there any sign of damage to the bamboo spikes along the top of the fence.

"That fence sure is high, isn't it?"

"Yes, the inspector who was here last night said it wouldn't be easy to scale a fence like that. He didn't think, either, that the intruder had used a ladder or climbed down the tree. So according to him, it's unlikely the person entered the house from the garden. But even if he's right, the murderer must have escaped this way — and yet the gate was securely locked from inside. It sure beats me. . . ." Jūzō looked around the garden helplessly, his gloom deepening.

"That's right. Climbing over such a tall fence without damaging any of those bamboo spikes or the branches of the tree wouldn't be child's play."

Hanshichi just couldn't imagine a merchant's daughter performing such a feat. No, the perpetrator must be a hardened criminal. And yet, the three women who ran to the scene said they were positive it was Okiku whom they'd seen from behind. He couldn't help feeling that somehow they must be mistaken.

To satisfy his suspicions, Hanshichi slipped on a pair of wooden clogs left at the edge of the veranda and made a thorough inspection of the small garden. A large stone lantern stood in its east corner. It looked to be of a considerable age, for its roof and base were covered entirely in a thick carpet of dark-green moss whose musty smell seemed to bespeak the long history of the Kikumuras' shop.

"That's a fine lantern. Has it been moved recently?' Hanshichi asked casually.

"No, it's been in that exact spot for as long as anyone can remember. The mistress was always very particular in warning us not to touch it, on account of its beautiful coat of moss."

"Is that so?"

On the roof of this ancient stone lantern, which no one might touch, Hanshichi had chanced to notice the faintest suggestion of a human footprint. The only evidence that remained was a tiny indentation, possibly made by someone's toe, in the plush green moss.

[3]

The impression in the moss was indeed very small. Only a boy could have left such a mark, unless . . . Somehow, it looked to Hanshichi as though it had been made by a woman. So perhaps he'd been wrong when he concluded that the culprit was an experienced burglar. But did this mean Okiku was guilty after all?

Yet even supposing she had used the stone lantern as a spring-board, it still seemed improbable that a young city girl would have been nimble enough to scale such a high fence.

Struck with an idea, Hanshichi left the Kikumuras' shop and headed for Ryōgoku's main plaza, Hirokōji,[8] a place many times more congested and chaotic than Asakusa Park is today.

It was noontime, and performances at the kabuki and vaude-ville theaters along Hirokōji, and at the sideshow stalls across the river in Mukō Ryōgoku, were about to get into full swing. The little makeshift theaters made of reed mats stood with their dusty picture signboards illuminated by the sun's gentle winter rays, their faded banners flapping overhead in the cold wind blowing off the river. The leaves had all fallen from the willow trees standing by the gates of a row of teahouses, their bleak skeletons signaling that the short, frosty days of winter were fast approaching. Waves of humanity, hailing from who knows where, were starting to pour into the popular entertainment district. Hanshichi threaded his way through the throng and entered one of the teahouses.

"How are things? Business thriving as usual, I see."

"Ah, nice to see you, Inspector!" said the fair-complexioned young woman who came over to pour him a cup of tea.

"Hey, young lady—I've got a question for you. You know that acrobat who calls herself 'Little Willow of the Spring Breeze' and performs at that theater over there? What's her husband's name?"

The girl laughed. "Her? Why, she's not married!"

"Husband, lover, brother, whatever . . . I mean the guy who hangs around with her."

"You mean Kin?" the girl answered.

8. *Hirokōji* refers to a public square formed by the widening of a major street. There were three major *hirokōji* in Edo (present-day Tokyo): in Asakusa (in front of Sensō Temple), in Shitaya at the southeast corner of Shinobazu Pond, and at the western approach to the Ryōgoku Bridge over the Sumida River.

"Yeah, that's it. Kinji . . . isn't that right? His house is just across the river. I guess she lives there with him?"

She laughed again. "What do *you* think?"

"Is Kinji still just loafing around?"

"Last I heard he was working at a big kimono dealer's — that's how he met her, when he took some material from the shop around to show her so she could place an order. He's much younger than she is . . . seems a really nice fellow."

"Thanks a lot. That's all I needed to know."

Hanshichi left the teahouse and walked next door to one of the makeshift theaters. It was home to a troupe of acrobats. On stage, the woman who called herself Little Willow was performing death-defying feats such as tightrope walking and turning somersaults in midair. She had gone to great lengths to make herself look as young as possible, applying a thick masklike layer of white face makeup, but in fact she must have been nearly thirty years old. Her beautiful, seductive eyes, their lids shaded with rouge and eyebrows darkened with ink, roved over the audience incessantly. Even in the middle of a stunt, she frequently cast lewd glances in the direction of her assembled admirers, who reacted with apparent rapture, mouths agape. Hanshichi watched her act for a while, then went out into the street again and crossed the bridge over the river into Mukō Ryōgoku.

Kinji's house lay down a side street near the butchers' shops by Komatome Bridge.[9] When he found it, he called out two or three times through the lattice door, but no answer came from inside. Reluctantly, he gave up and went to inquire at the neighbor's house. There he was told that Kinji had stepped out to the local public bath, leaving the house open and unattended.

"In that case I'll just wait inside for him to return — you see,

---

9. *Momonjiiya*, of which there were many in this part of Edo, sold boar meat and venison. The eating of beef did not come into practice until after the Meiji Restoration.

I've come all the way downtown to see him," he informed the lady of the house.

With that, Hanshichi opened the lattice door and went in. He sat down on the step inside and began smoking his pipe. Suddenly, struck by a thought, he quietly slid open the shoji just a fraction. Beyond, he saw two rooms, one six mats in size and the other four and a half. The nearer, six-mat room contained a rectangular charcoal brazier. In the four-and-a-half-mat room there appeared to be a foot warmer cut into the floor, for the edge of the quilt covering it was protruding from between the incompletely shut sliding doors.

Hanshichi leaned forward slightly from where he was sitting and peered into the house. Wasn't that a woman's yellow-striped kimono hanging on the wall of the four-and-a-half mat room? He slipped off his straw sandals and crept in on all fours. Looking into the room from the opening between the sliding doors, he saw that he had not been mistaken. Moreover, one of the sleeves of the kimono was still damp. Maybe someone had hung it up there to dry after washing out Otora's blood. Nodding to himself, Hanshichi returned to the front entrance.

At that moment, he heard the sound of someone approaching over the gutter boards in the street, and a man's voice greeted the woman next door.

"What's that — someone's waiting for me inside? I see . . ."

Hanshichi realized that Kinji had returned. At that moment, the lattice door rattled open and a stylishly dressed young man of about Hanshichi's age stepped inside, a damp towel in his hand. Hanshichi's face was by no means unfamiliar to Kinji, who was a small-time gambler and general man-about-town.

"Hey, if it isn't Hanshichi from Kanda! This is indeed an honor. Won't you come in?"

Kinji made a show of greeting this special visitor with great hospitality. He led the detective inside and sat him down in front of the brazier. But as they exchanged the usual pleasantries, it became clear to Hanshichi's trained eye that there was something unnatural about the way Kinji was behaving.

"You know, Kinji, I owe you an apology."

"An apology? What do you mean, Hanshichi?"

"Yeah, I'm afraid so. I may be an inspector and all that, but it still doesn't give me the right to enter someone's house and go snooping around while he's out. Do you think you can manage to forgive me?"

At this, Kinji, who had been poking at the charcoal in the brazier with a pair of tongs, paled and went mute, his hands trembling so violently that the tongs they held started to clatter.

"Does that kimono belong to Little Willow? I know she's a performer, but isn't it a bit gaudy even for her? But then, I guess when a woman finds a beau as young as you, she's bound to start dolling herself up a bit." He laughed. "Hey, Kinji. What's wrong, cat got your tongue? Well, aren't you a sourpuss! Don't you want to take me out for a drink so you can gush about your lovely Little Willow? Come on, say something. I know you're being kept by an older woman who takes care of your every need. So I can understand you may well have to go along with anything she asks, even if you're not happy about it. I've already got that figured out, so I'll try to get them to go easy on you. How about it . . . you want to tell me the truth?"

Still trembling and pale even to his lips, Kinji prostrated himself abjectly on the floor.

"I'll tell you everything, Hanshichi!" he cried.

"Ah, you're showing some sense for a change. That kimono belongs to the Kikumuras' daughter, doesn't it? So, when did you abduct her?"

"It wasn't me," Kinji replied, peering up at his interrogator's face with an imploring look. "Actually, three days ago, Little Willow and I went to Asakusa just before noon. She has a habit of getting drunk, then saying she's going to take the day off— stubbornly refuses to come home however hard I try to persuade her. That flashy job of hers pays well, but she spends money left and right. And since I haven't being doing so well myself lately, we've gotten up to our necks in debt. With the end of the year approaching, the loan sharks have been beating on our door. Even

Little Willow seems to be getting a bit desperate, so the other day I didn't have any choice but to humor her. Just past noon, we were in Asakusa, strolling around Okuyama, when we saw a young clerk come out of a teashop. He was followed a few minutes later by a well-dressed young woman. 'Why, that's the Kikumuras' daughter from Nihonbashi!' Little Willow exclaimed. 'She acts all prim and proper, but she's having a tryst with a clerk in a place like this! I think we might have hit the jackpot.'"

"How would Little Willow know anything about the Kikumuras' daughter?" interrupted Hanshichi.

"Because she sometimes goes there to buy rouge and powder. The Kikumuras' is an old establishment, you know. Anyhow, after that I went to find a palanquin to take us home. I don't know what Little Willow said while I was gone to induce the young lady to come with us, but she emerged onto Uma Street with her in tow. There were only two palanquins available, so Little Willow and the girl got inside and went on ahead, while I followed them home on foot. When I got back, the girl was in tears. 'Stick a gag in her mouth and shove her in the closet.' Little Willow said. 'We don't want the neighbors to hear her.' I felt sorry for the girl, but Little Willow turned on me angrily. 'Well, what are you waiting for, you coward?' she said. So, I helped her put the girl in the back closet."

"My — I'd heard that Little Willow was a bad egg, but I'd no idea she was *that* evil!" said Hanshichi. "So what happened next?"

"That night she went straight ahead and called in a white slave trader,[10] a woman who offered to pay us forty *ryō* by the end of the year to ship the girl off to Itako.[11] Little Willow thought it wasn't enough but she reluctantly agreed. The next morning she

---

10. *Zegen,* someone who sold girls into prostitution.

11. A town on the Tone River near the coast about 50 miles (75 km) northeast of Edo that served as an important transfer point for goods entering Edo from northern Japan. Its thriving licensed red-light district was established in 1682.

put the girl in a palanquin and sent her off with the slave trader — but until the woman returns from Itako we won't see any of the money. Well, the year-end debt collectors were beating at the door every day like a pack of hungry demons. Getting desperate, Little Willow came up with a new plan. Before sending her off to Itako, she'd stripped the girl's yellow kimono off her and dressed her in her own best outfit. 'No one wants an unattractive set of goods,' she said. The girl's kimono has been hanging here ever since."

"Hmm. So Little Willow disguised herself as the girl in order to sneak into the Kikumuras' house. I guess she was after money then?"

"That's right." Kinji nodded. "She'd threatened the girl into revealing that her mother kept some cash in a small chest in the living room."

"So that was what she was after from the very beginning?"

"I don't know, but Little Willow was desperate — she said she had no choice. But night before last she returned looking upset . . . things hadn't gone well. Then, yesterday evening, she went out again. 'Tonight I won't fail!' she said. But once again she came back empty-handed. 'I blew it again — and not only that,' she said. 'The missus started screaming, and I panicked and stuck a knife in her guts.' I tell you, I started shaking like a leaf and couldn't say anything for a while. I knew she wasn't lying, because there was blood on her sleeves. 'What a mess she's gotten me into!' I thought. But Little Willow wasn't the slightest bit worried. 'Relax. The only thing people saw was this kimono and scarf I was wearing, so everyone will naturally assume that the daughter murdered her.' Then she proceeded to wash out the blood and hung the kimono up here to dry. Today she went off to work as though nothing had happened."

"Well, you've got to admire her nerve. That lover of yours is sure full of spunk!" Hanshichi said with a wry smile. "Anyhow, I appreciate your being straight with me. It was your bad luck that an evil woman like that fell for you. Well, her head will be on a stake before long, that's for sure. But provided you testify against her, at least you'll be able to keep yours. Fear not!"

"I'm at your mercy, Hanshichi. I'm a coward through and through . . . last night I hardly slept a wink. As soon as I saw your face a moment ago, I knew I was done for. I know I'm being disloyal to Little Willow, but for someone like me the best thing really is to make a clean breast of it all."

"Well, I'm afraid you're going to have to come along with me to Kanda to see my boss. You might be locked up for a while, so you better make sure you have everything you need."

"Thank you."

"Since it's broad daylight, I'll spare you the indignity of tying your hands," Hanshichi said gently, "for the sake of appearances."

"Thank you," Kinji replied gratefully. Hanshichi saw the helpless look in his eyes, which were moist with tears.

Reflecting on their similar ages, Hanshichi couldn't help pitying the weak young man he was taking into custody.

[4]

"Well, well . . . will wonders never cease! You've pulled off a real coup, you know."

Upon hearing Hanshichi's report, his boss, Kichigorō, could not have looked more surprised if Hanshichi had told him he'd caught a whale down at the Kanasugi seashore.

"Aren't you the sly one—here I was thinking you were still wet behind the ears. Well done! Well done, indeed! Don't worry, I'm not going to steal your thunder. I'll give a full account of your performance to my superiors. You can count on that. For the moment, we've got to track down Little Willow and arrest her right away. For a woman, she's a real nasty piece of work. You never know what she might do next. Hey, someone else go along with Hanshichi and help him."

DUSK WAS ALREADY gathering on that short winter day when Hanshichi set out again for Ryōgoku followed by two veteran detectives. The little makeshift theater was just winding down for the night. Hanshichi left the men waiting outside and went in alone. Little Willow was backstage in her dressing room, changing into her kimono.

"I've been sent by Inspector Kichigorō in Kanda—my boss wants to see you about something," Hanshichi said nonchalantly. "I apologize for the inconvenience, but would you mind coming with me, miss?"

A dark cloud descended on Little Willow's face. Nevertheless, she remained surprisingly calm. With a sad smile she replied, "Your boss . . . what a nuisance. What does he want?"

"No doubt he's taken a fancy to you—you've got quite a reputation, you know."

"Hmm, very funny. What's he really after? You've got a pretty good idea, haven't you?" Draping her supple body over a wicker clothesbasket, Little Willow peered at Hanshichi with a pair of snakelike eyes.

"I've no idea at all, actually. I'm simply a messenger, miss. Anyhow, I'm sure it won't take up very much of your time, so why don't you come along without making a fuss?"

"In that case, I'd better go with you, I guess. If your boss wants to see me, I can't very well run and hide, now can I?" Little Willow said, taking out her tobacco pouch and quietly taking a puff on her pipe.

On the other side of the partition, a drum signaled the end of the day's acrobatic performances. Wearing anxious expressions, the other performers observed the two of them from a distance, straining to overhear their conversation. The cramped dressing room had grown completely dark.

"The day's coming to an end—my boss's temper will come to an end too, miss. If we don't get a move on, I'm the one who's going to get in trouble. So could you hurry it up a bit, please?" A note of impatience was creeping into Hanshichi's voice.

"All right, all right. I'll be with you in just a moment."

When Little Willow finally emerged from her dressing room, she saw the two detectives standing there in the dark. She shot Hanshichi a vexed look.

"My, it's chilly!" she exclaimed, clasping her sleeves together. "When the sun goes down it sure gets cold quickly."

"All the more reason to hurry!"

"I don't know what your boss wishes to discuss with me, but if it's going to take a while I'd like to go home first. Could we stop at my house on the way there?"

"Kinji's not there, if that's what you're thinking," Hanshichi said coldly.

Little Willow stopped and closed her eyes. When she finally opened them again, Hanshichi saw what might have been taken for dewdrops on the ends of her long lashes.

"Kinji's not at home, you say? All the same, I'll need to stop off and prepare a few things — I am a woman after all."

The party crossed Ryōgoku Bridge, Little Willow surrounded by the three men. Every once in a while, her shoulders shook and she broke into plaintive sobs.

"Do you love Kinji that much, miss?"

"Yes."

"Somehow he doesn't seem your type."

"Please judge for yourself."

By the time they'd reached roughly the midpoint of the long bridge, a few scattered lights were beginning to glow yellow on the riverbank. A gray mist hung over the waters of the Sumida River, and far downstream the pale light reflected from their surface heightened the feeling of cold. The lantern outside the bridge guardsman's hut already emitted a faint flicker of candlelight. A flock of geese honked as they flew over the roofs of the government boathouses, perhaps a sign that there would be frost that night.

"What would happen to Kinji if I were to die?"

"Then everything would hang on his testimony."

Little Willow silently wiped the tears from her eyes. Then, without warning, she cried out, "Forgive me, Kinji!"

Pushing Hanshichi aside with all her might, Little Willow darted away from the men as quick as a sparrow in flight, too fast in her acrobat's agility for the eye to follow. Before Hanshichi could realize what was happening, Little Willow had grabbed the railing of the bridge, and the next thing he knew, her body had plunged headfirst into the river and disappeared beneath its waves.

"Damn it!" muttered Hanshichi through clenched teeth.

Hearing the splash of water, the bridge guardsman emerged from his hut. Informed by Hanshichi that he was on official business, the guardsman immediately ordered the local boatmen to search the waters; but Little Willow did not resurface.

The next day, a mass of long black hair was spotted entangled like a clump of seaweed in the pilings on the opposite bank of the river. When it was hauled ashore, the body proved to be that of Little Willow. A coroner came and inspected the frozen corpse as it lay atop the morning frost. The news quickly spread throughout Edo that the great female acrobat had at last fallen from the tightrope of life, and Hanshichi's fame grew accordingly.

The Kikumuras immediately dispatched someone to retrieve Okiku, who was safe at the brothel in Itako; she was still in training, not yet having been put to work.

"Thinking back on what happened," she later said, "it seems like it was all a dream. After Seijirō left the teahouse and went home, I got rather lonely, so instead of waiting for Otake to return, I wandered out into the street. There, standing under a large tree, was that acrobat, Little Willow. To my horror, she informed me that Sei had suddenly fallen ill and told me to come with her. Then she said he had already been taken to a doctor's house. She forced me into a palanquin. When we arrived at our destination, I was led inside a dark house, and Little Willow's demeanor suddenly changed. She and another young man treated me very roughly; then they sent me off somewhere far away. I was in a complete daze, like I was half dead. I couldn't think straight . . . I didn't know what to do." This was the account that Okiku gave when questioned by an official after returning to Edo.

Seijirō, the clerk, was let off with a stern reprimand.

Little Willow had escaped punishment by taking her own life, but even in death she could not prevent her head being placed on a stake at Kozukappara.[12] As for Kinji, he should have met the same fate himself, but instead was granted special clemency and banished to a distant island. Thus the case was finally laid to rest.

"AND THAT WAS WHAT launched my career," old Hanshichi added. "Three or four years later, my boss, Kichigorō, was done in by heatstroke. Before he died he made a will in which he entrusted to me his daughter, Osen, and all his affairs, with a request that I should continue as his successor. So in the end his other deputies chose to stay on, with me as their new boss. That marked my start as a full-fledged detective.

"You say you want to know how I homed in on Little Willow as my prime suspect? Well, as I said earlier, it was because of the stone lantern. That impression in the moss looked to me to have been left by a woman. Even so, most women wouldn't have been able to clamber over a high fence like that with such ease. I knew it had to have been someone lightweight and agile. Then it struck me — an acrobat. There weren't very many female acrobats in Edo. I'd heard some bad rumors about one in particular named Little Willow who performed in Ryōgoku and kept a young lover. I had a hunch she was the one I was after, so I checked her out. From there, the pieces fell into place more easily than I'd expected.

"I heard later that Kinji received some sort of pardon and returned to Edo from his place of exile on one of the Izu islands.

---

12. Edo's execution ground on the northern outskirts of the city, in Senju.

The clerk, Seijirō, married the Kikumuras' daughter and carried on the business there for a while, but it seemed that they couldn't shake their bad luck. Despite being an old and reputable firm, they just couldn't make a go of it. Seems they had to leave downtown Edo and move to Shiba at the end of the Tokugawa era. I don't know what happened to them after that.

"No matter how you look at it, Little Willow was already as good as dead, but nonetheless, it's a shame she threw herself into the river. It was my own fault — I was so intent on catching her that when I finally did, I let down my guard. It's a common mistake, and criminals sometimes get away because of it. . . .

"What's that? You want to know if I have any more interesting stories? Sure — I could go on and on bragging about my exploits. Come see me again sometime," Hanshichi said, laughing.

"I'll be sure to do so."

And with that promise, I bid Hanshichi good-day.

The Death of Kampei

KAMPEI NO SHI

[1]

One day, I went to call on T—one of our great literary figures and a master of the Japanese historical novel[1] —at his home in Akasaka. After hearing all he had to say about life in Edo long ago, I felt an urge to see old Hanshichi once again. It was three in the afternoon when I left T's house. All along Akasaka's main thoroughfare, men were setting up pine-branch decorations for the New Year outside gateways and shop fronts. A group of seven or eight people crowded outside a confectionery shop. All the sights and sounds of Tokyo at year-end melded together in a great flurry of activity—posters and signboards advertising year-end sales, red lanterns, purple banners, the muddied tones of brass bands, and the shrill strains of gramophones.

"Only a handful of days left in the year now," I reflected. The thought made me, as a mere idler, feel guilty to be strolling around, descending on people left and right, at such a busy time. I changed my mind about visiting Hanshichi, thinking it best to head straight home. But then, as I was strolling toward the nearest trolley-car stop, who should I chance to run into among the oncoming throng but the old detective himself.

"How've you been? I haven't seen you for some time," Hanshichi said, beaming cheerfully as always.

---

1. Tsukahara Jūshien (1848–1917). Like Okamoto, Tsukahara was a journalist turned literary figure. When Okamoto joined the staff of the Tokyo *Nichinichi Shimbun* in 1890, Tsukahara was the paper's drama critic. Two years later, the paper serialized his first historical novel, *Kataki-uchi jōruri-zaka*, to great acclaim.

"As a matter of fact, I'd been thinking of dropping in on you, but then I decided it would be an imposition at this time of year."

"Don't be ridiculous! After all, I'm in retirement. Obon, Christmas, New Year's . . . it's all the same to me! Why don't you stop in for a while — that is, as long as you haven't anything more important to do."

Meeting old Hanshichi like this was a godsend if ever there was one. Setting aside earlier compunctions, I followed him home. When we arrived, he slid open the lattice door and showed me inside.

"We have a visitor!" he called out to his old housekeeper.

I was shown through to the usual six-mat room. Tea was brought — a high-quality variety, as always. Delicious cakes were served. The two of us — one at the end of his career, the other just starting out — proceeded to talk at leisure until dusk, as though we inhabited a timeless world far removed from the fast-paced, frenetic one outside.

"It was at this time of year, during the annual amateur theatricals at the Izumiya in Kyōbashi . . . ," the old man said suddenly, as though recalling a distant memory.

"Huh? What was?"

"That year, quite a shocking incident occurred. Even I had to rack my brain pretty hard to solve the case. . . . If I'm not mistaken, it all started on an unseasonably warm night in the twelfth month of 1858. The Izumiya was a large ironmonger's located in Kyōbashi's Gusokuchō district. The entire household was crazy about the theater — that's what brought about the whole messy affair. . . . What's that? You want to hear all about it? Well, all right, here goes — another of my 'great exploits'!"

AS THE FIFTH YEAR of the Ansei era[2] drew to a close, a warm spell set in that lasted four or five days. After breakfast one morning, Hanshichi decided he would head over to Hatchōbori to see

---

2. 1854–1860.

his boss, the chief inspector, and pay his year-end respects. Just then, his sister, Okume, appeared at the back door of his house, which opened onto the kitchen. She seemed to be in somewhat of a hurry. A teacher of samisen-accompanied ballads in the To-kiwazu style, she had a house below the Myōjin Shrine where she lived with their mother, Otami.

"Good morning, miss," the maid greeted her. "Yes, your brother's up already."

Hanshichi's wife, Osen, who was also in the kitchen, smiled.

"Oh, Okume. Come in. What are you doing here so early?"

"I came to ask my brother a small favor," Okume replied, glancing back over her shoulder.

"All right, then, come in."

Standing despondently in Okume's shadow was a fashionably dressed, matronly woman of around thirty-six to thirty-eight. Osen could tell that she was one of Okume's fellow musicians.

"Er . . . please do come in too, madam." Removing the cords she used to tie back the sleeves of her kimono when doing house-work, Osen bowed, whereupon the woman advanced timidly into the room and gave a polite bow in return.

"Are you the mistress of the house? My name is Mojikiyo. I live in Shitaya. I'm always grateful to my colleague here, Mojifusa[3] — Okume, that is — for her help."

"Not at all. It's kind of you to say so. Okume is still quite young, so I'm sure she must cause you a lot of trouble."

During this exchange, Okume had gone into the adjoining room and come back again. Looking tense and pale, Mojikiyo was led in to see Hanshichi. He noticed that she had headache plasters on her temples and that her eyes were slightly bloodshot.

"Hanshichi, I'll come straight to the point," Okume said, giving him a meaningful look as she introduced her pallid-faced companion. "Mojikiyo here has a special favor to ask you."

---

3. Okume's stage pseudonym. The prefix *moji-* ("word") in both women's names probably refers to the ballads that they perform.

"Hmm, is that so?" Hanshichi replied, turning to look at Okume. "Well, madam, I don't know what it is you want to discuss, but I may not be of any use to you. Why don't you tell me the whole story first?"

"I'm most terribly sorry to burst in on you unannounced like this, sir. I've been at my wit's end lately, and my good friend Mojifusa here graciously offered me her assistance. That's why we've come to see you this morning." Placing her hands on the tatami in front of her, Mojikiyo bowed her head to the floor. "As you are probably aware, the Izumiya in Gusokuchō held its year-end amateur theatricals on the night of the nineteenth."

"Ah, yes. I hear something went tragically wrong this year."

Hanshichi knew all about the incident at the Izumiya. The whole family was mad about kabuki and at this time each year they invited the entire neighborhood and all their regular customers to a performance celebrating year's end. It was an exceedingly grand affair—they removed the partitions between three large adjoining rooms and set up a stage nearly twenty feet wide at the front. The costumes and sets were always quite elaborate. The actors, from the narrator right down to the musicians, were all enthusiastic amateurs recruited from among the Izumiya's employees and neighbors.

The program for that night's performance consisted of five acts: acts 3, 4, 5, 6, and 9 of the perennial classic *The Treasury of Loyal Retainers*.[4] The scion of the Izumi house, Kakutarō, was to

---

4. *Chūshingura*, a dramatic adaptation of historical events surrounding a vendetta carried out in 1703 by 47 *rōnin* (masterless samurai) to avenge the wrongful death of their lord. Competing versions of the play were written, originally for the puppet theater, by Namiki Sōsuke (1695–1752) and Takedo Izumo II (1691–1756) in 1741 and 1748, respectively. The latter, whose full title is *Kanadehon chūshingura*, is the more famous of the two, and probably the one performed here. Due to the extreme length of the play—its eleven acts would take many hours to perform in their entirety—abbreviated performances were common, and usually omitted acts 2, 8, and 10. The play sets the action in the fourteenth century so as to evade the government prohibition on depicting recent events.

play the part of Hayano Kampei.[5] Aged nineteen, he was slender and graceful, a dashing figure who had the reputation among the young ladies of the neighborhood of being the spitting image of a certain kabuki actor. That evening, there was no doubt in the audience's mind that the young master would acquit himself superbly in the role of Kampei.

The first three acts — from the scene of the fateful quarrel to the encounter on the Yamazaki Road[6] — went off without a hitch. When the curtain for the sixth act went up that winter's night, it was just after eight o'clock. Latecomers had been trickling into the audience since the beginning of the previous act, avowing — perhaps this was part flattery — that they would not for all the world have missed seeing the young master in the role of Kampei. The audience was packed in so tightly that there was no place even to set a candelabra or a charcoal brazier. An almost suffocating aura of women's face powder and hair oil hung in the air, and a dense haze of tobacco smoke swirled about the room. Loud bursts of laughter, spilling out into the street, made passersby stop and wonder.

But the joyous shouts were soon to be transformed into tears of sorrow. When Kakutarō, in his role as Kampei, plunged his sword into his belly to commit suicide, his costume turned bright red as blood oozed from the wound. It was not, however, the fake stage blood provided for this purpose. The audience watched in admiration as Kakutarō's face assumed an expression of horren-

---

5. Kampei (based on the historical character Kayano Sanpei) is one of the forty-seven *rōnin* in the play and commits suicide, mistakenly believing that he has accidentally killed his father-in-law.

6. The first three acts — here acts 3, 4, and 5 of the play — depict the quarrel between Kō no Moronō and Enya Hangan; the order for Hangan to commit suicide for having drawn his sword in the shogun's palace; the forty-seven *rōnin*'s decision to take vengeance on Moronō for bringing about their lord's death; and Kampei's nighttime encounter with a bandit who has just murdered his father-in-law on the Yamazaki Road.

dous pain; but when he slumped over onto the stage, unable to finish his line, their reaction turned to disbelief, and the room erupted into chaos. The scabbard had contained not the intended tin-plated bamboo prop sword but a genuine blade. Kakutarō's act of seppuku had in fact been entirely real. He had plunged the sword into his side with all his might, and the tip had pierced deep into his abdomen. Writhing in agony, the actor was carried offstage to his dressing room. There was no question of the show going on. The evening's year-end festivities disintegrated into horror and disbelief.

There, still in full costume, Kakutarō was treated by a doctor. Beneath his white face paint he was already deathly pale. His wound was stitched up, but he had already lost a large amount of blood and his prospects for recovery did not look good. In terrible pain, he clung to life for two days and two nights, but then, in the middle of the night of the twenty-first, he met his tragic end. The funeral was held at the Izumiya shortly past noon on the twenty-third.

That had been yesterday. . . .

It was not at all clear to Hanshichi what connection there could possibly be between the Izumiya and this woman Mojikiyo who now kneeled before him.

"This matter is most distressing for Miss Mojikiyo," Okume chimed in. Enormous tears were rolling down Mojikiyo's pale face.

"Inspector, please help me avenge this wrong."

"Avenge . . . what wrong?"

"My son's death . . ."

Hanshichi peered into the woman's face through a haze of tobacco smoke. Mojikiyo looked up, and her eyes, filled with tears, narrowed as they met his. Her lips were contorted and quivered as though in anger.

"You mean the young master was your son?" Hanshichi asked, incredulously.

"Yes."

"Hmm. This is the first I've heard of it. And Mrs. Izumi wasn't Kakutarō's real mother?"

"No, I was. I guess I'd better explain. Exactly twenty years ago, I was living in Nakabashi and teaching Tokiwazu just as I am now. The master of the Izumiya often did me the honor of visiting and . . . well, you know how these things are — the following year I gave birth to a boy. That was Kakutarō, rest his soul . . ."

"So, the Izumiya took the boy in?"

"That's right. When the mistress heard about it, she said that, since they didn't have any children yet, she would like to have him. . . . Of course, I didn't want to let Kakutarō go, but I figured that if I did, he would grow up to inherit that fine business of theirs. In other words, I did it so that he would have a better life. I handed him over shortly after the birth. Then, I was told that it wouldn't do anyone's reputation any good — least of all my son's — if it were known that I was the real mother, so I accepted the generous allowance they offered me and promised never to see my son again. Later, I moved to Shitaya, and I've been living there ever since, teaching Tokiwazu as always. But it's true what they say — the bond between mother and child is unbreakable. You can never forget the child you gave birth to, not even for one day. I heard rumors that my son had grown up to be a fine young gentleman, and I was secretly very happy for him. Then this awful thing happened . . . it's enough to drive one mad."

Her nails almost digging into the tatami in her despair, she began wailing loudly.

[2]

"Well, I'll be . . . ! So that's what happened? I'd absolutely no idea!" said Hanshichi, tapping his pipe out against the side of the brazier. "But in any case, wasn't Kakutarō's death an accident? It seems to me that you don't have to blame anyone . . . or is there more to it than that?"

"Yes, there is. It was the mistress who killed him — I'm sure of it."

"Mrs. Izumi . . . ? Now, why don't you calm down and explain everything. It seems to me that she wouldn't have agreed to take the boy in the first place if she was going to kill him."

Through her tears, Mojikiyo gave Hanshichi a terrible smile, almost as though she were sneering at his stupidity.

"Five years after I handed Kakutarō over to the Izumiya, the mistress became pregnant with a daughter. Her name is Oteru and she turned fifteen this year. Listen, Inspector. Put yourself in her shoes for a moment. Which child would you love more — your own or someone else's? Would you want Kakutarō to take over the family business? No matter how good people behave most of the time, deep down human beings are evil. Don't you think she'd be capable of devising a plan to get Kakutarō out of her way? Besides, Kakutarō was her husband's illegitimate son, so somewhere down inside she was probably still the jealous woman. When you take all that into consideration, isn't it natural for me to suspect her? She could either have done it herself or had someone do it for her — I mean, sneak into the dressing room amid all the comings and goings and exchange the prop sword for a real one. Please, Inspector, what do you think? Are my suspicions groundless?"

Hanshichi had had no inkling whatsoever that the Izumis were hiding this secret concerning their son. So Kakutarō was the Izumis' stepson, and the master's illegitimate child to boot! Given that, even if Mrs. Izumi had made a gracious show of taking the boy in, there could be no doubt that, in her heart, the whole affair must have left a bitter aftertaste. And later, when she had given birth to her own child, it was understandable that maternal instinct would make her want to pass her fortune on to Oteru. All these factors together could well have led her to devise extreme measures for removing Kakutarō. Hanshichi had dealt with enough criminal cases to know very well the terrible things of which people were capable.

Under the circumstances, Mojikiyo's firm conviction that Mrs. Izumi was her son's sworn enemy was natural enough.

"Inspector, please try to understand. I can't take it any longer. . . . Sometimes I feel like bursting into the Izumiya with a carving knife and hacking that bitch to pieces!"

Mojikiyo was gradually getting more and more worked up. Before long, she was in an absolute frenzy. Hanshichi felt sure that at the least incitement she would lose control and set on someone like a mad dog. He sat smoking his pipe in silence, not daring to contradict her.

At last, in a quiet voice, he said, "I understand completely. Don't worry. I'll look into the matter thoroughly. I'm sure I don't need to tell you not to talk about this to anyone for a while."

"However much she says she treated Kempei like her own child, I won't let her get away with murdering him. You'll help me get revenge on her," Mojikiyo pressed, "won't you?"

"Yes, yes, I understand. Just leave everything to me."

Once Hanshichi had calmed Mojikiyo down and gotten rid of her, he began making preparations to go out. Okume had stayed behind, talking to her sister-in-law, Osen.

"Hanshichi, thanks so much for your help," she said as he was about to leave. "Do you really think," she added almost in a whisper, "that Mrs. Izumi did what Mojikiyo says?"

"I really don't know. That's what I've got to find out."

Hanshichi headed straight for Kyōbashi. He might be an inspector, but it wouldn't do for him to go barging into the Izumiya without any evidence and start interrogating people. So he walked past the ironmonger's without stopping and dropped in on the head of the local neighborhood association instead. Unfortunately, the headman himself was out, so Hanshichi exchanged a few words with the man's wife and left again.

What should he do now? He was standing in the street planning his next move when he became aware of someone hurrying up behind him. Turning, he saw a man of about fifty whom he judged from his clothes to be a merchant, and one of considerable means at that. He edged up to Hanshichi and greeted him politely.

"Forgive my rudeness, but aren't you that inspector from Kanda? I'm an ironmonger, have a business in Rogetsuchō over in Shiba — the Yamatoya. Jūemon's the name. I was just going over to speak to the headman about something when I saw you having a chat with his wife. When you left, I . . . well, she told me who you were, so I thought this might be a good opportunity and hurried after you. I hope you don't mind. Would it be too much trouble to come somewhere with me so we can talk? It won't take very long. . . ."

"Surely. Where shall we go?"

At Jūemon's invitation, the two men entered a nearby eel restaurant. They were shown to a small private south-facing room upstairs. Gentle sunshine streaked in as though spring had already arrived. A row of elegant potted damson trees, outside on the veranda, cast interesting shadows that looked like an ink painting on the closed shoji. The two men ordered, and while they waited for the food to arrive, took turns politely replenishing each other's saké cups.

"Since you're a detective, I'm sure you know all the circumstances surrounding the tragic death of the Izumis' son. The fact is, I'm Mrs. Izumi's older brother. As far as this incident is concerned, I'm afraid there's nothing more to be done for the deceased, but our family's future reputation is quite another matter — you know how idle tongues will wag. My sister is terribly worried about what people will say."

Jūemon's voice trembled with emotion. It seemed that Mojikiyo, Kakutarō's real mother, was not the only person who had her suspicions about Mrs. Izumi. It appeared that someone else very familiar with the Izumiya, someone who had an inkling of the family's secret, was also beginning to cast aspersions upon the mistress of the house. Deeply troubled, Jūemon had gone to the local headman that day to discuss the matter.

"I thought I'd ask him to find out how the fake sword came to be replaced by a real one . . . if people started exchanging malicious gossip, it would be most regrettable for my sister. For what it's worth coming from her older brother, she's an honest and upright woman. She always treated Kakutarō as if he were her own son; to think that people might accuse her of being an evil stepmother is simply outrageous! At any rate, now that yesterday's funeral is out of the way, I thought I'd better begin inquiring into the cause of the tragic mishap. As long as it remains a mystery, my sister will be open to suspicion. She's oversensitive and likely to drive herself mad with worry. I feel awfully sorry for her . . ." Jūemon took out a tissue and blew his nose.

Mojikiyo was going mad. Mrs. Izumi was likely to go mad. Were Mojikiyo's accusations true? Was Jūemon lying? Even Hanshichi was perplexed by it all.

"You were in the audience on the night of the play?" he asked, putting down his saké cup.

"Yes, I saw the performance."

"I suppose there were lots of people backstage?"

"Yes, it was quite crowded in the dressing rooms. There must have been about ten people in the eight-mat room and two more in a separate four-and-a-half-mat room . . . and that's only counting the actors. There were quite a few assistants, too. And the rooms were so full of wigs and costumes there was hardly room to walk. But it was only us common folk—no samurai —so it's not as though anyone had a sword they could have left lying about.[7] At the beginning of the performance, Kakutarō inspected each of his props carefully as they were handed to him. There couldn't have been anything amiss at that point. Either he picked up the wrong sword or someone switched it before he went out on stage."

"I see." Hanshichi sat with arms folded, hardly touching his saké. Jūemon fell silent and stared down at his knees. They could

---

7. Only samurai were permitted to own swords.

hear the faint pitter-patter of a fly walking busily across one of the paper screens.

"Was Kakutarō in the eight-mat room or the smaller one?"

"He was in the four-and-a-half-mat room. There were three men from the shop with him — Shōhachi, Chōjirō, and Kazukichi. Shōhachi was helping with the costumes and Chōjirō was in charge of bringing tea and hot water. Kazukichi was playing the role of Senzaki Yagorō."

"One more thing. This may sound like a strange question, but did the young master have any hobbies besides the theater?" Hanshichi asked.

Jūemon replied that Kakutarō had had a strong aversion to popular pastimes such as go and chess, nor, as far as he knew, had he been a ladies' man.

"And there was no gossip about a prospective bride?"

"That's a private family matter," Jūemon replied, looking a trifle annoyed. "But since it's come to this, I might as well tell you — the fact is, Kakutarō had been having an affair with one of the maids, a girl named Ofuyu. She's an attractive girl with a decent disposition, so my sister and her husband talked it over and decided to find a respectable couple to act formally as her godparents. They were going to announce the engagement before any rumors leaked out. Then, out of the blue, this tragedy occurred. I guess you could say fate frowned on both him and the girl."

Hanshichi pricked up his ears at the mention of this love story.

"How old is this Ofuyu and where is she from?"

"Seventeen. She's from Shinagawa."

"How about it — would it be possible for me to meet Ofuyu?"

"Well, you know how young girls are. Kakutarō's sudden death has hit her very hard. She spends all her time sitting around staring vacantly into space. I don't think you'll get anything coherent out of her, but if you wish, I could arrange a meeting anytime."

"The sooner the better. If it's not too much trouble, would you take me to her right away?"

"Certainly."

The two men agreed to head straight over to the Izumiya as soon as they had had their meal. Jūemon clapped his hands impatiently to call the waitress, but at that very moment she at last arrived with the eel they had ordered.

[3]

Jūemon at once picked up his chopsticks and tucked in, but Hanshichi barely touched his food. Instead, he asked the waitress to bring him another bottle of warmed saké.[8]

"You're fond of drink, are you, Inspector?" Jūemon asked him.

"What, an unrefined fellow like me? No . . . can't hold my saké. But today I thought I'd make an exception. Getting a bit tipsy might liven things up, don't you think?" Hanshichi said with a big grin on his face.

Jūemon gave him a quizzical look and again fell silent.

The waitress arrived with a flask of saké, which Hanshichi proceeded to pour into his own cup little by little until he had drunk it all. Soon, flush from the saké and warmed by the noontime sun streaming into the room, Hanshichi's face and extremities took on a crimson hue resembling the New Year's lobsters for sale outside in the street.

"What d'ya think? Ever seen a mug as red as this?" Hanshichi said, stroking his warm cheeks.

"It's quite an impressive color, I must say," Jūemon said with a reluctant smile.

Jūemon began to have misgivings about taking a drunk like Hanshichi over to the Izumiya, but it was too late now to refuse.

---

8. Typically saké is only drunk before a meal. When drinking with others, it is customary to take turns pouring saké into the other person's cup, hence Hanshichi's drinking alone while Jūemon eats is unorthodox behavior.

He paid the bill and led Hanshichi out into the street. A bit unsteady on his feet, Hanshichi nearly collided with a shop boy walking toward them carrying a large salmon.

"Inspector. Are you all right?"

Hanshichi staggered along, Jūemon holding his hand. The latter seemed to be regretting having consulted such an impossible person on such a delicate matter.

"I'll slip in through the back door, if you don't mind," Hanshichi said. Jūemon hesitated for a moment, thinking it highly unlikely that Hanshichi could even make it that far. But Hanshichi popped into the alleyway at the side of the shop and darted down it toward the back of the house. Nothing about his gait suggested that he was drunk. Jūemon followed him, struggling to keep up.

"Get Ofuyu for me right away."

Entering the house, Hanshichi passed through the spacious kitchen and peeked into the maids' room, where three ruddy-faced women were sitting in a huddle. None fit the description of Ofuyu.

"Where's Ofuyu?" Jūemon asked, gently sliding open the shoji. The ruddy-faced girls looked in his direction. Ofuyu had taken sick the night before, they said, so the missus had instructed her to sleep in a separate room until she felt better. It was the same four-and-a-half-mat room that Kakutarō had used as his dressing room on the night of the nineteenth.

As they passed along the veranda toward the inner part of the house, Hanshichi noticed a large nandina laden with bright red berries growing in a small garden. Jūemon halted in front of a pair of shoji and called out. The paper screens were drawn open from inside. There, seated at Ofuyu's bedside, was a young man, presumably the person who had let them in. Ofuyu was buried so far under the bedclothes that not even her hair could be seen. The man was small of stature and had a swarthy complexion, a narrow forehead, and thick eyebrows.

The young man greeted Jūemon and quickly left the room.

"That's Kazukichi, the man I mentioned earlier who played the role of Senzaki Yagorō," Jūemon said to Hanshichi.

Ofuyu pulled back the covers and sat up in bed. Her face was even more wan and haggard than Mojikiyo's had been that morning. She was like a zombie, her replies to their questions vague and incoherent. At the very mention of Kakutarō's death, she broke down and wailed uncontrollably, as though the mere thought of the nightmarish events of that dreadful night was more than she could bear. Nearby, the singing of a caged bush warbler—tricked by the spell of warm weather into thinking that spring had arrived—only intensified her grief.[9]

The fire of love ignited in Ofuyu's heart had burned itself out and the ashes scattered. She would not speak of the past, of her memories of being happy and in love. She did, however, reply to Hanshichi's questions about her current misery, albeit in an incomplete and fragmented fashion. She said the Izumis' had shown her great sympathy and were being altogether too good to her. Of the shop employees, Kazukichi was the kindest. He had already come to look in on her twice that morning when he'd had a free moment.

"So, that was him who was here just now? What did you talk about?" Hanshichi asked her.

"I said that because of what happened to the young master it had become very difficult for me to remain in service here, so I was thinking of giving notice. Kazukichi told me not to say such things and urged me to be patient, at least until next year when our contracts run out."

Hanshichi nodded.

"Well, thank you very much, miss. I'm sorry for barging in on you like this while you're trying to rest. Please take care of yourself. Jūemon, would you be kind enough to take me to the shop for a moment?"

---

9. Perhaps because *uguisu* (bush warbler) was a colloquial term for "funeral."

"Yes, certainly."

Jūemon led the way toward the shop, Hanshichi staggering along behind him. The alcohol appeared to be catching up with him again. His cheeks were increasingly flushed.

"Are all the employees here at the moment?" Hanshichi asked Jūemon, gazing out across the shop from the bookkeeping office. The head clerk, a man in his forties, sat nearby. Next to him, two junior clerks were running their fingers over abacuses: Hanshichi recognized Kazukichi and another, middle-aged man. In the shop itself, four or five shop assistants were opening packages of iron nails.

"Yes. It seems everyone's here," replied Jūemon, seating himself in front of the charcoal brazier.

Hanshichi strolled into the shop and plopped himself down cross-legged on the tatami in the middle of the floor, whence he began casting suspicious glances around the faces of the clerks and shop assistants.

"Look here, Jūemon. Gusokuchō's is famous for two things: the Seishōkō Shrine[10] and the Izumiya. It's one of the most prosperous merchant houses in all of Edo. But if you don't mind my saying so, security's a bit lax here, isn't it? I mean, just look at all these brawny, murderous-looking chaps! Here you are taking good care of them, fattening them up and lavishing money on them!"

The shop employees exchanged glances with one another. Even Jūemon seemed a bit flustered.

---

10. A shrine dedicated to Katō Kiyomasa (1562–1611) on the grounds of Kakurin Temple, where Kiyomasa's mansion once stood. Kiyomasa was a retainer of Toyotomi Hideyoshi, who became lord of Higo Province in Kyūshū (present-day Kumamoto Prefecture). He distinguished himself in several major campaigns, including Hideyoshi's invasion of Korea, and was known for his ruthlessness. After Hideyoshi's death, he became one of Tokugawa Ieyasu's closest allies and helped him consolidate his control of Japan. His writings on *bushidō*, *The Precepts*, lay down the disciplines and austerities that a samurai must follow. Worshipping at his shrine is believed to help one achieve victory in any competitive endeavor.

"Please, Inspector. Not so loud . . . people outside can hear you."

"What does it matter if someone hears me? Sooner or later people are gonna find out you're harboring a condemned criminal," Hanshichi replied. He chuckled to himself. "Hey, you lot. Listen, I know you're up to no good. Do you think you can just go about your work, pretending you don't know there's a murderer among you? You pack of liars! Mark my words, one of you is gonna be crucified! Mr. Izumi must be blind as a bat . . . letting a blackguard into his house to murder his precious son, all on account of some coddled young girl. You know what I'm gonna give him for New Year's? . . . some medicine to cure his stupidity! Hey, Jūemon! Your eyes don't seem to be too good either . . . why don't you go to the storeroom and wash them out with lye a few times?"

Hanshichi cut an intimidating figure and, what's more, was extremely inebriated. The others had no choice but to sit quietly and put up with it. Getting no response, Hanshichi hit his stride and began hurling still more abuse.

"To tell the truth, I'm as happy as a clam about all this. When I nab the murderer I'll be able to make a nice year-end present of him to my boss in Hatchōbori. You all look pretty smug right now, but rest assured, I've already sniffed out the skunk among you. If you think I'm as blind as that tomfool master of yours, you've got another think coming. Don't go cursing me when you suddenly find your arms bound behind your back, or whine about 'the long arm of the law' or any of that nonsense, like Chūbei in that dreadful play *The Courier for Hell*.[11] This is no joke — better just accept your fate and go quietly!"

---

11. *Meido no hikyaku*, written by Chikamatsu Monzaemon for the puppet theater and first performed in 1711. Chūbei is an adopted son whose family owns a courier service. He falls in love with Umekawa, a courtesan, and steals 300 *ryō* in order to buy out her contract and elope with her. At the end of the play, he is apprehended and led away to be executed.

Unable to stand it any longer, Jūemon timidly sidled up to Hanshichi.

"Inspector. I think you've had a little too much to drink, so why don't you go back inside and take a bit of a rest? People might think badly of our establishment if you raise your voice like that inside the shop. Kazukichi, get over here and take the inspector inside."

"Yes, sir," Kazukichi replied, trembling as he prepared to take Hanshichi by the hand. The next moment, he felt a crushing blow land on the side of his face.

"Hey, what's the big idea? I don't need any help from a bunch of condemned men like you. Why the hell are you looking at me like that? Didn't you hear what I said? You're all gonna be crucified! Do you know what they do to murderers? They put you on a horse bareback and parade you all over Edo. Then they take you to Suzugamori[12] or Kozukappara and string you high up on a wooden cross. Next, two men stand on either side of you, shouting and thrusting their spears right in front of your face. But that's just to scare you . . . remember that! Once they're done scaring you, they start jabbing their spears into your sides for real!"

Listening to this gruesome account of the punishment for murder, Jūemon grimaced in discomfort. Kazukichi, too, blanched visibly. The others all gasped and cowered in fear. To a man, they sat quiet and unblinking for a while, as though each of them had just received a death sentence.

Outside the shop, the winter sky was crystal-clear and bright sunshine flooded the street.

[4]

In due course, Hanshichi, seemingly overcome by alcohol, passed out on the floor. The Izumiya's employees were mortified

---

12. An execution ground south of Edo, near Shinagawa.

at the idea of customers seeing him asleep in the middle of the shop, but no one could summon the nerve to touch him.

"Well, there's nothing we can do. Just let him be for a while."

Jūemon withdrew inside the house to speak with Mr. and Mrs. Izumi. One by one, the men in the shop returned to their work.

After he had judged that half an hour had passed, Hanshichi — who'd been feigning sleep all this time — suddenly got up.

"Ugh, what a hangover! I think I better go to the kitchen and get a drink of water. That's all right . . . don't mind me. I'll get it myself."

But Hanshichi did not stop at the kitchen, heading instead straight through to the inner part of the house. He jumped nimbly off the veranda into the garden and lay down on his stomach, like a frog, in the shade of the large nandina. After a short while, Kazukichi appeared on the veranda and tiptoed along it until he reached the shoji giving onto Ofuyu's four-and-a-half-mat room. For a moment he stood and peeped inside. Finally, he slid the paper screens open and entered, whereupon Hanshichi stuck his head out from behind the nandina.

He could hear Kazukichi's tearful voice emanating from the room. So muffled was the sound, however, that he could not make out the words. He soon became impatient. Emerging from his hiding place, he crept like a cat burglar up to the veranda.

Kazukichi's voice was, in fact, very hushed. Moreover, he seemed to be choking back tears.

"You're right, I killed the young master. But I did it because I loved you. I never had the nerve to tell you, Ofuyu, but I've been in love with you for a long time. All I could think about was how much I wanted us to become husband and wife. Then you and the young master went and . . . I heard the two of you were to be married soon. How my heart ached! Ofuyu, please try to understand! But even then, I never hated you. Even now, I don't hate you. But I couldn't help hating the young master. I didn't care that he was my boss, I couldn't bear it any longer. I must have been mad . . . I realized the year-end play gave me the perfect opportunity. I bought a ready-made sword in Hikagechō and exchanged it for the prop one, just as the curtain was going up on the sixth act. My plan went off perfectly . . . but when the young master was brought backstage covered in blood, I felt as though a bucket of cold water had been poured over my head. For the next two days and nights, until he died, I was scared out of my wits. Whenever I went to his bedside, I just sat there, trembling. Then I thought: once he was gone, sooner or later, you would be mine . . . I didn't know whether to laugh or cry. So now you know what I've been going through. . . . Ah, I don't think I can take it any longer! That detective is clever — I'm sure he suspects me."

Even on the other side of the shoji, Hanshichi could picture Kazukichi's deathlike face and trembling limbs. But Kazukichi blew his nose and continued his story.

"That detective came to the shop, pretending to be drunk and shouting about one of us being a murderer. He even went into a long rigmarole about how they crucify people. It was so horrible, I couldn't bear it. That's why I've resigned myself to my fate. I won't let myself be hauled out of here in ropes, thrown into jail, paraded through the streets, and crucified. I'll end my own life first. Like I said, I don't hate you, Ofuyu. But if it weren't for you, I wouldn't be in this position. Of course, you might think of it as retribution for killing the young master. But please, try to imagine how I feel and take pity on me. It was wrong of me to kill him. Forgive me, I beg you. After I'm dead, all I ask is that you burn a stick of incense for me — just one, that's all. That's my dying wish. I've managed to save up more than two *ryō.* I want you to have all of it and . . ."

His voice slowly trailed off and Hanshichi was unable to catch anything more. Just occasionally, he could hear the sound of Ofuyu's sobbing. The bell in Kokuchō sounded two o'clock . . . Hanshichi heard someone in the room stand up as though startled by the sound, and he returned to his hiding place amid the foliage of the nandina. Soon, he heard footsteps approaching listlessly along the veranda, and the dejected figure of Kazukichi passed by and disappeared like a shadow. Hanshichi dusted off his feet and stepped up onto the veranda.

He made his way back to the shop, but Kazukichi was nowhere to be seen. He chatted for a while with the head clerk in the office, but still Kazukichi did not reappear.

"By the way, you haven't seen that clerk Kazukichi, have you?" Hanshichi asked innocently.

"Hmm, I wonder where he could have gotten to?" the clerk said, shaking his head. "He can't be out on an errand . . . do you want to see him about something?"

"No, nothing in particular. But would you mind finding out where's he's gone?"

The clerk sent one of the shop assistants inside the house, but he soon returned and reported that Kazukichi was neither in the kitchen nor anywhere else in the house.

"Well, is Master Jūemon still around?" Hanshichi asked again.

"Yes, he's inside talking to the mistress."

"Would you mind telling him I'd like to have a word?"

Jūemon was in the living room at the back of the house with Mr. and Mrs. Izumi. All the doors to the room were tightly shut, and inside it was dark even though it was still the middle of the afternoon. The three were seated around a large charcoal brazier talking about something in hushed tones. Mrs. Izumi was an attractive woman of about forty. Her plucked eyebrows were drawn into a frown. Hanshichi was shown into the room and sat down.

"Forgive me, sir, but I've learned who killed your son," Hanshichi whispered.

"What?" all three turned to look at him, eyes flashing.

"One of the employees."

"An employee?" Jūemon said rising up on his knees. "So what you said earlier was true?"

"I'm afraid I said some inexcusable things during that drunken charade, but I found out that Kazukichi is the murderer."

"Kazukichi?"

The three looked at one another in disbelief. Just then, one of the maids came rushing into the room. She had gone to the storeroom to fetch something and found Kazukichi's body — he had hanged himself.

"Well, I figured he'd either hang himself or throw himself into the river," Hanshichi said with a sigh. "You see, earlier when I spoke with Jūemon, my attention was drawn to the relationship between Kakutarō and Ofuyu. Then I found that this Kazukichi had been in the same room with the young master during the play. It seemed likely that there was some sort of romantic entanglement between the three of them. So I first went to see Ofuyu and casually asked her about Kazukichi. She said he'd been very kind and frequently came to look in on her. I found that a bit odd, so next I went to the shop and deliberately started hurling abuse at the employees. I'm sure Jūemon must have thought I was behaving like a boor, but to be honest I was doing it for the good of the Izumiya . . . I could have arrested Kazukichi then and there, but he would have been thrown in jail and interrogated. He'd have been branded a criminal and paraded through the streets of Edo. All sorts of things about the Izumiya would have come out during his interrogation, foremost among them that you'd been harboring a depraved murderer. It would have been a blot on your reputation, and naturally your business would have suffered. That's why I didn't want to arrest him. I thought it would be better for Kazukichi if he ended his own life rather than being crucified, so I deliberately went and put the fear of god into him. What's more, seeing that I didn't have any concrete evidence that pointed definitively to him, I was only more or less grasping at straws in making those rash accusations: if he was innocent, then my words would have no effect on him; but if he had a guilty conscience, he wouldn't be able sit and take it calmly like the others. Everything went according to plan. Kazukichi soon realized the game was up. If you want all the details, please talk to Ofuyu."

The other three people in the room listened in stunned silence. Jūemon was the first to speak.

"We're very grateful to you, Hanshichi. Instead of doing your job according to the book and arresting the murderer, you swallowed your pride and prevented the good name of the Izumiya from being tarnished. I don't know how to thank you. Now, I wonder if we might beg your indulgence and make one further request? So that we can keep this matter private, if you could let it be known that Kazukichi went insane . . ."

"Very well. As parents, and as an uncle, you must naturally feel that even crucifixion would have been too good for him. But however cruel the punishment, nothing would have brought the young master back to life. Please think of it as some sort of karma, and dispose of Kazukichi's remains in some decent manner."

"Of course. Thank you again."

"I'll keep the matter strictly confidential, sir, but I must warn you before it's too late that there is one person in all of Edo who needs to be told the truth," Hanshichi stated forthrightly.

"One person?" Jūemon said, with a puzzled look on his face.

"It's rather a delicate subject, I'm afraid, but I'm speaking of Mojikiyo, a music teacher in Shitaya."

Mr. and Mrs. Izumi looked at one another.

"You see," Hanshichi went on, "she seems to be laboring under a grave misapprehension in regard to this matter, and the only way for me to put her mind at rest is by telling her everything. I understand that while the young master was alive things might have been rather awkward, but considering all that has transpired, please try to keep an eye on her and invite her to visit you. She's never married after all these years, and it's sad to see a woman without anyone to depend on as she grows old."

At this heartfelt speech, Mrs. Izumi burst into tears.

"Oh, I've been so insensitive! I'll call on her immediately and from now on I'll treat her as my own sister."

"IT'S GOTTEN completely dark."

Hanshichi rose and turned on the overhead light.

"Ofuyu remained in service at the Izumiya, and not long after that Jūemon arranged for her to marry someone in Asakusa, with the Izumis acting as her godparents. Mojikiyo became a regular visitor to the Izumiya. Two or three years later, she retired from teaching and married someone in Shiba, also thanks to the Izumis, of course. He was a kind and generous man, the master of the Izumiya.

"The Izumis' younger daughter, Oteru, married a very enterprising young fellow. When the Tokugawa era ended and Edo became Tokyo, he immediately turned the Izumiya into a clock dealer's. The business is still going strong. I sometimes go uptown to see them and talk about old times.

"As you know if you've read Ryūtei's *Eight Laughing Men*,[13] amateur kabuki was all the rage in Edo, and the fifth and sixth acts of *The Treasury of Loyal Retainers* were universal favorites, perhaps because they don't require much in the way of costumes and sets. For one reason or another, I've been obliged to attend such performances on many occasions, but strangely enough, since what happened at the Izumiya, the sixth act is no longer staged. I guess it just doesn't go down well with people anymore."

---

13. *Hanagoyomi hasshōjin,* a comic novel by Ryūtei Rijō (d. 1841), published in installments from 1820 to 1849, recounting the escapades and idle pursuits of a group of friends in Edo.

The Room over the Bathhouse

YŪYA NO NIKAI

[1]

On another occasion, I again paid old Hanshichi a visit around New Year's.

"Happy New Year!" I sang out unceremoniously.

"New Year's felicitations to you, too, my good fellow, and best wishes for health and happiness."

The formality of Hanshichi's greeting took me, as a young student, slightly aback. But then he produced the customary bottle of New Year's mulled saké. Since the old man had a low tolerance for alcohol, and I was a virtual teetotaler, it was not long before both our faces had taken on a springlike flush, and the conversation grew more and more animated.

"Could you tell me one of your usual stories — something suitable for spring perhaps?"

"That's a tall order!" the old man said with a laugh, rubbing his forehead thoughtfully. "Almost all the stories in my repertoire are about murderers and thieves. I don't know if I have any that are light and cheerful! Now, let me see . . . I did slip up rather badly a few times. We detectives aren't gods, you know — we don't always get our man. Sometimes we miscalculate. Sometimes we just plain make mistakes. You might say that detective work is a comedy of errors. I'm always bragging about my great deeds, so today, why don't I confess one of my blunders instead? Looking back on it, it really is quite a laughable story!"

THE YEAR WAS 1863. The New Year's pine-tree decorations had already been taken down. Early in the evening of the sixth — the day people used to call "The Sixth Day of New Year's" — a deputy by the name of Kumazō paid Hanshichi a visit at his home in Kanda's Mikawachō district. Kumazō ran a bathhouse in Atagoshita, so the other deputies had given him the nickname Bathhouse Kuma, or "Bathhouse Bear." He tended to do things in a slapdash manner and often fouled things up, turning in reports that were utter nonsense and making the most outrageous assertions. For that reason, he was also known familiarly as "Boastful Bear."

"Good evening."

"What's up, Kuma?" Hanshichi asked, seated in front of the charcoal brazier. "Got any interesting stories for the New Year?"

"Er . . . matter of fact, boss, that's what I came to see you about . . . there's something I need to tell you."

"Well, out with it. Not another one of your cockamamie stories, is it, Boastful Bear?"

"No . . . not at all," Kumazō replied. "This time there isn't even a hint of boastfulness in it. You see, this past winter — around the middle of the eleventh month — a couple of men started coming every day to use the room over my bathhouse. I felt there was something peculiar about them . . . just odd, if you know what I mean."

People who have read Shikitei Samba's *The Bathhouse of the Floating World* will understand what Kumazō was talking about.[1] From the Edo period on into the early years of the Meiji era, most bathhouses had a room upstairs where young women served tea and cakes. Lazy fellows went there to take naps. Idlers sat about playing chess. Some fast types even went there, wasting their money, just so they could gawk at a pretty woman. Kumazō had just such a room on the second floor of his bathhouse, where he

---

1. *Ukiyo-buro,* a comic novel published in installments from 1809 to 1813.

employed an attractive girl by the name of Okichi to serve his customers.

"Get this, boss — the men are samurai. Don't you think that's strange?"

"There's nothing strange about it. Samurai take baths, too, you know."

When a samurai went to a public bathhouse, he was required to take his swords upstairs and check them before entering the bath.[2] There was always a sword rack on the second floor for this purpose.

"But they come every single day without fail!"

"They've been sent up from the provinces,[3] I imagine — and probably have designs on Okichi!" said Hanshichi, laughing.

"If you don't think it's a bit strange, then listen to this. . . . They've been coming every day for nearly two months. They even showed up on New Year's Eve, New Year's Day, and the day after that! I don't care if they are just provincial samurai stationed here in Edo — no samurai spends the New Year's holidays lazing around in a bathhouse! It doesn't make sense. Not only that, but these two usually show up together in the morning, then come and go as they please during the day. But as soon as it gets dark, they always leave together. And I'll say it again — this has been going on day in and day out since the beginning of winter. Don't you think that's peculiar? I can't help thinking these aren't your usual samurai."

"I see what you mean," Hanshichi said thoughtfully, looking more serious.

"What do you think, boss? What do you suppose the two of them are up to?"

"Imposters, perhaps . . ."

---

2. Samurai carried two swords, one long and one short.

3. As part of the system of *sankin-kōtai,* or "alternate attendance," mandated by the shogun in 1631, provincial lords were required to maintain a residence in Edo and live there every other year. These "secondary residences" were staffed with retainers from the lord's own domain.

"Exactly!" Kumazō exclaimed, clapping his hands. "That's what I figured! Just pretending to be samurai as a cover for some sinister purpose. They probably meet at my place during the day to hatch their plans, then go out at night and get up to no good. I'm sure that's it."

"It's quite possible. What do these two men look like?"

"They're both young. One guy — must be twenty-two or -three — he's kinda pasty but not bad-looking. The other one . . . same age, a little taller . . . he doesn't look too disreputable either. I guess you could say they're your typical well-heeled playboys. You know the type . . . tip well, don't go prattling on to Okichi about sardines and whale meat like country bumpkins. Matter of fact, I think Okichi's a bit sweet on that pasty one . . . can you believe it? I asked Okichi what those two were always talking about up there, but I don't think she's being straight with me. Today I climbed halfway up the ladder and listened to see if I could catch anything. I heard one of them say, 'We can't just cut him down with our swords. We'll try to talk some sense into him, but if he puts up a fuss, we'll just have to get rough and grab him. . . .' Well, what do you think of that? Sounds like they're up to no good!"

"Hmm . . ." Hanshichi remained pensive.

Lawlessness had been rife in Edo ever since the sails of Commodore Perry's "black ships" were spotted off the coast of the Izu Peninsula in 1853. Gangs of self-styled *rōnin* roamed the streets of the capital threatening rich merchants into handing over money as contributions to a so-called military fund for quelling the barbarian invaders. Needless to say, few of these men were true *rōnin*. Most were corrupt retainers of the shogun, dissolute second sons from good families, or simply common city scoundrels. Birds of a feather, they had banded together to rob people indiscriminately and force them to loan them money in the name of a patriotic cause. Hanshichi imagined that the two shady characters at Kumazō's bathhouse were in fact using it as their base for just such operations.

"Well, I guess tomorrow I'll have to go check it out myself."

"I'll be expecting you. If you come around noon, they'll be there for sure," Kumazō promised.

The next morning, before going out, Hanshichi marked the end of the New Year by eating the traditional bowl of rice porridge flavored with spring leaves. Then he dropped in to see his boss in Hatchōbori, who advised him that, due to a public outcry, they were under orders to step up their ongoing investigation of a string of burglary-arsons; Hanshichi was to give it top priority. He grew even more suspicious of the goings-on at Kumazō's bathhouse.

It was eleven o'clock by the time Hanshichi left his boss's house, whereupon he made a beeline for Atagoshita. Though New Year's was long past, the streets were still full of people out making belated New Year's calls. He could hear the lively accompaniment of a lion dance being performed in the street.

Arriving at the bathhouse, Hanshichi slipped in via the back entrance. He found Kumazō waiting for him inside.

"You're just in time, boss. One of the men is here — he's taking a bath right now."

"Is that so? Well, then, maybe I'll just have a dip myself."

Hanshichi went back around to the front and paid the entrance fee like an ordinary customer. At midday, the bathhouse was practically empty. Painted on the low doorway leading through to the bath itself was a picture of a fearsome warrior. Inside, someone could be heard cheerfully singing a popular love song. Entering, Hanshichi saw four or five other men already there. He had a quick dip to warm himself up, then threw on a kimono and went upstairs. Kumazō quietly followed him.

"Was it that fellow closest to the tub?" Hanshichi asked, sipping his tea.

"That's right. The young one."

"He's no imposter — that's for sure."

"So you think he's a genuine samurai?"

"Just look at his legs."

A samurai always wore a pair of swords — one short, the other long — on his left side, which tended to make his left leg more muscular and the ankle thicker than the right. Having had the chance to observe the man without his clothes on, Hanshichi had no doubt about his credentials.

"So, you figure he's a shogunal retainer?"[4]

"No, his topknot is tied differently . . . he must be a samurai from a provincial fief."

"I see," Kumazō nodded. "Then listen to this, boss — this morning I saw him hand Okichi something to take care of. It was a bundle wrapped in cloth . . . seemed pretty heavy. Shall we take a look at it?"

"By the way, where is Okichi? I haven't seen her."

"Things are slow in here right now, so she's gone out front to watch the lion dance . . . she likes that kind of childish stuff. This would be the perfect time to sneak a peek at that bundle before anyone shows up. There's no telling what kind of clue we might find."

"Good point."

"I think Okichi stuck it in the clothes cupboard . . . wait here a second."

Kumazō went back to search the shelves. He returned with a bundle wrapped in a dark-blue cloth, which he proceeded to untie. Inside, there was another, yellowish-green cloth wrapped around what appeared to be a pair of boxes.

"I better take a quick look around downstairs . . . I'll be right back."

Kumazō climbed down the ladder. He returned a moment later.

"It's all right. I told the attendant downstairs to cough to let us know when the guy comes out of the bath."

---

4. *Gokenin*, a direct vassal of the shogun, similar to a *hatamoto* but lower in rank (and income) and without the privilege of having audiences (*ome-mie*) with the shogun.

Unwrapping the second cloth, they found two old lacquer boxes of the kind used for storing Noh masks. Each was tied shut by a flat, charcoal-gray length of cord, which was attached to the bottom of the box, crossed over the lid, and knotted tightly. Full of eager curiosity, Kumazō hurriedly undid one of the knots. Even with the lid removed, neither man could make out exactly what was inside. Whatever it was, it was wrapped in some sort of stiff, yellowish substance like fish skin or oil paper.

"What the hell . . . !"

Kumazō could not suppress a cry of astonishment as he undid the wrapping. There, before their eyes, was a severed human head. It was clearly ancient, but so shriveled that it was impossible to tell how many hundreds — if not thousands — of years old it was. The skin had a blackish-yellow hue like decaying leaves. It was not even apparent whether the head was male or female.

For a while the two men just stared at the grotesque object, hardly able to breathe.

[2]

"What do you think it is, boss?"

"Beats me. Anyhow, let's look in the other box."

Kumazō opened the remaining box with obvious distaste. Another carefully wrapped head came tumbling out. This time, however, it was clearly not human but seemed to belong to some monstrous creature — a dragon or a serpent, perhaps — with a large mouth, fangs, and small horns on its head. The flesh was black and shriveled like the first, and as hard as wood or stone.

The combined effect of these two grotesque discoveries left the two men feeling extremely shaken.

"Maybe he's some sort of huckster," Kumazō suggested. The man probably went around exhibiting the bizarre heads at sideshows and such places. Hanshichi, however, was disinclined to accept this theory, adhering to his belief that the man was a genuine samurai. Even so, why in the world would a samurai carry such objects around with him? And why had he casually deposited them with a woman on the second floor of a bathhouse? And what exactly were the objects, anyway? Hanshichi found his wits sorely tested by this riddle.

"I'll be damned if I can figure it out," he admitted.

Just then, they heard the attendant downstairs clear his throat loudly. Hurriedly, the two men returned the objects to their boxes and shoved the bundle back in the clothes cupboard. The lion dance had moved on, its music fading into the distance. Okichi came back inside. Soon, the samurai appeared at the top of the ladder with a damp towel in his hand. Hanshichi put on an innocent look and sat sipping his tea.

Okichi, who knew Hanshichi by sight, had somehow managed to discreetly tip off the samurai to the detective's presence. Without speaking to anyone, the man went and sat in a corner. Kumazō tugged at Hanshichi's sleeve and together they went downstairs.

"I saw Okichi give that fellow a meaningful look, and he tensed up," Hanshichi said. "He's on his guard now, so I don't think we'll get anywhere today."

"Well, I'll keep a close eye on what they do with those boxes," Kumazō whispered to Hanshichi, clearly annoyed.

"What do you think has happened to that other fellow?" said Hanshichi.

"Yes, he's late today — I wonder why?"

"Anyway, keep your eyes open. I'm counting on you."

With that, Hanshichi left the bathhouse and headed over to Akasaka to look into another case. As he walked through the streets, absorbing the hustle and bustle of early spring, Hanshichi was racking his brains all the while for the key to the riddle of the boxes. But no convincing explanation presented itself. "Perhaps those two samurai practice black magic, and the heads are for incantations or casting spells or something.... Or could they be Christian outlaws?"

Since the arrival of the American Black Ships, the government had stepped up its persecution of Christianity.[5] If the two men were indeed adherents of that faith, then the matter demanded serious attention. Whatever the explanation, Hanshichi felt that the two samurai should be closely watched.

His business in Akasaka concluded, Hanshichi returned home. The rest of the evening proved uneventful and he soon went to bed. But the next morning, before it was even light, Bathhouse Bear came bursting into the house.

"Boss! Boss! Something awful's happened! They've finally done it! We were too slow, and now they've gone and . . ."

According to Kumazō's report, the previous night two men dressed as samurai had burst into a pawnshop called the Iseya, not far from Kumazō's bathhouse, and demanded that the proprietor hand over all his available cash for the "military fund." Meeting with some resistance, the men had drawn their swords and wounded the pawnbroker and his head clerk. Then they'd grabbed all the money they could find — about eighty *ryō* — and fled. Their faces had been covered, but their general descriptions matched those of Kumazō's two suspicious customers.

"It was them. There's no doubt about it now — they've been using my place as a base for their raids. We've got to do something quickly!"

"Yes, I suppose we oughtn't to let them get away," Hanshichi said as though to himself.

"*Suppose* . . . ? Look, boss — if someone else catches them before we do, you won't be the only one who comes off looking bad. I and my bathhouse will lose face, too."

This was enough to catapult Hanshichi into action. There was

---

5. Christianity had won many converts, primarily in southern Japan, since Portuguese missionaries first arrived in 1549. The Tokugawa shogunate tried various measures to limit the influence of missionaries and eradicate Christianity from the 1610s onward, including confining foreigners to Nagasaki and persecuting large numbers of Japanese converts. In 1639 all missionaries were expelled from Japan, and the remaining Japanese Christians were forced to practice their religion in secret at the risk of execution.

nothing he hated more than having a case he was working on swiped from under his nose. On the other hand, he couldn't very well arrest the two men at the bathhouse without any evidence. They were samurai after all, and one had to tread carefully; to go butting in might very well bring retaliation later.

"All right, Kumazō. I want you to go home and keep your eyes open to see if the two samurai show up today. I'll head over there as soon as I'm ready."

After sending Kumazō home, Hanshichi had a hasty breakfast, then got ready to go out. Before going to Atagoshita, however, he had something else he wanted to do along the way. He was passing through Hikagechō when he caught sight of a young samurai, seated in front of a swordsmith's called the Aizuya, engaged in some sort of negotiation with the clerk. Looking more closely, he realized it was the owner of the bizarre boxes whom he'd seen yesterday in the room over the bathhouse.

Hanshichi paused and observed the man from a distance. After a while, the clerk handed the samurai some money, and he hurried off. Hanshichi's first instinct was to follow him, but deciding he might learn more if stayed, he retraced his steps and entered the swordsmith's shop.

"Good morning."

"Ah, Inspector. Good morning." The clerk recognized Hanshichi.

"Pretty cold this spring so far, isn't it?" said Hanshichi as he sat down. "Hope you don't mind my asking, but was that samurai who just left here an acquaintance of yours?"

"No, I've never seen him before. He'd been going around trying to sell this. He was turned away from two or three places before he managed to foist it off on me." The clerk gave a wry smile. Next to him lay some sort of hard object wrapped in oil paper.

"What is it?"

The clerk unwrapped the package to reveal what appeared to be a fish covered in blackish mud. He explained that it was a sharkskin to be used for covering sword hilts and scabbards.

"Sharkskin, you say? It looks pretty disgusting if you ask me."

"Well, it hasn't been cleaned up yet," the clerk replied, turning the sharkskin over to show Hanshichi. "As you know, these sharkskins are imported from overseas. They're covered in mud when we get them, but by the time they're washed and polished, they're beautiful and white. It's a time-consuming business, and if we're not careful, we stand to lose quite a bit of money. Because of all the mud, we can't tell if they've got any scrapes or bloodstains on them until we've cleaned them. We can deal with scrapes, but bloodstains are a big problem. You see, when the sharks are killed, blood sometimes seeps from the wound into the skin. No amount of washing and polishing will get it out, and no one wants to buy white sharkskin with black spots on it. Of course, we can hide the spots by staining the skin with lacquer, but then it's not worth half as much. If we buy a sheaf of, say, ten sharkskins, we figure on finding three or four bloodstained ones. We average those into the total price that we're willing to pay. But until they've been cleaned, you never know for sure what you're getting — that's why it's a tricky business."

"I see." Hanshichi nodded as though impressed. To the untrained eye, it seemed incredible that a dirty bit of skin could be polished, like a jewel, into the lustrous beauty of a sharkskin hilt.

"You mean that samurai came to sell you this?" Hanshichi said, turning the sharkskin over and inspecting it.

"It seems he purchased it in Nagasaki.[6] We were haggling over the price — he wanted me to pay quite a lot for it. It's not that I didn't want to buy it, seeing that this is what I do for a living, but I'm a bit uneasy about purchasing something like this from a rank amateur — even if he is a samurai! You can see how muddy it is, and it's just one skin. If I got stuck with a bloodstained one, I'd feel I'd really been had. Well, I tried refusing him, but he was insistent, said he'd take anything for it, so I ended up paying a

---

6. Nagasaki was Japan's main port of foreign trade. From 1616 to 1859, it was one of only two ports open to non-Chinese foreign ships.

very modest sum. Even so," the clerk concluded with a rueful laugh, "my boss will probably yell at me."

The man seemed too disheartened about the whole affair to reveal how much he'd actually paid. For his part, Hanshichi refrained from asking. Rather, he was pondering the strange array of objects that the samurai seemed to possess: two shriveled heads — one human and one belonging to some monstrous creature— and now this grubby piece of sharkskin. He sensed that there must be something behind it all.

"Well, I'm sorry to have bothered you."

Gulping down the cup of coarse tea, which a shop assistant had served him out of a large pot, Hanshichi left the Aizuya and headed straight for Atagoshita. When he reached the bathhouse, Kumazō darted out to meet him as though he'd been eagerly awaiting his arrival.

"Boss, that young guy who was here yesterday showed up a while ago and went out again straightaway."

"Was he carrying anything?"

"He had a long, narrow bundle with him, but I don't know what it was."

"Is that so? I saw him on my way over. What about the other fellow?"

"Like before, the tall one hasn't shown up yet."

"All right, Kuma. I'm sorry to send you off like this, but I want you to go back to the Iseya and find out exactly what was stolen from the pawnshop apart from the money."

Having issued his instructions, Hanshichi went upstairs, where he found Okichi sitting idly in front of the charcoal brazier. This was the detective's second appearance in two days, and a look of unease seemed to creep into her eyes, but she forced herself to smile.

"Hello, Inspector," she greeted him affably. "Cold today, isn't it?"

She brought him tea and cakes and hovered over him attentively. But Hanshichi paid her scant attention. Instead, he filled his pipe and lit it; then he took out some money wrapped up in paper and gave it to her, saying it was a tip because he'd troubled her so much of late.

"Thank you very much, sir."

"By the way, are your mother and brother well?"

Okichi's older brother, he knew, worked as a plasterer, and her mother was in her fifties.

"They're both well, thank you."

"Your brother's still young, but your mother's getting on in years, isn't she? So remember the old saying: 'Don't postpone filial piety until your parents are in their graves.' Now's the time to be a good daughter, you hear?"

"Yes, sir," Okichi blushed, her eyes downcast.

For some reason, she seemed to be embarrassed, guilty, and frightened all at the same time. But Hanshichi pressed ahead.

"By the way," he said in a bantering tone, " I heard some talk of a romance in your life. Is it true?"

"Oh, Inspector . . . really!" Okichi blushed an even deeper shade of red.

"Actually, everyone's talking about it — they say you've become real pally with one of those two samurai who started coming in here last year."

"Well, you could put it like that."

"What do you mean, 'put it like that'? Actually, Okichi, that's what I've been meaning to talk to you about. What fief are those two samurai from? They look like west-country types to me."

"So I've heard," Okichi answered vaguely.

"Well, I'm sorry to say this, but sooner or later I might have to ask you to come down to the watchpost with me. I just wanted to warn you in advance."

Okichi did not miss the note of intimidation in Hanshichi's voice, and a look of fear crept into her eyes again.

"What is it you want to ask me, Inspector?"

"About those two samurai. Or would you prefer to tell me everything now, without having to come to the watchpost?"

Okichi tensed and fell silent.

"Tell me, what line of work are they in? All right — so they're in service to some provincial lord here in the capital. But you can't expect me to believe they spend all their time loafing around on the second floor of a bathhouse, day in and day out — even at New Year's! They're running some shady business on the side, aren't they? Now, don't tell me you don't know anything about it — I know you do. C'mon, why don't you come clean? What's in those boxes they left in that cupboard?"

Okichi trembled and her face turned from red to ashen.

[3]

Although she worked in a bathhouse, Okichi was still just a naïve young girl. Hanshichi's threats so terrified her that she could scarcely breathe. She still maintained, however, that she knew nothing about the two men's identities.

"I heard them say their lord's residence is near Azabu, but I swear I don't know anything else," she insisted. But Hanshichi continued to coax and cajole her, and at last she offered up one more piece of information.

"It seems they're on a vendetta."

"A vendetta," Hanshichi said, bursting into laughter. "You must be joking! This isn't kabuki, you know. These days a couple of samurai don't just launch a vendetta in the middle of Edo! All right, though . . . for now, let's just say that they are on a vendetta. Do you mean you have no idea where they live?"

"None whatsoever."

Hanshichi continued to press Okichi, but when it seemed he would get nothing more out of her, he fell quiet and sat thinking for a while. At that moment, Kumazō's head appeared above the opening in the floor at the top of the ladder.

"Boss!" he called out excitedly. "Could you come down here for a minute?"

"What's all the fuss about?"

With self-conscious calm, Hanshichi descended the ladder. Kumazō sidled up to him and whispered, "It turns out that three old kimonos and five sharkskins were taken from the Iseya in addition to the cash."

"Sharkskins," Hanshichi repeated, his pulse quickening. "Had they been cleaned already, or were they still covered in mud?"

"Hmm, I didn't ask them that . . . guess I'd better go back and find out, huh?"

Kumazō left again in a hurry. He returned to report that they had been white, polished sharkskins, which the pawnbroker had received from a hilt maker in Rogetsuchō. Hanshichi was a bit disappointed at this news; it meant that he could no longer link the samurai who broke into the Iseya the previous night with the man who sold the sharkskin to the Aizuya that morning.

"Well, it beats me," he said.

In any case, it was already nearly noon, so he and Kumazō went out for a meal at a nearby restaurant.

"It seems Okichi is really stuck on that samurai," Hanshichi said, laughing.

"That's just it — that's why we can't get anywhere. Why don't we go lean on her a bit?"

"No, I already scared the life out of her — that's enough for now. It won't do us any good to overdo it, so let's just leave her alone for a while."

The two men left the restaurant, toothpicks still drooping from between their lips. As they approached the bathhouse, they spotted one of the young samurai parting the curtain on his way out. No mistake, it was the man Hanshichi had seen in Hikagechō. He was carefully holding something wrapped in a yellowish-green cloth. It appeared to be one of the boxes.

"There's that fellow now! Looks like he's making off with a box," Kumazō said, drawing himself up with a glint in his eyes.

"No doubt about it. Go and follow him."

"Right."

Kumazō headed off in pursuit. Hanshichi entered the bath-

house and went upstairs to check on the boxes. Okichi was nowhere to be seen. An inspection of the cupboard revealed that
both boxes were indeed missing.

"They're gone!"

He climbed back down the ladder and asked the attendant
what had become of Okichi. The man told him that she had descended the ladder only a few moments earlier and disappeared
into the back of the house. Hanshichi headed in the same direction. According to the man stoking the fire that heated the baths,
Okichi had said she was stepping outside for a moment, then had
rushed out of the back door into the street.

"Was she carrying anything?"

"I dunno."

The man was a country bumpkin, totally oblivious of what
was going on around him. Hanshichi clicked his tongue in frustration. Undoubtedly, the samurai and Okichi had happened to
return to the bathhouse just as he and Kumazō were out eating
lunch, and quickly decided to abscond with the boxes, one of
them slipping out the front door and the other out the back.

"I've really gone and bungled it!" Hanshichi thought. He could
have kicked himself for his carelessness. "If I'd known this was
going to happen, I'd have hauled that Okichi girl off to the watchpost in the first place."

Hanshichi returned to the front of the house and asked the bath
attendant where Okichi lived. Her house was located in Shiba just
outside the main gate of the Shinmei Shrine, he was told; so he
headed straight over. Okichi's brother was out at work, but her
mother, an honest-looking woman, was alone, mending some
well-worn clothes. Okichi had gone out as usual that morning,
she said, and had not returned home since. There was no trace of
duplicity in the woman's face. Moreover, it seemed unlikely that
Okichi could be hiding anywhere in such a small house.

His spirits deflated, Hanshichi left. By the time he reached the
bathhouse, Kumazō had already returned. He directed a look of
disappointment at Hanshichi.

"Bad news, boss. I ran into a friend along the way, and was just having a word with him when that guy gave me the slip."

"Idiot! How could you stop to shoot the breeze with a friend when you're in the middle of a case!" But he realized that bawling out Kumazō wouldn't do any good. Hanshichi chafed with frustration.

"After what's happened today, I don't know whether to laugh or cry. I want you to watch carefully to see if Okichi returns. And if the other samurai comes, I want you to trail him . . . and make sure you find out where he lives this time! This investigation was all your idea — let's see if you can take your job seriously for a change."

Hanshichi left Kumazō and went home. He was still so wound up, however, that he spent a restless night.

IT WAS FREEZING the next morning. Splashing cold water on his face in his usual routine, Hanshichi hurried out of the house, only to find the alleyway in back, where the sun hadn't reached, covered in a sheet of ice. Some local children had apparently emptied the neighbor's rain barrel onto the street as a prank; the ice looked two or three inches thick and was hard as steel.

It was so cold that Hanshichi could see his breath as he hurried toward Atagoshita.

"Well, Kuma? Any new developments since last night?"

"Boss, Okichi seems to have eloped. She never went home last night. Her mother came by this morning to ask after her because she was worried," Kumazō spoke in a hushed voice, frowning.

"Is that so?" Hanshichi replied. His brow, too, was deeply furrowed. "Well, there's nothing we can do. Let's just set our nets and be patient. There's still a chance the other fellow will show up."

"I guess so," Kumazō responded in a vacant and desultory manner.

Hanshichi went upstairs. Since Okichi had not shown up that morning, there was no heat in the room yet. Kumazō's wife appeared, offering her apologies, and brought in the charcoal brazier and some tea. No other customers were upstairs yet and Hanshichi sat there alone, absentmindedly smoking his pipe, shivering as he felt the spring chill creep under his collar.

"That Okichi's been so flighty of late she hasn't even mended the paper screens," Kumazō said, tut-tutting disapprovingly as he turned to look at the tattered shoji.

Lost in thought, Hanshichi made no response. The grotesque heads he had found there in the bathhouse the day before yesterday . . . the mud-covered sharkskin he had seen yesterday in Hikagechō — the three objects fused together and raced round and round in his mind like a revolving picture lantern. Was it black magic, Christianity, or just plain old-fashioned robbery? Hanshichi could find no easy solution to the conundrum. Moreover, he was still kicking himself for allowing the samurai to get away the day before. It was all his own fault for having asked a nincompoop like Kumazō to trail the man rather than doing it himself.

Seeing the disgruntled look on his boss's face, Kumazō simply sat quietly whiling away the time. Presently, the bell on the hill in Shiba struck ten o'clock. At that moment, they heard the lattice door downstairs open and the voice of the attendant greeting a customer. Then they heard him clear his throat as though sending a signal to the two of them upstairs. Hanshichi and Kumazō looked at each other.

"He's here!" Kumazō exclaimed, jumping up excitedly and peering downstairs. At that very moment, the taller of the two young samurai came climbing swiftly up the ladder carrying his swords.

"Ah, come in!" said Kumazō, smiling affably. "Another cold day, isn't it? Have a seat. The young lady has taken the day off, so I'm afraid it's a bit messy up here."

"Taken the day off?" the samurai said, cocking his head slightly to one side as he placed his swords on the sword rack. "Is Okichi sick?" he asked in a meaningful tone.

"Well now, she didn't say exactly. She's probably caught some bug that's going around."

The samurai nodded silently for a moment, and then took off his kimono and went downstairs.

"Is that the other one?" Hanshichi asked in a low voice.

Kumazō nodded. "What should we do, boss?"

"Well, we can't very well arrest him just like that. Listen — when he comes back, think of a good way to ask him about his partner without arousing his suspicions. What we decide to do after that will depend on his answer. Don't forget, he's a samurai. Better hide his swords somewhere — things could get tricky if he started brandishing them about."

"All right. Should we call in some reinforcements?"

"That shouldn't be necessary. There's only one of him, after all. We'll handle him somehow," Hanshichi said, feeling inside his kimono to check that he had his truncheon.[7]

The two men waited in great suspense.

[4]

"It's a silly story, I'm afraid," old Hanshichi said to me with a smile. "Looking back on it now, it all seems so ridiculous!" Then he continued.

"We waited for the samurai to return, whereupon Kumazō, with an innocent air, started asking him questions. His answers were pretty vague, and it seemed to me he was hiding something. I chimed in a few times to try to find out more, but a lot of what he said just didn't make sense. Finally, I got so impatient that I whipped out my truncheon. My, what a stupid thing to do!" Hanshichi laughed. "One should never be too hasty. But the samurai seemed to realize he was cornered and finally confessed what they had really been up to. It was just as Okichi had said — they were on a vendetta!"

---

7. *Jitte.* A forked metal instrument used to ward off sword blows and subdue criminals.

"A vendetta . . . ," I echoed. Hanshichi gave me a big grin. "A genuine, honest-to-goodness vendetta! But wait — it gets even stranger. Listen to this . . ."

THE SAMURAI WHOM Hanshichi had threatened with his truncheon, Kajii Gengorō by name, was from a fief in the west country. His lord had a mansion in Azabu, and Gengorō had been sent to Edo the previous spring to serve there. He was a man who enjoyed the good life; he became close friends with a colleague, one Takashima Yashichi, and the two together would make the rounds of the pleasure quarters in the Yoshiwara and Shinagawa. Gradually, they came to feel very much at home in Edo.

Then, at the beginning of November, they invited two of their fellow retainers, Kanzaki Gōsuke and Mobara Ichiroemon, to visit a brothel in Shinagawa with them. While they were there, Gōsuke and Ichiroemon got drunk and started a quarrel. Gengorō and Yashichi intervened and managed to effect a reconciliation. But Gōsuke declared that he'd had enough and wanted to go straight home. Gengorō and Yashichi tried to prevent him from leaving; it was already well past their curfew, so he'd have to spend the night there and go back in the morning, they said. But Gōsuke was adamant.

They couldn't very well let Gōsuke go home alone, so in the end all four men had left the brothel together. It was past eight o'clock when they approached the coast at Takanawa. Torches aboard two or three fishing boats floated forlornly in the darkness of the ocean, and a sobering north wind blew frost in their faces. Packhorses hurried along past them on the road heading for the next station, the sound of their bells ringing out in the night seeming to magnify the chill. For some time, Gōsuke had been walking quietly beside them, but at some point he must have fallen a step or two behind the others and unsheathed his sword. No sooner did Ichiroemon see something glimmer in the darkness than he cried out and fell to the ground. Withdrawing his sword immediately, Gōsuke set off running at full speed in the direction of Shiba.

For some time, Gengorō and Yashichi stood dumbstruck, rooted to the spot. Ichiroemon had been cut down with a single stroke that ran from his shoulder diagonally across his back. He had died instantly. It was too late to do anything for him, so they loaded his body into the first free palanquin they could find and transported it back to Azabu, arriving in the dead of night. The murder of a fellow samurai as the result of a drunken brawl at a house of ill-repute was an inexcusable offense that could not go unpunished. A search was immediately mounted, but five days passed, then ten, and still no one had any clue as to Gōsuke's whereabouts.

The murdered man, Ichiroemon, had a younger brother named Ichijirō, who immediately requested permission from their lord to undertake a vendetta.[8] Ichijirō's request was granted. He was told, however, that officially he could not be released from service to carry out the vendetta. Instead, he was granted leave so that he could return his brother's ashes to his place of birth — and was also told that it would not hurt if he stopped along the way to worship at temples or pay visits to relatives. In other words, he was given tacit permission to pursue his brother's killer under the guise of these other activities. After expressing his gratitude and making the proper obeisances, Ichijirō set off from Edo carrying his brother's remains.

Gengorō and Yashichi were censured for having entered a brothel district, an act unbecoming to a samurai. It was also noted that in regard to the bloodshed on the night in question, they had shown extreme negligence in allowing the murderer to get away, and for that they were severely reprimanded. Moreover,

---

8. It was official policy that anyone wishing to undertake a vendetta *(kataki-uchi)* had to apply to the government for permission. The practice was outlawed in 1873.

for this act of carelessness they were ordered to assist Ichijirō in his vendetta, with the proviso that they could not set foot in any other clan's domain. "Search every inch of Edo for a hundred days and find the murderer," they were ordered.

It was far from clear, even, whether Gōsuke was in fact hiding in Edo, but the two men had their orders: they must walk the length and breadth of Edo from dawn to dusk, day after day, searching for him. For the first ten days or so, they conscientiously carried out their duty, but then their resolve began to flag due to the enormity of their task. In the end, they came up with a plan for shirking their duty: they would leave their lord's estate each morning at the usual hour and spend the entire day amusing themselves at teahouses, storyteller's halls, and bathhouses. One day, they would go to Asakusa's busy shopping district, the next they would visit the samurai mansions of Hongō — in these ways they idled away the time, afterward returning to the estate to report on the supposed progress of their search. Needless to say, they made no attempt to ascertain Gōsuke's whereabouts.

Because they spent all their time amusing themselves, the two samurai were obliged by financial necessity to choose places that were inexpensive. They eventually settled on the second floor of the bathhouse as their headquarters, only venturing out from time to time for the sake of appearances. It was while they were there that one of them, Yashichi, became a little too friendly with Okichi. "Stop this vendetta business — it's dangerous," she was forever urging him, concerned for his safety.

There was little chance that they would ever track Gōsuke down in this manner. Even were they to discover his whereabouts, they had not steeled themselves for the task of assisting Ichijirō in carrying out his vendetta. As time went by, they could not help thinking more and more about their own future. In the event that the one-hundredth day came and they still had not found Gōsuke, their ineptness would be exposed. It was unreasonable that they had been ordered to track Gōsuke down within a stipulated period of time, given that it was far from certain he was still in Edo. Nevertheless, there was nothing they could do about it. They thought it unlikely that they would be dismissed outright from their lord's service, but they accepted the fact that they would be sent back to their provincial domain for dereliction of duty. As they lazed away the days, their anxiety about their impending exile from Edo began to weigh on their minds like a heavy stone.

"Well then, I'll become a *rōnin!*" Yashichi declared one day, with Okichi hovering in the background. He dreaded the day when he would be sent back to his domain and would no longer be able to see her. Gengorō, too, was apprehensive about being sent home, but in the absence of any similarly compelling motive, he could not summon the courage to cut his ties with his master. Unlike Yashichi, who was all alone in the world, Gengorō had a mother, an older brother, and a younger sister waiting for him back in the provinces.

"Now, don't be so hotheaded, Yashichi," said Gengorō soothingly. But when spring came, Yashichi seemed to have made up his mind once and for all. Every morning when he left the estate, he removed a few of his important personal effects and took them to Okichi's house. It was around the same time that the owner of the bathhouse, Kumazō, began to look askance at him. Okichi had whispered in Yashichi's ear that her boss was a detective's deputy, and Yashichi, fed up with being regarded with suspicion, was becoming increasingly restless. Now, it looked as though he and Okichi had absconded. Alarmed when Yashichi had not returned to the estate the previous night, Gengorō had come to the bathhouse that morning to look for his friend.

Listening to his story, Hanshichi understood the reason for their vendetta and for Yashichi and Okichi's elopement. But what about the suspicious boxes that Yashichi had deposited with Okichi?

"Those are his family heirlooms," Gengorō explained.

When Toyotomi Hideyoshi decided to conquer Korea,[9] a certain Takashima Yagoemon — Yashichi's ancestor ten generations back — had followed his lord and signed on with Hideyoshi's invading army. Subsequently, as his share of the spoils, Yagoemon had received the objects in question — two shriveled heads, one human and one belonging to some unknown creature, which a Korean priestess had used for performing black magic and chanting spells; it seemed they were considered extremely sacred. Never having seen anything like them before, Yagoemon had brought them back to Japan with him, but no one could tell him exactly what they were. Be that as it may, they had been passed down from generation to generation along with other family treasures. There was no one in their home province who had not heard of them. Once, Yashichi had even allowed Gengorō to look at them. Presumably, this unusual treasure was the first thing that Yashichi had given to Okichi for safekeeping when he decided to leave his lord's mansion.

Gengorō knew nothing about the sharkskin, he said. Yashichi's grandfather had been stationed in Nagasaki for a long time, so he'd probably acquired it from a foreigner. Yashichi must have sold it because he needed the money, but the other two items would have been impossible to sell. Moreover, as old family heirlooms, Yashichi would probably have wanted to take them with him when he and Okichi eloped. Where were the two of them now, as they wandered about the countryside carrying the heads of a human being and a dragon? Somehow, it was both amusing and pathetic at the same time. Certainly, it was a "lovers' journey" to rival any in the kabuki drama of the past.

---

9. The invasion was ordered by Hideyoshi on April 24, 1592, and an army of nearly 200,000 troops was assembled. The Japanese invaders captured Seoul on June 12 of the same year, but retreated in May 1593 under an onslaught by Korean guerilla fighters and a Chinese army.

"I HAVE TO ADMIT now it was too late for me to back out,"
old Hanshichi said, rubbing his forehead. "There I was, waving
my truncheon about the place — it was most inexcusable. But
that samurai Gengorō was very understanding about it all. In
fact, we had a good laugh together afterward, and that put an
end to the whole affair. The other one, Yashichi, never did return to the mansion in Azabu, nor was Okichi ever heard from
again. There were rumors that their journey took them as far
as Kanagawa, where they went into hiding. I wonder what happened to them after that? I never heard, either, what became of
that fellow Ichijirō and his vendetta. Gengorō was not sent back
home after all, and he often used to drop by the bathhouse to
say hello. The *rōnin* who robbed the pawnbroker's turned out
to be entirely different people — they were later arrested in the
Yoshiwara. During the Meiji era, I once asked someone about
that bizarre human head, and he said he thought it was probably
some sort of mummy; but I really wonder. . . . Anyhow, it was the
strangest thing I've ever seen in my life."

The Dancer's Curse

OBAKE SHISHŌ

[1]

My work had kept me busy since February, and I'd neglected to call on Hanshichi for the better part of half a year. Feeling rather guilty, I sent off a letter at the end of May apologizing for my remissness. I immediately received a reply inviting me to visit Hanshichi the following month during the festival at the Hikawa Shrine,[1] when he would be serving the customary festive *kowameshi*.[2] Filled with anticipation at the thought of seeing the old man again, I set out for Akasaka on the day of the festival. Along the way a light, misty rain began to fall.

"I'm afraid it's started to rain," I said upon my arrival.

"It's not surprising," Hanshichi said, looking up at the sky gloomily. "The rainy season's almost upon us. Even so, it's annoying. This year's festival isn't the usual abbreviated version, they say — it's going to include all the proper ceremonies, no expense spared. Ah well, I don't expect this rain will amount to much."

Just as Hanshichi had promised, a sumptuous meal of *kowameshi* with boiled vegetables was served, with saké to accompany it. I ate and drank to my heart's content, while Hanshichi gossiped about the floats carrying dancers that were to appear in the festival parade. The rain started to fall harder and harder, so the

---

1. In the Edo and Meiji periods, the festival was held on June 15. Today it is held on September 15.

2. Sticky rice cooked with red beans.

old servant woman hurriedly began bringing in the lanterns and artificial flowers that decorated the house's eaves. Gradually, the music emanating from the neighborhood floats waiting in the street to start the parade was drowned out by the rain.

"What a nuisance! It's really coming down now," Hanshichi said as the servant woman began clearing the plates and dishes with remaining food on them. "At this rate, we'll have to forget about seeing the floats. Well then, tonight let's just have a good chat. Perhaps I'll tell you one of my stories about the old days."

For me there was no greater pleasure than listening to Hanshichi reminisce — not even seeing a festival or eating *kowameshi* — so I leapt at the offer and begged him to recount one of his tales.

"Another great exploit, then?" the old man said eventually with a broad grin, giving in to my solicitations. "Are you afraid of snakes?" he went on. "I mean, I know nobody actually likes them, of course, but some people turn pale at the mere thought. As long as you don't dislike them that much, then I'll go ahead with tonight's story. It happened, if I remember rightly, in 1854, the year before the Great Ansei Earthquake. . . ."

IN THE DIM LIGHT of early morning on the tenth day of the seventh lunar month, Hanshichi went to the temple of Kannon in Asakusa. Praying at the temple on that day is said to earn the worshipper forty-six thousand days of merit. He arrived to find the temple's five-storied pagoda veiled in a damp, early-morning mist. There were few other worshippers around; even the pigeons that usually flocked there to collect the beans people scattered around had not yet arrived. Unhurriedly, Hanshichi paid his respects and set off home again.

On his way, as he approached Onari Street in Shitaya, he spotted a group of seven or eight men standing around on a side street next to a swordsmith's, talking among themselves as though something had happened. Ever the inspector, Hanshichi halted abruptly and peered down the alleyway, whereupon a slightly built man in a blue-and-brown-striped cotton kimono broke away from the group and dashed toward him.

"Where are you off to, Inspector?"

"I've been to Asakusa to pay my respects."

"You've come along at a good time. Something rather odd has just happened."

The man spoke in a subdued voice, his brows knitted. Genji by name, he was a tub maker by trade — and a *shitappiki*.

["Now, a *shitappiki* was what today you might call an informant," explained old Hanshichi, interrupting his story. "In other words, he worked for an inspector's deputy in an unofficial capacity. The *shitappiki* had regular jobs — like being a tub maker or a fishmonger — but in their spare time they'd come to the deputy with bits of information. They worked in the shadows and never received official recognition, always pretending to be just straightforward tradesmen. But without people like them, we'd never have been able to catch criminals. Below us detectives there were deputies, and below the deputies were these informants. We all worked together as a team."]

Genji, who'd lived in that particular neighborhood for a long time, had a reputation among his fellow *shitappiki* for being sharp-witted. So when he said something odd had happened, Hanshichi knew it was serious.

"What is it? What's up?"

"Someone's dead . . . the Haunted Teacher."

The "Haunted Teacher" . . . this rather bizarre sobriquet belonged to a dance instructor by the name of Mizuki Kameju. Kameju had taken a young niece under her wing, raised her as her own daughter, trained her in her art, and bestowed on her the professional name Kameyo. She had intended Kameyo to succeed her when she retired, but the previous fall the girl had died, aged just eighteen. That was when Kameju acquired her nickname.

Kameju's youthfulness and elegance belied her forty-eight years. Considering her profession, it was not surprising that she was rumored to have spent a flighty youth. Over the past ten years, though, she had pursued her career with a single-minded ambition that had earned her an unfavorable reputation in the neighborhood. In adopting her niece, she had harbored an ulterior motive, eventually making the girl completely subservient to her own interests.

To an observer, Kameju seemed strict to the point of cruelty in her training of the girl. Perhaps because of the ill-treatment she'd received ever since she was small, Kameyo was sickly. Yet if nothing else, her aunt's strict training had turned her into a skilled dancer. And she was pretty too. Since the age of sixteen, Kameyo had from time to time filled in for Kameju as a teacher. Her greatest asset was her beauty, and the small school had been besieged by an unusually large number of male pupils. As a result, Kameju's financial situation improved considerably, but her avarice was such that she was not satisfied with what she received from her students in monthly tuition, not to mention the fees she charged them for such things as charcoal to heat the room and wear-and-tear on the tatami. Instead, she hatched a scheme to use Kameyo, this beautiful young creature, as bait to catch a much larger fish.

Just such a fish had come swimming along the previous spring. The caretaker at the mansion of a provincial lord from western Japan had implored Kameju to allow him to marry the girl. The dance teacher had put him off once, knowing this would only increase the man's desire. She could not part with Kameyo, she said, because she was counting on the girl, as her only daughter, to take over the running of her small school. To this the caretaker responded with an offer to bestow a considerable monthly allowance on the girl if she would agree to become his mistress. He had even said that he was prepared — provided they could work out certain details — to hand over 100 *ryō* in gold coin to cover any initial expenses the girl might incur. In those days, 100 *ryō* was a huge sum of money. Kameju had agreed to these terms on just the second offer.

"We're both going up in the world," she'd whispered to Kameyo, her demeanor toward the young girl softening.

But Kameyo had refused.

"Mother, this is one thing you mustn't ask me to do," she'd said with tears in her eyes. She knew she wasn't strong, she said: the dancing alone was almost too much for her nowadays, what with all the students she was taking on from morning to night. She simply couldn't put up with taking a lover as well. It wasn't as though they couldn't make ends meet without her having to bear this indignity. She'd work herself to the bone so that Kameju wouldn't want for anything. "But please," she'd implored, "don't let this man make me his mistress."

Kameju, of course, didn't take the girl's protests seriously, but Kameyo, docile though she was, was adamant, and no amount of threatening or cajoling would induce her to agree. Kameju was growing increasingly annoyed with the girl, when the summer rainy season set in and Kameyo's health began to decline. Soon she was no longer able to teach everyday and fell into the habit of staying in bed one day out of three. The man was put out that no final response to his offer was forthcoming, and at some point negotiations had been broken off. The big fish had gotten away.

Kameju was bitterly disappointed: it was all due to Kameyo's selfishness that this man whom she had cultivated had slipped through her fingers, and she began to loathe the girl for it, scolding Kameyo for lolling about in bed.

"Get up, then, and work yourself to the bone!" she yelled, throwing Kameyo's own words back in her face. She dragged the girl, pale and wan, from her bed, forcing her to give dance lessons from morning till night. Naturally, she never allowed the girl to see a doctor. A young woman named Onaka who accompanied their lessons on the samisen took pity on Kameyo and secretly brought her medicine, but the oppressive heat of late summer was taking its toll on Kameyo's frail body. She wasted away until she was only a shadow of her former self, but still Kameju drove her relentlessly without a day's rest. As Onaka watched Kameyo day after day, teetering about on the stage more dead than alive, an intense anger welled up inside her. But her employer's fierce gaze was always turned on her, and she was helpless to do anything.

Shortly past noon on the ninth day of the seventh month — just two or three days before the Obon holiday was due to begin[3] — Kameyo, utterly exhausted, collapsed as she was performing the Dance of the Mountain Witch.[4] Soon after that, the beautiful young dancer, finally succumbing to the cruel harassment of her foster mother, departed this world in the early autumn of her eighteenth year.

On the first night of Obon, as the long streamers attached to the traditional white paper lanterns fluttered in a cool breeze, Onaka clearly saw Kameyo's ghost wandering disconsolately in the shadows. Trembling, she related the incident in hushed tones to one of the neighbors. The story spread, and people not kindly disposed toward Kameju embellished it further. Disturbing rumors began to circulate telling how, late at night, the sound of a foot rhythmically tapping out a beat could be heard emanating from the empty stage in the dance teacher's home. Kameju's house, everyone concluded, was haunted. As word of the haunting spread through the neighborhood, more and more students stayed away. Onaka, too, turned in her notice and left.

And now, the Haunted Teacher, too, was dead.

"How did she die?" Hanshichi asked. "Knowing her, I wouldn't be surprised if it was something she ate," he said, his voice dripping with sarcasm.

"No, nothing like that," Genji whispered. He stared straight ahead, a hint of fear in his eyes. "She was strangled by a snake."

"A snake!" Hanshichi exclaimed, startled.

"The maid, Omura, found her this morning. She was lying

3. The Festival of the Dead, or the Lantern Festival, when the souls of one's ancestors are said to return home for several days and are welcomed by lighting lanterns.

4. *Yamamba*, a legendary old hag, or "mountain witch," said to live in the mountains with her son, Kintarō, who became the famous warrior Sakata no Kintoki — a story that inspired many dramatic adaptations for Noh, puppet theater, and kabuki. The dance here was one performed in the kabuki play *Takigiō yukima no ichikawa*, also known as *Shin yamamba* (New Yamamba), by Mimasaya Nisōji, first performed in 1848.

in bed underneath the mosquito net with a black snake coiled around her neck. Weird, isn't it? The neighbors are saying it's Kameyo's curse. . . . They're pretty shaken up about it."

Genji himself seemed to find it all very uncanny, too. Was it possible that Kameyo's ghost had possessed the snake in order to exact revenge on her cruel foster mother? Hanshichi shuddered at the thought. No matter how one looked at it, the idea that the Haunted Teacher had been strangled by a snake was enough to send shivers down anyone's spine. . . .

[2]

"Well, let's go take a look."

Hanshichi set off down the alleyway, followed by an anxious-faced Genji. A crowd of onlookers was gradually gathering in front of Kameju's house.

"The young teacher died exactly one year ago."

"I knew something like this would happen. How horrible."

The bystanders whispered among themselves, fear in their eyes. Parting a way through the crowd, Hanshichi and Genji entered the dance teacher's house through the rear entrance. The rain shutters remained closed, so the house was dark inside. A mosquito net still hung from the ceiling in the room where Kameju had slept. Next to it, in a small, four-and-a-half-mat room, Omura, the maid, and the landlord sat in utter silence, as though almost afraid to breathe.

Hanshichi recognized the landlord immediately.

"Hello," he greeted him. "Nasty business this, isn't it?"

"Ah, is that you, Inspector?" the landlord said. "Here's a nice mess! I told the local duty-man to rush over to the watchpost and make a report, but so far no one's come to investigate, and I haven't been able to touch a thing. This gossip about the teacher being strangled to death by a snake — what a lot of nonsense! It's too much!" He was obviously annoyed by the way the case was being handled.

"Are there many snakes in this neighborhood?" Hanshichi asked.

"As you know, in a heavily built-up place like this you hardly ever see frogs, let alone snakes. Not only that, but the garden outside is only twelve feet square, so there could hardly be snakes living in it. I've no idea how it could have gotten in here. And the neighbors are saying a lot of other things besides."

No doubt he had Kameyo's ghost in mind.

"Is it all right if I take a look under the mosquito net?"

"As you wish." Aware of Hanshichi's official standing, the landlord raised no objection.

Hanshichi got up and went into the next room. It was six mats in size, with an old scroll depicting the deity Taishaku hanging over a low platform about three feet wide that had been placed in one corner.[5] The mosquito net had been spread out to cover the entire room, probably in order to alleviate the lingering summer heat that had been afflicting the city for the past two days. Kameju had laid a sleeping mat on top of her futon, and a thin cotton blanket had been pushed down toward the edge of the mattress. She had been sleeping facing south and her pillow was shoved over to one side. The body lay face up as though she had been about to get out of bed. Her braided hair was disheveled as though someone had been tearing at it. In death, the traces of her last agonizing moments were clearly inscribed upon her face — the furrowed brow, the contorted lips, the protruding white tongue. Her night robe had been torn half off, revealing her body from shoulder to chest and exposing small, pinkish breasts that might easily have been taken for a man's.

"Where's the snake?" Genji asked, following Hanshichi into the room and peering at the body.

Hanshichi pulled up the mosquito net and went inside.

---

5. An ancient deity of Indian origin found in both Buddhism and Hinduism, known in Sanskrit as Indra.

"It's dark in here. Open one of those rain shutters," he said.

Genji got up and opened one of the shutters, which faced south onto the garden. It was now past six o'clock, and morning sunlight flooded into the room, illuminating the pale folds of the mosquito netting, which appeared to be quite new. In the light, the dead woman's face looked even more pale and sinister. Beneath the paleness of her chin, something black and shiny was visible, covered with what looked like scales. Peering in through the net with a strange fascination, Genji instinctively recoiled.

Hanshichi bent down to get a closer look. The snake was not very large. It appeared to be about three feet in length, and its tail was loosely coiled around the woman's neck. Its flat head rested limply on top of the futon; it appeared to be dead. Wondering whether it was so in fact, Hanshichi tapped the head lightly with the tip of his finger. The snake quickly raised its head and stretched out its long neck. Hanshichi thought for a moment, then took out a piece of folded tissue paper from inside the breast of his kimono. With it, he lightly pressed down on the snake's head, whereupon the creature recoiled submissively and lay its head down again on the futon.

Hanshichi emerged from under the mosquito net and went out onto the veranda. He washed his hands in the washbasin at the edge of the garden and returned to the four-and-a-half-mat room.

"Learn anything?" asked the landlord, who had been eagerly awaiting Hanshichi's return.

"Well, it's hard to say just yet. No doubt when the inspector comes to have a look he'll form his own opinion. For the time being, I must be going."

Leaving the landlord looking somewhat disappointed by his vague response, Hanshichi quickly went outside and circled around to the front of the house, followed by Genji.

"So, Inspector. What do you think?"

"That maid looked quite young—around seventeen or eighteen, wouldn't you say?" Hanshichi asked abruptly.

"I hear she's seventeen. But you're not telling me you think she did it?"

"Hmm . . ." Hanshichi thought for a moment. "Well, I can't say if she did or she didn't. But I'll tell you one thing — that snake certainly didn't kill the teacher. Someone strangled her first, then coiled the snake around her neck. Better keep that in mind and keep a close eye on the girl, as well as anyone else who often came to the house."

"So it wasn't the dead girl's ghost taking revenge, then?" Genji asked, still looking dubious.

"That may have something to do with it, too, but there's one thing we can be sure of: this case has more to do with the revenge of the living. I've an idea I want to follow up on, so I'd like you to keep an eye on things here while I'm gone. Oh, and one more thing — would you say the teacher was rich?"

"That miserly woman? I'm sure she had a little something stashed away."

"Any sign of a lover?"

"No, lately all she seemed to care about was money."

"I see. . . . All right, then, I'm counting on you."

Hanshichi was about to say something else when he happened to glance back at the house and saw a young man standing close at hand, only a short distance from the throng of horrified by-standers. He seemed to be trying to eavesdrop on Hanshichi's conversation and occasionally stole a glance at the two men's faces.

"Say, who's that? Do you know him?" Hanshichi asked Genji in a quiet voice.

"That's Yasaburō, the local paperhanger's son."

"Did he ever visit the dance teacher's house?"

"He took lessons there every night until last year — he stopped going when the young teacher died. But he wasn't the only one. Most of the male pupils dropped out. They'd all had designs on her."

"Hmm. Where's Kameyo buried?"

"Myōshin Temple . . . on Kōtokujimae Street. I know it pretty well because last year I went there for the funeral with the other people from the neighborhood."

"Myōshin Temple, huh?"

Hanshichi left Genji and started out along Onari Street, but a sudden thought made him turn back, this time in the direction of Kōtokujimae. Autumn was just around the corner and a late summer sun glimmered on the water inside a wide ditch beside the road. A large yellow dragonfly brushed against the tip of Hanshichi's nose and darted swiftly over a low earthen wall. On the other side of the wall was Myōshin Temple.

On his left as he entered the gate of the temple, he saw a stall selling flowers. Obon was only a few days off, and there seemed to be many worshippers at the temple. A tall pile of *shikimi* leaves made it impossible to get anywhere near the front of the stall.[6]

"Excuse me — anybody there?" Hanshichi called out.

A bent-backed old woman who'd been virtually buried under the pile of leaves straightened up and turned to squint at Hanshichi.

"Ah, good day, sir! On your way to worship, are you? This early-autumn heat is something awful, isn't it?"

"I'll take a few of those *shikimi* leaves. . . . Could you tell me the direction to the dancer Kameyo's grave?"

Paying for the leaves he didn't need, Hanshichi got the location of Kameyo's grave from the woman. He also asked her whether people often came to visit it.

"Well, now. In the beginning, her students dropped by to pay their respects from time to time, but lately they've stopped coming. Except for the paperhanger's boy — he comes without fail every month on the day she died . . ."

"The son of the paperhanger comes every month?"

---

6. A Japanese anise tree, whose leaves are placed at the graves of one's relatives.

"That's right. A fine lad he is for his age. . . . He was here just yesterday, in fact."

Hanshichi put some water and the *shikimi* leaves into a bucket and went to see the grave. It had a small stone plinth beneath which the mortal remains of successive generations were kept. A member of the Nichiren sect of Buddhism, Kameyo had been cremated and her ashes deposited there. The grave was shaded by the branches of a large maple tree that stood between it and its neighbor. From its branches sounded the dying fall of the voices of autumn cicadas. The flower holder in front of the grave contained fresh bellflowers and goldbaldrians,[7] no doubt placed there tearfully by the paperhanger's grieving son. Hanshichi added his own offering and joined his palms together in prayer. As he did so, he heard a rustling sound behind him and instinctively turned to look. There, gliding rapidly through the autumn grasses as though chasing something, was a small snake.

"Maybe you took her away," he muttered in a rather puzzled tone, half to himself, as he watched the snake slither away. Then, quickly correcting himself, "No, that's impossible."

Returning to the flower stall, he asked the old woman whether Kameyo had ever visited the family grave while she was alive. Yes, she told him; the girl had been unusually pious for her age, and had in fact come frequently. Sometimes she'd even come together with the paperhanger's son.

Pondering what he'd heard, Hanshichi began to feel that there must have been some deep bond between the tragic young dancer and the paperhanger's son who came to weep at her grave.

"Thank you. I'm sorry to have bothered you."

Hanshichi left the temple, placing a few coins in the offering box as he went.

---

7. *Kikyō* and *ominaeshi*, respectively, sometimes paired together in poetry and literature as harbingers of autumn.

[3]

Hanshichi headed back in the direction of Ueno. On the way he ran into a tall, willowy man. His name was Matsukichi and he was a deputy, known familiarly as Hyoro Matsu, or "Lanky Pine."

"Hey, Lanky. Fancy meeting you here — I was just thinking of stopping by to see you."

"What about?"

"Haven't you heard? The Haunted Teacher is dead."

"What?" Matsukichi exclaimed, looking surprised. "No kidding! That dance teacher, dead huh?"

"C'mon, pull yourself together — she lived practically next door to you!" Hanshichi said, scolding him. "When are you going to start taking your job a bit more seriously?"

The circumstances of Kameju's death, once he had heard them from Hanshichi, left Matsukichi still more wide-eyed in astonishment.

"You don't say! So there is justice, after all. Kameyo's ghost finally got its revenge."

"Well, that's as may be. But listen here. I want you to find out where the Chiryū snake-amulet salesmen stay around here. I don't think it's Bakurochō. Try around Mannenchō. Anyway, be quick about it. It shouldn't be too difficult."

"Okay, I think I can manage that."

"Do your best. And don't forget, I want to know how many there are and a description of each one."

"Right, boss. Got it."

Hanshichi watched the other man's tall, lanky form disappear into the distance toward the foot of Ueno Hill, then headed home to Kanda.

The oppressive heat lingered throughout the day. In the evening, Genji paid a visit to Hanshichi and told him that the inspection of the crime scene had taken place that morning, but with no definitive conclusion as to whether Kameju had been killed by a person or by the snake. Either way, it seemed that the inspectors, given that no one in particular was mourning the death, were willing to accept it as the result of a curse and save themselves the trouble of further investigation.

"When's the funeral?"

"Tomorrow morning at seven," said Genji. "Seems she had hardly any relatives to speak of, so the landlord and the neighbors will have to see to it that everything's taken care of."

No word came from Matsukichi that night. In the morning, Hanshichi went to look in on the funeral at Myōshin Temple. There, he found a crowd of thirty or forty former students and neighbors who'd arrived along with the teacher's body, which had been carried there in a palanquin. Among them was Genji, keeping a close watch on the proceedings. The paperhanger's son, Yasaburō, was there, looking pale, and Hanshichi spotted the small figure of Omura, the maid. He made no sign of recognition, but went and sat at a respectful distance to one side.

Once the sutras had been read, the body was removed to be sent to the crematorium. For a while, as the mourners trickled out, Hanshichi deliberately remained seated. Then, going out himself, he slipped around the back and headed for the cemetery. There, in front of the very same grave Hanshichi had visited the day before, a young man was praying. It was the paperhanger's son. In his straw sandals, Hanshichi tiptoed quietly over to a large stone plinth just behind Yasaburō, hoping to catch what he might be saying, but the young man stood praying in silence. Finally, as Yasaburō was turning to leave, Hanshichi poked his head out from his hiding place and the two men's eyes met for the first time. Yasaburō looked flustered and hastily moved away.

"Just a minute. I'd like to speak to you," Hanshichi said quietly. Yasaburō halted, clearly unnerved.

"There's something I'd like to ask you. Come over here a moment."

Hanshichi led him back to Kameyo's grave and the two men

squatted down on the grass. The sky was cloudy and the cold morning dew soaked into the soles of their sandals.

"I hear you come every month without fail to pray at this grave," Hanshichi began in a casual tone.

"Yes, I took dance lessons with the young teacher for a short time," Yasaburō replied politely. He seemed to have a good idea who Hanshichi was from the previous morning.

"All right. Listen—I won't beat about the bush. I take it you were in love with Kameyo?"

Yasaburō paled. He looked down in silence and tugged at some blades of grass by his knees.

"C'mon, tell me the truth. You were crazy about her, right? But then she met that terrible end. Now, exactly one year later, Kameju is dead. Call it fate if you like, but it's an odd kind of fate. And odd doesn't begin to explain what's happened. People are saying that somehow you killed her to take revenge for what happened to the young teacher. Even the authorities have got wind of the rumor."

"That's absurd. Why would I have . . . ?" Vehemently Yasaburo denied the accusation, his lips trembling.

"No, I know you didn't do it. . . . By the way, my name's Hanshichi—I'm an inspector from Kanda. I wouldn't be so heartless as to arrest an innocent man based on idle gossip. On the other hand, if you won't tell me the truth, I can't help you. Understand? Now then, about this matter—you were in love with the young teacher, right? See her grave there? You wouldn't tell a lie in front of it, would you?" With a touch of menace, Hanshichi pointed at the tombstone.

The bellflowers and goldbaldrians that had been placed there yesterday were already fading, their leaves dry and drooping. As Yasaburō sat staring at the flowers, tears appeared on his eyelashes.

"Inspector, I'll be honest with you. The truth is, the summer before last I started going to Kameyo's dance lessons every night, and she and I . . . but you must believe me, sir, I never laid a finger on her. She was so frail and sickly, and as you can see, I'm not the dashing lover type. The most we ever did was have a good long talk when together in private . . . and even that was only once, in the spring of last year. We'd come here together to visit this grave. That was when she told me she couldn't bear to stay in that house any longer — she wanted me to take her away somewhere. Thinking back on it, I wish I'd had the nerve to do it, but I had my parents and my younger brother and sister to think about. I couldn't just run off and elope. I tried to console her, that was all, and saw to it that she got home safely. It was soon afterward that she suddenly took to her bed — and then she died. I blamed myself day and night for not having done anything to help her, and I started coming here to her grave every month to apologize. But that's all I did — I had nothing to do with what happened to the head teacher. When I heard that Kameju had been killed by a snake, it sent shivers down my spine . . . I mean, coming on the anniversary of Kameyo's death and all. . . ."

It was just as Hanshichi had guessed: behind the bizarre events there was a tragic love story involving the young dancer and the young paperhanger. As he watched the young man sniffling unabashedly, Hanshichi was convinced that there was absolutely nothing false in Yasaburō's outpouring.

"You haven't been to the teacher's house since Kameyo died, have you?"

"No," Yasaburō mumbled.

"Don't hold out on me. This is really important. Are you sure you haven't been to the house?"

"Well, that's what's rather strange."

"What's strange? Tell me."

Under Hanshichi's watchful eye, Yasaburō began to fidget, but finally he seemed to make up his mind to confess what had happened. About a month after Kameyo's death, Kameju had dropped by the paperhanger's shop and asked for Yasaburō, who was working inside, to come out front. She said she wanted to consult him: it would soon be the thirty-fifth day after her daugh-

ter's death, and she had to distribute return gifts to the people
who had brought tributes to the funeral. Would he come to her
house that night to discuss it? So Yasaburō went, and found that
the talk of gifts had just been an excuse. Suddenly, Kameju asked
him if he would become her son-in-law. She had depended upon
her daughter, she said, and now that Kameyo was gone, she was
extremely lonely. She implored him to let her adopt him.

Yasaburō was appalled by the proposal. As he was expected to
take over the running of his own family business, he naturally
declined her offer and returned home. But Kameju would not
give up. She obstinately pursued him, even going so far as to
visit his shop and call him out on some pretext or other. Once,
she waylaid him in the street and, ignoring his protestations,
dragged him to a teahouse in Yushima, where she plied him with
saké, despite his being a virtual teetotaler. She soon drank herself
tipsy and began saying all sorts of suggestively outrageous things
about how she would gladly accept him as either her son-in-law
or her husband. The timid Yasaburō recoiled in astonishment.
Finally, with an all-out effort, he managed to make his escape.

"When did this scene in the teahouse take place?" Hanshichi
asked with a smile.

"This past New Year's. Then, in the third month, I ran into
her in Asakusa, and she tried to drag me off somewhere again,
but I managed to shake her off and get away. The next time I
saw her must have been around the end of the fifth month. I'd
gone to the local bathhouse after sunset, and as I was coming out
of the men's bath to go home, I ran straight into Kameju coming out of the women's. She said she wanted to talk to me and
asked me to come home with her. I had nowhere to run to this
time, and I ended up following her to her house. She threw open
the front door and we went in, and there, seated in front of the
charcoal brazier, was a man. He was about forty — six or seven
years younger than the teacher — and had a dark complexion.
When she saw him she froze for several moments as though she
couldn't believe her eyes. Anyway, for me, this unexpected visi-

tor was a stroke of luck, and I used it as an excuse to get away quickly."

"Hmm. Is that what happened?" Hanshichi said, barely able to contain a smile. "So don't you have any idea who the man was?"

"None at all. I heard later from the maid, Omura, that the two had an argument and then the man left."

It appeared that Yasaburō had told him everything he knew, so Hanshichi brought the conversation to a close and said good-bye with these parting words: "For the time being, don't tell anyone about our meeting today."

[4]

As he was leaving the temple, Hanshichi ran into Matsukichi outside the gate.

"I was just at your house, boss. They told me you were here, so I came right over. After we talked yesterday I went to Mannenchō, but couldn't find a single amulet salesman. So I walked all over, looking everywhere I could think of. I finally located one this morning in a flophouse in Honjo. What should we do now?"

"How old would you say he is?"

"Hmm . . . twenty-seven or -eight, I'd guess. The owner of the place told me that the heat has got him down and he hasn't been out for the past four or five days — just lies around doing nothing."

Hanshichi was disappointed to hear that the man was considerably younger than the one Yasaburō had described. Not only that, but the fact that he'd been holed up in his lodgings for the past four or five days ruled out any need to investigate further.

"Is he traveling alone or with someone?"

"There's one other guy, but he seems to have headed uptown early this morning on business. He's about forty and . . ."

Without waiting for Matsukichi to finish his sentence, Hanshichi clapped his hands triumphantly.

"Great! You go on ahead and wait for him to return to his lodgings. I'll follow along later."

As soon as Matsukichi had left, Hanshichi hurried over to Kameju's house. The maid, Omura, had apparently gone to the crematorium with the neighbors, and he found two women he didn't know sitting in the house. He wanted to ask Omura about the man who had come by and gotten into an argument with Kameju, so he decided to wait for her. But after a while, when she still hadn't returned, he grew impatient and headed over to Genji's house. However, he too was out; he must have stopped off somewhere on his way home from the funeral, his wife told Hanshichi, looking rather peeved. He was exchanging a few bits of gossip with her when the bell at Ueno sounded ten o'clock.

If that amulet salesman has gone uptown, he probably won't return till past noon, Hanshichi reflected. In the meantime, he decided, he would stop in at two or three other places to take care of some unfinished business. With an abrupt farewell he left Genji's house, made his other calls at breakneck speed, stopped for lunch, and reached the ferry crossing at Onmayagashi shortly before two o'clock in order to catch the boat over to Honjo. He'd not been waiting there long when a handsome, dark-complexioned man of about forty, wearing a sedge hat, wrist guards, leggings, and straw sandals, arrived carrying a small box. Hanshichi could tell at a glance that he was a Chiryū amulet salesman, and despite his years of experience in detective work, his pulse quickened.

Hanshichi was certain it was the same fellow Matsukichi had told him about, and his age squared with what Yasaburō, the paperhanger, had said. But he couldn't very well interrogate the man officially without firm evidence. Either way, once he'd ascertained that the man was returning to his lodgings, he would try to find an opportunity to question him. Hanshichi made a show of casting furtive glances at the man's face, which was partially covered by his wide-brimmed hat. Noticing, the man moved away and took refuge beneath a willow tree, where he opened his shirt a little and began fanning himself.

Since noon, the thin layer of cloud hanging over the city had gradually dispersed, and the sun was shining on the roof of the main hall of the Komagata Temple. There was no breeze to speak of that day, and even out on the waters of the Sumida River the heat was oppressive — in the ferry, which was rowing across from the opposite bank, Hanshichi could see the passengers holding white fans and towels up to their foreheads to shield themselves from the sun. The red shadow cast by a small girl's parasol bobbed on the waves alongside the boat.

When the group reached the shore, the amulet salesman waited impatiently as they filed off the boat, then quickly climbed aboard. Hanshichi jumped in after him.

"We're leaving!" the ferryman bawled to a group of latecomers, consisting of a woman leading a child by the hand, an old woman dressed for a pilgrimage, a shop boy carrying a bag of sugar, and five or six other men and women. In response, they all rushed toward the boat and clambered over the side, rocking it to and fro. When the boat finally pulled away from the shore, the amulet salesman suddenly seemed to take notice of a man who had climbed on at the stern. He pushed his way through the other passengers and grabbed the man by the collar.

"You thief! You're the one who stole my wares. The god of the Chiryū Shrine will punish you for that!"

The object of his torrent of abuse was also a man of about forty. He wore a coarse, unlined blue kimono. And he was not about to take this public affront lying down.

"What?! A thief . . . how dare you! What did I steal from you?"

"Don't play dumb with me! I remember your face as clear as can be! You sneaking bastard, you won't get away with it!"

Still holding onto the man's collar, the amulet salesman punched him several times with all his might. The man grabbed the salesman's other hand and twisted it, trying to loosen his grip. The little boat began to pitch dangerously from side to side. Women and children began to cry.

"No fighting in the boat! If you want to fight, wait till we get ashore!" the ferryman shouted at them. The other passengers all chimed in, persuading the amulet salesman to calm down, and reluctantly he released his grip. But he continued to glare angrily at his adversary, indicating that he wasn't about to let the matter drop.

When the boat arrived on the bank at Honjo, Hanshichi leapt out nimbly, followed by the man who had been accused of being a thief. Then the amulet salesman rushed ashore in hot pursuit of the latter and grabbed him by the sleeve. Frantically, the man shook him off and was about to make off when Hanshichi took hold of his arm.

"Hey! What do you think you're doing?" said the man, struggling to get free.

"Take it easy. I'm a detective."

At Hanshichi's sharp, peremptory tone, the man froze and went limp. The amulet salesman, too, who'd been preparing to give full chase, stopped dead in his tracks.

"What did this man steal from you?" Hanshichi asked the amulet salesman. "Was it a black snake?"

"That's correct."

"I want you two to come with me."

With the two men in tow, Hanshichi made his way to the nearest watchpost. The old man on duty was out in front, spreading clamshells over the mud. He threw his basket aside and made way for Hanshichi.

"All right — tell me the whole story," Hanshichi said, glaring at the accused thief. "That 'Haunted Teacher' who lived near Onari Street, she was your lover . . . or was she your wife? Let me see now . . . you went to her house after a long absence and caught her bringing a young man home, right? That didn't sit well with you, did it? You flew into a jealous rage and accused her of being unfaithful. Afterward, you made up your mind to kill her, so you stole a snake from the amulet-salesman's box to use as a prop in your little act. You have quite a flair for the theatrical, don't you? You knew about her scandalous reputation, so you crept in and strangled her, leaving the snake coiled around her neck to make everyone think her death had been the result of the daughter's curse. You thought you could pull the wool over everyone's eyes with a page out of one of Hayashiya Shōzō's horror stories, eh?[8] Well, I saw through your little charade. C'mon, now, fess up. . . . No? Well, aren't you the cool customer! If you want to play rough I won't show any mercy. Cat got your tongue, huh? Well, open your mouth wide like you do when you stuff food in and start talking! Idiot! Don't you know who you're dealing with? Get on the wrong side of me, and I'll knock the living daylights out of you!"

"BACK THEN, things were different than they are now," old Hanshichi explained. "This was typical of how interrogations were handled at a watchpost in Edo. The city magistrate was different, but the rest of us—from the deputies and detectives all to way up to the officials in Hatchōbori—knew how to give suspects a good tongue-lashing. And it wasn't as though we just read them the riot act. If they gave us any grief, we'd slap 'em around pretty hard."

"So did the man confess?" I asked.

"After what I said, they were so terrified they both spilled their guts. The first man was a former priest from Ueno. He was younger than Kameju, but he fell under her spell and left the religious life—about ten years earlier he'd gone off to Kai Province.[9] But in the end he grew homesick for his native Edo, and when he returned after all those years in the provinces he went straight to Kameju's house. But she was coldhearted, wouldn't even give him the time of day. What's more, when he saw her bringing home that young greenhorn of a paperhanger, the priest was so

---

8. 1781–1842. A comic storyteller famous for his ghost stories.
9. Present-day Yamanashi Prefecture.

bitter he swore he'd get revenge. He moved into the flophouse and spent more than two months watching and waiting for his chance. Just then, he heard rumors about how her adopted daughter had died the year before and her house was haunted. Deep down he still thought like a priest, so he soon hit upon the idea of strangling Kameju and making it look like the dead girl's ghost was to blame. The brilliance of his plan was in using the snake."

"So he stole the snake from the amulet salesman?"

"The salesman just happened to show up at the flophouse while the priest was staying there, so he took one of his snakes. If it hadn't been for the snake, he probably would never have gotten the idea. It was a stroke of bad luck for both Kameju and the priest, you might say. Obon and the anniversary of the girl's death were only a few days away — the timing was perfect. The priest sneaked into Kameju's house through the kitchen, killed her, coiled the snake around her neck, and there you have it — a ghost story made to order! At first I suspected the maid, Omura, but later it turned out she'd been sound asleep at the time and hadn't heard a thing."

"But how was it that you thought of looking for a Chiryū snake amulet salesman in the first place?" This was the only part of the story that didn't make sense to me. Hanshichi gave me another big grin.

"I see what you mean. People today probably wouldn't understand. In the old days, as soon as summer arrived, hucksters would appear out of nowhere selling amulets to keep away snakes and vipers. The most famous ones hailed from the great shrine in Chiryū, but there were a lot of frauds from all over. They walked around with a snake inside a box hanging around their necks, and once they'd gathered a crowd of people together, they took out the snake and rubbed its head with an amulet, and the snake would recoil. Real Chiryū salesmen were on the up-and-up, but swindlers typically used snakes that had been conditioned using an amulet with a needle in it, so that when they tapped the snake on the head it recoiled in pain; snakes trained in this way would recoil if you just rubbed their heads with a bit of paper. You'd see these hucksters walking around Edo with their boxes and their live snakes, shouting 'Step right up and witness the miraculous power of the amulet!'

"When I saw that snake in the dance teacher's house, it didn't strike me as a normal snake . . . it was timid. Then I remembered those amulet con men. I took out my handkerchief and rubbed the snake's head. Sure enough, it recoiled immediately. That's how I knew it belonged to one of them. Then, all I did was follow up that lead, and the man I was after fell right into my lap. . . . What's that? What happened to the priest? Why, he was put to death of course."

"What about the amulet salesman?" I asked.

"Well, he wasn't really from Chiryū. Nowadays, I guess, if someone was caught selling fraudulent merchandise, they'd be punished, but in the old days it wasn't so. People figured that if you were stupid enough to get swindled then it was your own fault. But he must have had a guilty conscience, because when I ran into him at the ferry crossing, he got flustered and moved away to avoid my glances. Not, of course, that Chiryū amulet salesmen were the only con men around in those days — Edo was full of them."

"Where is the Chiryū Shrine, anyway?"

"It's on the Tōkaidō in Mikawa Province.[10] I expect it's still going strong. . . . Ah, it looks like it's stopped raining. Things are livening up again outside. Now that you've come all this way, why don't we go out for a stroll to see all the lanterns lit up in the street? Festivals are always best at night."

The old man took me around his neighborhood, showing me all the festivities. That night, when I got home, I leafed through a guidebook of famous places along the Tōkaidō. There was a

---

10. The eastern half of present-day Aichi Prefecture.

detailed passage about the Chiryū Shrine in the post town of Chiryū in Mikawa. "Chiryū snake amulets," it read in part, "originated at the Bettō Shōchi Shrine. People far and wide swear by their powers. When carried while walking in mountain forests in summer and autumn, they are said to ward off vipers. . . ."

The Mystery of the Fire Bell

HANSHŌ NO KAI

[1]

It was a rainy day in early November when I went to pay old Hanshichi a long overdue visit. He had just returned from the Hatsutori Festival in Yotsuya,[1] he said, and was holding a small rake, roughly the size and shape of a woman's ornamental comb, that he'd brought from the shrine for good luck.[2]

"If I'd been any later I'd have missed you," he said, "Anyway, won't you come in?"

The old man reverently placed the rake on the household Shinto altar, then took me into the usual six-mat room. He was talking about how much the festival had changed since the old days, when somehow the subject of fires came up — it was the time of year when they often occurred. Hanshichi showed himself to be extremely knowledgeable on the subject of fires in Edo times, perhaps because it had been tangentially related to his line of work. Arson, of course, was an extremely serious crime in the old days; back then, according to Hanshichi, even looting during a fire had been a capital offense.

---

1. A festival held at the Ōtori Shrine on the first Day of the Rooster (under the sexegenary cycle) in the eleventh month (each month having two or three such days).

2. *Kumade.* Such objects were sold as good-luck charms and were decorated with propitious symbols, such as ersatz gold coins.

And that launched the old man, with a chuckle, into another of his stories.

"Life sure is full of the unexpected," he began. "This particular incident occurred in Edo's old downtown area — I won't mention the name of the neighborhood where it happened because it's still something of a sensitive subject there. Suffice it to say, it was not far from where the 'Haunted Teacher' — that dancer I once told you about — lived. A very strange series of events that took place there set the whole neighborhood on its ear for a while."

THE FESTIVAL AT Kanda's Myōjin Shrine had ended and a cold spell had set in. From morning till night, it was so cold that even a lined kimono was not enough. It was the time of year when baked sweet potato vendors set up their stalls at night, hanging out lanterns that glowed in the darkness and were inscribed with the words, in big, fat brushstrokes: "As sweet as roasted chestnuts."[3] The white smoke rising from the fires of the bathhouses somehow caught the eye more than usual, and the winds that blew down from Chichibu[4] in the autumn were a source of uneasiness for the residents of fire-prone Edo.

It was from the end of the ninth month through the beginning of the tenth that the neighborhood fire bell began tolling from time to time.

"Fire! Fire!" people would shout, running into the streets, only to find to their astonishment that there was no smoke to be seen. The same thing was repeated night after night — some nights just once or twice, some nights as many as three or four times. Sometimes it was only a single-ring alarm, sometimes a double

---

3. *Hachiri-han* ("eight-and-a-half leagues"), a pun on the word "chestnut" (*kuri*), which can also mean "nine leagues." The idea here is that sweet potatoes are "close" in taste to chestnuts, which were a great delicacy.

4. A mountainous region northwest of Edo along the Arakawa River, which becomes the Sumida River where it flows into Edo Bay.

one; but at other times it was a continuous clamor, a warning that the fire was very near. As the sound of the bell carried from one neighborhood to the next, the residents there too would hasten to sound their own alarms. Firemen would rush to the scene — in vain.

These disturbances often occurred in the dead of night, when not even the bathhouse fires were alight, and the firemen, none the wiser as to what had caused the false alarm, would simply withdraw again. Ultimately, the locals grew used to it and decided that it must be someone's idea of a prank. However, because of the serious nature of the matter, a full-scale investigation to catch the culprit was launched.

Disturbing the peace of the shogun's capital for no good reason . . . needless to say, this was an extremely serious offense in those days. The people most adversely affected were the men on duty in the neighborhood *jishinban* — the watchpost.

["Now, a *jishinban* was what we'd call a *hashutsujo* nowadays," Hanshichi explained, "only it was bigger. There was one in every neighborhood. In areas where the samurai had their mansions they were called *tsujiban,* or 'corner-posts,' but in the working-class neighborhoods they were known as *jishinban.* A lot of people referred to them simply as *ban'ya* — posts. Longer ago still, each homeowner kept watch at night for himself, which is supposed to be why they were called *jishinban* — literally, 'keeping one's own watch.' But eventually, the homeowners in each neighborhood pooled their responsibilities, entrusting the job to a head watchman assisted by two or three other guards. In a large *jishinban* in Edo, there might be as many as five or six men on duty at any one time. In those days, there was a ladder on the roof of the *jishinban* with a bell at the top. When a fire broke out, either the watchmen in the *jishinban* or the duty-man making his rounds in the street would climb the ladder and sound the alarm. If for some reason the bell was rung by mistake, it was ultimately the men in the *jishinban* who had to accept responsibility."]

In the small *jishinban* in this story, there was a head watchman named Sahei and two guards. Sahei was an unmarried man of about fifty who invariably suffered from colic in the wintertime. The other two men were named Denshichi and Chōsaku, both of them single and in their forties. Because these three were on duty at the time of the first incident, they bore the brunt of the local officials' anger. Thereafter, they took turns keeping an eye on the bell at night. So long as they remained vigilant, nothing out of the ordinary took place. But as soon as they relaxed a bit and lowered their guard, the bell would begin clanging away by itself as though remonstrating with them for their laziness. The local officials came and inspected the bell, but they could find nothing amiss. It was only at night that the bell rang spontaneously in this way.

Even in that day and age, when many people believed in the supernatural, the idea that a fire bell could ring all on its own was hardly credible. And seeing that the bell never rang so long as it was being watched, everyone agreed that it must be a prank. There seemed little doubt that the miscreant's intent was to spread panic, taking advantage of the fact that winter was drawing near and people were increasingly nervous about the threat of fire. No one would be able to rest easily until the culprit was caught.

But even assuming the nightly ringing to be the work of a prankster, some people took it as an omen that a major conflagration was about to occur. The more hasty among them packed up their belongings, ready to leave at a moment's notice. Others remained constantly on the alert. Some even hustled their elderly family members off to stay with relatives in the countryside. The tiniest puff of smoke was enough to strike fear into their hearts and set them trembling like leaves, so frayed were their nerves. No longer could they rely on the watchmen in the *jishinban* or the senile old duty-man who did the rounds of the streets. All the mature men in the neighborhood, and most of the younger ones too, took to patrolling the streets every night in a body, concentrating their efforts on the area around the fire bell.

The prankster was apparently scared off by this elaborate display of security, for the alarm did not sound for the next five or six days. In the tenth month, after the anniversary of the birth of Nichiren on the thirteenth,[5] a cold, hard rain began falling. Lulled into complacency — the fire bell had not been heard for a while and the rain continued to fall steadily — the townspeople slackened their vigilance. But then one day, as though prompted by this, an unexpected calamity befell one of the local women.

The young woman's name was Okita and she lived down one of the neighborhood's small side streets. She had once been a geisha in Yanagibashi, but the head clerk of an emporium in Nihonbashi had purchased her freedom and set her up in modest accommodations as his mistress. On the day in question, he had visited her around noon and stayed until eight o'clock, after which she had gone out to the local bathhouse. Half an hour later, having finished her bath, she set out for home. It was a rainy night. There were few people in the street, and most of the shops had half closed their shutters. In addition to the rain, there was a slight wind.

As she was about to turn into her street, Okita's umbrella suddenly went as heavy as a rock in her hands. "How strange," she thought, letting it tilt to one side. Just then, she heard the sound of the umbrella ripping open as an unseen hand suddenly reached down and grabbed her chignon. She screamed and staggered toward the side of the road, where she stumbled on one of the planks covering the drain and fell. Hearing her cry, some neighbors rushed out into the street to find her already lying on the ground, unconscious. One of the planks had flown up and struck her forcefully in the side.

They carried Okita home and tended to her, and before long she regained consciousness. She had been too frantic at the time to recall exactly what had happened. All she could remember was that her umbrella had felt strangely heavy, then seemed to split apart of its own accord, and someone had grabbed her by

---

5. The founder of one of Japan's principal Buddhist sects (lived 1222–1282).

the hair. Once again the entire neighborhood was plunged into panic.

A rumor began to spread that there was a ghost in the neighborhood. Women and children stopped going out after dark; even the sound of the temple bells of Ueno and Asakusa at sunset set them trembling as though they were signals that demons were at large in the streets. In the midst of all this, another incident occurred.

One day when the winter rains had finally let up, the women of the neighborhood were busily doing their laundry by the side of the communal well. Under the blue sky, white sleeves and red skirts were hanging from the laundry poles, fluttering in the breeze. Then as night fell, the clothes gradually disappeared inside, until all that remained were two red children's kimonos hanging outside the seal cutter's house, coldly spreading open their sleeves like New Year's kites that had fallen from the sky. Perhaps the mistress of the house intended to leave them there to dry overnight. . . . But then one of the kimonos took on a mind of its own and walked off into the night.

"Look! Look at that kimono!" a passerby began shouting. People rushed out of their houses and looked up to see one of the red kimonos leaving the laundry pole and wandering unsteadily through the dark as though possessed by a demon. It moved from rooftop to rooftop — not, seemingly, being swept along by the wind, but walking on two legs. The onlookers emitted cries of utter disbelief. One of them picked up a stone and threw it at the wayward garment. The kimono, too, seemed taken aback; its skirt dragging along the ground, it took flight, then disappeared out of sight behind the pawnbroker's large storehouse. The seal carver's wife stood there pale and trembling.

By this time the whole neighborhood was in an uproar. The kimono was eventually found caught in the branches of a tall tree in the pawnbroker's garden. The ensuing debate among the neighbors split along two lines. On the one hand, the attack on Okita might suggest that there was an invisible poltergeist at work. On the other hand, in light of the theft of the seal carver's kimono, it was conceivable that the culprit was human. In the latter case, of course, no one had actually seen who it was. But that did not rule out the possibility that someone had been concealed in the dark folds of the garment.

Ghost or human? It was no easy task to choose between the two points of view, but one strong piece of evidence weighed in the latter's favor. A mischievous lad by the name of Gontarō, apprenticed to the local blacksmith, had been seen clambering over the fence at the side of the pawnbroker's house that evening.

"No doubt about it . . . it's that rascal Gon."

Everyone jumped to the same conclusion: that the prankster terrorizing the neighborhood was Gontarō. He was fourteen years old, and his reputation for mischief was undeniable.

"The boy's a good-for-nothing scamp. This is an outrage against the neighborhood!"

The blacksmith and Gontarō's fellow apprentices ganged up on him and hauled him off to the *jishinban,* where the guards tried to force a confession out of him, but Gontarō firmly protested his innocence. He claimed that he had sneaked into the garden next to the pawnbroker's house to steal some tasty-looking persimmons; he vociferously denied ever having rung the fire bell or made off with any laundry. No one believed him. The more he protested the more everyone despised him. The watchmen beat him with sticks, and he was thrown, hands bound, into a six-mat room with a hard wooden floor.

[2]

Thinking the problem had been resolved, the whole neighborhood breathed a sign of relief. In the middle of the night, however, people were astonished to hear the fire bell once again, its clear tones seeming to proclaim Gontarō's innocence. Somehow, someone was ringing it just as before, despite the fact that the wooden bell hammer had already been removed as a precaution.

It now appeared that the disturbance was not the act of a human being after all. Again sensing a threat, the neighbors reverted to keeping a collective watch on the fire bell. But so long as they remained vigilant, the bell quietly behaved itself; as soon as they took their eyes off it, the bell cried out. After this unsettled state of affairs had gone on for about a month, everyone was exhausted, at a loss what to do next.

It was a drizzly day in early November, much like the day on which old Hanshichi was telling me his story.

"Cold, isn't it?" Hanshichi said as he stepped into the watch-post.

"Ah, Hanshichi. Come in!"

The owner of the building, who was on duty, smiled grimly as he greeted the detective. A charcoal fire was blazing away in the large stove inside the door. Entering, Hanshichi spread his hands out in front of the fire.

"What's all this fuss I've been hearing about? Sounds as though you've got a real problem on your hands."

"I take it you've been apprised of the situation," said the owner, frowning. "I must say, we're at our wit's end. What do you think? Can you shed any light on it?"

"Hmm . . . well, now," Hanshichi said, tilting his head to one side. "The fact is, I haven't heard the full story, but I take it it's not that rascal Gon, or whatever his name is."

The other launched into a long recounting, finally ending up:

". . . and while Gon was in custody the bell rang anyway, so that was that. We sent him back to the blacksmith's."

Hanshichi closed his eyes in thought.

"I don't have the answer yet, but let's see if I can figure something out. It's too bad I couldn't come by sooner, but I was held up on another case. Well, first I'd like to take a look at that fire bell. Do you mind if I go up?"

"No, no. By all means."

The owner stood up and led Hanshichi outside. Pensively, Hanshichi glanced up at the bell, then scrambled up the ladder. He quickly inspected the bell and came straight down again. Next, he went to have a look around the neighborhood. About three doors away from the watchpost there was the narrow alleyway where Okita—the kept woman who claimed to have been attacked by a ghost—lived. Beyond her house there was a sizable vacant lot in one corner of which stood an old Inari shrine. Crouched beside it, one of the neighborhood boys was spinning a top. Returning to the alleyway, Hanshichi noticed that Okita's house had a "For Rent" sign out front. The fainthearted mistress, the watchpost owner informed him, had cleared out three days after her ordeal.

Next, Hanshichi stopped in front of the blacksmith's. Peering inside, he saw a man of about forty, who appeared to be the master, giving directions as three workers sent sparks flying from a hot crowbar. Next to them stood a boy absentmindedly working the bellows. This, the owner informed Hanshichi, was the hapless Gontarō. His square face was covered in soot, but the mischievous glint in his eyes was enough to tell Hanshichi that he was indeed, as people maintained, a "little devil."

"Thanks for all your help," Hanshichi said as he left. "I still have some other business to attend to, but I'll be back in two or three days."

He was working on another case that demanded his attention, so the "two or three days" stretched into four, then five, with no chance for him to revisit the neighborhood. During that time, still more disturbing events took place.

The second person to be attacked was the daughter of the tobacconist, a seventeen-year-old named Osaki. She'd been returning home at around seven in the evening after visiting a relative in Honjo. The winter sun had set long ago, but even in the dark she could see the north wind blowing fine particles of white sand down the street. As she approached her own neighborhood, where so many strange things had happened of late, the young girl's heart began to beat faster. Regretting not having returned home earlier, she held her head down and clasped her sleeves tightly to her chest. As she gradually quickened her pace, she heard a faint footfall behind her, as though she were being followed. A chill like ice water went down her spine, but she was not brave enough to turn around and look. Feeling weak in the knees she redoubled her pace.

Just as she was turning the corner into her neighborhood with a sigh of relief, a whirlwind of white sand enveloped her from chest to foot, and she instinctively held her sleeves up to her face. At that moment, whatever strange being it was that had been following her ran at her like a bat out of hell and sent her flying.

Hearing the girl's shrieks, the neighbors came running over and found her on the ground in a faint. Her chignon was pitifully disheveled and her knees slightly grazed, but otherwise she was unharmed. Even after coming to, she still sat there looking dazed from the shock. That night, she took to her bed with a fever and did not get up again for three days.

Ghost or human? Again the townspeople gathered to debate the question. It had been Osaki who had witnessed Gontarō, the blacksmith's apprentice, climbing over the fence at the pawnbroker's. Suspicions were voiced that he might have followed her to take revenge for giving him away, as a result of which he would run afoul of the local authorities. But these allegations were quickly quashed. The blacksmith attested to the fact that Gontarō had been in his shop at the time of the attack on Osaki, and someone else stepped forward to say he had seen Gontarō at work that night. However mischievous Gontarō might be, so long as there was only one of him, there was no way anyone could hold him responsible. In the end, no one at the meeting was able to shed any light on this latest mystery.

"From now on, dears, we mustn't go out at night," worried mothers told their young ones.

This time, the women and children really did stay indoors after dark. But to everyone's surprise, the third victim was a man. It was Sahei, head watchman of the *jishinban,* who was dealt the next blow.

Sahei's archenemy was winter. Since the end of the previous month, he'd been plagued by his old nemesis, colic. In spite of his obvious discomfort, he did his best to be present at the meetings of local officials that, due to the disturbances in the neighborhood, were now being held every day. But the pain had finally become more than he could endure. By placing heated stones inside his kimono he was able to make it through the day, but at night the cold penetrated right into his stomach. He stood now beside the fireplace, groaning and clutching his abdomen, whence the spasms came.

"Shall we go fetch the doctor?" Denshichi and Chōsaku finally asked, unable to bear the sight of his suffering any longer.

"No, I think I can hold out."

In those days, watchmen were notorious penny-pinchers. Sahei dreaded having to pay for a doctor and would rather have made do with over-the-counter medicine. But as the night wore on, his pain worsened until money was no longer a question. Hating to do it, he finally relented and said he would see the doctor.

"I'll go with you, then," Denshichi volunteered.

Sahei's cramps were so bad that he could not walk without assistance. When they got outside, they saw that a night frost was settling over the city. Taking his hand, Denshichi led the sick man to a doctor's house in the next neighborhood. The doctor gave Sahei some medicine and told him to keep warm and go to bed. It was nearly ten o'clock by the time they thanked him and prepared to leave.

"I hear there's been some trouble in your neighborhood. Take care on the way home," the doctor cautioned them on their way out the door.

The well-meant words made the cold seem all the more piercing to the two men. Once again, Denshichi took Sahei's hand and helped him along.

"Let's hurry back before they close the gates," he said. "It'd be annoying to get locked out and have to wait for Chōsaku to come and open them for us."

It was a windless, moonless night, so silent one could almost hear the frost falling. Most of the lights in the neighborhood had gone out. Sahei walked along stooping and clutching his stomach. The two men had entered the neighborhood and passed two or three houses when suddenly a dark shape appeared from behind a rain barrel outside the pawnbroker's house. Before they could tell what it was, the shape ran toward them as though crawling on all fours and latched onto Sahei's leg. Sahei slipped and fell. Denshichi, who'd been on edge from the beginning, shrieked and fled.

Denshichi ran and reported to Chōsaku what had happened. The latter took a stick and set out with trepidation from the watchpost. Denshichi grabbed a weapon for himself and returned with him to the scene of the attack, but the black shape was nowhere to be seen. Sahei had hurt his knee in the fall. In addition, there was a mark on the left side of his forehead as though a stone had grazed it, though whether his assailant had inflicted it or whether he had hit his head when he fell wasn't clear.

Inquiries revealed that Gontarō had a rock-solid alibi that night and had not been outside at the time of the attack. Thus suspicions as to the mischievous boy's involvement were slowly diminishing, while uneasiness as to a possible supernatural cause was mounting. The cowardly Denshichi declared it might have been a *kappa*,[6] but no one took him seriously — *kappa*, he was assured, never ventured into the middle of town like that.

"It must be a human being," they concluded.

Around this time, food began to disappear from people's houses. Given the similar nature of the assaults on Osaki and Sahei, everyone agreed that the mysterious perpetrator of these

---

6. A *kappa* is a water sprite, believed to live in rivers, which grabs children who come too near the water and pulls them under.

acts was beginning to seem more and more human. In fact, there now seemed little doubt that a stranger bent on creating mayhem was in their midst. The townspeople resolved to redouble their nightly vigilance.

[3]

From then on, not a peep was heard from the fire bell. It just hung there, indifferent, high against the wintry sky.

New tenants moved into Okita's house but cleared out after a single night. The wife said her lamp had suddenly gone out during the night and that someone had grabbed her by the hair and dragged her out of bed. Nothing in the house was missing. The landlord searched the empty house, thinking someone or something might be lurking there, but he came up empty-handed.

"Maybe it's a ghost after all. . . ." Again the rumors spread. Not knowing whether the author of their affliction was human or supernatural, people were at a loss how to respond. While the bell overhead no longer rang, down on the ground, as though to compensate for its silence, the bizarre events persisted.

The next human sacrifice was Okura, the duty-man's wife.

["I don't suppose you young people know what a duty-man is," old Hanshichi said, interrupting his narrative to explain. "Simply put, a duty-man in the old days — that is, a *bantarō* — was someone who did odd jobs in the neighborhood, though his primary task was to signal the time of day using wooden clappers. His house was usually next door to the watchpost, and he kept a shop where he sold straw sandals, candles, charcoal, paper fans, and that sort of thing. In other words, it was kind of a five-and-dime store. In summertime he'd also sell goldfish, and in the winter baked sweet potatoes. Although it wasn't a particularly lofty line of work and people used to scorn him, his wide range of activities was enough to make many a *bantarō* quite a rich man."]

Next door to the duty-man's house was a small brush maker's shop. Just after six o'clock that evening, the brush maker's pregnant wife suddenly went into labor. Rushing next door, Okura found the brush maker standing around looking helpless, so she immediately dashed off to fetch the midwife. One of the perquisites of being the duty-man's wife was that she could sometimes earn a little extra cash by running such errands.

Okura was a stouthearted woman. Slipping on her clogs, she raced out without a moment's hesitation, secure in the thought that it was only just after dusk and that the neighborhood patrols were on high alert. The midwife's house was four or five blocks away, so she went as fast as she could. Judging from the sky, it looked as though there would be a frost that night. The lanterns lining both sides of the narrow streets cast pale shadows. She reached the midwife's house and asked her to come at once. The woman agreed, and together they set off.

The midwife, over sixty and slow-footed, plodded along with a scarf pulled over her face. She prattled on about trivialities, and Okura, walking beside her, had to suppress her impatience. Soon, driven by anxiety, she was practically dragging the other woman along, making only inattentive responses to her remarks. Just ahead of them, she could see the lights of her own neighborhood.

On the edge of the neighborhood stood two large storehouses, and just beyond them lay a lumberyard. Along this nearly twenty-yard stretch there were no lanterns, and the wintry darkness loomed before the women like a pool of black lacquer through which they must pass in order to reach Okura's neighborhood. It was about here, Okura thought to herself, that the tobacconist's daughter had met with misfortune, and she urged the midwife on even faster. Just then, a dog or some such creature crawled out of the shadows behind a pile of lumber.

"My! What's that?"

With the midwife in tow, it was impossible for Okura to flee. As she peered bravely into the darkness trying to make out what it was, the bizarre creature crawled toward them on its stomach and suddenly lunged at Okura's waist.

"Get off me!" she shrieked.

The first time, she was able to push the creature away by sheer force, but the second time it got hold of the sash of her kimono and loosened it so that it began to unravel. Okura panicked and started screaming for help at the top of her lungs. The midwife, too, began shouting hoarsely. Hearing their cries, the neighbors came running. At the sound of their footsteps, the creature also panicked, scratching Okura on the right cheek before it fled. She chased after it for four or five yards, but it quickly disappeared from sight.

"It was no ghost, that's for sure — it was a man," Okura said. "I couldn't see his face in the dark, but he must have been about sixteen or seventeen years old." The brave woman's testimony convinced the townsfolk once and for all that the culprit was human, but they still had no idea who it might be.

If the creature was human after all, the neighborhood officials reasoned, then there must be some way of capturing him. Meeting again at the watchpost, they discussed the best way to hunt the villain down. Just then, though, they received a report about another strange event that had occurred about an hour after Okura's encounter.

The wife of the seal maker — whose kimono it was that had been stolen — had been in her kitchen when she heard something clattering around on the roof. Thinking it was probably a cat or a rat, she stepped outside and tried shooing it away, but the noises persisted. Still shaken from the incident with the kimono, she felt a slight chill go down her spine. But spurred on by a morbid curiosity, she untied the rope attached to the door of the skylight and slowly began pulling it open. At that point, she saw something and let out a shriek, almost tripping over herself as she fled into the next room.

According to her story, she'd seen two large, gleaming eyes staring at her as she peered out of the skylight onto the roof — whereupon, she said, still trembling, she'd lost her nerve and run screaming into the next room.

This piece of news left people even more perplexed.

"Okura's story can't be trusted. This suggests that the creature isn't human after all." That night, the neighborhood council meeting ended inconclusively.

During this period of anxiety and confusion, Hanshichi had been winding up other cases. Then a morning came when he told himself that, at last, he could look into the matter of the fire bell. Even then, a sudden visitor showed up and detained him, so it was two o'clock in the afternoon before he left his house in Kanda and set foot again in the gloomy little neighborhood where the haunted fire bell kept watch.

"Perhaps it's just my imagination, but this is a pretty dismal place," he thought to himself.

Though not windy, the day was cold. A faint gleam of sunshine would start to break through the overcast sky only to disappear suddenly, as though blown out like a candle. So overcast was it that even the crows had become confused, cawing as they hurried home to their roosts.

His hands burrowing for warmth into the breast of his kimono, Hanshichi first headed over to the blacksmith's. As he approached, a shower of tangerines came flying out into the street, where they were scooped up by a crowd of children. Ah, yes, Hanshichi remembered, it was the eighth day of the eleventh month—the day of the Festival of the Bellows.[7] From where he stood behind the children, he could see the blacksmith inside, energetically tossing tangerines into the street. Gontarō and the older men who worked there were busily carrying in baskets filled with more tangerines.

Hanshichi stopped by the *jishinban* and swapped gossip with the owner of the house as he waited for the tangerine tossing at the blacksmith's to finish. So long as the problem of the fire bell remained unresolved, the owner was obliged to take his turn on

7. *Fuigo-matsuri,* said to originate with fire festivals *(ohitaki-matsuri)* held at shrines in the Kyoto region in early November to celebrate the harvest.

duty in the watchpost. He hoped, he complained self-centeredly to Hanshichi, it all would be settled soon so that he could get back to doing other things.

"Don't worry," Hanshichi assured him, "I'll have the matter cleared up in short order."

"We'd be very much obliged. It'll be winter very soon, and people here in Edo are scared to death when they hear a fire bell," the owner said dejectedly.

"I understand. Please be patient a bit longer. I wonder if you could tell young Gontarō to come here once that little ceremony at the blacksmith's is finished?"

"So you think that boy's the culprit after all?"

"Not necessarily, but there's something I want to ask him. You needn't intimidate him — just bring him here without any fuss."

The number of tangerines rolling into the street was dwindling. As soon as all the children had dispersed, the watchpost owner went and called Gontarō. Hanshichi puffed at his pipe, gazing outside. The leaden sky was becoming even heavier, with dark, demonic clouds hastening by overhead. The cry of a street vendor hawking sea cucumbers echoed coldly through the air.

"Gontarō, say hello nicely to Inspector Hanshichi from Kanda," the owner said, hauling Gontarō into the *jishinban* and sitting him down. Probably on account of the festival, Gontarō had changed his usual filthy black working clothes for a fresh kimono of rough cotton, and his face was relatively clean of soot.

"So you're Gontarō, eh? What's your boss up to right now?" Hanshichi asked him.

"They're just about to have a big party."

"So I guess you're free then. Did you get any tangerines today at the festival?"

"Ten," Gontarō said, shaking his sleeves to show they were full of tangerines.

"I see. Well, we can't talk here. Come with me to that empty lot over there."

When they emerged into the street, it was hailing sporadically.

"Just our luck," Hanshichi said looking at the sky, then added, "But it's not that bad. C'mon, hurry up."

[4]

Gontarō obediently trailed along after Hanshichi, who turned into the alleyway and drew to a halt in front of the Inari shrine in the vacant lot.

"Here, Gonta — was it you who rang that fire bell?"

"Nope," Gontarō answered nonchalantly.

"And stealing the kimono from the seal carver's house — that wasn't you either?"

Gontarō again shook his head.

"Did you scare that geisha who lived over there?"

Gontarō denied this allegation, too.

"Do you have any siblings, or a best friend?"

"I don't have any real close friends, but I've got an older brother."

"How old is he? Where's he now?"

The hail had started to come down hard. It was too much even for Hanshichi. He took Gontarō's hand and led him under the eaves of the vacant house where Okita had lived. The front door was unlatched, and it opened easily when Hanshichi tugged at it. He stepped into the dirt-floored area for removing one's shoes; then, using his handkerchief to wipe off the wooden step placed just inside, he sat down and invited Gonta to sit beside him.

"Have a seat, Gonta. Now, tell me, does your brother live at home?"

"No, he's an apprentice at a clog maker's . . . he's seventeen."

The clog maker's house, he said, was five or six blocks away. Then, in a suddenly subdued voice, he explained how their mother had gone off after their father had died, orphaning him and his brother. Hanshichi was deeply touched.

"So, it's just you and your brother, eh? Does he look after you?"

"Yeah. He comes to see me every year on his day off," Gontarō stated proudly. "He takes me to the Enma Temple and buys me lots of things to eat."[8]

"He's a good brother. You're a lucky kid."

Then, changing his tone, Hanshichi gave the boy a long, hard look and changed his tone.

"What would you do if he went to jail?"

Gontarō started to cry.

"Don't, sir, please!"

"If you do something bad, you go to jail . . . that's all there is to it."

"But I didn't do anything wrong and they put *me* in jail! It made me so mad!"

"So mad you did what? Huh? Don't hold out on me, Gonta. Tell me the truth. Don't force me to use my truncheon! You were so mad you asked your brother to do something, right? C'mon, out with it!"

"I didn't ask him! He was so upset about what they did to me that he . . . I was innocent—they had no right to treat me that way."

"That was because you're always up to no good! After all, you stole those persimmons, didn't you?" Hanshichi shouted.

"Well, what do you expect? I'm just a kid, after all! They coulda just bawled me out. I can put up with the boss beating me, but those guys in the *jishinban* hit me with sticks and tied me up. My brother said tying someone up is very serious—they can't just do it anytime they want," Gontarō was trembling, and there were tears in his voice.

---

8. Enma (Sanskrit, *Yama*) is the god who presides over the underworld and passes judgment upon the dead. It was believed that, on the fifteenth day of the seventh month (Obon), Enma opened the furnaces of Hell once a year to relieve the suffering of the damned. This was also one of two annual holidays (along with New Year's) when apprentices were granted leave by their employers to return home to visit their families, and hence many of them went to pay their respects at temples dedicated to Enma for releasing them from *their* suffering.

"I might as well tell you everything. My brother was so angry he said he'd get revenge for me. It was that bigmouth girl at the tobacco shop who blabbed on me for climbing over the fence. And it was that batty old watchman who beat me up. My brother said he'd see to it they got what was coming to them, so he watched and waited for his chance."

"So it was your brother who attacked the tobacconist's daughter, Sahei the watchman, and the duty-man's wife, huh?"

"Please let him off, sir!" Gontarō said loudly, breaking into tears again. "My brother's not a bad person. He only did it for me. If you arrest anyone, arrest me! He's always looked after me, so I don't mind going to jail for him. Please, sir. Let him off and take me instead!" He pressed his small body against Hanshichi and clung to him, crying.

Hanshichi was deeply moved by this display of emotion. Deep down, then, the boy the locals condemned as a rascal had a gentle, innocent heart!

"All right, all right. I'll forgive your brother," Hanshichi said gently. "I'll keep what you told me a secret . . . I won't tell anyone. In return, will you do exactly as I say?"

He need not have asked. Of course, the boy swore he'd agree to anything. So Hanshichi whispered something in his ear. The boy nodded, and immediately left the house.

The hail had stopped but the clouds had sunk even lower in the sky, and a cold shadow hung over everything. Even at that time of day, the entire street was silent as the grave, with no sign, even, of the usual dogs scavenging scraps from the piles of garbage. Stealing out of the vacant house, Gontarō crept over to the Inari shrine. Taking out five or six of the tangerines he had in his sleeve, he carefully tossed them through the lattice doors on the front of the shrine. Then he lay flat on the ground and did his best to hold his breath.

Hanshichi remained seated inside the vacant house and waited for a while, but when Gontarō didn't return to make his report, he grew impatient and went outside.

"Hey, Gonta—did you find anything?" he called out quietly. Gontarō's head rose from where he was lying and shook from side to side. Hanshichi looked disappointed.

Hail began clattering down again, so Hanshichi hastily took out his handkerchief and put it over his head. It bothered him to see Gontarō lying obediently on the ground being struck by the hail, so he motioned with his chin for him to come over. Slowly, Gontarō got up and came back.

"Were there any noises coming from inside the shrine?" Hanshichi asked. "Any thumping or anything like that?"

"Not a sound—doesn't seem to be anything in there," Gontarō whispered disappointedly. The two returned to the vacant house.

"Do you have any more tangerines?"

Gontarō took out three tangerines and handed them to Hanshichi, who quietly slid open the shoji behind him. The vestibule was two tatami mats in size. Next to it, through the partially opened doorway, he glimpsed what appeared to be a maid's room of about three mats. Hanshichi crawled into the vestibule and opened a pair of sliding doors on the opposite side. Beyond lay a well-appointed, rectangular six-mat room, but even in the dim light Hanshichi could see that the shoji facing onto the veranda were severely damaged. In a number of places, the wooden lattices were broken and the paper was torn. Hanshichi rolled two tangerines into the room. Then he tossed another into the maid's room. Finally, making sure that the shoji opening onto the vestibule were tightly shut, he stepped down into the dirt-floored area just inside the front door.

"Quiet!" he cautioned Gontarō.

The two waited with bated breath. The hail outside began to let up again. There was no sound at all from inside and Gontarō grew impatient.

"Maybe there's nothing here . . ."

But just then a thumping noise came from inside. The two looked at one another. It sounded as though something had clambered through the broken shoji into the six-mat room. From the sound as it walked, it might have been a cat. Slowly, the noise of claws scraping on the tatami mats came closer. Then, straining their ears, they caught the sound of the creature munching on the tangerines Hanshichi had thrown into the room.

"He's eating my tangerines!"

Hanshichi smiled and shot Gontarō a glance. Picking up their sandals, they pushed the shoji open all the way. Then they threw open the door to the six-mat room and plunged inside. There in the dimly lit room lurked the creature. It let out a hair-raising cry and tried to escape through the shoji onto the veranda, but Hanshichi chased after it and hit it on the head with his sandal. Then Gontarō joined in. Enraged, the creature threw itself at Gontarō with its fangs bared. This was where Gontarō's untamed nature came in handy — without a second thought he grappled with the strange beast. It let out a bloodcurdling growl.

"Hang in there, Gonta!"

As he cheered the boy on, Hanshichi took off the handkerchief he had spread over his head and, standing behind Gontarō's adversary, wrapped it around the creature's neck. Being strangled seemed to take some of the fight out of the monster; it flailed its arms and legs in vain, and Gontarō was at last able to pin it down. The quick-witted boy loosened his sash, swiftly wound it around the creature's limbs, and tied it tight. In the meantime, Hanshichi wrenched open the rain shutters on the veranda, allowing the pale light from the overcast sky to flood into the vacant house.

"Damn, just as I thought!"

The monster that Gontarō had captured alive was a large monkey. As souvenirs of his struggle with the beast, his face, legs, and arms bore several claw marks.

"This is nothing. Doesn't hurt a bit," Gontarō said, gazing triumphantly at his prey. In its desperation, the monkey shot him a murderous look.

"IMAGINE IF the hero of this tale had been the legendary swordsman Miyamoto Musashi or someone like that," said old Hanshichi with a laugh. "I'm sure it would have been immortalized by storytellers and in plays as 'Musashi Vanquishes the Baboon,' or something like that, eh?

"Anyway, when we dragged the creature back to the watchpost, everyone was amazed. The whole neighborhood turned out to see it. What's that? How did I figure out the culprit was a monkey? Well, when I inspected the bell, I noticed there were claw marks all over the ladder. Somehow I didn't think they could've been made by a cat, but it suddenly struck me that a monkey might have got up to just such tricks. Jumping onto the geisha's umbrella, running off with a kimono someone had hung out to dry . . . that seemed like a monkey's handiwork. Then I asked myself where a monkey might be hiding, and I thought of the Inari shrine.[9] Well, I was wrong there. In the beginning, though, he probably was in fact hiding inside the shrine and eating the offerings of food people left there. But then he grew more brazen and started causing real mischief. When the former geisha's house became vacant, he moved his base of operations there and continued to pursue his fiendish ways. The person who suffered the most was poor Gontarō. His reputation for delinquency weighed against him. I was the only one who ever found out about his brother. In the end, of course, the monkey got blamed for everything. And Gontarō became a local hero for having vanquished the beast. In time, he became a full-fledged blacksmith."

"So where had the monkey come from in the first place?" I asked.

"Well, that's the funny part. It had been performing in a monkey show in Ryōgoku. Somehow it escaped and went climbing over rooftops and underneath people's houses until it stumbled

---

9. Inari is the god of the harvest, and people often leave offerings of food such as tangerines or rice at shrines dedicated to him.

upon the neighborhood where it set off such an uproar. When I started making inquiries, I found that the monkey specialized in female roles and had been playing the part of Oshichi the Greengrocer's Daughter![10] Isn't that a laugh? His role was to climb up a fire tower and beat a drum as hard as he could. So he pulled the same kind of stunt with the fire bell. He just ran up the ladder and rang it for all he was worth. Hilarious, isn't it? A real ham, that monkey was! I filed a lot of reports in the course of my career, but nothing got a bigger laugh than that!"

"What happened to the monkey in the end?" I asked, brimming with curiosity.

"The monkey's owner was fined a thousand copper pieces. For having disturbed the peace, the monkey was put on the next prison boat leaving from Eitai Bridge and banished to Hachijō Island. He was probably happier there in the wild than he had been cooped up in some little sideshow hut. Since he was an animal, the officials on the island weren't about to keep him locked up, so they just let him run free."

A monkey banished to a remote isle . . . had anyone ever heard such a strange tale? Once again, I left Hanshichi's house feeling that my visit to the old man had been well worth my time.

---

10. A young woman who fell in love with a handsome young monk while taking shelter at his temple during a great conflagration in Edo in 1682. Later, she allegedly committed arson in the hope of seeing him again, was apprehended, and put to death. The story was immortalized in popular song, literature, and plays.

The Daimyo's Maidservant

OKU JOCHŪ

[1]

I returned to Tokyo in the dog days of August after spending a fortnight in the countryside away from the heat. Bearing a small souvenir of my vacation, I went to Hanshichi's house and found him just back from his evening visit to the bathhouse. He was seated on a straw mat on the veranda, energetically fanning himself. A cool breeze blew through the tiny garden, and a caged grasshopper could be heard chirping from the window of a neighbor's house.

"As far as keeping insects is concerned, it's grasshoppers that always make me think of Edo," the old man said. "I know they're inexpensive and don't have the prestige value of pine crickets or bell crickets, but somehow they seem to typify the old city. When I pass by a house and hear a grasshopper calling from a window or under the eaves, it immediately brings back memories of Edo in the summertime. Insect sellers would hate to hear me say this, because crickets fetch a lot more money, but the grasshopper is the only true Edo insect.... It's what people these days would call the 'common man's insect.' No, there's nothing that says 'Edo' like a grasshopper."

Thus launched into a lecture on grasshoppers, Hanshichi sang the praises of this humble insect, though today, he said, it was little more than a child's toy, selling for a few pennies. If I wanted to keep an insect as a pet, he declared, I should make it a grass-hopper. Having exhausted the subject of insects, he switched next to a discussion of wind chimes. And then, he pointed out that, according to the new calendar, tonight was the night of the fifteenth day of the eighth month.[1]

"But even though they call it the eighth month, look how hot it is still. It's because we've switched over to the Western calendar. Under the old calendar, the mornings and evenings would be much cooler at this time of year."

The old man then started to reminisce about moon-viewing festivities in the old days. And in the course of that, he was reminded of the following story, which I added to the collection in my notebook.

THE YEAR WAS 1862, and it was the evening of the fourteenth day of the eighth month. Hanshichi returned home earlier than usual, had dinner, and was thinking of popping out to the local loan association, when a woman of about forty with her hair done up in a small bun appeared, looking very troubled.

"Good evening, Inspector. I'm sorry I've not been round to see you for so long. I hope you've been keeping well?"

"Ah, Okame — quite a stranger! My, what a fine young lady that daughter of yours has turned into! I hear Ochō's a real hard worker. As her mother, that must put your mind at ease."

"No — as a matter of fact, it's on account of Ochō that I've come to see you this evening. I'm at my wit's end."

Looking at the furrows on the middle-aged woman's brow, Hanshichi felt fairly certain what had happened. Okame and her daughter, Ochō, who was now seventeen, ran a teashop at one end of Eitai Bridge. Ochō's elegant beauty, marred only by a somewhat taciturn and retiring nature, was a great asset in

---

1. The Western calendar was adopted in Japan in 1872. Under the lunar calendar previously in use, the fifteenth day of the eighth month fell in mid-autumn and was the night of the Moon Viewing Festival (o-tsukimi), now held in mid-September on the night of the full moon.

attracting young male customers. Okame was proud of having given birth to such a beauty, and one didn't need to be a detective to guess that concern about her daughter could mean only one thing: someone had replaced Okame in the filial Ochō's affections and was creating friction in their relationship. But that was to be expected given the kind of business she was in, and Hanshichi found it rather vulgar to come griping to him about such things.

"What is it? Has Ochō been up to no good? Causing you grief, is she? But you know," Hanshichi added jovially, "it's best to overlook these small things. Young people need to have some fun once in a while or they'll lose interest in their work. Don't you remember what it was like at her age? You mustn't go on at her too much."

Okame gave him a long, hard look. She was not amused.

"No, sir, that's not it at all. If it were just something silly like having a boyfriend . . . well, just as you say, I generally turn a blind eye to that sort of thing. But this is something much more serious. Ochō herself has been crying her eyes out about it."

"That does seem strange. What's happened, then?"

"You see, she disappears from time to time . . ."

Hanshichi could not repress a smile at this. A young teahouse girl disappearing from time to time? Such things hardly ever developed into anything serious. Seeing the look on Hanshichi's face, Okame hastened to correct his assumption.

"No, no. It's got nothing to do with a man, or anything like that. Anyway, let me explain. It all started just prior to the fireworks festival at Ryōgoku in the fifth month.[2] One day, a very impressive-looking samurai was going past our teahouse with his attendant, when he happened to glance in and see Ochō. He

---

2. *Kawa-hiraki* (lit. "river opening"), a festival celebrating the beginning of the summer season on the twenty-eighth day of the fifth month, when the Sumida River was opened to pleasure boating and other summer activities. The fireworks display on that day was famous, dating back to 1733.

wandered in, ordered tea, and sat there drinking it for a while. Then he got up, leaving a silver coin[3] on the table, and left. All in all, a very respectable customer. Then, about three days later, he appeared again, and this time he was with an elegant woman of about thirty-five or -six — a real lady. But I didn't get the impression they were husband and wife. The woman asked Ochō her name and age, and then, just as before, they put a coin down on the table and left. Three days later Ochō disappeared."

"Hmm," Hanshichi nodded, rapidly appraising the situation. No doubt the pair were kidnappers passing themselves off as upper-class types in order to abduct attractive girls.

"And your daughter hasn't come home yet?"

"She has — about ten days later she returned as it was getting dark, looking white as a sheet. I can't tell you how relieved I was! Of course, I immediately asked her to tell me what had happened. It had been just before dark the day she disappeared, too, and I'd stayed behind in the teahouse to clean up after she left to go home. She was walking past the stone yards along the riverbank in Hamachō when two or three men jumped out from behind a pile of rocks and grabbed her. They gagged and blindfolded her, tied her hands together, and shoved her into a waiting palanquin. It moved off, and Ochō was tossed around inside, scared half out of her wits . . . she had no clue which way they were heading. Eventually they arrived at what seemed to be a huge mansion and the men took her inside. She doesn't have the slightest clue where it was, nor even how long it took to get there."

Ochō was led to a room in the inner recesses of the house. Someone undid her blindfold, removed the gag from her mouth, and untied her hands. In due course, the elegant woman whom Ochō had met at the teahouse appeared. "I know this must be quite a shock for you," she said, "but there's no need to be afraid. Just be a good girl and do exactly as we say." She treated Ochō very kindly. Realizing that the young girl was too frightened to

---

3. One *shu,* about ten times the cost of a cup of tea.

say anything, the woman adopted a still more soothing tone. "Just relax here for a while," she said, and brought Ochō tea and cakes. A short while later, she told Ochō to take a bath. Several women came to escort her to the bathroom and she went with them, still in a daze.

After her bath, Ochō was shown to another large room where a beautiful plush cushion had been placed on the floor for her. In the alcove, fringed pinks were arranged demurely in a vase. A koto leaned against the wall. Utterly overwhelmed by her surroundings, she could make neither head nor tail of it all.

The elegant woman reappeared and instructed Ochō to get undressed. Then, assisted by the same women as before, she took a very fetching long-sleeved kimono from the clothes rack and draped it over the cowering Ochō's shoulders. The women tied it with a sash made of thick brocade. Ochō felt so unlike her usual self that she simply stood there in a daze, hardly knowing what to do with her own body. Next, they took her by the hand and led her over to the cushion, where they pressed her down into a kneeling position. Then a small writing desk like the ones used for copying sutras was brought out and placed in front of her. On it sat two or three imposing-looking books. Next, the women brought an incense burner and placed it on the floor by the desk. A purplish trail of smoke gently wafted up from it, and Ochō was gradually intoxicated by a wonderful fragrance that seemed to penetrate her very being. A silk lantern painted with autumn grasses shone dimly overhead. Ochō sat rigidly in the formal manner, feeling as though she were in a dream.

The women opened one of the books on the table in front of her and told Ochō to bow her head and begin reading it. Ochō felt herself unable to resist, as though she no longer had any will of her own. Like a puppet in a play, her body was under another's control. As she gazed obediently down at the pages of the book, one of the women began fanning her gently with a silk fan. "You look hot," she said to Ochō.

"You mustn't speak," the elegant woman cautioned her quietly. Ochō sat perfectly still.

After a while Ochō heard, outside on the veranda, the muffled footsteps of what seemed to be three or four people approaching the room. "Keep your head lowered," the woman warned her again. Ochō thought she heard the sound of the shoji quietly sliding open just a little.

"Don't look!" the woman whispered sternly.

What sort of fearsome being is watching me? Ochō thought, cowering down with her eyes fixed to the desk. Presently, she heard the shoji slide quietly shut, again followed by the sound of footsteps, this time receding along the veranda. She breathed a sigh of relief. Cold beads of sweat from under her arms were dripping down her sides like rain.

"You did very well," the woman said kindly. "You can relax now."

The oil lamp was turned up, bringing sudden brightness into the dimly lit room. The other women entered bearing two gorgeously decorated lacquer dinner trays, and Ochō was directed to sit in front of one of them. "You must be famished," they said, politely serving her. But to Ochō, who felt as though there was a huge lump in her throat, it seemed unlikely she would be able to swallow anything. She picked up her chopsticks and began halfheartedly picking at the lavish array of food in front of her. Once the meal was over, the elegant woman rose from her seat. "Rest here a bit longer," she said to Ochō as she left the room. The other women collected the trays and disappeared as well.

Left alone in the room, Ochō began for the first time to feel like herself again. But the more she thought about it, the more it all seemed like a dream. It simply didn't make sense. Perhaps, she wondered, she'd been bewitched by a fox? What possible reason could her captors have for bringing her here, dressing her in beautiful clothes, giving her delicious things to eat, and installing her in a palatial room where they waited on her hand and foot? She began to suspect that she was to be sacrificed in someone else's stead — just as in one of those puppet theater or kabuki plays — and her head handed over to her captors' enemies.

Either way, the place was scary, and she wanted to get away as fast as she could. But how should she go about trying to escape? She had no idea of the way out.

"If I can just make it to the garden, I'll probably find a way out from there." Summoning up all her courage, Ochō held her breath and tiptoed silently across the slippery tatami. Her fingers trembled as she touched the shoji. But at that moment the door slid open unbidden and she found herself face to face with one of the women. Ochō recoiled in alarm. "If you would like to use the lavatory, allow me to show you the way," the woman said, turning and leading Ochō out of the room. Stepping out onto the veranda, Ochō saw that it overlooked a spacious garden. It was a moonless night, and fireflies flitted in and out of the pitch darkness of a stand of trees. Far off, she heard the plaintive cry of an owl.

Returning to the room, Ochō found that a futon had been laid out for her. A pure-white mosquito net embroidered with a "flying goose" crest hung over it, cool and inviting. The elegant woman reappeared out of nowhere.

"Please go to bed now. I must warn you, though — no matter what happens during the night, do not lift your head from the pillow."

Ochō was led across the room and the mosquito net raised as she was helped into bed. A quilt as white as driven snow was laid over her. Somewhere a bell sounded the hour of ten. Like ghosts, noiselessly, the two women vanished.

Ochō spent the night in terror.

[2]

It was impossible for Ochō to sleep with her nerves so on edge. The bedding was softer than anything she had ever slept on before, but it felt strangely rough against her skin and the sensation of floating on air was mildly disconcerting. In addition, it was a hot, muggy night and her forehead and the back of her neck were covered in an unpleasant, sticky sweat. Again and again, she adjusted the position of the pillow, with its long red tassels, beneath her heavy head.

How much time had passed? She couldn't tell, but it must have been quite late, for the house was deathly quiet, when she heard a faint footfall gliding across the tatami in the next room. Feeling as though her blood had turned to ice, Ochō pulled up the covers as high as she could and lay with her face pressed against the pillow. Even so, she could hear the large, lacquer-framed door leading to the next room slide smoothly open, followed by a faint rustling sound as of a kimono skirt trailing along the floor. She held her breath.

Whoever it was who had entered the room came and stood noiselessly beside the dimly glowing lamp and peered at Ochō's apparently sleeping face. Had the creature come to suck her blood, Ochō wondered, or to devour her flesh? Half convinced that she was already dead, she clutched the edge of the quilt with all her might. At last, she heard the swishing of silk retreating into the next room. As though waking from a nightmare, Ochō wiped the sweat from her forehead with the sleeve of her robe, carefully opened her eyes and looked around the room. The sliding door was shut and all was quiet — not even the buzz of a mosquito from outside the net.

After a restless night, Ochō dozed off toward dawn as the air finally turned cooler. She awoke to find the women from the day before patiently waiting by the side of her pillow. They helped her change into a fresh kimono and brought a lacquered basin for her to wash her face. When she had had breakfast, the elegant woman reappeared.

"I'm sure you feel very confined here, but please be patient a little longer. If you're bored, why not take a stroll in the garden? We'll show you the way."

One woman on either side of her, Ochō slipped on a pair of wooden clogs and stepped down into the spacious garden. Wending their way through copses and thickets, they came to an enormous pond covered with aquatic plants. Tall green reeds and pampas grass grew at the water's edge. "A giant catfish lives at the bottom of this old pond and guards it," one of the women told Ochō, who felt a chill go down her spine.

"Hush!" the first woman hissed at them suddenly. "Keep your eyes on the pond. Don't look away!"

Ochō suddenly had the feeling that someone, somewhere, was watching her, and her body went stiff. She stood rooted to the spot, her eyes fixed on that terrifying pond that was said to harbor a guardian spirit. After a few moments, the other women relaxed their vigilance, and they quietly set off walking again.

On returning to the room, Ochō was again told to rest. The women brought some storybooks for her to read. After lunch, one of the women came and played the koto. Though it was the sixth month and the day was hot, they had not allowed the shoji leading onto the veranda to be opened; the other sliding doors were also, of course, kept tightly shut. Ochō passed the long day feeling like a prisoner in a luxuriously appointed jail. When evening came, she was taken for her bath and, on returning to the room, made to change into yet another kimono. The lamp was lit and Ochō was told to sit at the desk. This time, she did not sense that she was being watched, but still she felt she couldn't afford to let her guard down.

"I wonder if whoever it was will come back again tonight?"

She went to bed again around ten o'clock, slipping under the mosquito netting with a feeling of dread in her heart. Since dusk a light rain had been falling gently, and the frogs in the pond croaked incessantly. Again, she found it impossible to sleep. She was thinking it must be quite late when she noticed that the lantern by her pillow, whether naturally or by human agency, had gradually grown dim and was now almost out. Opening her eyes and looking around, she made out a vague white shape that entered the room through the white sliding door and drifted like a phantom up to the white mosquito netting.

"Ah, a ghost!" Quickly, she pulled the covers over her head and started fervently reciting under her breath prayers to Kannon,

Suiten,[4] and the other familiar gods. After about half an hour, she timidly peered out from under the covers to find that the white apparition had disappeared. Somewhere she heard a cock crowing.

In the morning, she washed her face, braided her hair, applied her makeup, and was taken for a walk in the garden after breakfast, all exactly as on the previous day. That night, she sat at the desk, went to bed, and again saw the ghostly apparition hovering by her bedside. This went on for the next seven or eight days. From morning to night she felt trapped and frightened, and soon began to look as wan and emaciated as a ghost herself.

Eventually, she resolved that she'd sooner die than suffer like this any longer. With tears in her eyes, she pleaded with the elegant woman to let her go home just once. From the expression on her face, the woman was clearly annoyed, but Ochō's insistence must have convinced her that if she pushed the girl too far, she might well throw herself into the pond. On the evening of the tenth day, she finally relented and agreed to let Ochō return home for a while.

"But you must not speak of this to anyone. I expect we will send for you again soon. I want you to promise me now that you will come back."

Ochō had no choice but to agree, knowing that they would not let her go home otherwise. "I promise," she said, without really meaning it. Commiserating with Ochō over her ordeal, the woman gave her a small packet wrapped in thick handmade paper. At sunset, as the sky was growing dark, Ochō was blindfolded and a gag was placed in her mouth. Then she was put in a vehicle like the one in which she had arrived. The route they took was nearly deserted, and after bouncing along for a while,

---

4. A Buddhist deity of Indian origin (Sanskrit *Varuna*). Once considered the creator and preserver of heaven and earth, and the supreme divinity, he later was identified more specifically as the god of water, the form that he assumes in Buddhism.

they reached the riverbank at Hamachō. Ochō was put down in front of the stone yards and the bearers made off again with the empty palanquin as though in a hurry to get away.

Ochō stood there for a moment in a daze, like a person who has just been released from a fox's spell. Then, suddenly gripped again by fear, she started to run. Not until she had reached her house, dashed inside, and seen her mother's face did the feeling that it was all a dream leave her. Had she been spirited away by a fox? asked Okame. But Ochō reached into the breast of her kimono and produced the packet the elegant woman had given her: it was real after all, not just a tree leaf with a fox's spell cast on it! Unwrapping it, Ochō found it contained ten shiny gold coins, each one the size and shape of a child's identity tag.

"Look, there are ten *ryō* here!" Okame exclaimed, wide-eyed in astonishment.

Even an honest person is not without avarice. In those days, the going rate for a man's mistress was barely one *ryō* a month, and here Ochō had been paid that much per day for doing nothing more than wearing a beautiful kimono and eating fine meals! Nice work if you can get it! rejoiced Okame. But Ochō only shuddered in horror at the memory. "There's no way I'm going back to that creepy place," she said, "not even for a *ryō* a day, not even for ten."

For the next two weeks, Ochō had the pallor of an invalid. Okame had at first been thrilled when she saw the money, but the more she thought about it the more uneasy she became. She even started to feel that Ochō was justified in loathing the situation.

"We've got our ten *ryō*—it doesn't matter if our customers come or not. It'd be best if you stayed at home and didn't come to the teahouse for a while."

Afraid her daughter might be taken from her again, Okame had decided that Ochō should stay away from the teahouse. Then, one evening toward the end of the month, Okame returned home after closing the shop to find that Ochō, whom she'd left minding the house, was not there. None of the neighbors had seen her either. Okame guessed her daughter had been abducted and taken back to the samurai mansion, but of course she had no idea where that was.

Day after day, Okame wondered what she should do. Then, ten days later, Ochō returned again, looking dazed and disoriented. Once again, she was carrying ten *ryō* wrapped in paper, and her story was exactly the same as before.

"I see. Well, it's not a bad way to earn a living, but strange all the same. I'm not surprised your daughter isn't too pleased about it," Hanshichi said, his brow furrowing as Okame concluded her bizarre tale.

"And then she disappeared again at the end of last month. It seems they always wait until I'm out of the house before snatching her away. She'll step out into the street and find a palanquin waiting there, and the next thing she knows she's been blindfolded and put inside. So she still has no idea where they're taking her."

"And this time she came back safely again?"

"No, not yet," Okame said. "This time it's been more than ten days, and I was starting to get rather worried because I hadn't heard from her. Then, early this morning, a woman came to the house — the one from the teashop who looks like a samurai lady. She said they wanted to keep my daughter for a while and wanted me to agree not to see her. In return, I'd receive 200 *ryō*. I didn't know what to do. I mean, I can't just sell my darling daughter to some stranger. I tried to refuse, but she wouldn't take no for an answer. 'I know we're asking a lot of you,' she said, 'but please give us your consent.' Then that grand lady, she actually prostrated herself before me! I really didn't know what to do. I said I couldn't give her an answer right away, I needed a day or two to think about it. And finally I got her to leave. Oh, Inspector — what do you suppose this is all about?"

Okame's voice trembled. She was clearly desperate.

[3]

"Yes, I can see why you're worried," said Hanshichi. "From the sound of it, I'd say you're dealing with a high-ranking *hatamoto* or a *daimyo*. But I wonder why someone like that would do such a thing? I mean, it's not as though a daimyo couldn't take the daughter of a teahouse as his mistress if he wanted to, especially one as beautiful as Ochō. Why not just come out and say so — ask to take her into his household? It doesn't make sense." Then, after he'd thought for a few moments, he added, "But now the jewel's been snatched away, and there's not much we can do about it. We don't even know where this mansion is, so we've got nothing to go on. We're stuck."

Seeing Hanshichi cross his arms in perplexity, Okame's expression turned to one of utter helplessness.

"What shall I do if my daughter doesn't come back?" she asked, wiping her eyes with the sleeve of her summer crepe kimono, faded from repeated washings.

"At any rate, I expect the samurai lady will be back in a day or two," Hanshichi said comfortingly, "so I'll be waiting at your teahouse and try to get a look at her. Then maybe I'll think of something."

"It would be a great comfort to me if you were there. I'm sorry to trouble you, but please come by tomorrow if you can."

After repeating the request several times, Okame finally left.

The next day was the fifteenth. The sky was clear and blue. A blustery autumn wind was blowing. Early in the morning, Hanshichi heard a vendor out in the street hawking pampas grass.[5] Until lunchtime, he had other business to attend to, and it was around two o'clock in the afternoon when he went to see Okame. Her house was located down a side street near the riverbank in Hamachō. A greengrocer's at the entrance to the street was piled

---

5. *Susuki,* one of seven plants *(nana-kusa)* placed in the home on the night of the full autumn moon.

high with pampas grass and green soybeans in their pods. The autumn cicadas could be heard singing in the grounds of a large estate in the neighborhood.

"Ah, Inspector—I'm glad you could come," Okame said, as though she had been expecting him for some time. "Before you say anything, I must tell you my daughter returned last night."

While Okame was at Hanshichi's house, Ochō had been brought home in the usual fashion and deposited at the stone yards near the riverbank. "We've already explained the whole situation to your mother," the samurai lady had told her, "so go home now and talk things over carefully with her."

The fact that Ochō had been sent home in good faith demonstrated that they were dealing with reasonable people who bore them no ill will. Ochō was sleeping off her fatigue in a small three-mat room in the back of the house. Okame went and fetched her. From her, Hanshichi heard the whole story in great detail, but he still had no idea what to make of it all. Judging from Ochō's story, it seemed to him that the mansion in question was probably the secondary residence of some daimyo.[6] But since Ochō could not tell him where or even in what direction it lay, it was anyone's guess as to who that daimyo might be.

"Someone will probably be along soon. Let's wait and see," Hanshichi said, settling down on the veranda as though for a long stay.

The days had been getting shorter, and by the time the evening bell sounded six, the tiny house had become quite dark inside. Okame came out onto the veranda bearing a flask of saké, some dumplings, and a few sheaves of pampas grass, whose fronds rustled in the evening breeze that blew chill through Hanshichi's unlined kimono. It was time for dinner, so Hanshichi had Okame buy him some broiled eel from a local shop, then, feeling bad about eating alone, offered some of it to her and her daughter.

---

6. *Shitayashiki*, a residence typically reserved for a daimyo's dependents other than his primary wife and heir, or one used by him after he has retired and turned his affairs over to his eldest son.

Once he had finished eating, Hanshichi returned to the veranda with a toothpick dangling from his lips and gazed up at the vast ocean of deep-blue sky stretching over him, divided up irregularly by the overlapping eaves of the houses in the narrow street. The full moon had not yet risen, but to the east a pale yellowish glow on the fringe of some clouds foreshadowed its arrival. The dew that had started to fall while he was inside eating glistened now on the withered leaves of two potted morning glories that had been exiled to the garden, apparently no longer welcome in the house.

"You'd better come out here to see the moon—it'll be rising any minute now," Hanshichi called inside to the women.

But, just then, he heard footsteps on the planks covering the drain in the street and saw a man stop in front of the lattice door to the house. Okame immediately went to see who it was. He was indeed a samurai, though not one she had seen before. After confirming that she was Ochō's mother, he informed her that his mistress had arrived.

"Don't let on that I'm here," Hanshichi said. Hurriedly grabbing his straw sandals, he went to hide with Ochō in the three-mat room at the back of the house. Soon, peering through a crack between the sliding doors, he saw a woman of about thirty enter, from her appearance a lady-in-waiting in a samurai house.

"It's a pleasure to meet you," she said politely. Okame responded appropriately in a faltering voice.

"I'll come straight to the point," the woman went on. "I understand that yesterday another lady from our house came here and discussed the matter of your daughter, Ochō, with you in some detail. With your consent, madam, I have come to take her back with me tonight."

The woman's tone was abrupt. Okame hesitated, intimidated, unsure how to respond.

"I have been sent here to secure your consent. Once again, I urge you to consider our offer."

"Actually, my daughter hasn't felt very well since coming home last night. She's spent the entire day in bed, so I haven't really had the chance to talk it over with her yet . . ."

Okame's tone was evasive. It seemed she'd hoped to wriggle out of the situation somehow, but the woman was not about to give up that easily. Her manner became more highhanded.

"I'm sorry, but that will not do. We sent her home to you last night specifically so that you could discuss the matter with her. Now you say that, contrary to our wishes, you have not as yet spoken to her about it? Well, you will not get rid of me so easily, madam. Ask your daughter to come out and let all three of us discuss the matter together. Call Ochō here at once!"

Her harsh, imperious tone made Okame panic even more. Then the woman took out two bundles of gold coins wrapped in silk cloth and placed them side by side on the floor in front of the dimly glowing lamp.

"I have just placed before you the sum of 200 *ryō*, the payment that you were promised. Now, please bring your daughter here."

"Er, yes . . ."

"So you give your consent? For your information, if I am unable to fulfill my duty, I will be forced to kill myself here and now."

The woman took what appeared to be a small dagger wrapped in cloth from the sash of her kimono and showed it to Okame. Seeing the cold, unwavering gleam in her eyes, Okame paled visibly and began to tremble. The negotiations had reached a stalemate.

"Do you know that woman?" Hanshichi whispered to Ochō. She shook her head silently. He thought for a moment, then crawled from the three-mat room into the kitchen and quietly slipped out the back door and around to the front of the house.

Out in the alleyway the moon shone brightly. In front of the pawnbroker's warehouse four or five doors away, a palanquin rested on the ground. Next to it stood the two bearers and the samurai whom Hanshichi had seen at the door earlier. Keeping an eye on them, Hanshichi opened the latticed front door of Okame's house and went inside. Without saying a word, he sat down opposite the woman. She had a long, narrow face lightly powdered, bright eyes, and a prominent nose. Hanshichi could tell at a glance that she was strong-willed. Her hair was done up in the samurai style with a circular band of hair held together at the top with a long, ornamental hairpin.

"Evening, ma'am."

With regal composure, the woman responded to Hanshichi's casual greeting by bowing silently.

"Okame here is a relative of mine," he said. "I hear you've expressed an interest in her daughter. As an only child, Ochō is naturally expected to marry someone who will take the family name and help her run the business. But given the nature of your request, we would not rule out the possibility of allowing her to enter his lordship's service."

Okame looked at Hanshichi in surprise. He continued: "Of course, I understand you must have your reasons for asking Okame to relinquish the right to see her daughter, but try to understand her feelings as a parent. At the very least, won't you let us know the name of the lord in whose house she is to serve? If you could just tell us that . . ."

"I understand your concern, but I am not at liberty to disclose his lordship's name. Suffice it to say, he is a daimyo whose fief lies in southwestern Japan."

"And you are employed as . . . ?"

"I am acting as his lordship's liaison."

"I see," Hanshichi said smiling. "Well, I'm sorry to inform you, then, that we must decline your request."

The woman shot Hanshichi a piercing look.

"And why do you refuse to give your consent?"

"Forgive me for being rude, but I do not care for the manner in which his lordship manages his house."

"Is that so? What would you know about the inner workings of his lordship's household?" the woman asked, shifting her knees on her cushion.

"His lordship's rules must be rather lax for his liaison to have a callus on her little finger!"[7]

The woman blanched noticeably.

"Good evening! May I come in?"

From outside the lattice door came the sound of a woman's voice.

[4]

"Do come in. This way, please."

Okame went out to the front door looking slightly flustered and beckoned the newcomer to enter, but the latter hesitated.

"I see you have other guests."

"Yes . . ."

"I shall return later, then."

The woman turned to leave, but Hanshichi called to her from inside.

"Excuse me, madam — would you please wait a moment? I wonder if you would be so kind as to take a look at this woman who is impersonating you, and give us your opinion."

The first woman turned even more pale, but quickly seemed to regain her composure and broke into a broad grin.

"Inspector — so it's you! I'm sorry I didn't recognize you at first, but as soon as you came in, I knew you weren't just anybody. You're that inspector from Mikawachō, aren't you? Well, I guess I can drop pretenses. The game's up."

"Just as I expected," Hanshichi said, smiling. "When I was out front I saw that your supposed master had sent a hired palanquin

---

7. Specifically, a callus formed by holding a plectrum used for playing a musical instrument — not an activity in which a servant in her supposed position would normally engage.

to fetch Ochō — now that would be a real first for a daimyo! And a lady-in-waiting with a callus on her little finger? It looked like a bad act to me. So where did you two appear from in those getups? Your acting was pretty good, but the staging left a lot to be desired."

"You've got me there," the woman said, with a slight bow of the head. "I thought this would be a tricky performance, but I worked up enough courage to go through with it. I thought I had the plan all worked out — but I didn't count on running into you, Inspector. So I suppose I'd better just confess everything.

"You see, I was born right here in Edo in Fukagawa — my mother was a teacher of old samisen ballads. . . ."

As it turned out, her name was Oshun. Her mother had wanted her to follow in her footsteps and had devoted herself to training her daughter from childhood to sing ballads. But no sooner was Oshun old enough to wear a full-length kimono than she went boy-crazy and caused her poor mother no end of grief before finally running away from home. She spent the next two or three years up north as a traveling minstrel, wandering all over the Jōshū, Shinshū, and Echigo areas. When she at last returned to Edo her mother was already dead. Some of her old acquaintances still lived in the neighborhood, so she set herself up teaching ballads and began to attract a few students. But the quiet life wasn't for her. She had a weakness for penniless wastrels and, needing money, learned how to entrap married men and blackmail them. She stole people's belongings from bathhouse changing rooms. Then, one day she happened to hear a rumor about Ochō from the neighborhood fishmonger.

Oshun was on good terms with the fishmonger, whose daughter was friends with Okame, so naturally the news of Ochō's mysterious abductions reached Oshun's ears. Oshun knew that Ochō was a beauty, so she hatched a crafty scheme to use the story of the kidnappings to get hold of the girl herself. Following Oshun's instructions, a man named Yasuzō, her regular accomplice, had been loitering in the vicinity of Okame's house for the past two or three days, spying on its occupants. From him, she also learned of the negotiations to retain Ochō in lifetime service at the samurai mansion and of Ochō's return the previous night. So she and Yasuzō had come, disguised as a samurai and a maidservant, to retrieve her. Of course, the 200 *ryō* that she had placed in front of Okame was nothing but counterfeit coins made of cheap metal.

"The problem was, we were in too much of a hurry. I said that if we dilly-dallied any longer, the real samurai would come and whisk Ochō away. We didn't have time to prepare properly and couldn't get hold of a suitable vehicle — that's how we ended up in this laughable mess!" She spilled the whole story with the true bravado of the hardened criminal that she was.

"It all makes perfect sense now," Hanshichi said nodding. "Well, I'm sure you won't feel happy about getting nabbed over something like this, but I can't just close my eyes and send you merrily on your way. I'm sorry, but you're going to have to come with me."

"It can't be helped. Well, I hope you won't be too hard on me."

The only thing Oshun asked was to be allowed to send home for a plain cotton kimono so she didn't have to be led through the streets in that awful getup, which made her look like an actor in a second-rate play. Hanshichi consented, but told her she must accompany him to the local watchman's house, as it wouldn't do to stay there at Okame's. He was about to march her off when the samurai lady, who had been standing just inside the front door since her arrival, came all the way into the house.

"If this matter becomes public it will reflect badly on his lordship's name. It's fortunate that this ill-advised plot was foiled before anyone got hurt. I would kindly ask you, therefore, to forgive this woman's offense for my sake."

The woman pleaded her case so fervently that Hanshichi found himself unable to refuse. He guessed that she was in a very awkward position, so in the end he agreed to let Oshun go.

"Oh, thank you, Inspector!" said the latter. "I'll be sure to drop in later with a token of my appreciation."

"I don't need your appreciation — just see that you don't cause any more trouble."

"Yes, of course."

Oshun hurried off with her tail between her legs. So the imposter had been unmasked, but what was behind the mask of the genuine article? Indeed, the samurai woman seemed to realize that because of this new complication, it would only arouse suspicions further if she continued to conceal the truth from Hanshichi and Okame, thus ruining her chances of bringing the matter to a successful conclusion. Turning to them, she began to divulge her secret.

Unlike the imposter Oshun, she really was a lady-in-waiting in the Edo residence of a provincial daimyo. Her lord had returned to his estate in the north, but his wife had of course remained behind in Edo as the law required.[8] Her mistress's best-beloved daughter — a beautiful girl with an equally beautiful disposition — had been carried off by smallpox that spring at the age of just seventeen. The girl's mother was driven mad with grief. Prayer and medication were equally ineffective. She called her daughter's name continuously from morning to night, sobbing hysterically, begging to be reunited with her. No one in the house could do anything to alleviate her suffering. Unable to bear seeing such pain and misery any longer, her steward and her senior maidservant met to discuss the matter and decided to hire a replacement who closely resembled their mistress's late daughter. They reasoned that if the girl were done up to look like the daughter, her ladyship's feelings might be soothed by the sight of her. But if word of what they were up to leaked out, it would bring shame upon his lordship's house. Two or three men, sworn to secrecy, were dispatched to search for a suitable candidate.

---

8. Under the law of "alternate attendance" *(sankin kōtai)*, a daimyo was required to leave his wife and children in Edo as "hostages" of the shogun to ensure his loyalty.

In those days, people were more patient than they are today. The men conducted an exhaustive search, in the course of which one of them stumbled upon Ochō at her mother's teahouse near Eitai Bridge. In age and physical appearance she seemed to him a perfect match, so he returned with Yukino, the lady-in-waiting in question, to obtain the latter's opinion. No one would know the difference, she agreed; thus, for better or for worse, Ochō passed muster.

Now that a suitable person had finally been found, the household staff was divided over how to bring her to the mansion. The moderates held that abducting someone's daughter against her will amounted to kidnapping, so they should, in the strictest confidence, inform the girl of what they were doing and secure her consent. But some objected: they were, after all, dealing with a woman who worked in a teahouse — no matter what they did to keep her quiet, she could not be trusted with their secret. It would be most unfortunate if, for example, she later tried to blackmail them. No, it might seem an unsavory way of doing things, but the safest course was to dash in and spirit her away. The main thing was to protect his lordship's reputation.

In the end, the latter view prevailed. The samurai assigned to the duty found themselves in the position of kidnappers, a role most unsuited to their status.

The hard-fought debate finally paid off, and their plan succeeded brilliantly. From time to time during the day and night, her ladyship would look in on Ochō, her daughter's stand-in, and her madness seemed mitigated by the idea that her late daughter's soul had been called back to this world. Her bad temper became a thing of the past. But the effect was only temporary — if she did not see Ochō for a few days, she flew into a rage and demanded to see her daughter. Even so, they couldn't very well keep the girl under house arrest indefinitely. Once again, the staff was at a loss.

At just that point, a new problem arose. In the seventh month, the shogun proclaimed that the families of daimyo would be free to return to their provincial domains if they wished. The ruling clans were overjoyed. Having been forced to live in Edo for so many years as virtual hostages, sons and wives of the various feudal lords joined in a great rush back to their hometowns. His lordship's wife was of course no exception, so what would happen if the madwoman had one of her fits on the way home? And how would they all cope once she was there? These concerns weighing heavily on their minds, the staff held another meeting. The conclusion was that they had no other choice but to take Ochō back to their domain with them.

This time, however, the arrangement would have to be more or less permanent, which meant that they couldn't abduct Ochō against her will. They decided to discuss the matter with the girl and her mother and obtain their agreement to a lifetime service. It was Yukino who had been charged with that duty, which was why she had paid a call at Ochō's home the previous day. If she had only been straightforward with them from the very beginning, they might have been more receptive to the idea. But all Yukino could think of was his lordship's family honor, and her impatience to secure their consent while keeping everything cloaked in secrecy only aroused their suspicions. On top of that, the imposter Oshun's interference had further complicated the situation.

On hearing all the facts, Hanshichi could not help but feel pity. A mother's madness brought on by the loss of her child; the desperate efforts of her servants to assuage her sorrow — how could he find harsh words for this?

Ochō at last emerged from her hiding place in the three-mat room. Wiping tears from her eyes, she spoke.

"Everything is clear to me now. Mother, if someone like me can be of any use, please let me go back to their home with them."

"So you really agree to come with us!" Yukino exclaimed, taking Ochō's hand and touching it reverently to her forehead to express her gratitude.

The full moon moved across the southern sky until its light flooded into the tiny house from the garden.

"OCHŌ'S MOTHER finally relented and agreed to let her daughter go into service," old Hanshichi said. "Then, as they talked things over further, the samurai woman proposed that Okame also should come along with them. After all, she reasoned, Okame had no close relatives in Edo, and as she grew older it would be best if she were near her daughter. So Okame closed her shop and went off to the daimyo's domain in the provinces. It seems he set them up in a little house in the town near his castle, and she passed her remaining years in comfortable retirement. Her ladyship died not long after the beginning of the Meiji era, and Ochō was finally released from service. I heard a rumor that the family arranged for her to marry into a very prominent family. She's still alive, I imagine. That good-for-nothing Oshun, I hear, went on the skids and drifted to Sumpu,[9] where she was eventually locked up for good."

---

9. Present-day Shizuoka city.

The Haunted Sash Pond

OBI-TORI NO IKE

[1]

t's been filled in and there's nothing left now, but long ago this used to be the 'Haunted Sash Pond.' It was still there during the Edo period. Take a look. Here—"

Old Hanshichi opened a map of Edo printed in 1860 and showed it to me. There, west of Gekkei Temple in Ichigaya and just below the secondary estate of the Owari[1] clan was a large blue area labeled "Haunted Sash Pond."

"I've heard that there's a pond with the same name in Kyoto, but if you need proof that one existed in Edo, just look at this map. The pond got its name from an old legend. It was said that travelers passing the pond had often seen a beautiful brocade sash floating on its surface, but when they approached and tried to grasp it, the sash wrapped itself around them and dragged them to the bottom of the pond. Some people asserted that the guardian spirit of the pond transformed itself into a sash in order to lure passersby into its depths. Of course, this was all a long, long time ago."

"Perhaps it was really a large python[2] that lived in the pond," I said, trying to sound knowledgeable.

"Yes, that's a possibility," Hanshichi said, nodding. "But some

---

1. A domain located in the western half of present-day Aichi Prefecture, containing the city of Nagoya.
2. *Nishiki-hebi* in Japanese or, literally, a "brocade snake."

people maintained that a big snake like that couldn't live at the bottom of a pond. They believed it must have been a bandit — someone who was a skilled swimmer and could conceal himself underwater, then, using the sash as bait, jump out and drag people into the pond, stealing their clothes and all their belongings. Anyway, whichever theory you chose to believe, it was an eerie spot. In the distant past, the pond had been much larger, but during the Edo period it slowly dwindled in size. In my day, the edges were more like a swamp where reeds grew in the summertime. But the old legend lived on and no one would go there to swim or fish. Then, one day, a woman's sash was seen floating on the surface of the pond and all hell broke loose."

IT WAS EARLY IN the third month of 1859. The cold winter weather had dragged on longer than usual that year, and the reeds around the edges of the pond were putting out new shoots. One day, a local resident was passing by and happened to spot a woman's sash lying in the shallow water at the pond's edge. The long, colorful garment trailed off across the water toward the middle of the pond. Even in an ordinary pond, such a discovery would have been cause for concern, and it was all the more so in this case because of the bizarre legend that had given the pond its name. Rumors of the discovery spread rapidly, and in no time everyone in the neighborhood was talking about it. The more timid onlookers came to gawk at it from a safe distance, fearing that if they strayed too close something awful would happen to them; no one dared venture near enough to get a good look.

Before long, two or three samurai emerged from the Owari estate. Tucking the skirts of their *hakama* into their waistbands, they waded down to the pond's edge. Then, standing knee-deep in mud with the bright spring sunshine beating down on them, they tugged at the long sash, which swished across the surface of the pond as they reeled it in. It was not the pond's guardian spirit but an ordinary sash, made of crepe, dyed in three bands of green, red, and purple, and tie-dyed with a pattern of white hemp leaves — a typically gaudy thing of the kind young women wore in those days.

"Who would throw such a thing away?" This was the first question that people asked. The sash was new and of fine quality. In those days it would have cost a pretty penny. Who could have tossed such a valuable item into the pond? Various scenarios were advanced. According to one, a bandit stole it but found it too awkward to carry; or perhaps he had feared it might be used later as evidence of a crime. Someone else suggested that it was the work of a prankster who, knowing the legend of the pond, had put the sash there hoping to spread panic. But practical jokes had already gone out of fashion by that time. Unlike in the 1830s, few people were willing to go to such elaborate lengths to spread mayhem just so they could sit back and watch gleefully from their hiding place. So the former explanation was more widely accepted: it was the work of a bandit. But where had the theft occurred? No one came forward to claim the sash. For the time being, it was deposited at the local watchpost.

Then, two days later, an astonishing fact emerged: the sash had belonged to a beautiful young woman by the name of Omiyo who had lived on a back street behind the saké shop at the bottom of Kappa Hill in Ichigaya. She had been found strangled to death. Once this became known, the sash's fame spread.

Omiyo had been eighteen years old and had lived in comfortable circumstances with her mother, Ochika, in a rented rowhouse. For a dwelling of that kind, it was quite neat and attractive, with about four rooms including a vestibule. Omiyo's mother had a reputation for fastidiousness, and the lattices on the front of the house were always spotlessly clean. But the neighbors wondered just whose largesse it was that allowed the pair to live so well. Ochika let it be known that she had an older son working for a downtown emporium who sent her a monthly allowance, but no such person had ever been seen frequenting the house, so none of the neighbors gave much credence to the story. Rumors spread that Omiyo had taken a rich lover; and because she was a beauty such suspicions were not surprising. But Ochika and her daughter paid little heed to this idle chatter and were on good terms with their neighbors.

The day before the sash was found floating in the pond, Omiyo and her mother asked the neighbors to keep an eye on their house for a few days, saying they were going to stay with relatives in Nerima to help out with a funeral. They had locked the front door when they left, so none of the neighbors could have gone inside during their absence. About four days later, Ochika returned home alone. After stopping to greet the neighbors on either side, she unlocked the lattice door and went into the house. Moments later, she came rushing back out into the street sobbing.

"Omiyo's dead! Come quick, everyone!"

The neighbors hurried over in alarm to find Omiyo lying face up on the floor of a six-mat room at the back of the house. The landlord came as soon as he heard the news. A doctor arrived shortly. He examined the body and announced that Omiyo had been strangled. The strangest fact of all was that Omiyo was dressed in the same clothes she had been wearing when she left home with her mother, but her crepe sash tie-dyed with a hemp-leaf pattern was missing. Otherwise, everything was in good order, and it was obvious that Omiyo's body had been carefully rearranged after she had been murdered.

"When did Omiyo return home?" This was everyone's first question. According to Ochika, her daughter had disappeared on their way to Nerima. The girl had been complaining bitterly about having to go to their relative's house in the first place, and her mother naturally assumed that Omiyo had given her the slip and gone home. As she was in a hurry to get to Nerima, she couldn't very well turn back and search for her daughter, so she simply went on ahead without her. The wake and funeral took three days, and on the morning of the fourth day she had promptly left for home. On arriving, she found the front door unlocked and supposed that her daughter, as she'd thought, had come home already. She opened the front door and entered to find the interior pitch dark, though it was broad daylight outside. Grumbling to herself, she opened a shutter — and the first sight that met her eyes was her poor daughter's corpse. Ochika had crumpled to the ground in shock.

"I can't understand it . . . it's like a bad dream," Ochika said, sobbing uncontrollably.

The neighbors, too, felt it must be a dream. When had Omiyo returned, and when had she been strangled? Not even the next-door neighbors had seen or heard anything. And who had re-moved her sash? Enquiries revealed that it had been found float-ing in the pond one morning two days prior to the discovery of Omiyo's body. As soon as Ochika saw it, she burst into tears and identified it unmistakably as her daughter's. In that case, had someone strangled Omiyo, removed her sash, and taken it all the way to the pond, just to throw it in? If so, why had they taken the sash in the first place? Hardly for material gain — there were many items in the house of greater value. And why leave the kimono? There must be a reason for whoever it was to focus on the sash and choose to dispose of it in that way. Or could it be — unlikely though it seemed — that the guardian of the pond had taken a fancy to the beautiful Omiyo? However one looked at it, there were no easy answers.

Much to the annoyance of the neighbors, the authorities ques-tioned everyone living on the street. Ochika was singled out for special scrutiny. They suspected her of strangling her own daughter and leaving home for several days to hide her crime; but she protested her innocence. Her neighbors, too, testified that they had seen Omiyo and her mother leaving home together. Moreover, they said, mother and daughter had always been on good terms. No one could think of any reason why Ochika would have wanted to murder Omiyo.

Thus the secret of the stolen sash remained as shrouded in mystery as the eerie old legend of the pond itself.

[2]

One night about seven days later, Hanshichi was at home in Mikawachō when Matsukichi, his deputy, came bursting in.

"Boss, I've got it! The case of the stolen sash . . . the neighborhood rumors were true — that girl Omiyo had a rich patron after all. The man's a retired *hatamoto*. She visited him from time to time on the sly. Her mother did her best to keep it hushed up, but I put the squeeze on her — she came out with the whole story in the end. What d'ya think? This should provide some clues, shouldn't it?"

"Uh-huh. The fact alone is very suggestive." Hanshichi nodded. "So you put the squeeze on her, eh? Hardly something to brag about but quite a feat for you, I guess, Lanky. Omiyo seemed all sweetness and innocence, but if she was the type to take a rich lover, she probably had all sorts of other problems, too. So, what's your next move?"

"Well, I dunno. That's why I came to you. I don't figure that *hatamoto* killed her. What do you think, boss?"

"I agree . . . it's highly unlikely," Hanshichi replied, cocking his head to one side. "But stranger things have happened. We can't afford to rule out anything. So who is this *hatamoto* and where is he living now?"

"His name's Ōkubo Shikibu. He's got an income of 1,000 *koku* and lives in retirement on his secondary estate in Zōshigaya."

"Well, we'd better get over to Zōshigaya and have a look around. You never know what we might stumble across."

The next morning, Hanshichi waited at home for Matsukichi to come by, then the two set out together from Kanda. It was the middle of the third month, and the weather was ideal for cherry-blossom viewing. As the two strolled along enjoying the brilliant sunshine, a light perspiration stood out on their foreheads. When they reached Zōshigaya they headed for Ōkubo's estate. As one might expect for a samurai of his rank and fortune, the house he had retired to turned out to be a grand affair with a small drainage ditch running along the front.

"What a mansion!" Matsukichi exclaimed.

Indeed, the residence was set back from the road, with plenty of space between it and the house in back. There was just the one building on the property, with entrances at both front and back and spacious fields on both sides. When Hanshichi made inquiries, the neighbors told him that a retired gentleman of about sixty lived in the house along with a staff consisting of a steward, a young retainer, a manservant, and two live-in maids. Wending his way through the fields of rape blossom, Hanshichi gave the sides of the house a quick once-over.

"This guy didn't kill her."

"You don't think so?"

"Look at the size of this place: it's set apart from the rest of the neighborhood with lots of space on either side. If he wanted to do his mistress in, he'd have done it here in the house, or as she was on her way home. No need for him to go barging into her house and kill her there. Anyone can see that."

"I guess you're right, boss. So this was just a wild goose chase after all," Matsukichi said, disappointment written on his face.

"Perhaps. In any case, I haven't been in this area for a while. Now that we've hiked all the way up here, we might as well go pay our respects to Kishibojin[3] then grab some lunch."

The two took a road cutting through paddy fields and came out onto the long thoroughfare in front of Kishibojin Temple. The bark of several large zelkova trees that lined the road glittered in the bright spring sunshine as though to reflect the lively atmosphere of the place. The number of worshippers at the temple had declined over the previous twenty years, but as one might expect it was crowded now, for spring had arrived and the cherry

3. Also called Kishimojin (Sanskrit, *Hariti*), a female deity prayed to for safe childbirth and the health of children.

blossoms were in bloom, an event in the temple's calendar second only to the celebration of Nichiren's birth in the fall. At a teahouse specializing in dumplings, people sat outside fanning themselves and talking noisily. It was too early for the vendors who later in the year would be selling souvenirs in the shape of sharp-beaked horned owls woven from pampas grass, but the temple's famous pinwheels were for sale, spinning away in the gentle spring breeze. There were the equally familiar straw geisha dolls, too, attached to stalks of bamboo grass and stuck into bundles of straw, their red sleeves flapping lightly in the wind. And there were the butterflies cut from paper, their white wings all aflutter in the breeze. In short, it was a typically amiable springtime scene. Walking beneath the zelkova and cherry trees, the two men came to a stop in front of the temple's main hall.

"Lots of worshippers here today, eh, boss?" Matsukichi said.

"It's because it's the cherry-blossom season. I imagine a lot of people just stopped by on a whim . . . like us. Well, we've come all this way to pray — let's make the most of it."

Matsukichi soberly followed Hanshichi into the hall and each man paid his respects. Then the two of them went to eat lunch. The once-famous restaurants of Yabusoba and Kōkōtei had vanished without a trace, so they settled on the Myōgaya. Matsukichi ordered some saké and Hanshichi had one or two cups to keep him company. By the time they got up to leave they were both slightly red in the face. At the entrance on their way out, they ran into a stylish young woman of twenty-three or -four. She was carrying a bag of sweets from the Kiriya and was accompanied by a girl of about fifteen who looked to be her younger sister. The girl was carrying, attached to a stalk of bamboo slung over her shoulder, a straw doll of a Sumiyoshi dancer.

"Oh, it's you, Inspector." The young woman stopped and smiled pleasantly at Hanshichi.

"You're very pious, I see," he said with a polite bow, smiling back at her. The younger girl, too, greeted him and smiled. "Come for lunch, have you?" Hanshichi went on. "I wish you'd arrived a littler earlier — you could have poured our saké for us. Bad luck!" He smiled again.

"Yes, what a shame!" The woman laughed, too. "My sister and I don't usually come out together and leave the house empty, but today I was asked to say a prayer at the temple on someone else's behalf, so I didn't have any choice. You see, it would have been greedy of me to pray for two people all by myself, so I brought her along. We agreed that I'd pray for myself and she'd pray for the other person."

"Your old man's sick, I suppose?" Matsukichi said, giving her a wink. The woman's shoulders quivered with a suppressed giggle.

"You're making fun of poor old me . . . still unmarried at my age! Actually, I came to pray for the mother of our local used-clothing dealer. My, that doesn't sounds very grand, does it? The truth is, his sister comes to take lessons from me, you see."

"So she's a pious lady too," Hanshichi observed casually.

"Well, I suppose she's as pious as the next person. . . . But there's something that's bothering her, actually. About ten days ago her son went off and didn't return, so she went to consult a couple of fortune-tellers. One of them told her that her son had met with 'misfortune by sword.' Then the other said no, it was 'misfortune by water' — that got her all worked up. So just now I went to the temple and drew an oracle stick from the box for her — sure enough, it came up 'bad luck!'" Her delicate brows knitted in concern.

The woman's name was Otoku. She was a samisen teacher of the Kineya school who lived down a back street on the north side of Naitō Shinjuku. She knew what line of work Hanshichi and Matsukichi were in and was glad she'd run into them, she said. Would they let her know if they came across any clues as to the whereabouts of the used-clothing dealer's son? Hanshichi cheerfully agreed to do so.

"I feel so bad for his mother," Otoku said sympathetically. "His sister is still just a child. He's the family breadwinner, and they'll be in a real dilemma if he doesn't come back."

"That's too bad," said Hanshichi. "What's his name and how old is he?"

Otoku launched into a detailed account of the son's situation. His name was Senjirō. In the spring of his tenth year, he'd been apprenticed to a pawnbroker's at the bottom of Kappa Hill in Ichigaya. On completing his apprenticeship, he spent the obligatory additional three years in service there. Last spring he'd opened his own little used-clothing store in Shinjuku. He lived together with his mother and sister, and was a hard worker. He was twenty-five years old, but looked about two or three years younger on account of his fair complexion and slight build.

As he listened to her story, Hanshichi watched the expression on Otoku's face carefully. Then, when she'd run out of things to say, he said quietly: "Well, Otoku. I guess it goes without saying that we'd better find Senjirō as soon as possible."

"Yes. The sooner the better," Otoku responded imploringly. "I can't tell you how worried his mother is about him." A dark cloud had descended over her face beneath the light makeup.

"Well, there're a few more things I'd like to ask you, so seeing as you were on your way inside, why don't we both join you?"

"But that doesn't seem right . . ."

"Don't worry about it. C'mon, I'll show you the way."

They all filed into the Myōgaya behind Hanshichi, sat down, and ordered a fair amount of food and sake. He waited until Otoku and her sister had finished eating and then, seeing his chance, led her to one of the other small rooms.

"Now, about this matter of the young man who runs the used-clothing store. . . . Since you've asked me to look into it, I want you to tell me everything you know. So far, you haven't given me much to go on."

Hanshichi looked at her with a broad grin on his face, and Otoku, already rather flushed from the alcohol, turned even redder. Pressing a piece of tissue paper to her lips, she looked down at the table.

"Listen, Otoku. Why are you acting all prim and proper?

From what you said earlier, I can pretty much guess what's on your mind. Someday you'd like to be sitting side by side with that used-clothing dealer in his shop, measuring up the merchandise together, isn't that right? After all, he's good husband material — young, honest, hardworking. Isn't that so? You're an entertainer, he's a merchant — it's not as though you'd have opposition from your family about marrying him. So what are you afraid of . . . what's making you so secretive? Why, when the time comes I'll show my friendship by giving you a nice fish or something as a wedding present. So, why don't you tell me the whole story? I won't even mind if you start gushing about how wonderful your beau is. I'll just sit here and listen quietly."

"I'm sorry . . ."

"You don't need to apologize. I realize you two were just trying to keep up appearances," Hanshichi said, still smiling. "Of course, this Senjirō isn't a playboy who leaves broken hearts wherever he goes . . . you're his special someone, aren't you?"

"Well, I'm not sure of that," Otoku said with a hint of jealousy in her voice. "I don't have any solid proof, but ever since he was at the pawnbroker's, I've had the feeling that something's on his mind. It made me rather uneasy, so I tried asking him about it from time to time, but he always says nothing's the matter."

She had no reason to believe that Senjirō ever stayed out all night. She knew that he never even socialized except on business. He'd been a devotee of Kishibojin ever since he was an apprentice at the pawnbroker's, and he went to the temple two or three times a month to pray. Only once had anything happened to arouse her suspicions: she'd discovered him reading what appeared to be a letter from a woman. Of course, he'd torn it up right away, so Otoku herself hadn't seen what it said. After that, though, she watched him more carefully and noticed that he seemed to be troubled about something. She had the feeling he was hiding something from her; it had begun to bother her, and about a fortnight ago they'd quarreled. She'd even put pressure on him to hurry up and marry her as soon as possible. He disappeared not long after that.

"Is that so?" said Hanshichi, nodding to himself seriously. "That doesn't sound good. . . . Look here, Otoku," he went on. "You really had me fooled with that story about feeling sorry for his poor mother! You're not without sin yourself, remember that!" He laughed.

Otoku reddened and, innocent creature that she was, looked like she wanted to shrink under the table.

[3]

Hanshichi sent Otoku and her sister home with some food wrapped in bamboo leaves and remained behind in the Myōgaya with Matsukichi.

"Well, Lanky. If this isn't a case of dumb luck, I don't know what is! We didn't waste our time coming to Zōshigaya after all. I think we've found ourselves a clue as to what happened near Kappa Hill. Call the waitress, would you?"

Matsukichi clapped his hands, and a middle-aged waitress promptly appeared.

"What can I do for you, sir?"

"I just wanted to ask you something. Have you ever had a customer by the name of Sen, a former clerk at a pawnbroker's in Ichigaya?"

"Yes, he's been in."

"Comes two or three times a month, I suppose?"

"My, sir — you're well informed!"

"Is he always alone," Hanshichi asked, smiling, "or does he come with a pretty girl?"

The waitress smiled but said nothing. Pressed further, though, she told him that Senjirō had started coming to the restaurant about three years earlier. He showed up two or three times a month together with an attractive young woman. Sometimes he came during the day, sometimes in the evening. Actually, about ten days previously he had come on his own and waited there by himself for a while until the girl appeared, around noon. They left together toward dusk. The two always acted very shy in front of the waitresses—they never said anything while there was anyone else in the room, so even after all this time no one knew the young woman's name.

"The last time she came here, was she wearing a red sash dyed with a hemp-leaf pattern?" Hanshichi asked.

"Yes, that's right."

"Well, thanks miss. We'll be sure to come back again to show our appreciation." He handed her several small objects wrapped in paper.

Matsukichi followed Hanshichi out of the Myōgaya and into the street, then whispered in his ear: "Boss, you were right—it looks like we've got a lead. We ought to arrest that fellow Senjirō, don't you think?"

"Yeah," Hanshichi nodded. "But he's not a hardened criminal. He can't hide forever. Once all the fuss has died down he'll come drifting back to Shinjuku—mark my words. I want you to go there and keep an eye on the used-clothing store and the samisen teacher's house."

"Right. Count on me."

After leaving Matsukichi, Hanshichi thought of heading home to Kanda, but decided instead to have a look around Ichigaya, as he hadn't so far set eyes on the scene of the crime. By the time he reached the neighborhood below Kappa Hill, the sun was already starting to set. He made his way around behind the wine merchant's shop and peered into Omiyo's house through the lattice door. Then he stopped in to see the merchant, who owned the house. The man, who had been in the back office when Hanshichi entered, became exceedingly polite when he learned who the detective was.

"It's very good of you to come. How may I be of assistance?"

"The girl who lived behind your shop . . . has anything out of the ordinary happened since the incident?"

"Actually, Inspector Chōgorō stopped in this morning and asked me all about it."

Chōgorō was an uptown cop from Yotsuya in whose jurisdiction the neighborhood lay. Hanshichi knew that he shouldn't trespass on Chōgorō's turf while an investigation was in progress, but since he'd come all this way, he thought he might as well ask the man a few questions before leaving.

"What did you tell Chōgorō?"

"That Omiyo wasn't murdered," the wine dealer said. "You see, yesterday morning when Ochika, the girl's mother, went to open the middle drawer of the charcoal brazier, she found it was stuck — she'd been so upset at the time of the incident that she hadn't noticed. She said something seemed to be caught in the back of the drawer. Finding it odd, she forced it open, and there, wedged at the back, was a piece of paper with something written on it. She pulled it out and read it. It was her daughter's suicide note. It was a short, scribbled message, which said something like: 'I can't bear to go on any longer. Forgive me, mother, for this unfilial act.'

"Well, it gave Ochika a nasty shock, and she immediately came running over here clutching the note. I recognized the girl's handwriting, and her mother said there was no doubt her daughter had written it. So it seems Omiyo hanged herself for some reason she couldn't bear to name. Of course, I immediately went and filed a report at the watchpost. Then, when Inspector Chōgorō came by to see me this morning, I told him the whole story."

"This is a rather unexpected development. What did Chōgorō have to say?" Hanshichi asked.

"The Inspector shook his head incredulously, but he said that since it was a case of suicide there was nothing more he could do."

"That's true enough. I guess there's no point in continuing the investigation."

Hanshichi asked the merchant a few more questions about Omiyo's usual behavior, then left. But he still wasn't convinced.

If Omiyo had hanged herself, then who had arranged the body so neatly? He couldn't know what Chōgorō was thinking, but it seemed to him that it would be too hasty simply to accept a verdict of suicide and close the investigation. Assuming that Omiyo's suicide note was not a forgery, then it was indisputable that she had planned to kill herself. Contemplating a number of reasons why a young woman might want to hasten her own death, Hanshichi had a sudden idea. He went straight home to Kanda to await news from Matsukichi.

One afternoon five days later, Matsukichi appeared, looking sheepish.

"Boss, it's no good. I've had that house staked out since I last saw you, but no one's caught any sight of the fellow. Do you think he's left Edo and gone into hiding?"

According to Matsukichi, the used-clothing dealer and the samisen teacher both lived in cramped, one-story houses — neither seemed big enough to conceal someone. Senjirō's mother spent the whole day in his shop. Otoku had been at home every day giving lessons. There was nothing at all unusual to report.

"What day does the teacher hold her monthly rehearsal?" Hanshichi asked.

"The twentieth. She canceled it this month — said she had a cold."

"The twentieth ... that was the day before yesterday," Hanshichi said thoughtfully. "What does she eat? The fishmonger and the greengrocer must call at her house. . . . What has she ordered these past two or three days?"

Matsukichi hadn't bothered with such details, but he told Hanshichi what he knew: the day before yesterday, at lunchtime, Otoku had ordered one serving of weatherfish cooked in a pot from the local eel restaurant, and yesterday she'd asked the fishmonger to prepare sashimi.

"Why didn't you say so? What more do you need?" Hanshichi all but yelled at Matsukichi. "She's hiding Senjirō in her house. That's perfectly obvious. Kappa Hill may be close to Shinjuku

but it's a backwater these days. How could a teacher like her afford to order sashimi and other fancy food like that day after
day? She's hiding her lover-boy and has been scraping the bottom of her purse to buy nice things for him to eat. On top of that,
she canceled a scheduled rehearsal — that's the ultimate proof! I
imagine there's a stage somewhere in the house where she holds
those rehearsals, right?"

In fact, the teacher's house consisted of two rooms: one of
four-and-a-half mats, the other six. The six-mat room, which was
at the back of the house, had a section of raised wooden floor a
dozen feet in length, Matsukichi explained. It was typical for
such floors to have a storage space underneath. It was there, in
Hanshichi's expert opinion, that Senjirō was hiding.

"All right, Lanky — let's get over there right away. Who knows
what they'll do when they run out of money?"

The two men headed for the north side of Shinjuku.

[4]

"Oh, it's you, Inspector. I'm very sorry we imposed on you like
that the other day. I've been meaning to come by and thank you,
but you know what they say: 'No rest for the weary.' On top of
that, I haven't been very well lately," Otoku laughed.

The samisen teacher greeted Hanshichi with a smile, straight-
ening the collar of her old, threadbare housecoat. Matsukichi
had gone around and hidden by the back entrance, but of this
she seemed completely unaware. She took Hanshichi inside and
invited him to sit in front of the small ornamental alcove. In the
four-and-a-half mat room next door, a charcoal brazier, a chest,
and a tea cupboard sat in a row. The six-mat room at the back
was clearly used as her practice studio — Hanshichi could see
several samisen and boxes of music books lying on the floor. It
was a little before two in the afternoon. Otoku's pupils must still
be in school, for not one had shown up yet.

"Where's your sister?"

"Oh, she's gone to the temple again today."

"Kishibojin?" Hanshichi said with a wry smile, sipping at a cup of cherry-blossom tea, which Otoku had brought for him. "What a devout young woman! But perhaps she ought to pay her respects to me rather than to Kishibojin. You see, I've figured out what's become of Senjirō!"

Otoku's eyebrows rose almost imperceptibly. Then, as though trying to match Hanshichi's jovial tone, she gave a big smile.

"How right you are, Inspector! Ask you to grant a wish, and before you know it, it's done!"

"I'm not kidding. I really know what happened to him. I came all the way up here to tell you. Otoku — are we alone?"

"Yes . . ." Otoku stiffened and stared at Hanshichi.

"I don't like having to tell you, but when Senjirō was working at the pawnbroker's, he got involved with a young woman named Omiyo who lived behind the saké shop at the bottom of Kappa Hill. She's the other woman you were always worried about. Anyway, for some reason — I'm not sure why — they resolved to commit suicide together. He was going to strangle her, then kill himself."

"Oh, no!" Otoku blanched. "Is it true he meant to die with her?"

"It's not a matter of truth. I think he wanted to die, but once he had killed her he got cold feet. Had a sudden change of heart. He ran off and hid somewhere. My, but that dead girl's ghost must be very angry with him!"

"Do you have any proof it was meant to be a lovers' suicide?"

"No mistake about it — we found the woman's suicide note."

As the words left his mouth, Hanshichi noticed tears welling up in Otoku's clear, sorrowful eyes.

"If he loved her enough to commit suicide, that means he was playing me for a fool, doesn't it?" she said.

"I know how you must feel, Otoku. . . . But, yes, in a nutshell, I guess you could say that."

"Oh, why am I such an idiot?"

She seemed unable to contain her emotions any longer. Her body trembling in anger, she wiped her eyes with the sleeve of her undergarment. Out by the back door, a dog had come up and started barking at Matsukichi, whose voice Hanshichi heard trying to chase it away, but Otoku was totally oblivious to the commotion. Eventually, she wiped the tears from her eyes and asked Hanshichi a question.

"What will happen to Sen when they learn where he is?"

"Well, seeing as the woman is dead, it won't go well for him."

"Will you arrest him if you find him, Inspector?"

"It's a thankless job, but someone has to do it."

"All right, then, go ahead and arrest him."

Otoku suddenly got up, walked over to the raised wooden floor, and threw open the sliding door of the storage space. Hanshichi could see a man's pale face cowering in one corner. Just as I suspected! Hanshichi thought to himself. Otoku grabbed the man's hand and hauled him up out into the room.

"Sen, you deceived me! Three days ago you came and told me you were afraid you were going to get in trouble for selling some bad merchandise — said you needed somewhere to hide for a few days. But that was a bald-faced lie! Now I hear you tried to commit suicide with some woman from Ichigaya. You weren't satisfied with deceiving me all this time — now you've lied to me . . . I hate you! Here, Inspector, take him. Tie him up. Throw him in jail. Do whatever you like with him!"

Otoku glared at the man, tears of rage in her eyes. He looked away from her, only to find Hanshichi's piercing gaze turned on him. Prostrating himself on the floor, he buried his face in the worn and tattered tatami, as though wishing he could melt away into nothingness.

"That's enough," Hanshichi said admonishingly. "Cut the act, Senjirō. C'mon, out with it! I don't want to have to drag you over to the watchpost and knock you around. Tell us exactly what happened!"

"Forgive me!" Senjirō's face was like a death mask.

"You and Omiyo had a suicide pact, didn't you? It was you who strangled her — isn't that so?"

"No, Inspector! I didn't kill her."

"Liar! I'm not a woman — you can't deceive me. You'll be in serious trouble if you go telling a pack of lies to an officer of the shogun. Or have you forgotten who you're talking to? Don't forget — Omiyo left a suicide note."

"But Omiyo's note didn't say anything about a lovers' suicide — she killed herself all on her own," Senjirō protested tremulously.

Hanshichi was flummoxed. The lovers' suicide had been his own hypothesis — true enough, the note itself had made no mention of any such thing — but he still refused to believe there was no connection between Senjirō and Omiyo.

"In that case, how do you know what her note said? You couldn't know unless you'd been there with her. More to the point, how do you know Omiyo died by her own hand? Tell me that!" Hanshichi said, pressing home his advantage.

"I can explain everything."

"Is that so? Well, hurry up then."

Otoku was glaring at Senjirō with a look of utter contempt. It made him falter somewhat, but at Hanshichi's urging he summoned up his resolve and launched into his confession.

While in service to the pawnbroker in Ichigaya, Senjirō had happened to take up with Omiyo, who lived in the neighborhood. But since she had become the property of a samurai, the two feared his wrath should their relationship be exposed. So they took care to meet secretly, two or three times a month only, at the teahouse in Zōshigaya. They continued to meet even after Senjirō opened his used-clothing shop in Shinjuku. It was then that his sister began taking lessons in *nagauta* from Otoku,[4] and the latter and Senjirō developed more than a nodding acquaintance. Unbeknownst to Otoku, though, he still continued to see his old lover.

---

4. *Nagauta* is vocal narration accompanied by samisen music performed for kabuki.

This was already a disaster waiting to happen, but then an even more terrifying threat reared its head: someone from Lord Ōkubo's mansion spotted Senjirō and Omiyo together at the teahouse in Zōshigaya. Omiyo had heard a rumor that the samurai had murdered his previous mistress when he discovered she had been unfaithful to him and, innocent girl that she was, trembled at the prospect of impending death. Having previously arranged to meet Senjirō at the teahouse, she gave her mother the slip on the way to Nerima. When she saw him, she wailed that her life would no longer be worth living when her master learned of their secret.

Her words struck terror in the cowardly Senjirō's heart. There was no telling what horrors awaited him as her partner in this illicit affair when, inevitably, the samurai came and marched the two of them off to his mansion. Neither, though, did he wish to commit suicide with her. When she hinted at such a thing, he worked hard to allay her fears, and eventually persuaded her to return to Ichigaya that evening. But on his way home he began to have second thoughts. He turned back and headed straight for her house. But by the time he arrived it was already too late: Omiyo had hanged herself from a beam in the kitchen with her hemp-leaf patterned sash. Next to the charcoal brazier there were two suicide notes, one addressed to him and the other to her mother. She seemed to have written them in a hurry, for neither of them was sealed. He opened both and read them.

For some time, Senjirō was paralyzed by shock and grief, but gradually he regained his composure. Taking hold of Omiyo's body and lowering it to the ground, he carried her to the back room, removed the sash from around her neck, and neatly arranged the body with her head pointing north.[5] Then he wept and prayed over her. Finally, he placed the suicide note addressed to her mother in the drawer of the charcoal brazier and slipped the other one into the breast of his kimono. He resolved to hang

---

5. *Kita-makura*, the traditional position for arranging the dead in Buddhist practice, in imitation of the Buddha, who is said to have died lying on his side facing west with his head pointing north.

himself then and there; but then he changed his mind, thinking that to die there beside Omiyo would be cruel to his other lover, Otoku. In a kind of trance, he slipped out the front door of Omiyo's house, carrying her sash, and went in search of somewhere to end his life.

Somehow, he wound up at Haunted Sash Pond, not knowing where he was or how he'd gotten there. He stood for a while, debating whether to hang himself using Omiyo's sash or throw himself into the pond. But each time he was about to reach a decision, someone would happen along and he missed his chance. It was a cloudy night, but a few stars flickered dimly in the sky. As he gaped vacantly up at them, the night air fell chill on his skin, and suddenly he was afraid of death. He threw the sash he was holding into the pond and set off running at full speed down the dark road.

Even then, wracked with uncertainty, he couldn't bring himself to go straight home. Though he hadn't killed Omiyo with his own hands, he feared he would be held accountable for her death, and he also feared Lord Ōkubo's wrath. At that point, he remembered that a former colleague of his from the pawnbroker's lived in Horinouchi and set off at once for his house. On some plausible pretext, he got his friend to let him lie low there for ten days. Finally feeling he'd outstayed his welcome, he cadged a little travel money from his friend and headed back to Edo. That was the night after Hanshichi had run into Otoku in Zōshigaya.

Senjirō didn't have the courage to tell either his mother or Otoku the truth, so he made up another lie about having sold some inferior merchandise and wanting to stay out of sight for a while to avoid trouble. After talking things over with his mother, Otoku decided to give her lover refuge in her house.

But Hanshichi had seen through her little subterfuge and, what's more, revealed Senjirō's awful secret to her. Furious with rage and blinded by jealousy, she thrust the very man whom she had been protecting into the detective's hands.

"WHAT HAPPENED in the end?" I asked old Hanshichi.

"What else is there to say?" Hanshichi replied with a smile. "If Senjirō had been party to a lovers' suicide, I would have arrested him for murder, but since Omiyo had taken her own life, there wasn't anything in particular I could do. If I'd wanted to make the case public, I could have turned him over to the local official for a reprimand. But I felt too sorry for him to do that, and anyway it would have meant a lot of trouble for me. So I just gave him a good tongue-lashing on the spot and . . . well, I forgave him. But to my surprise, about a month later, he and Otoku came by together to see me. They'd patched things up and wanted to thank me. Otoku said she was relieved at how things had turned out in the end: if Senjirō had been found guilty of a grave offense, she'd never have forgiven herself for turning him over to me. When I teased her for saying such a thing, her face went all serious and she said, 'That's how we women are, Inspector.'"

Hanshichi burst out laughing.

Snow Melting in Spring

HARU NO YUKI-DOKE

[1]

Since you're a fan of kabuki, you're no doubt familiar with that scene from *Kōchiyama*[1] where the courtesan Michitose[2] goes to a convalescent home in Iriya[2] to recover her health, and her lover, the samurai Naojirō, sneaks in to see her. Now, what was the name of the Kiyomoto[3] ballad performed during that scene? Ah, that's right—*Snow Melting in Spring: A Secret Rendezvous.*[4] Every time I see that play, I'm reminded of something that happened a long time ago. Of course," old Hanshichi added, launching into another of his stories, "the plot is completely different, but the setting's the same. There was even a blind masseur with a scarf over his head who appeared near Iriya's rice fields on a snowy spring night— just like the actor Matsusuke as Jōga in that scene from the play.

---

1. A play by Kawatake Mokuami, first performed at the Shintomiza Theater in 1881. The play's proper title is *Kumo ni magou ueno no hatsu hana,* but it was popularly known as *Kōchiyama,* after the play's main character, Kōchiyama Soshun.

2. An area of agricultural land located on the northeastern outskirts of Edo near the licensed quarter known as the New Yoshiwara.

3. A style of narrative music performed in kabuki that was founded by Kiyomoto Enju (1777–1825).

4. *Shinobi-au haru no yuki-doke,* a scene from the play in which Naojiro meets the blind masseur Jōga at a soba restaurant and entrusts him with a letter for Michitose prior to sneaking in to visit her.

Anyway, let me tell you all about it. I'm afraid it won't be as entertaining, though, since my version doesn't have musical accompaniment, and, of course, it won't be sung in the inimitable voice of the great master from Hamachō."[5]

IT ALL BEGAN near the end of the first month of 1865. Hanshichi had gone to see someone living near Ryūsen Temple in Shitaya. It was about five o'clock in the evening when he left the person's house. Though spring had officially arrived, the days were still short and it was already getting dark as he headed home. The skies had been gray ever since morning, and it looked as though, at any moment, white flakes might come spilling from the cold darkness above. Night was closing in quickly. His host in Shitaya had offered to lend him an umbrella as he was leaving, but Hanshichi had declined, saying he could make it home without one. He walked along with his hands shoved into the breast of his kimono. As he approached Iriya's paddy fields, big white flakes began falling in front of his face like goose feathers plucked from the sky. Quickly taking out his handkerchief, he tied it around his head, covering his ears, then forged on ahead into the cold wind that blew across the fields.

"Tokuju, wait!" came a woman's voice. "Why are you being so stubborn? Come here a minute . . ."

Hanshichi glanced over his shoulder. In front of the elegant gateway to what appeared to be some sort of high-class boardinghouse stood a stylishly dressed woman of about twenty-five or -six who looked to be a maid. Tokuju was a blind masseur, whose sleeve she'd grabbed in an effort to drag him toward the house.

---

5. Kiyomoto Enju IV (1832–1904), who composed numerous ballads for Mokuami's plays. He was married to Kiyomoto Enju II's daughter, Oha, who composed the balled for the scene mentioned here.

"No, Otoki. I can't. I'm sorry, but I have an appointment in the Yoshiwara,"[6] said the masseur, trying to shake himself free. The woman addressed as Otoki continued to tug at his sleeve.

"You're making things so hard for me, Tokuju! There are lots of masseurs, but you're my mistress's favorite. She won't have anyone else. What will I do if you leave?"

"I'm extremely grateful that your mistress favors me . . . I always tell her so, but, like I said, today I have a previous engagement and I . . ."

"Liar! That's what you've been saying every day of late. I don't believe you, and neither does the mistress. Stop stalling and come on in! Oh, how tiresome you are!"

"But I can't. You must excuse me just this once."

The two of them were equally obstinate. It didn't look to Hanshichi as though the dispute would be easily resolved, but neither did he feel any duty to intervene. Ignoring them, he went on his way. The snow did not last long and had let up by the time Hanshichi arrived home, but for the next couple of days the sky remained cloudy. On the third day, something came up that required Hanshichi once again to return to the house near Ryūsen Temple.

"Today the sky really *does* look threatening," he said to himself as he was getting ready to go out.

This time he brought his umbrella with him. Sure enough, large snowflakes had begun to fall when Hanshichi took leave of his host. It was after five o'clock, and by the time he reached Iriya, the entire area was covered with a white blanket of snow. Walking along with the umbrella resting on his shoulder, Hanshichi came to the house he had passed the previous evening. Just then, as luck would have it, the front strap of one of his

6. The original Yoshiwara, established in 1617, was located in central Edo in the vicinity of Nihonbashi. Destroyed in the Meireki Fire of 1657, it was moved to an isolated spot just north of Asakusa and renamed the "New Yoshiwara" (*Shin Yoshiwara*). Here it is referred to simply as the Yoshiwara.

wooden clogs broke. Cursing to himself, he leaned up against a fence by the side of the road and began trying to fix it. As he did so, he heard footsteps approaching through the snow, and the same woman as before emerged from the gateway along a path of stepping-stones.

"My, look at all the snow on the ground!"

Talking to herself, she stopped outside the gate with an air of expectation. She was without an umbrella, however, and soon the snowflakes landing in her hair became too much for her and she retreated inside the house.

His hands numb from the cold, Hanshichi took a while to fix the strap. Finally, he got the clog back on his foot, and he was just removing the mud from his hands by rubbing them together in the snow, when the masseur came walking along at a brisk pace. The woman, who had apparently been lying in wait and had heard his footsteps approaching, came running out of the house. She'd evidently learned from her earlier mistake, for this time she was holding a partially opened umbrella.

"Tokuju! No running away this time!"

Hearing his name, the masseur stopped in his tracks with a frightened look on his face. But when the woman latched on to his sleeve, he again protested vociferously and tried to free himself. The tussle went on for a while and Hanshichi, finding it all rather amusing, pretended to fiddle with the strap of the clog he'd just repaired while watching them out of the corner of his eye. Once again, the masseur refused to yield, finally managing to shake the woman off and flee the scene.

"What an impossible fellow!" Grumbling to herself, the woman went back inside.

Hanshichi watched her disappear, then went off in pursuit of the blind masseur's white umbrella, which was now about ten meters ahead. "Hey, masseur!" he called out to the man from behind. "Hey, Tokuju!"

"Yes?"

Hearing the unfamiliar voice, the masseur stopped, his head

slightly to one side. Hanshichi came and stood next to him, their umbrellas touching.

"Cold, isn't it, Tokuju? The snow's coming down like blazes. Don't you remember me? I've had a few massages from you in the Yoshiwara—last time was on the second floor of the Ōmiya."

"Ah, is that so? I do apologize," Tokuju responded. "Age is catching up with me, and I'm afraid I've always been absentminded with my patrons. Are you on your way there, too, sir? A trip to the Yoshiwara's a special pleasure on a night like tonight, isn't it? You know what they say—'Let not a snow-laden umbrella hinder your pursuits'!"

He laughed heartily. He may have known Hanshichi was lying, but he responded affably enough to the detective's overtures.

"Anyway, it's damn cold, isn't it?" Hanshichi commented.

"Like winter again, these last two or three days."

"It won't be much fun going through those fields up ahead. What do you say we fortify ourselves by downing a bowl of hot soba noodles over there? Won't you join me? It's still a bit early to visit the Yoshiwara, anyway."

"My word, sir . . . that's very generous of you. I'm a teetotaler myself, but people who drink do say that having a cup of warm saké makes all the difference when crossing unsheltered land. Yes, indeed. Thank you very much."

They backtracked about one block and Hanshichi ducked into a small soba restaurant. Looking cold, Tokuju dusted the snow off his headscarf and went and huddled next to an old square charcoal brazier. Hanshichi ordered a flask of saké and two bowls of noodles in hot soup.

"This is *arare*,[7] isn't it?" said Tokuju, grinning from ear to

---

7. A dish of hot buckwheat noodle (*soba*) soup topped with strips of roasted seaweed and scallops. The white scallops and green seaweed are intended to resemble hailstones (*arare*) scattered on the grass, a seasonal signifier of early spring.

ear. "Now, this is what I call *real* Edo soba! This seaweed smells pretty good, too." He sniffed at the bowl of hot soup with a look of utter bliss on his face.

The wife of the restaurant's owner went and lit the lantern outside the front door. In its pale glow, Hanshichi could see huge flakes of snow, like cherry-blossom petals, drifting gently to the ground beyond the short curtain that hung over the doorway.

When he had drunk about half the saké in the flask, Hanshichi asked, "Tokuju, what's that place I saw you outside just now, talking to that woman?"

"Oh, were you there, sir? — I had no idea," Tokuju chuckled. "Well, that's a convalescent home owned by the Ise Dragon, a brothel in the Yoshiwara."

"So why are you always in such a hurry to get away when she asks you to come inside? A place like that must be full of good customers."

"Yes, but listen, sir. There's something about that house I don't like. It's not that they don't pay me properly or anything like that. I don't know how to explain it . . . it's just sort of creepy . . ."

Hanshichi put down the cup of saké he was sipping.

"Creepy? What do you mean, exactly? Don't tell me it's haunted!"

"No, I've never heard any rumors to that effect, but I just have a strange feeling about the place . . . I get shivers down my spine whenever I go there, and all I can think of is getting away as fast as I can." He wiped a bead of sweat from the tip of his nose with the back of his hand.

"How odd!" Hanshichi said, smiling. "I don't get it — I wonder what makes you feel that way."

"I don't understand it either. I just get this sensation all over my body like someone's poured ice water down my collar. . . . It's like there's something weird right next to me, only I can't see it because I'm blind . . . I can't explain it."

"So who's staying at this convalescent home, anyway?"

"A high-class courtesan[8] by the name of Tagasode. I hear she's a real beauty — about twenty-one or -two — at the height of her career. But last year in the eleventh month she took sick and went there to recuperate."

"It's spring now, and you say she hasn't been back to the Yoshiwara since last autumn? This illness of hers must be quite serious."

On the contrary — according to Tokuju — the courtesan didn't appear to be all that sick. Of course, being blind, he couldn't tell exactly how she looked, but it seemed to him she simply "had the vapors," as people said in those days. She would lie about in bed, getting up from time to time when she felt like it. All the same, Hanshichi couldn't understand why the masseur should find the convalescent home such a creepy place. Over Tokuju's protestations, Hanshichi pressed him to accept another bowl of noodles. Then, slowly sipping his saké, he calmly set about trying to elicit more information.

"Well, I just don't know how to describe it," Tokuju whispered, his brow furrowed. "I mean, this is how it was, sir. I'd go to the home — usually in the evening or at night — and be shown to a room. There, I'd set about massaging the courtesan's shoulders, and right away I'd get the feeling someone had entered the room and was sitting next to her. . . . No, not the lady's apprentice or a maid . . . someone like that would have said something . . . instead, there was just an eerie silence from beginning to end. To be honest, it felt like a ghost was in the room. Shivers would go down my spine, and after a while, I just couldn't stand it any longer. I feel sorry for the maid, Otoki, whom you saw outside with me tonight, but that's why I've been giving her the slip lately. I know I'm losing a good customer, but there's nothing I can do about it."

Silently, Hanshichi reflected on the blind man's ghostly tale, which was both logical and illogical at the same time. Outside the soba restaurant, the sun had set completely, but the snow

8. *Oiran,* the highest rank of prostitute in the Yoshiwara.

seemed not to have let up. From time to time, white petals of snow blew in through the front door and settled on the earthen floor of the entrance.

[2]

Despite providing him with no solid evidence to go on, the blind man's tale was something Hanshichi found he could not simply dismiss out of hand as a mere curiosity. He felt a compelling desire to find out what was behind the mystery.

That evening, after leaving Tokuju, Hanshichi went straight home. The next morning he sent for Shōta, one of his deputies who lived on Uma Street in Asakusa.

"Hey, Shōta — I've got a job for you. I know the Yoshiwara's not my turf, but I don't suppose Inspector Jūbei in Tamachi would mind if poked around there just a bit. There should be a brothel in Edochō⁹ called the Ise Dragon. I want you to find out what you can about a courtesan named Tagasode who works there."

"But hasn't Tagasode checked into a convalescent home in Iriya?" replied the well-informed Shōta.

"That's what I want you to look into. Something about it doesn't seem right to me. Find out if she has a lover, or if anyone's got a grudge against her. I think there might be some funny business going on at that brothel, so make sure you go inside and have a good look around."

"Got it. I'll check it out and get back to you in two or three days."

With this assurance, Shōta left. Despite his promise, though, four or five days passed, and still there was no sign of the deputy. "What's happened to him?" Hanshichi wondered to himself. But since there was no particular urgency about the case, he let it go. Then one day at the beginning of the second month Shōta sauntered into Hanshichi's house.

---

9. One of the Yoshiwara's three main streets.

"I'm sorry, boss. My kid's come down with the measles."

"That's too bad. Is it serious?"

"No, he should get over it pretty soon. Boss, about that matter of the Ise Dragon — I went over and checked it out, and . . ."

According to Shōta's report, the Ise Dragon had once been one of the most prosperous brothels in Edochō. But then the Great Ansei Earthquake of 1854 had come along. All of the prostitutes who worked there had died in the ensuing fire, locked up in the brothel's basement, unable to escape. The Ise Dragon had never recovered from this black mark on its reputation, and business was not good. As one of the Yoshiwara's oldest establishments, however, it had acquired a number of other properties in the area, so for the time being it was managing to keep its doors open.

The madam of the house was a woman named Omaki whose twenty-year-old son, Eitarō, helped her run the business. Unlike her late husband, Omaki had a sympathetic nature and enjoyed a good reputation. Since Omaki had taken charge of running the Ise Dragon, the place had had two very popular courtesans, Tagasode being the second, but she had been sent off to the convalescent home in Iriya just after the Ninotori Festival[10] in the eleventh month of the previous year. Tagasode had a most unfeminine appetite for alcohol, and it was rumored that too much drink had damaged her heart. She was twenty-one years old. According to the broker who had sold her to Omaki, she had been born in Shitaya's Kanasugi district.

Hanshichi nodded. "Good work, Shōta," he said. "That gives me a decent overview of the situation. But weren't you able to find out if Tagasode has a lover? If she's so much in demand, there must be someone."

"Well, it seems no one knows for sure," the deputy replied. "Of course, she's got lots of regular customers, but she's quite a

---

10. A festival held at the Ōtori Shrine on the second Day of the Rooster in the eleventh month.

smooth operator — not even the people who work in the brothel know who her real lover might be. I'm stumped there."

The information was not much for Hanshichi to go on.

"Too bad about your son," he said. "My old lady's not home at the moment, but when she gets back I'll send her around with something for the boy. Anyway, take this for now."

He handed Shōta a few coins and offered to treat him to lunch. Delighted, Shōta accompanied him to an eel restaurant. While they were eating, Shōta told Hanshichi another story.

"This is changing the subject a bit, but speaking of Kanasugi, there was this girl from there who used to come to the Yoshiwara every night and walk around hawking fortune crackers. She must have been about sixteen or seventeen . . . real pretty with a wonderful voice to boot. Even in the red-light district she could draw a crowd. The 'window-shoppers' — men who come to gawk at the prostitutes but never go into a brothel — were crazy about her. Then, for some reason, toward the end of last year she suddenly stopped coming. I know some fellows who started poking around and asking questions, but they didn't turn up anything. In the end, they figured she'd probably hooked up with a man and eloped or something. But now Inspector Jūbei seems to have taken an interest in the case — he's told his men to track down the girl."

"Is that so?" Hanshichi looked thoughtful. "I hadn't heard about that. Well, Jūbei doesn't mess about when it comes to protecting his turf, does he? So, the fortune-cracker salesgirl was a beauty, you say? Sixteen or seventeen. . . . Hmm, at that age, she's bound to have had a boyfriend. What was her name?"

"Okin, I think. Do you have an idea, boss?"

"Well . . . just a hunch. It'll probably be a waste of time, but I'd like to go over to Kanasugi. I'm sorry to bother you again, but do you mind coming with me?"

"All right."

They finished eating and headed straight for Kanasugi. It was a mild day and a reddish mist hung over the woods near Ueno.

"Tagasode's from Kanasugi, too, you know," Hanshichi said as they walked along. "I wonder where we should start? Why don't we begin with that fortune-cracker salesgirl, Okin? Shōta, do you know where her house is?"

He didn't. Resigned to having to search for the house for themselves, the two men sauntered along toward Kanasugi, the sun shining warm on their backs. Suddenly, Hanshichi came to a halt as though he'd made a discovery.

"Hey, Tokuju! What're you doing here?"

Clutching his walking stick, the blind masseur paused in the street. He obviously had good ears, for he immediately recognized the voice of his companion from the soba restaurant, and hastened to thank Hanshichi profusely for having treated him. Then he added: "What fine weather we're having! Where are you off to today, sir?"

"Actually, I'm glad I ran into you. You're from around here, aren't you? Do you happen to know where a fortune-cracker salesgirl named Okin lives?"

"What a coincidence! As a matter of fact, Okin used to live in my neighborhood. But last year she ran off somewhere."

"I don't suppose she lived alone, though, did she? Doesn't she still have parents or siblings in the area?"

"Well, now . . . it's like this, sir," Tokuju replied with an air of importance. "Okin lived with her older brother, Toramatsu. He's a smalltime gambler—a real playboy. About a fortnight after Okin disappeared, he also up and vanished somewhere in the middle of the night. I heard he wounded a man in a gambling dispute and ran off to avoid trouble. Their house has been empty ever since, though there's a rumor new tenants are moving in any day now."

It occurred to Hanshichi that Inspector Jūbei's interest in the case probably had more to do with Toramatsu than with the question of Okin's disappearance.

"What can you tell me about that courtesan named Tagasode who's staying at the Ise Dragon's convalescent home?" he asked Tokuju again. "I hear she's also from Kanasugi."

"Well, it's true that Tagasode was born in Kanasugi and grew up on the same block as Okin. But both of her parents are dead now, so she doesn't have roots here any longer."

With this, all of Hanshichi's possible leads had gone cold. But he did not despair completely, determined as he still was to squeeze some useful tidbit of information out of the masseur. Then as today, police work was not for the faint of heart.

"Listen, Tokuju. Didn't you tell me the other day you were Tagasode's favorite masseur — that as far as she's concerned, no one else will do? This might sound like an odd question, but why you? What is it that courtesan likes about you so much? I don't suppose it's just that you've got good hands. There must be some other reason."

"Well, now . . ." Tokuju said, grinning.

Hanshichi and Shōta exchanged glances. The detective reached into his wallet, took out a silver coin, and pressed it into Tokuju's palm. Then he said, "Come with me," and led the blind man down an alleyway to their left. Passing an estate belonging to Lord Yanagiwara on one side and Anraku Temple on the other, they emerged into a stretch of open land. Looking around, Hanshichi noted that there was no one about except for a child scooping for weatherfish in a narrow irrigation ditch.

"Okay, what're you hiding, Tokuju?" Hanshichi asked. "I don't want to have to play rough, but remember, I've got my truncheon with me and I wouldn't hesitate to use it."

Tokuju's face went pale and he bowed submissively.

"All right, I'll tell you everything I know," he responded, his voice quavering.

"Good . . . give it to me straight. Tagasode asked you to secretly deliver letters for her, didn't she?"

"Forgive me," Tokuju replied, bowing his head and closing his sightless eyes. "It is just as you say."

"Who did she ask you to deliver the letters to?"

"The master of the Ise Dragon."

Hanshichi and Shōta again looked at one another.

[3]

This was Tokuju's story:

Since the previous autumn, Tagasode had been carrying on a secret affair with Eitarō, the son of Omaki, owner of the Ise Dragon. It was forbidden in the Yoshiwara for employers to consort with their prostitutes, and there would have been trouble if Eitarō were found out. So Tagasode often feigned illness and went to stay at the convalescent home in Iriya. There, Eitarō was able to sneak in to see her. Omaki was more indulgent than other brothel owners, and since Tagasode was the Ise Dragon's star attraction, she gave her leave to stay at the home almost without question. Tagasode's maidservant, Otoki, handled everything concerning Eitarō, and no one was any the wiser.

Though nominally head of the house, the young Eitarō was still under his mother's thumb and was not free to leave it and wander off on his own anytime he liked. Even when Tagasode was in Iriya, he was not able to visit her every day without fail. This vexed Tagasode enormously. If Eitarō did not show up for two days, she would immediately dash off a letter summoning him. She had recruited Tokuju to act as her messenger, so it was little wonder that she was so attached to him.

"But if she was so fond of you, why did you make such a fuss about going in that night?" Hanshichi asked him. "Were you afraid of getting mixed up in something?"

"That's part of it.... Though Omaki's a decent person, and I don't think she'd cause trouble for me, even if she found out what's been going on. But like I said before, whenever I'm around Tagasode, something makes my skin crawl... it's unbearable...I simply can't understand it." Tokuju looked genuinely perplexed.

"Have any of the women at the brothel died recently?"

"Not as far as I know. A lot were killed in the earthquake, but since then I don't think they've lost a single one. Unlike the late master, Omaki and her son are both kind people — I've never heard it said they mistreat the women in the brothel; nor have there been any love suicides."

"I see," said Hanshichi. "Now, Tokuju, I don't want you to tell anyone what we talked about today." With this warning, he let the masseur go on his way. Then, turning to Shōta: "What we've got to do now is track down Toramatsu."

Hanshichi located the back-street tenement where the siblings had lived, and spoke with the landlord. The man said he had no idea what had become of Okin and her brother, but related a rumor that Toramatsu had appeared out of nowhere at the end of the year and donated a large sum of money to the local temple.

Hanshichi and Shōta lost no time in visiting the temple. At first the head priest was evasive, but in the end he admitted that Toramatsu had come on the fifteenth day of the twelfth month and made a donation of five *ryō* in gold coins.

"Toramatsu's parents are interred here at our temple," he said, "but in all the years he lived in the neighborhood, that ne'er-do-well son never once made an offering — not even at New Year's or Obon. So you can imagine my surprise when he showed up one day to request we hold a memorial service and handed me five *ryō!* And then the young man said his sister had recently vanished without a trace, and he assumed she was dead. 'Consider the day of her disappearance as her death anniversary,' he told me. He was overjoyed when I agreed to pray for her. Then he thanked me profusely and left," the head priest recounted in amazement.

After leaving the temple, Shōta turned and whispered to Hanshichi:

"You were right — Toramatsu's definitely up to no good."

"Uh-huh. We'll have to nab him. If he's a gambler he must have friends in the area. Shōta, I want you to track him down somehow."

"Right, I think I can manage that."

"I'm counting on you." With this, the two men parted.

The next day, when Hanshichi's wife went round to Shōta's house on Uma Street to see how his child was getting on, she found that it was a worse case of measles than she had feared. The boy's parents had their hands full looking after him, and

Hanshichi realized that the Toramatsu affair would probably not be resolved anytime soon. Sure enough, he had no word from Shōta for some time.

With the arrival of the second month there came a period of fine warm weather that continued for four or five days, fooling people into thinking that spring had finally arrived. Then one evening a cold spell set in. It must have started to snow during the night, for when Hanshichi awoke in the morning the world outside was white.

"Spring snow . . . won't last long, I expect."

No sooner had he said this than the snow began to ease up. By about ten o'clock, Hanshichi could hear the steady sound of water dripping to the ground outside as the snow melted on the roof. He had no work to attend to for the next two or three days, so as soon as he finished breakfast he left the house. Deciding he couldn't sit around any longer waiting for news from Shōta, he made his way through streets muddy from the melting snow, heading for Kanasugi.

When he arrived, he dropped in at Tokuju's house and called out quietly from the front door. The blind man appeared immediately.

"I'm afraid the streets are very bad today," Hanshichi said, "but would you mind coming with me to the place we went the other day? Here, take my hand."

"Don't worry, I'll be fine," replied Tokuju.

The two made their way past the mansion and the temple, stopping when they reached the road that ran alongside the fields, which was still covered with snow.

"I'll get straight to the point," Hanshichi began. "Have you been back to the Ise Dragon's convalescent home since I last saw you?"

"No," said Tokuju, shaking his head. "Since that last time, it seems Otoki's realized she's no match for me and has given up. That suits me just fine. Someone I know who works at the Ise Dragon tells me that Otoki's been fired but is refusing to go quietly. It seems trouble is brewing there."

"Where does Otoki live?"

"Honjo, I think, but I'm not sure."

"I see. Well, I'm sorry for dragging you all the way out here on a day like today. I'm working on a case, so you'll have to forgive me."

After seeing Tokuju home, Hanshichi pondered his next move. He had collected bits and pieces of information, but found himself unable to tie them together. He wasn't even sure what exactly he was investigating. He had only happened to learn of the missing fortune-cracker girl while looking into the masseur's vague account of strange goings-on at the convalescent home. But were the two cases connected? So far, he hadn't been able to establish even that. Despite all the effort he'd put into the investigation, Hanshichi wasn't convinced that he was likely to get any results. Even so, he wasn't ready to give up just yet. It wasn't mere curiosity that was driving him — he couldn't shake the feeling that there was more to things than met the eye.

"Even if it's a waste of time," he told himself, "I think I'll try probing a little further."

After taking care of some business in Ueno, Hanshichi was about to return home when he changed his mind and headed back to Iriya. The day had remained bitterly cold after the snowfall, and by the time he reached the fields the sun had gone down. Carrying an umbrella, he trudged along through the mud. As he neared the convalescent home, a woman emerged from the gate. He couldn't see her face clearly, but he had the impression it was Otoki. He quickly made after her and watched as she went into the noodle restaurant where he had eaten the other night.

Pausing for a moment, he thought, "Well, it's not as though she might recognize me," before himself ducking under the curtain and entering. In addition to Otoki, there was one other customer, a man, in the tiny restaurant. Hanshichi could tell at a glance that he was a shady character. Wearing a striped jacket tied with a narrow sash, he looked about twenty-five and had a swarthy complexion. A real child of Edo, thought Hanshichi. The man appeared to have been waiting for Otoki, and now sat facing her, drinking saké. Hanshichi went and sat in a corner, ordering something at random from the menu.

The man and the woman occasionally cast sidelong glances at Hanshichi, but didn't seem particularly concerned by his presence. Warming their hands at the charcoal brazier and speaking in low voices, they were engrossed in their conversation.

"... The way things stand now, this is our only option," the woman was saying.

"So, it's up to me to bring the curtain down on this show then," replied the man.

"Stop your dillydallying. If they commit suicide, we'll be stuck holding the bag," the woman warned in a low voice.

Hanshichi was unable to make out what was said next, but the mention of suicide sent his mind racing. Was Tagasode planning to kill herself? Now we're getting somewhere, he thought. He held his breath and tried as hard as he could to eavesdrop on their conversation, but the discussion seemed to be getting more involved and the woman lowered her voice still further. Close to them though he was, Hanshichi was unable to learn their secret. He could only watch in frustration and wait to see what they would do. Eventually, the two seemed to reach some sort of agreement; they got up, paid their bill and left.

After waiting for them to go, Hanshichi himself stood up.

"Was that Otoki from the Ise Dragon who left just now, ma'am?" he asked the woman who ran the restaurant as he paid for his noodles.

"That's right."

"Who's the fellow she was with?"

"He's called Tora."

"Tora?" Hanshichi said with a gleam in his eye. "You mean Toramatsu, the brother of Okin, the girl who sells fortune crackers? Well, I'll be ..."

"My, you know a lot, don't you?"

Quite suddenly, Hanshichi felt his mood brighten. Bidding the woman goodnight, he hastened out into the street. In the dim light reflected off the remaining snow, he could just make out two figures walking along the road side by side. He carefully began picking his way through the muddy slush that now covered the road. He watched as the two figures stopped in front of the Ise Dragon's convalescent home. There, they again began whispering to one another. Then the two figures parted, and the woman disappeared through the gate.

[4]

Hanshichi waited to see what the man would do next. He watched as Toramatsu turned around and headed back the way he had come, toward Hanshichi. Just as he was passing the detective, Hanshichi called out to him.

"Hey, Tora! Wait a moment."

Toramatsu came to a halt but said nothing.

"Hey, I haven't seen your face around for a while. Where've you been hiding?" Hanshichi said in a tone of familiarity.

"Who are you?" Toramatsu asked, peering cautiously at him through the darkness.

"I doubt you'd remember me . . . we've met a few times upstairs at The Peacock House."[11]

"Liar!" Toramatsu replied, drawing himself up. "You're that guy who was in the noodle shop just now. I knew there was something I didn't like about your face. I thought I'd seen all of Jūbei's henchmen, but I've never met you before. Well, I'm not gonna let you guys shake me down any more. If you wanna arrest me you better get Jūbei himself to come here!"

"My, full of spunk, aren't we!" Hanshichi laughed derisively. "Anyway, you'd better just cut it out and come along with me."

"Are you crazy? If I wind up in Tenmachō again I won't be

---

11. *Kujaku-nagaya.* According to historical records, this appears to have been an inexpensive boardinghouse in Asakusa.

comin' out alive! I'll be damned if I'm gonna let you cops give me another one of your beatings! You can't catch a peacock with a butterfly net, you know. If you wanna take me in, you're gonna need reinforcements!"

Hanshichi was taken aback by Toramatsu's defiant attitude. Clearly he was going to have to get his hands dirty, much as he disliked to. The snow would make things a bit tricky, but it shouldn't be too difficult to get the better of a punk like Toramatsu. He'd just have to haul him off by force.

"C'mon, Tora. I don't want to get all muddy over a numbskull like you. I'll give you a break — I've got a nice truncheon here, but I won't show it to you until I've got you tied up. So come along like a good boy."

He took a step toward Toramatsu, who took a step backward, at the same time reaching into the breast of his kimono. Only a rank amateur would have dared to draw a knife on an Edo detective. This guy's nothing to write home about, that's for sure, thought Hanshichi smugly. But sometimes a rank amateur can be more dangerous than a hardened criminal.

"In the name of the law, Toramatsu, give yourself up!" Hanshichi shouted, hoping to intimidate his adversary.

But at that moment someone stole up behind Hanshichi and placed both hands over his eyes. Taken by surprise, he had a moment of panic, but almost immediately he realized from the feel of the person's skin that it was a woman. And who else could it be but Otoki? Ducking his shoulder to one side, in a single motion he grabbed her arm and threw her to the ground at his feet. As he did so, Toramatsu stepped over her and came at him. Hanshichi saw the blade of a dagger flash in his hand.

"Stop, in the name of the law!" he shouted again.

Toramatsu's dagger stabbed the air two or three times. His body seemed to sway from side to side. Then, before he knew what had happened, the blade he'd been holding in his right hand was on the ground and Hanshichi's rope was wrapped around his left wrist. At the sudden realization that he was outmatched, a feeble moan escaped Toramatsu's lips.

"I underestimated you, Inspector. Please forgive me — I didn't mean to cause you any trouble."

"Well, maybe now you'll listen to me — Hanshichi's the name, I'm from Kanda," he said, introducing himself. "Anyway, let's not stand out here in the street talking. Hey, Otoki! This concerns you, too. Take us to your mistress's place."

Covered in mud, Otoki struggled to her feet. Hanshichi marched her and the bound Toramatsu off toward the convalescent home. As they entered, a girl ran up to them crying.

"Come quick! The young master and Tagasode . . ."

She led them to an eight-mat room at the back of the house. There, surrounded by an inverted[12] folding screen, lay Eitarō and the courtesan. Their throats had been slit with a razor.

"EVEN I WAS dumbfounded," old Hanshichi said. "True, I'd heard Otoki say something about a double suicide, but I didn't think anything would happen so soon. And there I was — I had two people in custody and two dead bodies on my hands. The convalescent home was thrown into absolute chaos. Rumors of the deaths spread like wildfire, and a crowd of people gathered outside the front gate and stayed there until late into the night."

"So why did Eitarō and Tagasode kill themselves? I asked. "Did Otoki and Toramatsu have anything to do with it?"

I was still completely in the dark, so old Hanshichi explained it to me in greater detail.

"Tagasode was a murderess. The blood of Okin, the fortune-cracker salesgirl, was on her hands. Why did she do it? Well, as I said earlier, Tagasode became deeply involved with Eitarō, the son of the Ise Dragon's owner. She didn't have any ulterior motive such as wanting to get out of her contract, or anything of that sort . . . she was just truly head-over-heels in love with the guy. But then, at some point, Eitarō took up with that popular

---

12. Done to signify death.

fortune-cracker girl, and when Tagasode got wind of it, she hit
the roof. Women in that line of work aren't like normal human
beings — when they get jealous, they don't mess around. The
maid, Otoki, who'd become friendly with Okin, waylaid the latter on her way home one night from the Yoshiwara and invited
her into the convalescent home. There, Tagasode gave her a good
tongue-lashing and then really set on her. She scratched and
knocked her around a bit, and eventually ended up strangling
her with her own sash. Even Otoki was shocked at first, because
she hadn't thought Tagasode would go that far. But Otoki is quite
a strong, level-headed woman, and besides, she'd been romantically involved with that no-good Toramatsu, Okin's brother, for
some time."

"My, what a tangled web!"

"That's how Okin got to know Otoki in the first place, and
why the girl blithely went into the convalescent home to meet her
terrible fate. Otoki immediately called in Toramatsu, told him
everything, and asked him what they should do. At first he was
shocked, but being the scoundrel that he was, as soon as his lover
told him he stood to gain handsomely if he kept the incident
under wraps, he agreed without giving a second thought to the
possibility of avenging his sister's death. So they dug a deep hole
underneath the house and buried Okin's body there. Then they
all went about their business as though nothing had happened.
Otoki gave Toramatsu 100 *ryō* as payment for his silence."

"But where did the money come from?" I inquired doggedly.

"From Eitarō of course," old Hanshichi said. "The day after
the murder, Tagasode called in Eitarō and told him everything
— how she had killed Okin in a fit of rage. If it was wrong of me,
do with me as you like, she appealed to him, prostrating herself
on the floor. Eitarō, it seems, went white and broke into a cold
sweat. But seeing that he himself was not blameless in the matter, the Ise Dragon would have to close its doors if it were to become public. In the end, he did as Tagasode suggested and paid
Toramatsu 100 *ryō* as hush money.

Well, you know the saying 'Ill-gotten gains are short-lived.' It wasn't long before Toramatsu lost his shirt at the gambling table. What's more, he got into a fight with the man who won the money from him, and had to skip town when he drew blood. Perhaps this made him see the error of his ways, or perhaps he was motivated by brotherly love, but as soon as he got hold of some more money, he paid a long overdue visit to his family temple and calmly handed the priests five *ryō* to pray for his sister's soul. Then he headed up north to Sōka[13] and hid out there for about a month. But an Edo man like him couldn't stomach the local diet of barley rice for long. He slipped back into the capital, where he shook Otoki down whenever he needed pocket money. He was hanging around Iriya when he attracted the attention of Jūbei, who found out about his relationship with Otoki. The Ise Dragon was on Jūbei's turf and he felt bad about subjecting them to an investigation, so he secretly advised Omaki, the mistress, to sack Otoki. That's when things turned from bad to worse."

"Otoki refused to leave quietly?"

"She wouldn't budge. She had Eitarō and Tagasode over a barrel . . . said she wouldn't clear out without being paid a nice chunk of change, not less than 200 or 300 *ryō*. She tried all sorts of threats, but there was no way Eitarō could get his hands on that much money until he came into his fortune, and Otoki had already hit Tagasode up for money a number of times. Even if the courtesan were to sell the clothes off her back, she couldn't raise that much. So the two of them were powerless to do anything. But meanwhile, Omaki — who knew nothing of all this — became rattled by the prospect of a police investigation and tried to force Otoki to leave immediately. So Otoki called Toramatsu to her aid. They went secretly and threatened Eitarō and Tagasode, saying they would have to expose Okin's murder if the two of them didn't do exactly as they were told. Realizing they were trapped, Eitarō and Tagosode resolved to kill themselves. Otoki

---

13. A city in present-day Saitama Prefecture.

had an inkling of this and knew that if she didn't act fast, the goose that laid the golden egg might soon be dead. She had just convinced Toramatsu that he'd have to take the matter to the person at the Ise Dragon who held the purse strings, when I came along and arrested the two of them. Tagasode was guilty of murder, so either way, there was no saving her life — suicide was probably a better way out. But Eitarō's crime wasn't severe enough to warrant a death sentence. It's a shame we weren't in time to save him."

Although I now understood the mystery of the Ise Dragon's convalescent home, there was still one doubt that lingered in my mind.

"So I guess Tokuju, the blind masseur, knew nothing about any of this?"

"Apparently he'd been telling the truth — he was simply Tagasode's messenger and had been kept completely in the dark."

"I wonder why he disliked going to the home so much? Do you suppose the blind man really sensed a ghostly presence next to Tagasode?"

"Well, now, I really haven't a clue. You're better qualified than I am to answer these difficult metaphysical questions. But we *did* find Okin's body buried beneath the floor of the convalescent home. . . ."

Old Hanshichi would not elaborate any further. In choosing to call this story "Snow Melting in Spring," I am merely borrowing Hanshichi's own words. In fact, I must admit that I find this tale more profoundly disturbing than that simple love story of the same name about the courtesan Michitose and the samurai Naojirō.

Hiroshige and the River Otter

HIROSHIGE TO KAWAUSO

[1]

f I were to write this story in the style of an old kabuki script, it might begin something like this.

[A platform sits atop the main stage. The set consists of a vermilion temple gate with guardian deities on either side. Through it, in the distance, one can see the precincts of the temple of Kannon in Asakusa with a large, well-placed ginkgo tree. Inside the gate, the Nakamise shopping street leading up to the temple is lined on either side with stalls selling various wares. Music of the kind heard in the local vaudeville theaters plays as the curtain goes up. An old man enters stage right, probably having just eaten at the Okada or some other well-known restaurant nearby. A young man enters stage left. Meeting in front of the temple gate, the two greet one another warmly.]

"Why, fancy running into you here! Come to see the cherry blossoms, have you?"

"Well, not exactly. It's such a fine day I just thought I'd go for a stroll."

"Is that so? Myself, I'm on my way to the temple in Hashiba. If I don't show my face there once a month my old lady gets lonely, rest her soul. That's what comes of having been on good terms with her when she was alive." He chuckled. "By the bye, have you had lunch?"

"Yes, I have."

"Well, then — if you're not busy, why not stroll with me over toward Mukōjima? I thought I'd walk off my lunch a bit."

"Splendid. Let's go." *[How he wishes he'd brought his notebook with him, the crafty youngster thinks to himself as he follows after the old man.]*

[The same music as before plays as the set begins to revolve. Now we see the riverbank at Mukōjima, with the opposite bank visible in the distance across the Sumida River. On the near bank stands a row of cherry trees that have shed their blossoms, with leaves just starting to bud. A faint lapping of waves can be heard. The set comes to a stop to the strains of a popular tune. The old man and the youth enter stage left, looking surprised to see that the blossoms have already fallen. One of them remarks that at least there are no crowds, and they stroll along toward stage right.]

By now, any reader will have guessed who the two main characters are: the older man is none other than Hanshichi and the youth is myself. On this occasion, at my behest, the old man talked about what Asakusa was like in the old days, touching upon such topics as the temple of Shōden[1] and the Sodesuri Inari Shrine.[2] The conversation slowly blossomed, and I persuaded Hanshichi to tell me another one of his adventures.

"Yes, indeed," he began. "A lot of strange things happened back then. Speaking of the Sodesuri Inari Shrine, for instance, I'm reminded of one case where . . . but let me tell you about it as we walk."

IT ALL BEGAN on the seventeenth day of the first month of 1858. The body of a three- or four-year-old girl was found lying face-down on the roof of the mansion of a *hatamoto* by the name of

---

1. Also known as Kangiten or Shōten (an abbreviation of Daishōkangiten), a Japanese version of the Hindu god Ganesha that typically depicts two elephant-headed deities (male and female) embracing. The particular image referred to here is housed in the temple of Honryūin on the riverbank just northeast of Sensō Temple.

2. Sodesuri, literally "sleeve rubbing," is a nickname given to this shrine on account of the narrowness of the shrine's entrance.

Kuronuma Magohachi located next to the Sodesuri Inari Shrine in Asakusa's Tamachi district. Because the body was on their own roof, the occupants of Lord Kuronuma's mansion didn't notice it at first. Then, at about eight o'clock in the morning, the people in the mansion next door alerted them to its presence, setting the Kuronuma household in an uproar. Some footmen and other members of the household got out a tall ladder, leaned it against the house, and climbed up on the roof, which still had a light dusting of morning frost, in order to have a look. It was indeed the body of a little girl, quite well-dressed and attractive in appearance. When they brought her down and took a good look at her, they found that she was wearing neither a waist pouch nor an identity tag, as children normally did, so they had absolutely no clue as to who she might be or where she came from. They looked at each other in puzzlement.

But the most perplexing question as far as the members of the household were concerned was less her identity than how her tiny body had come to rest upon the mansion's roof. Lord Kuronuma was a personage of considerable standing, with an income of 1,200 *koku*. More than twenty servants of various ranks lived under his roof — including a steward, footmen, butlers, and maidservants, not to mention ladies' maids, nursemaids, and the kitchen staff — yet not one of them recalled ever having seen the little girl before. Nor did any of the many tradespeople who frequented the house recognize her.

It was simply unfathomable how and why the unidentified child could have climbed onto the roof. Though it was a one-story house, the roof, as with all samurai mansions, was much higher than those of ordinary houses. Even supposing a ladder had been left leaning against the house, it seemed highly unlikely that such a small child could have managed to climb it. In that case, had she fallen from the sky? Had she been abducted by a *tengu*[3] who had dropped her out of the clouds? From summer

---

3. A flying, long-nosed goblin.

on into autumn the previous year, bright lights had been seen shooting through the sky over Edo, and there were stories that someone claimed to have seen a shiny flying object in the shape of a large ox. One member of the household put forward the explanation that the girl had been snatched by one of these strange flying objects, which had then deposited her body on their roof. But His Lordship Kuronuma Magohachi was not convinced. He was one of those sturdily rational samurai who denied the existence of *tengu* and all such fantastic beings.

No, there must be some other explanation.

Either way, Lord Kuronuma could not simply ignore the matter, so he ordered one of his men to report what had happened to the City Magistrate's Office. Usually, anything that occurred within a samurai's household would be settled in private, but in this case, Kuronuma decided to announce the incident publicly and seek the assistance of the city authorities in resolving the matter.

"A child as young as this cannot be without a family. Someone, somewhere, is certainly bewailing the loss of their daughter or sister. We must determine her identity so that we can hand her body over to her next of kin—that is the very least we can do. This is no time to be worried about our family reputation. Give a detailed description of the girl's clothing and her appearance to everyone who comes to the house and have them make inquiries."

Once he had expressed his opinion on the subject, no one in the household dared to contradict his lordship. Later that morning, his steward, Fujikura Gun'emon, headed for Kyōbashi to visit Chief Inspector Koyama Shimbei's official residence in Yaneyashindō. Always well up in the latest gossip, Shimbei had already gotten wind of the incident at Lord Kuronuma's house, but Gun'emon explained it to him in greater detail and begged him to do whatever he could to ascertain the girl's identity. Then he confided to Shimbei that, though Lord Kuronuma was intent on seeking the public's help in solving the mystery, in the steward's own humble opinion, this would have a deleterious effect on the family's reputation. The appearance of an unidentified body on the roof of his lordship's mansion just a few days into the new year was, at worst, inauspicious and at the very least reflected unfavorably on the Kuronuma name. You know how people talk, Gun'emon said. The rumor would grow wings and take on a life of its own. Truths and half-truths would be bruited about. Who knew what sort of trouble it would stir up? Wasn't there, he asked, some way to proceed with an investigation without making the matter public? The family would be satisfied if they could just discover the girl's identity and turn her body over to her relatives. In the interest of his lordship's good name, wouldn't he please, Gun'emon beseeched Shimbei, conduct the investigation in secrecy?

"I understand perfectly. We'll take whatever steps necessary to honor your wishes," Shimbei assured him straightforwardly.

After seeing Gun'emon off, Shimbei dispatched someone to Kanda to fetch Hanshichi. When the latter arrived, Shimbei gave him a brief overview of the situation.

"... and so that's how things stand," he concluded. "I know this is out of your jurisdiction, but I'd like you to check it out. You're just the man for the job. No, I'm not trying to flatter you — working with these samurai households can be a tricky business, and not everyone is cut out for it. Sorry to drag you out on a cold day like this, but I'm counting on you."

"Very good, sir," Hanshichi replied thoughtfully. "I'll see what I can dig up."

"I wouldn't put much stock in that *tengu* theory," said Shimbei with a smile. "There's a lot more to this than meets the eye. Once you scratch the surface, I think you'll find there's gold underneath."

"You're probably right. I'll head over to Tamachi right away and talk to Kuronuma's steward."

Leaving Hatchōbori, Hanshichi set off in the direction of Asakusa. Entering Kuronuma's residence by way of the main gate, he asked to see Gun'emon. The steward, who apparently had been expecting him, took Hanshichi to his private quarters.

"I hear you've got a difficult case on your hands — I hope I may be of service," Hanshichi said by way of greeting.

"You must appreciate our predicament," Gun'emon replied, deep furrows appearing on his brow below his somewhat receding hairline. "We're all very distressed about what has happened — it simply doesn't make any sense. We'd be perfectly within our rights, of course, simply to dispose of the unidentified girl's body, but his lordship will have none of it. He's ordered us to track down her family and return her to them without fail. That's all very well, but just how are we supposed to do it? To begin with, we haven't a clue as to how she wound up on our roof! We're at a complete loss. But you, now, are a professional — isn't there some way you can find out what happened?"

"Inspector Koyama has told me all about the case. I assure you I'll do everything within my power," Hanshichi replied. "Where is the body, by the way? Has it been sent to the local temple yet?"

"Not yet. It's being kept here until this evening. Please come and take a look at it."

The steward's quarters consisted of just three rooms, which were three, six, and eight mats in size, respectively. The girl's body had been laid out in a corner of the eight-mat room with her head pointing north in the customary manner. Someone had even thought to place offerings of water and incense beside her. Hanshichi edged across the floor to take a look at the body. He turned it over and examined it from head to toe so as not to miss anything.

"All right, I've seen enough," he said when he had finished, returning the body to its original position. He rose and went out onto the veranda, washed his hands in the outdoor basin, returned to the room, and sat thinking quietly for a while.

"Have you got the answer?" Gun'emon prodded.

"Not yet I'm afraid. But there's one thing I'd like to ask you. Can you think of anything at all unusual that happened between last night and this morning?"

"Nothing whatsoever," the steward answered without hesitation. He explained that Lord Kuronuma had hosted a card-playing party the previous evening attended by relatives and children from the neighborhood — about twenty people in all.[4] The fun had gone on until well past ten o'clock. Everyone was so exhausted afterward that they would have been too sound asleep to hear the girl climbing — or landing, as the case might be — on the roof. And since the body had not been discovered until one of the neighbors pointed it out to them that morning, they had no idea how long it had been there.

"And nobody has any clue who the child is?" Hanshichi persisted.

"I've never set eyes on her before, and there isn't a single person in the household we haven't questioned, but no one admits to recognizing her. Moreover, judging from her appearance, I'd say she must be a commoner."

"So would I," Hanshichi nodded. "She doesn't look as though she's from a samurai household, that's for sure. Now, if I might trouble you further, would you mind showing me the exact spot on the roof where the body was found?"

"Certainly."

Hanshichi followed the steward out of his quarters and over to the mansion's main entrance. There, Gun'emon called over two footmen and instructed them to lean a tall ladder against the wall to one side of the entranceway. Hitching up his kimono, Hanshichi clambered quickly up it and stepped onto the roof. After a moment, he waved his hand as a signal for someone to come up and join him. The smaller of the two footmen climbed up the ladder and pointed out to Hanshichi where the body had been found. He examined the spot and had a good look around before descending the ladder.

---

4. *Karuta-kai,* a game in which the first half of a poem is read out loud and then the players must pick from an array of cards on the floor one that is inscribed with the second half of the verse.

[2]

Hanshichi left Kuronuma's estate and made his way to Uma Street. There he called on his deputy, Shōta, to find out whether he knew any gossip concerning the samurai's household. But Shōta could recall nothing worth mentioning. The family had a reputation in the neighborhood for being stolid and upright; even their servants were beyond reproach, it seemed. In Shōta's judgment, the present incident most likely had no connection whatsoever with anyone in Kuronuma's household.

"Is that so? Well, that's that, I guess," Hanshichi said, gazing up at the huge, clear-blue sky of early spring. "Hey, Shōta — how about heading over to Jūmantsubo?⁵ It's such a nice day, and it's not all that windy out."

"Jūmantsubo?" Shōta said giving him a puzzled look. "Why would you want to go there?"

"I just thought I'd pay my respects at the Inari Shrine in Sunamura — haven't been for a long time. And since there doesn't seem anything else for me to do today, I've suddenly got the urge to pray. C'mon, join me — if it's not too much trouble, that is."

"I guess I might as well . . . I've got time on my hands, too. Anywhere you say."

The two men set off. Shōta found it strange that Hanshichi would want to go trekking all the way out to the far side of Fuka-gawa when it was already well past two in the afternoon, but he kept quiet and followed obediently. They crossed the Azuma Bridge, traversed Honjo, and by the time they reached the Inari Shrine in Sunamura, in the farthest reaches of Fukagawa, the bell at the Hachiman Shrine had already struck four o'clock. Though spring had already arrived, the days were still relatively short. Down by the river's edge a chilly evening breeze rustled through the yellowed leaves of the few reeds to have survived the winter.

---

5. An area of reclaimed agricultural land near the waterfront at the eastern-most edge of Edo.

"Getting pretty cold, isn't it, boss?" Shōta pulled up his collar.

"Yeah, now that the sun's setting."

After praying at the shrine, the two men ducked into a make-shift teahouse made of reed mats near the side of the road. The madam was obviously getting ready to close up for the day, but when she saw customers coming in, she broke into a smile.

"Pious gentlemen, aren't you, coming all the way out here in this cold! I'm afraid I haven't much to offer you, but I could warm up some dumplings."

"Anything will do — but let's have some hot tea first," Shōta said, sinking onto a stool, clearly exhausted.

The woman placed some grilled dumplings back on the fire to warm them and busily began fanning the coals beneath the kettle with a lacquered fan.

"Have a lot of worshippers been coming to the shrine lately, ma'am?" Hanshichi asked.

"Well, it's been so cold, you know . . ." the woman said as she brought them their tea. "Next month we shall be much busier around here."

"I expect so. Next month is Hatsu'uma after all,"[6] Hanshichi said, puffing on his pipe. "But even now I bet you get twenty or thirty customers a day, eh?"

"We're lucky if we get that many. Take today — we only had twelve or thirteen. And about half of them are people who come to the shrine everyday."

"So there really are people who come all the way out here to pray everyday, eh?" said Shōta admiringly, struggling to chew a tough bit of dumpling. "That sort of piety is kind of scary, isn't it? Once in a long while is enough for me."

"Piety takes people different ways. I feel really sorry for some of the ones I see. This morning, for example, a young lady from over Kiba way came in — a real sad case, she was. Imagine, wear-

---

6. According to the Chinese sexagenary cycle, the first Day of the Horse in the second lunar month. It is said to be the day upon which the god Inari visits shrines dedicated to him.

ing a thin cotton kimono in this weather! And she says she plans
to come here to pray in her bare feet every morning from now
on! She looked too thin and weak for it, if you ask me — I worry
she'll do herself harm. But I guess that's piety for you. The ones
who overdo it like that can't often keep it up for long, though."

"I wonder where she comes from, this young woman?" Hanshichi asked, obviously concerned. "What is it she's praying for?"

"That's what's so sad," the madam said, looking at Hanshichi
as she poured hot water into the earthen teapot. "It seems she's
the wife of a clerk in one of the lumberyards in Kiba — they got
married last fall. She's only nineteen, poor thing. She's his second
wife and he has a three-year-old child from his first marriage.
Well, yesterday evening, she took the child to visit her relatives
over in Hachirobei, and on their way home in the dark the child
somehow wandered off. She searched frantically all over, but to
no avail. She might wear a married woman's hairdo, but she's
only nineteen years old after all. She went crying home to her
husband all upset, but got no sympathy from him — said it was
her own fault. Of course, it was inexcusable to let the child stray.
The worst part of it is that the child's not her own daughter, just
a stepchild. So her mistake is that much more unforgivable. No,
not just unforgivable . . . suspicious minds will say she's the pro-
verbial wicked stepmother, that she deliberately abandoned the
child somewhere. It seems even her husband had his doubts. He
gave her a good tongue-lashing, of course — seems he even accused her of pushing the child into the river. She was so distraught
she rushed straight out of the house and off into the night. She
almost went and threw *herself* into the river to prove her innocence, but then she changed her mind and went home. She was
here this morning saying that from now on she'll come everyday
to pray to Inari. On top of everything else, it was her bad luck
that before setting out from home with the child, she'd dressed
the girl in her best going-out kimono but forgot to remove the
identity tag from her everyday sash and place it on her. So no one
will know who the child is when they find her. Of course, gossips

will say she forgot to attach the child's identity tag on purpose. I know you can't judge someone just on appearances, but if you'd seen how pale her face was and the tears welling up in her eyes, you'd know there wasn't an ounce of evil in her. I'm sure it was just an accident, but if the child doesn't turn up safe and sound, people will suspect the young wife, that's for sure."

As the woman finished her lengthy story, Hanshichi and Shōta exchanged glances.

"The child's a little girl, then, ma'am?" Shōta asked eagerly.

"It seems so. Her name's Ochō, they say — the father's name is Jirohachi. A small child like that couldn't have wandered off very far, and if she'd fallen into the river her body would have floated to the surface by now. I wonder what could have happened to her," the woman said with a sigh. "I've even prayed myself that merciful Inari might show her where her daughter is."

"What a terrible thing. Well, I'm sure your piety will be rewarded."

Hanshichi shot Shōta a glance and, paying for their tea, they both got up from their stools and left the teahouse. After walking a short distance, Shōta, turning to look back toward the teahouse, whispered to Hanshichi, "Say, boss. We really hit the jackpot there, didn't we?"

"Yeah — if this isn't a case of dumb luck, I don't know what is," Hanshichi answered with a big smile. "It explains everything."

"But there's one thing I still don't understand," Shōta said, looking at him inquiringly. "We know the child's identity, but how do you suppose she wound up on Kuronuma's roof? That's what puzzles me. I admit I thought it was strange when you suggested going to Jūmantsubo and visiting the shrine in Sunamura. I wondered, why's he want to go all the way out there? But I guess you had something in mind, huh?"

"Nothing I could put my finger on. I was afraid you'd laugh at me for clutching at straws, so I kept my thoughts to myself. But I dragged you all this way because I had a hunch we'd find something."

"But why here?"

"That's what's odd . . . let me try to explain," Hanshichi said, smiling again. "When I went to Kuronuma's mansion and the steward showed me the girl's corpse, I noticed there was hardly a mark on her. At first I thought perhaps she'd died of an illness and her body had been moved. But then I took a closer look and noticed faint, tiny scratches around her neck, underneath her collar. It didn't seem that they'd been made by someone's fingernails so much as the claws of some creature. I didn't seriously believe it was the work of a *tengu,* but if not, what else? Then, after leaving Kuronuma's mansion, I was strolling along when I passed a bookshop on my way to your house. And what did I happen to see displayed right out in front but a picture! It was a woodblock print from Hiroshige's series of famous views of Edo: a snow scene in Jūmantsubo.[7] Do you know the one I'm talking about?"

"Naw, I'm not one for that sort of thing," Shōta said with a wry smile.

"I know what you mean . . . I don't care much for the stuff myself. But it's my job to look at anything and everything. Anyway, it just happened to catch my eye. Like I said, it was a picture of Jūmantsubo, with the ground covered with snow and up in the sky, this enormous eagle spreading its wings in flight. Not bad, I thought; the composition's really rather interesting. And then it suddenly came to me — the body of the girl at Kuronuma's mansion! It wasn't a *tengu* that snatched her but an eagle! That would explain the marks around her collar. Anyway, it was just a passing thought, and I quickly dismissed it as crazy. Then, when we met, you told me that Kuronuma's household had a spotless reputation and you'd no reason to suspect foul play on their part. So I thought, what the heck, let's check out Jūmantsubo, just in case. Sure, I know — we're talking about a *bird* after all, so it could have come from anywhere. Why not go to Ōji, or Ōkubo

7. Andō Hiroshige (1797–1858), *ukiyo-e* printmaker. His series of famous views of Edo was published in 1832.

for that matter? But it was Hiroshige's picture of Jūmantsubo that put the idea into my head, so I thought maybe I'd figure something out once I'd had a look around.

"Well, when we got to Sunamura it turned out we hadn't wasted our time after all. The answer more or less fell into our laps. No doubt about it—that little girl, Ochō, got separated from her stepmother and wandered off in the dark. Then a big eagle suddenly swooped down, grabbed her by the collar, and flew up into the sky with her. There aren't many houses between Hachirobei and Jūmantsubo, and beyond that only the Hosokawa estate, so it's not surprising no one spotted her and the bird, especially in the dark, and no one would have heard the sound of the birds' wings either. Of course, I can't be sure, but the girl probably fainted from shock, which would be why she didn't cry out. Having caught its prey, the eagle must've realized after flying around a bit that the girl was too heavy—it dropped her and she just happened to land on the roof of Kuronuma's mansion. With luck, if she'd been spotted right away, her life might have been saved. Instead, she just lay there until morning, by which time it was too late. What a tragedy! A young life cut short.... Ah well, let the dead bury the dead. The main thing now is to tell her parents so they can come to terms with their loss. When they hear the story, though, there's bound to be more trouble—that young wife might even attempt suicide again. There's no saving the dead, but we must do what we can to help the living. We'd better get over to Kiba and explain things to them."

"You're absolutely right," Shōta promptly agreed. "It's bad enough that a four-year-old child is dead, but the stepmother's only nineteen herself. It'd be a pity if she lost her life, too."

"Now, you mustn't be too soft on young brides, Shōta," Hanshichi said with a laugh, "or next time it'll be you who becomes the eagle's prey!"

"Don't scare me! It's starting to get dark."

Walking along beside the river, the two men quickened their pace as they headed for Kiba, with its rafts of lumber afloat on the water.

"THAT'S PRETTY MUCH all there is to the story," old Hanshichi said. "It might have sounded more dramatic if somewhere along the way I could have stepped in to prevent the young wife from throwing herself into the river, but the truth wasn't so obliging." He laughed. "Anyhow, once we reached Kiba we tracked down Jirohachi's house and explained what had happened — they were flabbergasted. We immediately took the husband to see Kuronuma's steward, who turned the girl over to him with a huge sigh of relief. It was her all right. The father wasted no time in taking her body to the temple for the funeral.

"Of course, this case was different from my usual ones because I can't claim to have solved it beyond a shadow of a doubt. But in the absence of any better explanation, I decided the girl must have been snatched away by an eagle. I suppose you might say this case proves that Hiroshige's pictures have some redeeming value after all! Incidentally, that very same autumn Hiroshige himself died in the great cholera epidemic."[8]

[3]

At some point during the course of Hanshichi's story, we had passed the Mimeguri Shrine. The blossoms had already scattered from the cherry trees along the riverbank. For us this was a blessing, as it meant that there were few people about, even though it was Sunday. As we paused to catch our breath, I took out a pack of Evergreen cigarettes — a popular brand at the time — from the sleeve of my kimono. Lighting one, I offered it to Hanshichi, who bowed politely and accepted it, but winced slightly as he blew out a mouthful of smoke.

"Shall we have a rest somewhere?" I said, feeling a bit sorry for him.

"Good idea."

---

8. In addition to Hiroshige's, the cholera epidemic of 1858 claimed some 28,000 lives.

We found a teahouse and sat down outside. Now that the cherry-blossom – viewing season was over, the place was deserted. This time, the old man took out a bamboo tobacco case, lit his pipe, and puffed on it with obvious pleasure. With the sun shining brilliantly overhead, I sat enjoying the breeze coming off the river, only slightly apprehensive that a caterpillar might be swept out of the nearby treetops and land on me. My forehead grew damp with perspiration.

"I've heard that there used to be river otters around these parts," I said.

"That's right," Hanshichi nodded. "Not only river otters, but foxes and badgers too. Nowadays people invariably think of Mukōjima as the setting of those popular kabuki dramas in which lovers were forever coming here to commit suicide. But in fact there was more to Mukōjima than that. In the old days it was rather creepy at night."

"I imagine it *would* be scary to have river otters and such running all over the place!"

"Yes — they're nasty little devils, they are."

No matter what one asked Hanshichi, he was always happy to engage in conversation. He quite simply enjoyed talking, and he had a particularly soft spot for young people. When he reminisced about the past — as he frequently did — it wasn't only his great exploits that he talked about. As long as his listener was happy, he was happy, and he could go on talking and talking indefinitely. On this occasion, the old man couldn't resist telling me a story about a river otter.

"Of course, one thing that's really changed since the end of the Edo era is that there are far fewer wild animals in Tokyo. You hardly ever see a river otter these days, let alone a fox or a badger. They used to be everywhere, not just here in Mukōjima and in Senju. You could be sure to find one living in any decent-sized stream. You know the Sakura Creek in Atagoshita? Once a river otter built its nest there and would sometimes attack passersby. Whenever I heard someone blaming a *kappa* for having done such-and-such, I'd be pretty sure it was actually a river otter up to no good. Here's a story, then, about one such creature."

IT WAS A dark night in the ninth month of 1847, and the autumn rains had not let up for two or three days. A little before eight o'clock, a man flung open the front shoji of a household-goods store in Honjo's Kawaramachi neighborhood and dashed inside. Probably someone wanting some candles in a hurry, the mistress of the shop thought to herself. But the man, who was gasping for breath, asked for water. Then the woman caught sight of his face in the dim light of an oil lamp and let out a shriek. He was bleeding profusely from his forehead, his cheeks, and his neck, and his sidelocks were disheveled. A strange man bursting into the shop on a dark night with tousled hair and a bloody face — it was enough to give anyone a fright. Hearing his wife's cry, the proprietor emerged from the back of the house. His reaction, as a member of the stronger sex, was more muted.

"My, what's happened to you?" he asked the man forthrightly.

"Something flew at me from out of the darkness as I was walking along the canal toward Genmori Bridge. I couldn't see what it was, but it landed on top of my umbrella and did this to me."

Upon hearing his explanation, the woman and her husband seemed to relax.

"Ah, that would have been a river otter," the proprietor told him. "There's a nasty one that lives around here and sometimes does mischief. It happens all the time on rainy nights like this. Jumped on your umbrella and scratched your face, did it?"

"I guess so. I was in such a panic I didn't know what was happening."

Without further ado, the kindly couple brought some water, washed the blood off the man's face, and applied some ointment they had in the house. The man looked to be a merchant in his early fifties and was quite well-dressed.

"What a nasty accident. Where were you headed this evening?" the woman asked, lighting a pipe.

"Why, I was on my way to this very neighborhood."

"And you live . . ."

"In Shitaya."

"Well, you won't get very far with your umbrella all torn up like that."

"I can get a palanquin on the other side of Azuma Bridge," he replied. "Well, I'm sorry to have put you both to so much trouble."

The man handed the proprietor's wife a silver coin — a token of his appreciation he said. She tried to refuse it, but he was insistent. In the end, she gave him a new candle, which he placed in his lantern and, holding his battered umbrella over his head, set off into the rainy night. He had not gone very far when he turned around and went back to the shop. Standing in the doorway, he said to them quietly, "Please don't tell anyone about what happened tonight."

"No, of course not," the husband replied.

The next day, a retired tool merchant by the name of Jūemon who lived on Onari Street in Shitaya filed a report at his local watchpost. In it, he stated that he had been attacked while walking near the canal in Kawaramachi. The assailant had stolen his money pouch and inflicted multiple wounds to his face. In response to his report, two senior inspectors on duty in the City Magistrate's Office set out for Shitaya to look into the matter. The alleged attack had occurred in the vicinity of Lord Mito's estate, so the investigation was given high priority. Jūemon was called back to the watchpost for further questioning.

"Hanshichi, go ahead and ask your questions," the assistant magistrate said to the detective, whom he had brought along with him.

"Yes, sir. Now, Jūemon, this is an official inquiry. What you say must be the truth, the whole truth, and nothing but the truth." With this reminder, he asked the merchant for a full account of what had occurred the previous night. "Where were you headed and what was your purpose?" he began.

"I had gone to call on Lord Ōtsuki, a *hatamoto* residing in

Honjo's Motomachi neighborhood, on behalf of my son. I received payment in the amount of fifty *ryō* for some tools he had delivered to his lordship recently.

"If you were returning from Motomachi, I would have expected you to cross Genmori Bridge directly without walking along the canal. Did you go anywhere else before heading home?"

"Yes. I'm embarrassed to admit it, but I stopped to see a woman named Omoto who lives in Kawaramachi."

"You've been looking after this Omoto woman?"

"That's correct."

Jūemon had been seeing Omoto for over three years, but, according to him, she was a venal woman who was constantly trying to squeeze more money out of him. The previous night when he had visited her, he'd found her with a young man named Masakichi, whom she introduced as her cousin. She had insisted that Jūemon have a drink with them, but being a teetotaler he stubbornly refused. Then Omoto began pestering him to buy her some new clothes for winter. "C'mon," she said, "it'll be getting cold soon." But again he refused, saying he couldn't afford it at the moment, and then he'd left. It was on his way home, down by the canal, that the unfortunate incident had occurred. He knew that river otters had been seen around there before, so at first he assumed that one of them was responsible. But back home, he found that his pouch containing the fifty *ryō* for his son was missing. Thus he reasoned that it must not have been a river otter after all. "And I decided to file a report," he concluded nervously.

"How old is this Omoto?"

"She's nineteen. She lives with her mother."

"And her cousin Masakichi?"

"Twenty-one or -two, I'd guess. I understand he comes to the house quite a lot, but I'd never met him before last night, so I really don't know anything about him."

The inquiry concluded, Jūemon was shown out of the room. Based on his testimony, the inspectors' suspicions naturally fell on the nineteen-year-old Omoto and her putative cousin, Masa-kichi, who was undoubtedly her lover. They had probably found out about the money Jūemon was carrying and followed him in order to steal it. The two senior inspectors were unanimous in this assessment. Hanshichi himself could not think of a bet-ter explanation, but the simple fact that the money was miss-ing did not automatically mean that Omoto was guilty. Jūemon might have dropped it on his way home — or, indeed, carelessly left it inside the palanquin. Either way, Hanshichi decided he would pay a visit to Kawaramachi and find out all he could about Omoto.

Leaving the watchpost, Hanshichi first went to see the doctor who had treated Jūemon's wounds. The man was unwilling to give a definitive opinion on how they had been inflicted; he con-jectured that Jūemon had either been scratched repeatedly by a sharp set of claws or perhaps stabbed indiscriminately with some sort of small, blunt knife. Hanshichi left without having gained any insight into the matter.

In such criminal investigations, doctors in those days tended to be wary of committing themselves to any particular diagnosis for fear of getting into trouble later on. "It doesn't seem to make sense in this day and age," old Hanshichi commented, "but back then I was always running up against that sort of thing."

[4]

Had Omoto's lover attacked Jūemon and stolen his money, or had the merchant dropped his pouch somewhere along the way after having been wounded by a river otter? It had to be one or the other. Hanshichi headed over to Kawaramachi and made inquiries about Omoto's reputation in the neighborhood. He found that she was not the bad woman that Jūemon had made her out to be. Word had it that her older brother had died some years back, and that she used the money she received from the retired gentleman in Shitaya to take care of her elderly mother.

She was generally said to be high-minded and well-mannered, unlike other young women of her social class.

Hanshichi was rather puzzled by this latest information. He decided that the next thing was to go and confront Omoto herself. When he arrived at her house, a slightly built girl with a fair complexion answered the door. It was Omoto.

"Was the retired gentleman from Shitaya here last night?" Hanshichi asked lightly.

"Yes."

"Stayed long, did he?"

"No, he just came to the door," Omoto answered evasively, blushing slightly.

"So he went home without coming inside? Does he always do that?"

"No . . ."

"There was someone here last night by the name of Masakichi. Is he your cousin?"

Omoto hesitated, remaining silent.

It's no good beating around the bush, Hanshichi thought to himself, so he went ahead and identified himself.

"This is an official investigation, miss, so you'd better come clean. Masakichi went out somewhere after Jūemon left, didn't he?"

Omoto remained uncomfortably quiet.

"Don't hold back on me, Omoto. I won't mince words with you — Jūemon was attacked on his way home last night. Somebody beat him up pretty bad and took his money pouch. I've come to find out who did it. If I learn you're hiding something from me, you'll have a lot to answer for later. Better tell me everything you know, for your own sake."

Hanshichi gave her an intimidating glare that made Omoto blanch. No, she stated in a quavering voice, Masakichi had not gone out last night. From her nervous manner, Hanshichi immediately guessed that she was lying. "Really?" he prompted her. She repeated her assertion. But her face, which was looking more and more ashen by the minute, almost like a death mask, drew his attention. He could not bring himself to believe her.

"I'll ask you one more time. Are you sure you know nothing about this?"

"Yes . . ."

"Fine. If you insist on lying, you leave me no choice. There's no point in sitting here and talking about it any further. You'll have to come with me."

Hanshichi grabbed Omoto by the hand and was about to haul her out of the house when a woman of about fifty rushed into the room and seized the sleeve of his kimono. It was Omoto's mother, Oishi.

"Inspector, please wait! I'll tell you everything — you must forgive my daughter!"

"If you speak the truth, you'll be judged mercifully."

"The fact of the matter is, Masakichi *is* my nephew — he's a roof tiler. I promised to let him marry Omoto one day, but our financial situation being what it is, right now she has a patron who gives her a monthly allowance. My nephew came by last night while Omoto and I were sitting by the stove talking. To be frank, we were complaining that the gentleman from Shitaya is dreadfully tightfisted. He never gives us a penny more than the agreed monthly allowance, and now that the weather's turning cold, we'll soon be in a real fix. Just then the gentleman showed up, but either he overheard what we were saying from outside or he was put out to find that Masakichi was here, because he refused to come inside and rushed off with hardly a word. It was obvious he was upset about something, and I started to worry that we'd never see him again. Then we would *really* be in a fix. Masakichi was worried for us, too — he said it would be his fault if the master had gotten the wrong idea about him and gone off in a huff. So he said he'd go and call the gentleman back and explain everything to him. I tried to stop him, but he wouldn't listen. He grabbed his lantern and rushed out."

"Hmm . . . I see. Then what happened?"

"After a while my nephew came back..." Oishi said. She paused for a moment, but then, making up her mind, she continued with her story. "He said he'd lost sight of the master in the dark and rain. But then he said he found something on the ground — two gold coins."

Having listened sympathetically to his aunt's and cousin's complaints earlier in the evening, Masakichi produced the two coins and told them to use the money to buy themselves some winter clothes. But the honest Oishi and her daughter had felt uncomfortable about accepting the money. "Finder's keepers is what I always say," Masakichi had said wryly, urging them again to take it. They stubbornly refused. In the end, he'd lost his temper, grabbed the coins, and rushed out without a word. Despite Masakichi's claim to have found the coins, Oishi and her daughter had their doubts about the source of the money. They had been speculating about the matter that morning when Hanshichi came to make his inquiries.

"I see. Well, thanks for giving a statement. I'll leave your daughter with you for the time being, then. But don't go anywhere," he advised them. "I may need to ask you some more questions later."

Hanshichi now understood why Omoto had been protecting Masakichi. The two had been promised to one another, but because of her desperate financial circumstances, Omoto had betrayed her fiancé and taken another man as a patron. Even so, she'd covered up for Masakichi without fear of the consequences to herself. There was something about it all that Hanshichi found extremely touching. The two women were so honest that he felt safe leaving the two of them on their own. On his way home, he stopped in at the local headman's house and asked him to keep a discreet eye on them.

The next morning, Hanshichi's deputy, Shōta, arrested Masakichi as he was exiting the main gate of the Yoshiwara in the rain. Hanshichi was waiting at headquarters when Shōta brought him in, and the detective immediately proceeded to question him.

Regarding the source of the gold coins, Masakichi's statement corroborated that given by Oishi the day before: "The night before last I rushed off after the gentleman from Shitaya. I'd just reached the canal at Genmori Bridge when I noticed something shiny on the ground near the tip of my clog. I shone my lantern on it and saw two gold coins lying there in the rain. I guess I should have reported it to the watchpost, but I knew the money would mean a lot to my aunt and my cousin because they're so hard up right now. Luckily, there was no one else around, so I picked up the money and returned to the house. But those two were too honest to accept it . . . said it made them feel 'uncomfortable.' In the end, I got fed up. Suit yourselves, I said, and I took the money and left. Then I went to the Yoshiwara to enjoy myself. Since I found the money, I didn't consider it stealing."

In at least one respect Masakichi took after his aunt — he was an honest working-class type. Hanshichi didn't believe he was lying. And yet, even in those days, people knew better than to keep something they had found. It was the law of the land that one had to report lost property to the nearest watchpost. Even so, Hanshichi was not about simply to accept Masakichi at his word, and he decided to take him to the watchpost in Shitaya and have him confront Jūemon.

When they arrived, Jūemon admitted to recognizing Masakichi. Likewise, Masakichi admitted to recognizing Jūemon. But the retired merchant had been too flustered at the time of the assault to get a look at his assailant. Hanshichi was stumped. Then he suddenly remembered something.

"Someone who works in your son's shop said that despite the very serious injuries to your face and neck, most of the bleeding had stopped by the time you returned home," he said to Jūemon. "Did you receive treatment for your wounds along the way?"

"Well, when I reached Asakusa they gave me some water at the place where I hired a palanquin."

"Yes, I suppose that's true, but didn't you also stop for water at a household-goods store in Kawaramachi?"

Jūemon seemed taken aback. He looked down at the ground and did not answer.

"I don't see why you're hiding it. The household-goods store is the only place open around there at that time of night, so I went to ask if they knew anything. The proprietor and his wife were evasive at first, but in the end they came clean. The missus told me you even gave her a silver coin. That silver coin came from your money pouch, didn't it?"

"No, I had a separate coin purse with me. My other pouch had been attached to a string around my neck."

"Is that so? But then, like I said, why did you pay the household-goods dealer hush money?"

"I simply thought it would reflect badly on me if word about the incident got out. But when I discovered I'd lost the money, I knew I couldn't keep quiet any longer. I do apologize for causing you so much trouble."

Jūemon cast glances at Masakichi as he spoke, and the jealous glint in his eye did not escape Hanshichi's notice. He quickly guessed that the merchant had conspired to frame Masakichi for the theft. An old man's jealousy over his young mistress — in Hanshichi's estimation, that was what was at the root of the case.

But it was clear that Jūemon's testimony was not a complete fabrication, as witnessed by Masakichi's finding the two gold coins. So how much of Jūemon's story was true and how much of Masakichi's? Hanshichi found it difficult to gauge the veracity of their respective claims. Deciding he would get no more information out of them that day, he sent Jūemon back home and had Masakichi remanded over to police headquarters in Hatchōbori.

As things stood at that moment, Masakichi was in a very tight spot. No matter how much he proclaimed his innocence, there was still the evidence of the two gold coins he had kept, and it seemed unlikely that he could dispel doubts about his role. But luck was on his side. From the canal just below Genmori Bridge, a silent witness came forward to reveal the truth: a large river otter whose body was found floating in the water, a cord wound tightly around its neck. At the end of the cord was a pouch containing forty *ryō* in gold coins.

The husband and wife who owned the household-goods shop had been right when they guessed that Jūemon had been attacked by a river otter on that dark and rainy night. The mischievous creature had jumped onto his umbrella and scratched wildly at his face. As it did so, the cord of Jūemon's pouch had gotten caught on one of its claws and become entangled around the otter's neck. In the process, two of the coins had spilled from the pouch's opening. With the pouch hanging from its neck, the creature dove back into the canal, and the weight of the remaining coins pulled the cord tight. Desperately trying to free itself, the creature thrashed about with its front legs, but had merely succeeded in becoming more ensnared. The river otter had ended up strangling itself.

But the river otter's body did not float to the surface right away because of the heavy weight around its neck. When the rain finally let up four or five days later, the water level of the canal slowly began to ebb. As it did, the river otter's tail and legs became visible in the shallows near the water's edge, thereby testifying to Masakichi's innocence. The young man was let go with only a stern reprimand.

It turned out that Jūemon had suspected from the very beginning that his assailant was a river otter. But an idea popped into his head when he discovered that his money pouch was missing as he went to give the woman in the household-goods shop something by way of thanks. His jealousy prompted a desire for revenge: even if he could not frame Masakichi for the crime itself, at least the young man would be hauled into the watchpost under a cloud of suspicion — perhaps even bound and thrown into jail. It was a cruel, calculating plan whereby Jūemon would watch from a distance as Masakichi was subjected to hardships and humiliation.

Lacking incontrovertible evidence, however, Hanshichi could not bring any actual charges against Jūemon. But with Masakichi's innocence proven, Hanshichi treated Jūemon with the utmost contempt. For his part, the retired merchant must have felt ashamed about what he had done, for in the end he handed the forty *ryō* that had been recovered over to Omoto as severance money.

And once they had become husband and wife, Omoto and Masakichi dropped in on Hanshichi to thank him personally. . . .

"so I've prattled on and on again as usual. I know a few other stories concerning Mukōjima — about *kappa* and snakes that were caught here. But I'll save those for some other time. No, no . . . let me pay for the tea. You mustn't embarrass an old man like me," Hanshichi pulled a coarse cotton coin purse from the breast of his kimono and placed some money on the table.

In unison, the teashop waitress and I bowed politely.

"Well, shall we be going?" Hanshichi said. "Mukōjima's changed a lot since the old days, hasn't it?" he added as we went on our way.

[As the old man takes in the scene around him, a steam whistle at a factory somewhere in the distance echoes through the treetops. The curtain falls.]

In the old days, such a shrill sound would never have been heard in the kabuki theater. Mukōjima had indeed changed, I thought.

The Mansion of Morning Glories

ASAGAO YASHIKI

[1]

t was 1856—the sixteenth day of the eleventh month, if I'm not mistaken. A fire broke out in the Yanagiwara section of Kanda at about four in the morning. Four or five houses burned down before it was brought under control. Since I had an acquaintance in the neighborhood, I made my way through the dim light of early morning to see if he was safe, and stayed and chatted for a while before wending my way home. Then I took my morning dip at the bathhouse and ate breakfast, by which time it must have been nearly eight o'clock. A messenger arrived from headquarters in Hatchōbori saying that my boss, Chief Inspector Makihara, wanted me to come over right away. Wondering what he wanted at that time of the morning, I got ready to go out."

Old Hanshichi paused for a moment, the highly expressive corners of his eyes crinkling slightly as though he were conjuring up the memory of that moment long ago.

"The boss's house was on Tamagoya New Road. As I passed through the gate of his official residence, I saw the familiar face of Tokuzō, one of his attendants, who was standing at the entrance to the house. 'Hurry up and get inside,' he said. 'The boss is waiting.' I was shown straight through to a back room where Makihara was seated across from a very distinguished-looking samurai of about forty. This gentleman introduced himself as the steward of a *hatamoto* by the name of Sugino who lived in

Banchō and had an income of 850 *koku*. He handed me a calling card that read 'Nakashima Kakuemon.' I was in the process of reciprocating the courtesy when Makihara interrupted impatiently. 'The fact is,' he said, 'this gentleman has come in regard to a very delicate matter. It would be most unfortunate if it were to become public, so he wants us to conduct our investigation in the utmost secrecy. I'm sorry to spring this on you so close to the end of the year, Hanshichi, but I want you to take in all the particulars and give this job your full attention.' 'I am at your service,' I replied.

"The gist of Kakuemon's story was as follows."

IT HAD ALL BEGUN eight days earlier. Around that time every year, the Confucian school in Ochanomizu held its annual reading exams. These exams were administered to the sons of *hatamoto* and of *gokenin*.[1] According to the custom of the day, all boys from samurai families, regardless of rank, had to appear at the school when they were twelve or thirteen years old to be tested on the Nine Chinese Classics.[2] One was not considered a full-fledged samurai until one had demonstrated the ability to read through the texts without stumbling over the words. Samurai families were grouped according to rank, and one month before the exam an application had to be submitted to the head of one's group, whereupon a notice would be sent out telling the child to appear at the school by nine o'clock on the morning of the day. Each year there would be anywhere from a couple of dozen to as many as several hundred boys taking the exam. On the appointed day, the boys would arrive at the South Hall of the

1. Generally speaking, shogunal retainers with incomes of less than 200 *koku*.

2. *Shisho-gokyō*, sometimes called the Four Books and the Five Classics. The Four Books are the *Great Learning*, the *Doctrine of the Mean*, Confucius' *Analects*, and the *Mencius*. The Five Classics are the *I Ching*, the *Book of Odes*, the *Classic of Rites*, the *Classic of History*, and the *Spring and Autumn Annals*.

school, where one by one they would be called before the board of examiners, headed by Chief Scholar Lord Hayashi. There they would sit at a long, Chinese-style desk and be asked to read passages from the classics. The highest-scoring pupils received prizes of silver bars or bolts of cloth of a material befitting their rank.

Although the exam officially began at nine o'clock, the examinees were expected by long-established custom to enter the school gate by six. This meant that children who lived far away had to leave home before dawn. Even sons of samurai are at their most unruly at that age, and with so many together in one place, the din in the waiting area was overwhelming. Their samurai attendants would alternately threaten and cajole them in a strenuous effort to pacify their charges. The children wore short-sleeved jackets of black silk embroidered with their family crests, stiff-shouldered overgarments, and split skirts. Those from families whose status permitted them to have audiences with the shogun[3] wore a more formal version of this, made of finer material and more varied in color.

The son of Kakuemon's master, Sugino Daizaburō, was thirteen that year and had applied to take the exam. He stood out among the other families of his rank, being renowned for his handsome looks. A dashing figure in his black, stiff-shouldered overgarment and yellowish-green skirt, with his bangs combed over his forehead, Daizaburō on the day of the exam might well have been Rikiya in the kabuki play *A Treasury of Loyal Retainers*.[4] As the son of a high-ranking samurai, he had been accompanied by two men: a twenty-seven-year-old page named Yamazaki Heisuke and Matazō, a house servant. They had left

---

3. This privilege was called *ome-mie* (setting eyes upon [the shogun]) and was accorded only to *hatamoto,* who were referred to as *ome-mie-ijō* (above *ome-mie*). Gokenin, by contrast, were termed *ome-mie-ika* (beneath *ome-mie*).

4. The son of Oboshi Yuranosuke whose romance with Konami, daughter of Honzo, is one of the subplots of the play.

the mansion in Banchō at a little past four in the morning. There was a nip in the air that stung their eyes. Matazō had led the way carrying a lantern that bore the Sugino family crest, the morning frost scrunching beneath their straw sandals as the three of them walked.

The winter night had still not ended when the trio crossed Suido Bridge. As though frozen in place, a solitary pale star twinkled among the upper branches of a dark pine. Enveloped in a grayish mist, the surface of the river flowing from Ochanomizu reflected not a glimmer of light. The frost seemed to be especially thick in that spot, lying like a blanket of snow over the withered reeds growing along the high riverbank. From somewhere they heard the mournful cry of a fox. Their breath turned white before their faces as they clambered up the bank. Just then, Heisuke slipped on a patch of frost and, as he tried to recover his footing, one of the straps on his new straw sandals broke.

"What a nuisance! Matazō, shine your lantern over here."

While the servant held out his lantern, Heisuke crouched down at the foot of the bank and tugged at the strap of his sandal. "Okay," he said, once he had managed to mend it, glancing over his shoulder at where Daizaburō should have been standing. But the boy was nowhere to be seen. The two men were startled. How typical of a child to have left them and gone on ahead, they thought, and so they set off after him, calling out the young master's name as they went. But their walking half a block turned up no trace of him, and call as they might, they got no response. All they heard was the occasional cry of a fox.

"Do you suppose he's been bewitched by a fox?" Matazō asked, looking very uneasy.

"Don't be ridiculous!" Heisuke laughed scornfully. But he himself could think of no better explanation. Daizaburō had vanished in the short space of time he had spent fixing his sandal, with Matazō holding the lantern for him and looking down. The boy could not have gone very far. He should have answered when they called his name. There was no one about at that predawn hour who could have snatched the handsome youth and run off with him. Heisuke was at a complete loss.

"You know how kids are. He probably got cold and ran on ahead."

It was no good standing around wondering what to do, so the two of them hurried on toward the school. But when they arrived the official in charge told them that Master Sugino Daizaburō had not yet shown up. Again, the two men were dismayed. There was nothing for them to do but turn around and retrace their steps. They searched the route they had come by, but still no sign of the boy.

Eventually, even Heisuke began to have his doubts. "Maybe he really was bewitched by a fox — or perhaps spirited away," he said.

In those days, it was common for people to believe in spirit abductions.[5] It was not only children — even people well on in years might suddenly disappear and not be heard from for five days, ten days, sometimes half a month or more. In some cases it might even be six months to a year. Then, one day, they would suddenly reappear out of nowhere and wander back home. In rare cases, the person might be found passed out on the ground in front of their house, or perhaps standing in a daze outside the back door. In exceptional cases, someone might be spotted up on his own roof, laughing his head off. After being nursed back to health, most of them, if asked what had happened to them, would answer that they felt as though they'd awoken from a dream and were unable to remember anything. Others would say something about a strange mountain ascetic leading them deep into the hills. It was widely held that these "mountain ascetics" were in fact *tengu*. So while in principle Heisuke believed that a samurai should not believe such fantastic tales, doubts began to creep

---

5. *Kami-kakushi*, literally "hidden by the gods," most commonly used to refer to the disappearance of children.

into his mind: perhaps, in this case, the lord's son really had been spirited away by a *tengu – cum*-mountain ascetic?

Whatever the case, the crux of the matter was that the two men, having left home with the young master and then lost track of him, could not calmly go back to the mansion as though nothing had happened. Under the circumstances, Heisuke, to say nothing of Matazō, would be obliged to commit seppuku to atone for their negligence. The two men paled at the thought.

"This is it, then," they sighed. "The only thing we can do is return to the mansion and tell them the truth."

Steeling himself for the worst, Heisuke turned back in the direction of the house together with Matazō. They had spent quite a lot of time going to and fro, and by the time they dragged their tired feet across Suido Bridge, Matazō's candle had almost burned itself out. This time, it was a rooster, not a fox, whose cry they heard.

The strange report they made on returning to the Sugino estate threw the entire household into a panic. His lordship, Dainoshin, forbade anyone to speak of the matter, saying they must not irresponsibly broadcast the news to the world. A notice was sent to the school saying that Daizaburō had suddenly been taken ill and was withdrawing from the examination. Heisuke and Matazō were of course reproached in the harshest terms for this dereliction of their duty, but being an understanding man, his lordship had no desire to inflict any more severe retribution upon the two hapless servants. "Just see to it that you find my son as soon as you can," he commanded them.

Since Heisuke and Matazō were the ones responsible for the young master's disappearance, it naturally fell to them to track him down. They were not alone, of course. The members of the household split up and searched everywhere they could think of. The boy's mother arranged to have prayers said for him at the Hachiman Shrine in Ichigaya where she normally worshipped, as well as at the family's tutelary shrine in Nagatachō. One of the maidservants was sent running to consult a famous fortune-teller. While on the surface the household appeared to go about its business exactly as normal, underneath it was utter pandemonium.

In this way, three days passed, then five, and still they were no closer to learning what had become of the handsome Daizaburō. His lordship and his retainers had exhausted all the means at their disposal. Finally, the conclusion that an internal investigation alone would not solve anything had brought the steward Kakuemon discreetly to Hatchōbori to see Chief Inspector Makihara that morning. Kakuemon entreated him to investigate the matter in secret.

"The family's honor is at stake. Please use your utmost discretion," he stressed again and again.

"I understand."

Hanshichi then asked Kakuemon for a physical description of the boy so that he could recognize him. Next, he asked the steward to describe Daizaburō's personality and behavior, whereupon Kakuemon related proudly how the boy had learned to write at the age of five and had begun to study the classics at seven. His skills at reading and writing were such that when he had applied to take the examination, he had requested to be given unannotated copies of all of the required texts.[6]

From the tone of Kakuemon's remarks, Hanshichi received the impression that Daizaburō was a bit of a bookworm, something to be expected in a boy of his intelligence. His appearance and disposition, it seemed, were both highly pleasing.

"Does the young master have any brothers or sisters?"

"No, he's the sole heir. So you can understand why his lordship first and foremost, and indeed all of us, are in such a state."

An anxious look darkened the loyal steward's brow.

---

6. As the texts were written in Chinese, annotated texts *(tenbon)* contained phonetic syllables *(kana)* that enabled readers to pronounce Chinese characters in Japanese and a system of punctuation *(kaeriten)* to reconstruct sentences according to Japanese grammar.

[2]

Spirit abduction — Hanshichi, a product of the Edo era, was not entirely sure that such things were impossible. In this world, he believed, nothing was too strange to dismiss entirely. If this was indeed a case of spirit abduction, then it was quite beyond Hanshichi's powers to solve. But if there was some other explanation, he was confident of his ability to root it out. In any case, Hanshichi promised Kakuemon as he left that he would do his best.

He pondered the matter on his way home. By its very nature, the mansion of a *hatamoto* was a secretive world, closed to outsiders. It had seemed that the steward was being completely open with them, yet it was undeniable that Kakuemon would never have revealed anything potentially damaging to Lord Sugino; the possibility that there was more to the matter than met the eye could not be ruled out. If Hanshichi blindly based his assumptions on Kakuemon's story, there was a good chance he would go barking up the wrong tree. At the very least, he would be operating with blinders on if he did not head over to Banchō and make some inquiries about Lord Sugino's household for himself. So, on returning home, he immediately set out again and made his way up Kudan Hill.

When Hanshichi reached Banchō with its rows of samurai residences, he found Sugino's mansion to be an imposing edifice adjacent to a vacant area of reclaimed land. It was a little past noon and the winter sunshine shone brightly into the south-facing windows of the simple structures that were the servants' quarters. Just at that moment, a saké merchant making his rounds emerged from the gate. Hanshichi drew him aside and began inquiring discreetly as to the state of affairs inside the house, but the man's answers provided little useful information. However, Hanshichi had an acquaintance in the household of the neighborhood fire marshal, and it occurred to him that he might find out more over there. He left the saké merchant and had walked about fifty feet when he spotted a young woman who had just emerged from the large mansion next door, looking slightly flushed and carrying a set of stacked lacquer boxes.

"Hey, isn't that Oroku?"

Hearing her name, the young woman came to a halt. She was short and plump with a face like a toad plastered in white makeup. Strips of red cloth hung from the bangs over her forehead.

"My! — if it isn't the inspector from Mikawachō!" Oroku exclaimed coquettishly. "How've you been lately?"

"I see you're in a good mood today."

"Oh?" Oroku said, pressing the cuffs of her kimono against her cheeks. "Am I that red? They forced me to have a cup of saké in there just now."

She was one of those women who frequented the quarters of the low-ranking samurai within the great mansions of Edo. The boxes she carried contained edibles such as sushi, teacakes, and the like, but they were not the only things she had come to sell. She was far from being an attractive woman; but be it sweetmeats or sexual favors, she made up for her lack of beauty with rouge and powder, using her feminine wiles to satisfy her hungry customers. It was a stroke of luck running into Oroku here, Hanshichi thought. He pulled her aside and whispered in her ear, "Oroku, I suppose you often visit Lord Sugino's mansion, too?"

"No. I've never been there — not once."

"Oh, I see," Hanshichi said, clearly disappointed.

"I mean, everyone knows the place is haunted."

"Huh? A haunted house, is it?" Hanshichi cocked his head to one side. "Haunted by what?"

"I don't know what, but you won't catch me in there. People call it the 'Mansion of Morning Glories' — it's famous around here."

The Mansion of Morning Glories — the name jogged something in Hanshichi's memory. He'd often heard people speak of a haunted mansion called the Mansion of Morning Glories in

Banchō, but he hadn't realized it was Lord Sugino's place they were talking about. "Mansion of Morning Glories," "House of Blood" — tales of haunted houses in the upper-class areas of Edo abounded during that era. At the Mansion of Morning Glories, according to rumor, a distant ancestor of the current lord had once struck his mistress down with his sword for committing some minor offense. It had happened at the height of summer, and when the mistress was killed she had been wearing a light cotton kimono dyed with a morning-glory pattern. Thereafter, the house had suffered under a strange curse: whenever the morning glories in the garden bloomed, some calamity befell the family. Consequently, from summer until fall each year, the lord instructed his retainers to roam the sprawling estate — and even the vacant land next door — diligently pulling up any flowering vine they could lay their hands on, be it a morning glory, an evening face, or anything of that variety. It was even said that a merchant had been barred from coming to the house ever again after once presenting his lordship, as the customary midsummer's gift, with a paper fan depicting morning glories! Hanshichi had known of such rumors for ages, but it was news to him that Lord Sugino's residence was the place in question.

"I see. So *that's* the Mansion of Morning Glories."

"I've never heard of anything bad happening to outsiders, but all the same, it gives me the willies to think of going into an old haunted house like that," Oroku said, frowning.

"Yes, I suppose it would."

As he was speaking, Hanshichi glanced over and saw a samurai emerge from the main gate of the Sugino mansion and walk off silently in the direction of Kudan Hill. From his appearance, he looked to be a page.

"Oroku, do you know him?" Hanshichi asked, motioning toward the man with his chin.

"I've never actually spoken to him, but I hear his name's Yamazaki."

Hanshichi realized immediately that it must be Heisuke, the

page of whom the steward had spoken earlier. He bade Oroku goodbye and set off after him. Choosing a moment when they were both walking beside a long stretch of wall where there were few other passersby, he called out to Heisuke. "Excuse me! Excuse me, sir. Sorry to bother you, but you're from Lord Sugino's residence, aren't you?"

"That's correct," Heisuke answered, turning around.

"The fact is, your lordship's steward told me just this morning about the situation that's arisen there. I was most sorry to hear of it."

Heisuke watched Hanshichi cautiously while the latter described his meeting with Kakuemon. When Hanshichi had finished, he asked whether it was Yamazaki Heisuke to whom he was speaking. It was, Heisuke replied, but the look of uneasiness in his eyes did not abate as he stared into the face of the detective standing before him.

"Have you come across any clues as to the young master's whereabouts, sir?" Hanshichi asked.

"None at all, I'm afraid," Heisuke replied curtly.

"I wonder if it's a case of spirit abduction?"

"Well, I suppose that's not out of the question."

"Not much we can do if that's the case. Can you think of any other possibilities?"

"No, none."

Hanshichi followed this up with two or three more questions, but in keeping with the tone of Heisuke's perfunctory greeting, the page's whole manner showed that he was eager to avoid saying anything further. Kakuemon had bowed and scraped in seeking Hanshichi's help, and insofar as Heisuke was the person responsible for the whole unfortunate affair, one might have expected that he would turn to Hanshichi for support, confiding everything in him and asking for his advice. Instead, Heisuke eyed him with consistent suspicion and kept his remarks to an absolute minimum — but why? Hanshichi was puzzled. If worse came to worst, Heisuke might have to commit seppuku in order to make amends. His cold attitude toward Hanshichi therefore seemed quite extraordinary. Hanshichi scrutinized the man more carefully.

Heisuke was twenty-six or -seven years old, rather slightly built, and fair-complexioned. He had a steely gaze and the crafty look common to samurai of his station who served in the great houses of Edo. From years of experience, Hanshichi could tell at a glance that he wasn't the sort of numbskull who, charged with looking after his master's son, would lose track of him and then go on his merry way as though nothing had happened. This alone was enough to set off alarm bells in Hanshichi's mind.

"Well, as I just said, provided this isn't a real case of spirit abduction, I'll find that boy — mark my words. You needn't worry about that, sir," said Hanshichi briskly, as though covertly testing the other's reaction.

"So, have you any leads?" Heisuke shot back.

"Well, I haven't got my eyes on anyone just yet, but when you've been in this line of work as long as I have, you know something will turn up sooner or later. If he's alive, I'll find him."

"Is that so?" Heisuke replied, his eyes still giving nothing away.

"Which way are you heading now?"

"Nowhere in particular. I've just been walking all over Edo, day after day, trying to locate the boy as soon as possible. Please let me know if you find out anything."

"Certainly, sir."

Heisuke said goodbye to Hanshichi and walked briskly off, stopping occasionally and turning to look somewhat anxiously in Hanshichi's direction. The man's air of slyness had aroused Hanshichi's suspicions. But though tempted to go after Heisuke and tail him, he abandoned the idea, knowing that broad daylight did not afford the best opportunity.

[3]

Hanshichi was standing by the corner of an alleyway, contemplating his next move, when who should emerge from it but Oroku, laughing raucously, accompanied by another woman.

"Well, fancy meeting you again," Oroku greeted him, still smiling. Her companion gave him a polite bow.

"It must be fate," Hanshichi said, also smiling.

Oroku's friend was a slender girl of seventeen or eighteen who also carried a set of lacquered boxes. She wore a neat padded kimono of a coarse weave and, like Oroku, had strips of red tie-dyed cloth in her hair, which looked freshly braided. Her only flaw was a rather small nose. Apart from that, her face as a whole was much more attractive than Oroku's.

"Inspector, Yasu here's a regular at the Mansion of Morning Glories," Oroku said teasingly. She smiled and patted the girl on the back.

"Oroku, really!" The girl giggled, shrinking in embarrassment.

"What's the young lady's name again?"

"Yasu . . . that is, her name is Oyasu," Oroku took the girl's hand and held it out toward Hanshichi. "Inspector, give her a little talking-to. All she does is gush about her boyfriend . . . I can't stand it any longer."

"Oh, what nonsense, really!" Oyasu giggled.

Though there were few passersby, Hanshichi cringed at the thought of being seen standing there in the middle of the street listening to a couple of streetwalkers' inane prattle. For once, though, he'd have to make an exception, and he steeled himself for the challenge.

"Well, aren't you the lucky one! I suppose this boyfriend you've been gushing about works at the Mansion of Morning Glories?"

"He does," Oroku put in quickly on the other's behalf. "He's one of his lordship's personal attendants — an older guy, rather stylish. His name's Matazō."

Hanshichi pricked up his ears at the mention of Matazō's name.

"Hmm. Matazō, eh?"

"Do you know him?" Oyasu asked, looking somewhat embarrassed.

"I'm not completely unfamiliar with him," Hanshichi said, with corresponding seriousness. "He's a bit of a gadfly. I'd be wary of him if I were you."

"You're absolutely right," Oyasu nodded her head seriously. "He keeps stringing me along, telling me he's going to have a kimono made for me at the end of the year. I ask you! New Year's is only just around the corner. . . . If he really intends to have a spring kimono made for me, he should act like it and give me one *ryō* at least so I can go into a draper's shop and make a down payment. No one will give me the time of day otherwise. But he just keeps putting me off with whatever lie pops into his head: 'I'll give it to you tomorrow,' he says, or 'You'll get it in a couple of days.' . . . Oh, how I hate him!"

Hanshichi was taken aback at this outpouring of resentment, but nevertheless he tried to respond with a smile.

"There, there. Don't be too hard on him. I understand how you feel, but it's not easy for a man with an annual salary of three *ryō* to come up with one or two *ryō* in cash. You do love him, right? Then you mustn't judge him too harshly."

"But Mata keeps telling me he's going to receive a large sum of money any day now, and that's what's got my hopes up. Or perhaps he's just lying?"

"I wouldn't know how to answer that, but with a man in his position, there must be some truth to what he says. Why don't you just give him a bit more time?"

Seeing Hanshichi in an awkward position, Oroku came to his rescue.

"Come on, now, Yasu. Stop going on like that. You're being a pain in the neck for the inspector. Mata promised he'd give you the money tomorrow, so just relax."

Hanshichi seized this opportunity to prepare his escape. Not wanting the women to think he was rude for leaving in the middle of a conversation, he took two silver coins out of his change purse and handed them to Oroku.

"Here — just something for you to buy yourselves some soba noodles with."

"Oh, how kind! Thank you so much!"

Hanshichi turned and fled, followed by the voices of the two women profusely thanking him. Heisuke's shifty eyes, the rumor of Matazō's expecting a large sum of money, and the eerie tale of the Mansion of Morning Glories — Hanshichi tried various ways of connecting the three things, but nothing leapt to mind. Thrusting his hands into the breast of his kimono, he walked abstractedly down Kudan Hill.

Once at home, he sat down in front of the charcoal brazier and stared pensively at the ashes. The short winter's day was already drawing to a close. After a hasty dinner he went out, once again climbing the long slope to Banchō. As he entered the neighborhood from a side street, the roofs of the great mansions were bathed in the cold colors of dusk. At the ill-fated Mansion of Morning Glories, the great main gate was shut and barred, as though the house were deserted. Approaching, Hanshichi quietly addressed the guard on duty.

"Is Matazō around?"

He had just let Matazō out through the gate, the guard said. No doubt he'd gone to have a drink at a local bar called Fujiya. As for Heisuke, he'd gone out that afternoon and hadn't come back yet. Hanshichi thanked the guard and left.

The street was pitch dark. In the distance he could make out the faint red glow of a candle inside a paper lantern at the corner watchpost. He found the bar the guard had mentioned and peeked in through the entranceway. He saw a young man in the garb of a house servant nibbling on a dish of spicy peppers and sipping with obvious pleasure from a square wooden cup of saké.

Taking out his handkerchief, Hanshichi wrapped it around his head and cheeks, then hid behind a pile of kindling near the doorway and watched the man inside talking and laughing with the bartender. After a while the man got up and left without paying.

"Thanks for tonight. I'll be back in two or three days to pay what I owe for this time and last — with interest!" he said laughing.

He seemed well and truly drunk, happily humming a tune to himself as he walked off into the cold and windy night. Hanshichi trailed after him, walking as stealthily as he could in his straw sandals. The man didn't head for home but, on reaching the top of Kudan Hill, headed south down a street with *hatamoto* residences on one side until he came to the lonely open ground[7] of Chidorigafuchi facing the moat of Edo Castle. Just then, the pale wintry orb of the twenty-sixth-day moon appeared in the tops of some pines on the high bank across the moat, brightly illuminating the white form of another man standing in the open ground on this side. The keen-eyed detective immediately recognized it as none other than Yamazaki Heisuke. What could the two men be meeting to discuss, he wondered? At times like this, a bright moon could be both an advantage and a disadvantage. Hanshichi stole over to a large mansion facing the spot where the men were standing. He knew that the drainage ditch running past its gate was dry, so he got down on all fours and crawled into it. Keeping his face hidden behind a stone post used for tethering horses, he strained to overhear the conversation between the two men.

"Heisuke, it's simply not enough. You gotta help me out here."

"That's the most I can come up with right now. What happened to the five *ryō* I gave you the other day?"

"I lost it all at the fire marshal's place."[8]

---

7. Left undeveloped on purpose to act as a firebreak.

8. A samurai of *hatamoto* rank charged with overseeing fire prevention in his area. Matazō would not have been gambling with the fire marshal himself, but rather the lower-ranking samurai in his household.

"You and your gambling! A fool and his money are soon parted. . . . Idiot!"

"I know, I know. I won't try to make excuses. Now, don't get angry when I say this, but you know that broad I've been see-ing—Oyasu? She's been begging me to buy her a spring out-fit . . . I gave her my word as a man that I'd see to it."

"And what a man you are!" Heisuke retorted mockingly. "If it's a spring kimono she wants, have one made for her."

"Yes, well, that's why I've come to ask you a favor."

"Oh, aren't I lucky? Forget it. I'm not independently wealthy, you know. I've got enough to worry about, what with New Year's coming up, without looking after you as well."

"I'm not asking *you* for anything. Just speak to her ladyship on my behalf."

"How can I keep going to her for money? She's already given us ten *ryō* to settle this affair. You got half of it, so you can't complain."

"I'm not complaining. I'm begging you," Matazō persisted. "C'mon, I just need your help. This woman of mine won't let up —I can't take it any longer. You must have *some* idea what I'm talking about. Can't you find it in your heart to take pity on me?"

Heisuke said nothing, turning a deaf ear to these entreaties. Matazō became agitated and, in his drunkenness, his tone grew more aggressive.

"So you refuse to help, eh? You don't leave me any choice, then. I happen to know that his lordship's steward went to Hatchōbori this morning. I think I'll head over there too and tell them where the young master . . ."

"Threatening me, are you?" Heisuke said, smiling contemptu-ously. "Don't give me that tough-guy act you picked up at some second-rate theater over in Ryōgoku. Save it for someone else. I'm afraid you've come to the wrong place."

The night was still young, but the neighborhood was com-pletely quiet. Hanshichi caught every word of this tit-for-tat as though he were standing right beside the two men. He was

watching, doubtful that the altercation would be settled peace-
fully, when suddenly there was an exchange of sharp words and
the two shapes began grappling with one another. No match for
his opponent in a war of words, Matazō had decided to settle the
matter by brute force. But Heisuke was a samurai and no mean
hand, it seemed, at the martial arts. He pinned his opponent to
the ground and then, taking off one of his heavy winter sandals,
began beating Matazō with it.

"You little sneak! Go to Hatchōbori if you like! We're both of
us only hired help — his lordship will sack us without batting an
eyelid if this affair leaks out. If you've got a problem with that,
you can get lost!"

He brushed the mud off his kimono and calmly walked away,
leaving Oyasu's lover, bruised and battered, cowering on the
ground.

"You don't look too good, Matazō," Hanshichi called out to
him as he emerged from the drainage ditch after Heisuke had
gone.

"Who the hell are you? What business is it of yours?" Matazō
said, staggering to his feet, his face swollen. "If you don't shut
your trap I'll come after *you* next."

"There, there. Calm down," Hanshichi said, smiling. "What
do you say we go have a drink and celebrate better times? I'm
not a total stranger, you know — we've met once or twice at the
fire marshal's house."

Hanshichi removed the handkerchief from around his face.
Looking at him in the moonlight, Matazō gave a start.

"Inspector, it's you!"

[4]

The next morning, Hanshichi went around to Chief Inspector
Makihara's official residence. When he arrived, he again found
Lord Sugino's steward, Kakuemon, present. Ever the loyal ser-
vant, he had stopped by to ask whether they had turned up clues

on anything—however small—the previous day. The chief inspector found the man's impatience a trifle annoying, but seeing how earnest he was, had patiently explained the situation to him. At that very moment, Hanshichi appeared.

"His lordship's steward is still very worried," Makihara said as soon as he saw him. "How about it—have you found out anything yet?"

"Yes. I've got it all figured out," Hanshichi replied matter-of-factly. "You needn't worry any longer."

"You've figured it out?" Kakuemon exclaimed, edging forward eagerly on his knees. "So the young master is . . ."

"At his lordship's residence."

Gaping, Kakuemon stared into Hanshichi's face. Makihara scowled.

"What do you mean? How is that possible?"

"There's a samurai by the name of Yamazaki Heisuke in his lordship's employ, correct? The man who was accompanying the young master the other morning. I suppose he lives in the servants' quarters?"

Kakuemon nodded mechanically.

"You'll find the young master hiding in the closet of Heisuke's room. A street vendor named Oyasu sneaks food in to him three times a day."

Hanshichi's explanation did not seem to convince the two men.

"Why would anyone hide him there?" Makihara asked. "Whose idea was it?"

"Heisuke was following her ladyship's orders."

"Her ladyship!" Kakuemon echoed, more astonished than ever.

The news was so unexpected that even Chief Inspector Makihara, who thought he'd heard and seen everything, was left looking rather dazed. He sat there mute, eyes wide open, like a wooden puppet. Hanshichi continued to explain.

"I hesitate to bring this up," Hanshichi went on, "but his

lordship's residence is well known as the 'Mansion of Morning Glories.' I understand that the family has a profound abhorrence for that flower. But it seems that this past summer, one white flower bloomed in the garden. . . ."

Kakuemon made a sour face and nodded.

"In other words," said Hanshichi matter-of-factly, "that flower was the cause of the incident."

When the flower had bloomed in the garden, the whole household had felt anxious, convinced that some misfortune would befall the family. His lordship, however, had shrugged it off, not being one to pay heed to such things. In contrast, her ladyship had taken it to heart. She worried herself sick, praying day and night that nothing bad would happen. Then, the previous month, a very small incident pushed her to the end of her rope.

This is what had happened. One day, Master Daizaburō had gone with Matazō to visit one of the boy's relatives who lived in Akasaka. On their way home, they had passed a small compound of buildings in which several *gokenin* lived, men with incomes of just thirty to sixty bales of rice. Outside in the street, a group of four or five children were playing, the oldest of them a boy of about thirteen. In the excitement of the game, one of the children had run straight into Daizaburō and the two had landed in a heap by the side of the road.

Although quite aware that the child had not done it on purpose, Matazō voiced some insult about the child being from a humble family and accused him of knocking his young master down deliberately. He grabbed the child by the scruff of the neck and began slapping him. Of course, Matazō had been in the wrong. After all, the children *were* the sons of samurai, and they were enraged that Matazō had arbitrarily struck the boy without first ascertaining who was at fault. To make matters worse, Matazō's remark about the boy's lowly rank served to aggravate their own feelings of jealousy and inferiority toward others of higher status. They immediately summoned all the children within their group of families. Armed with wooden swords, a band of about fifteen of them had raised a war cry and set off in pursuit of Matazō and Daizaburō.

Among them was one youth carrying a spear with a padded tip, who appeared to be the boys' ringleader. Seeing him, Matazō gave a start. 'I suppose it's too late to apologize,' he mumbled, grabbing Daizaburō by the hand and fleeing as fast as he could. Having chased them all the way home, the band of children stood outside the gate of Lord Sugino's mansion, shouting in unison: "We won't forget this! Just wait until the exam!"

Daizaburō's face was white as a sheet as he tumbled through the front door of his house. When news of what had happened reached his mother, her already strained nerves became even more frayed. The children who had chased Daizaburō were all due to take the classics exam the following month. Whenever they gathered together to take the exam, even in the past, children from high-ranking and low-ranking families had not gotten along well with each other. Those whose family status did not permit audiences with the shogun were taunted with the nickname of "squids."[9] Not to be outdone, they retorted by calling the children of loftier status "octopuses." This battle between squids and octopuses went on year after year. Scuffles were frequent — a huge headache for their attendants and the exam officials. It was bad enough when the two groups just happened to run into each other, but much worse when one side lay in wait for the other, intent on getting revenge.

At any given exam, it was obvious that the low-ranking boys would outnumber the high-ranking ones. Lady Sugino might have been less worried if she could have known that her son was bold and confident by nature. But in fact he was gentle and retiring. She was convinced that in this lay the very misfortune foreshadowed by the morning glory that had bloomed that year.

Having already submitted the boy's application to take the

---

9. A pun on the word *ika,* meaning both "beneath" (see n. 3 above) and "squid."

exam, they could not withdraw it without a good explanation. Even if she voiced her concerns to her husband, Lady Sugino knew, given his usual attitude, that he would dismiss them, so she kept her worries bottled up inside. The day of the exam was fast approaching. As her anxiety mounted, she began having bad dreams night after night. She went to her temple and drew her fortune from the fortune-telling box, but even that came up "bad luck." Unable to stand it any longer, Lady Sugino secretly consulted her husband's retainer Heisuke about a way of preventing her son from taking the exam.

The product of this union between a woman's shallow wisdom and a mid-level samurai's mediocre intellect was the farce of Daizaburō's abduction. Because of his role in the earlier incident, Matazō was admitted to the plot over his own objections. The obedient Daizaburō was thoroughly briefed beforehand on what he must do. On the way to the exam, he slipped away and sneaked back into the house, where he was taken to Heisuke's quarters before dawn. The plan was to wait a suitable length of time before producing him in public and fabricating a story about a spirit abduction. To her accomplices in this scheme, Lady Sugino had forked over the sum of twenty-five *ryō,* from which the crafty Heisuke had deducted fifteen before splitting the remaining ten between Matazō and himself.

"For a job like this she gives us a measly ten *ryō?*" Matazō had griped.

"Don't complain. It was all your fault to begin with," Heisuke had countered.

Even so, Matazō had had an inkling that Heisuke was padding his own pocket, and he continued to come up with various excuses to get more money out of him. Being the more resourceful of the two men, Heisuke easily rebuffed his requests. But Matazō's resentment was compounded by distress over his lover Oyasu's repeated importuning. He became increasingly confrontational toward Heisuke, anger written all over his face, until the latter finally got fed up.

"You'll ruin everything if you go blabbing about it all over the house! Meet me tonight by the side of the moat."

The men agreed to meet at sunset at the appointed spot. The result was the scuffle that Hanshichi had witnessed. Afterward, he had concocted some pretext to get Matazō to accompany him to a local restaurant. There, in an upstairs room, Hanshichi had asked him one leading question after another. Finally, Matazō had bitterly recounted the entire story from beginning to end.

". . . Well, that's what happened," said Hanshichi in conclusion. "I hope I've managed to convince you. Seeing that it was all done with her ladyship's consent, I suppose it would only stir up trouble for you if we were to press charges. I'll let you decide how best to tie up any loose ends."

"Well, I can't thank you enough," Kakuemon said, heaving a sigh of relief as though he'd just awoken from a bad dream. "It all makes perfect sense to me now. But what do you suppose is the best way to bring things to a peaceful conclusion?"

Chief Inspector Makihara considered the steward's question carefully.

"Well, I guess spirit abduction is the answer after all!"

Lord Sugino would be most displeased, Makihara pointed out, if the truth were to reach his ears. He advised Kakuemon that it would be best, for the family's sake, to follow through with her ladyship's plan — to call it a spirit abduction and leave it at that.

"I see what you mean," the steward replied.

Kakuemon thanked them profusely and left. About three days later, he showed up at Makihara's residence bearing a substantial gift. He reported that Master Daizaburō had returned home safely.

"so lord sugino never learned what had really happened?" I asked.

"Apparently everyone accepted that the boy had been spirited away," old Hanshichi replied. "But it seems that in the end

Matazō grew uncomfortable, what with Heisuke and the steward giving him dirty looks all the time. So he grabbed something of value from the house and eloped with the street vendor Oyasu."

"And Heisuke continued in service without incident?"

"Now that's what's interesting. About a year later I heard that Lord Sugino had had him executed."

"Did the truth about Daizaburō's abduction come to light?"

"It wasn't as simple as that," the old man said with a wry smile. "You see, a lot of the samurai-for-hire who worked in the great mansions of Edo were unsavory characters. They would try to find a way to exploit people's weaknesses and draw them into their clutches. Terrible things happened. Apparently, after Heisuke was executed, her ladyship was sent back to her parents' house for having, in her maternal distress, fallen under the spell of that evil man. It's really very sad when you think about it. . . ."

"In that case, the curse of the morning glories didn't fall on the son so much as on the mother."

"You're probably right. You know, that house survived up until the Meiji Restoration, but sometime after 1868 it was torn down. Now there's just a row of tenements where it used to stand."

A Cacophony of Cats

NEKO SŌDŌ

[1]

Old Hanshichi had a small tortoiseshell cat. One warm February day I happened to stop by his house and found him outside on the south-facing verandah, stroking the small, furry creature curled up on his lap.

"What an adorable cat," I remarked.

"You say that because he's still just a kitten," Hanshichi replied smiling. "He hasn't even learned to kill mice yet."

The bright midday sun shone on the old roof tiles of the house next door; from somewhere there arose the clamor of a cat-fight. The old man looked up in the direction of the sound and smiled.

"Before you know it, this fellow too will be getting up to that sort of thing," he said. "A writer like yourself might compose a haiku on the theme — call it 'Cats in Love,' say. You know, cats are only cute when they're small. They're not so adorable any-more when they turn into big, nasty — not to say frightening — creatures. In the old days people used to say that cats could change their shape at will. Do you suppose that's true?"

"Well, I know there are lots of old stories about such things, but whether they're truth or fiction I don't know," I replied noncom-mittally. Old Hanshichi being who he was, he might well have had some actual proof, and I didn't fancy being nicely caught out for unthinkingly scoffing at those old legends.

As it turned out, though, the old man wasn't able to cite any specific examples of cats changing into something else. Lifting the tortoiseshell cat off his lap, he said: "That's true. There are lots of old stories along those lines, but I doubt if there's anyone who could say they actually witnessed such a thing. However, I did run across one very bizarre case. Don't get me wrong — I didn't see what happened with my own eyes, but it seems there was some truth to what I heard. Anyhow, two people died as a result of mischief by cats. In retrospect, it was rather frightening."

"You mean they were mauled to death?"

"No, not mauled. It's really a much more bizarre tale. Anyway, let me tell you about it."

Brushing aside the little kitten that kept clawing at his knee, the old man launched into his story.

IT ALL STARTED on the evening of the twenty-second day of the ninth month of 1862. Autumn was already drawing to a close, and the Ginger Festival at the Shinmei Shrine in Shiba had ended the previous day.[1] An old woman by the name of Omaki, who lived on a back street not far from the shrine, died suddenly. She was sixty-eight at the time, having been born in the year of the monkey during the Kansei era,[2] and had a devoted son named Shichinosuke. Her husband had died while she was still in her forties, leaving her to raise five children all on her own. However, her eldest child, a daughter who had gone into domestic service, had eloped, never to be heard from again. Her eldest son had drowned while swimming in Edo Bay at Shibaura, and her second son was carried off by the measles. Her third son she threw out of the house for habitual thievery from boyhood on. "I have rotten luck when it comes to children," Omaki was often heard to complain.

However, her youngest, Shichinosuke, had turned out admi-

---

1. Named for the many ginger sellers who set up stalls at the shrine during the festival. It ran for eleven days, starting on the eleventh day of the ninth month.

2. 1789–1801. Omaki would have been born in 1794, the sixth year of the Kansei era.

rably, and still lived at home with her. As though to atone for the sins of his siblings, he worked harder than anyone Omaki had ever known and took good care of his aging mother. "Isn't Omaki lucky to have such a dutiful son!" the neighbors all exclaimed.

Although Omaki bewailed the grief her children had caused her, she had over the years become quite the envy of the neighborhood. Shichinosuke was a fishmonger. Day in, day out, he could be seen hawking his buckets of fish here and there in search of customers. For a young man of only twenty, he was not in the least vain about his appearance, but would slave away outside in the sun until his skin was quite swarthy. He was only a humble street peddler, but he and his mother did not seriously want for anything, living alone together as happy as clams. Not only was he a devoted son, but his kind and honest disposition, so at variance with his rough-and-tumble profession, had endeared him to the neighbors.

His mother, Omaki, on the other hand, found her stock steadily declining in the neighborhood. She wasn't despised for any particular offense; it was her way of life, rather, that turned people against her. Ever since she was young she had liked cats, and her passion for them had increased as she grew older. At that time, she kept some fifteen or sixteen cats of all shapes and sizes. She had a right to keep cats, of course, and it wasn't that to which people objected. While the sight of so many cats crowded into a tiny house was distasteful to some of her neighbors, that alone hardly justified protest. The animals themselves, however, were not about to docilely accept being cooped up like that. Creeping off on the sly, they would raid the neighbors' kitchens. No matter how much food Omaki left out for them, she could not stop their thieving ways.

Here was ample cause for the neighbors to complain, and they were always coming by to tell Omaki of her cats' latest infraction. For her part, Omaki always apologized profusely. Even Shichinosuke apologized. The ceaseless caterwauling that arose from their house had led one of the more sharp-tongued residents of the neighborhood — no one knew who exactly started it — to nickname Omaki "the Cat Lady." Shichinosuke, to say nothing of Omaki herself, was mortified each time the sobriquet reached his ears. But he was too shy to take the matter up with his mother or, conversely, to stick up for her in front of the neighbors. So he said nothing and went mildly about his work, living a life surrounded day and night by a bevy of beasts.

Lately, the neighbors had noticed that every day when he returned home from work, Shichinosuke always had a number of fish left in his wooden buckets.

"No luck again today, eh, Shichinosuke?" someone finally asked.

"That's not it — I brought these home for the cats," Shichinosuke had replied, somewhat embarrassed. He explained that he deliberately didn't sell all the fish he bought down at the river market because his mother had instructed him to set a few aside to feed her cats.

"Expensive fish like this going for cat food?" the neighbor had responded in astonishment. "What a waste!" Soon all the other neighbors knew of it too.

"That boy's too easygoing, meekly doing whatever his mother tells him. If he puts aside that many fish everyday — and expensive ones at that — he won't be able to make ends meet no matter how hard he works. That old woman cares more about her cats than she does her own son. Poor fellow!"

There wasn't one of the neighbors who didn't sympathize with the filial Shichinosuke. Naturally, they came to harbor ill feelings toward the Cat Lady. The more they disliked her, the more she seemed to merit their contempt. The cats seemed to take the ill-feeling as a provocation, for the incidents of mischief began to increase. There was no house in the neighborhood that they had not dared to enter. In some, they tore the paper screens to pieces. From others they stole fish. Their yowling, going on day and night, was so horrendous that Omaki's neighbors in the adjoining rowhouse eventually packed up and left. Her neighbors on the other side were a young carpenter and his wife. The wife became so distressed about the cats that she could talk about nothing except how she, too, wanted to move elsewhere.

One of the other rowhouse residents finally, as though a dam had burst inside him, came out with what he felt: "We've got to get rid of those cats somehow; they're a burden to her son and a nuisance to the neighborhood!" Immediately, the other neighbors chimed in their agreement.

Seeing no future in discussing the matter directly with the Cat Lady herself, the head of the neighborhood association went to the landlord and explained the situation to him. Would he tell Omaki, in no uncertain terms, that if she didn't get rid of her cats she would be evicted? The landlord, or course, took their side. He summoned Omaki, told her that her cats were a neighborhood nuisance, and ordered her to get rid of them. If she refused, then she must immediately vacate the premises.

"I don't care where you go, just as long as you clear out," he added.

Faced with the landlord's ultimatum, Omaki had no choice but to agree.

"I'm terribly sorry to have caused everyone so much trouble. I'll get rid of the cats immediately." But Omaki, having lovingly raised and cared for the creatures herself, did not have the heart to dispose of them personally.

"I know it's an imposition," she wailed, "but please ask the neighbors if they will take them away somewhere and get rid of them for me." Considering this a not unreasonable request, the landlord passed the message on to the neighbors' representative. Shortly thereafter, the carpenter who lived next door to Omaki showed up at her house with two other men to collect the cats. A new litter had just been born, and altogether there were now twenty of them.

"Thank you very much. I appreciate your help."

Her face betraying no emotion, Omaki called all the cats in the house together and turned them over to the three men. They divided the cats equally among themselves. One man put his batch into an empty charcoal sack. Another wrapped his up in a large piece of cloth. As they set off down the street, each with a bundle under his arm, Omaki stood in the doorway and watched them go with an ambiguous grin on her face.

"I was watching her," the carpenter's wife, Ohatsu, whispered to the other neighbors afterward, "and there was something horrible about that smile."

The three men split up and went off in different directions, each choosing a lonely spot in which to abandon the cats.

"That should fix things," the neighbors declared, rejoicing that peace had returned to their little row of houses. They were surprised, then, to hear what the carpenter's wife reported the next morning.

"The cats are back. I heard them crying next door in the middle of the night."

Could that be possible?

A shock was in store for them when they went and peeked into Omaki's house. It looked as though the entire brood of cats had returned during the night. They filled the house, loudly meowing as though mocking the humans for their folly and stupidity. Little was to be learned from Omaki: she could only guess that at some point during the night they had crawled in through the lattice window in the kitchen or from under the raised floor of the house.

"Well, they do say cats can always find their way home," said someone.

At this, the three men agreed that next time they would abandon the cats somewhere whence they would never be able to return. Under the circumstances, they had little choice but to take a day off from work and set out again with the cats for the far-flung corners of Shinagawa and Ōji.

For the next two days, not a single cat was to be heard at Omaki's house.

[2]

It was one night during the festival at the Shinmei Shrine. The wife of a locksmith who lived in Omaki's row of houses had taken her seven-year-old daughter to pray at the shrine, and they were on their way home just before ten o'clock. It was a clear night, and on the rooftops dewdrops glistened in the bright light of the moon.

"Look, mother!" Catching sight of something, the girl suddenly stopped in her tracks and tugged at her mother's sleeve. Also coming to a halt, the locksmith's wife could see, on the roof of the Cat Lady's house, a small, white shape. She soon discerned that it was a cat and, more surprisingly, that the creature was standing straight up on its hind legs like a human being, with its front paws raised high in the air. She caught her breath. Whispering to her daughter to be quiet, she watched as the white cat sauntered along the shingled roof dragging its tail, almost as though it were performing a dance. Goose bumps rose on her skin and a chill went down her spine. When the cat reached the other side of the roof, its white form suddenly disappeared into one of Omaki's skylights. Quickly dashing into her own house, the carpenter's wife went around tightly closing all the rain shutters and skylights.

Returning home from the festival later that night, her husband was surprised to find the front door locked. When he knocked, his wife quietly got up to let him in and proceeded to tell him about the terrifying sight she had witnessed. Her husband, who was exceedingly drunk, did not believe a word of it:

"What utter nonshensh!"

Ignoring his wife's objections, he went outside and stole over to Omaki's kitchen window to try to get a look inside. Before long, he heard Omaki's voice cheerfully exclaim: "Oh, so you're back, are you? My, you're late!"

As though in reply, there came the sound of a cat's meow. The locksmith gave a start, then tiptoed back to his own house feeling somewhat more sober.

"It was really standing on its hind legs, you say?" he asked his wife.

"Both Yoshi and I saw it with our own eyes," she whispered, knitting her brow. This was confirmed, in a quavering voice, by their young daughter, Oyoshi.

The locksmith was overcome with a vague sense of foreboding. His role as one of the men who had disposed of Omaki's cats weighed on his conscience. He poured himself one more drink, then another and another, eventually passing out on the floor. His wife and daughter spent a wakeful night clinging to each other.

By morning, all Omaki's cats had come back again. When the locksmith's wife told the neighbors her story, they all stared at one another. No normal cat could walk on its hind legs. So, they reasoned, Omaki's cats must have supernatural powers. When the rumor reached the landlord's ears, he too was badly shaken. Again, he confronted Omaki and her son and threatened them with eviction. But Omaki did not want to leave the house where she had lived since before her husband died. "Get rid of the cats if you must," she pleaded, tears in her eyes, "but please let us stay." Not even the landlord could fail to be moved by this display, and he could not bring himself to throw her and her son out.

"Simply abandoning those cats somewhere won't work," he said. "They'll just come straight back again. This time, weight them down with rocks and throw them into the bay. As long as those feline devils are still alive, there's no telling what misfortune will befall us all."

At the landlord's suggestion, the neighbors decided to stuff the cats into straw sacks, tie large rocks to them, and sink them in the waters of Edo Bay at Shibaura. This time, all the adult men living in the rowhouses turned out en masse to take Omaki's twenty cats away. Omaki seemed resigned to the fact that not even her cats would ever rise from that watery grave, and turning to the group of men she made this appeal: "Since this is truly our final farewell, could you please wait a moment while I give my cats something to eat?"

Omaki gathered her twenty cats around her. Shichinosuke had taken the day off from work, and he helped her by boiling up some small fish. She put these, along with some rice, onto small plates, and placed one in front of each cat. As though on cue, they all began eating at once, their noses lined up in a row. First they ate the rice, then they devoured the fish. When there was nothing edible left, they gnawed on the bones. If there had been only one cat, it would not have been an unusual scene . . . but twenty! The sight of them purring away in unison, fangs bared as they gobbled their food, was scarcely heart-warming. Indeed, it struck terror into the hearts of the more sensitive of the men. Omaki, with her white hair and high cheekbones, kept her eyes lowered, watching her cats intently and quietly wiping away a tear from time to time.

Needless to explain the fate of Omaki's cats once she turned them over to the men: everything went according to plan — they were taken to Shibaura and given a live burial at sea. Five or six days passed and still the cats did not return. The residents of the rowhouses all breathed a sigh of relief.

Surprisingly, Omaki did not seem especially sad. As usual, Shichinosuke went off to work everyday carrying his buckets of fish. On the evening of the seventh day after the drowning of the cats Omaki suddenly died.

It was Ohatsu, the wife of the carpenter next door, who made the discovery. Her husband had not as yet returned from work and, following her custom, she locked the front door before going out to run errands in the neighborhood. The house on the other side of Omaki's was still vacant. As a result, there was no one around when Omaki died. But according to Ohatsu, she was walking down the street on her way home when she saw Shichinosuke's fish buckets and carrying pole lying in the doorway to Omaki's house. Supposing he had returned home from work,

Ohatsu called into the house as she passed by, but got no reply. Nor were there any lanterns lit inside Omaki's house on that autumn evening, though dusk was already gathering. The dark house was as quiet as the grave. Seized by a vague sense of unease, Ohatsu surreptitiously peeked inside. Someone seemed to be lying sprawled on the dirt floor of the entranceway. Stepping inside in great trepidation and peering through the darkness, she made out that it was a woman. In fact, it was none other than Omaki, the Cat Lady. Ohatsu screamed for help.

Hearing her cries, the neighbors came running. Word quickly spread through the rowhouses and into the next street. Alarmed by the news, the landlord rushed over. The rumor spread that Omaki had died suddenly, but in fact no one knew for sure whether she had been carried off by illness or murdered.

"By the way, what's happened to her son?"

Judging from the fact that Shichinosuke's buckets and pole had been left outside the door, it would seem that he'd already come home, but it was strange that he hadn't yet shown his face amid all the turmoil. People wondered where he was and what he was doing. In the meantime, they quickly summoned a doctor, who examined the body but found nothing unusual apart from what looked like a small scrape just in front of the crown of Omaki's head. It was unclear, though, whether someone had struck her, or whether she'd fallen from the step inside the entranceway and hit her head. In the end, the doctor concluded that Omaki had suffered a stroke. The landlord was relieved to hear this verdict, for it would entail less trouble for him. But there was still the question of Shichinosuke's whereabouts.

"What's become of that son of hers, I wonder?"

The neighbors were standing around Omaki's body gossiping about what had happened when, without warning, Shichinosuke walked in looking dazed, his face white as a sheet. He was accompanied by a man called Sankichi, a fellow fishmonger who lived one block away. Sankichi was a loud, jovial fellow in his thirties.

"Ah, hello everyone! Thanks for stopping by," Sanchi greeted them. "The fact of the matter is, Shichinosuke comes barging into my place just now looking like he's seen a ghost — says when he got home he found his mother sprawled out dead on the floor and asks me what he should do. I told him off: 'Why come talk to me? You should've gone straight to the landlord or the neighbors and let them take care of things.' But he's young, you know — just comes running to me all flustered and upset. Can't blame him, I guess. 'Anyway,' I said, 'let's get over there right now and talk to the neighbors.' So here I am. Well now, what do you suppose happened to her?"

"It's hard to say for sure — it seems she died of a sudden illness," the landlord replied calmly. "The doctor thinks it was a stroke."

"Is that right? A stroke, huh? Seeing as his old lady didn't drink, I never would've thought a stroke would get her. But like you say, she died suddenly, so there it is. C'mon, Shichinosuke," he added comfortingly, "crying won't do any good. You gotta accept that's how life is."

Shichinosuke sat rigid with his hands on his knees and his gaze riveted on the floor. Great tears welled up in his eyes. Knowing what a dutiful son he had always been, the neighbors felt tremendous pity for him, and in fact were more saddened by Shichinosuke's grief over the loss of his mother than by the actual death of the Cat Lady herself. Without exception, a dark shadow lay over each of their faces. The women began sobbing.

That night, the whole street gathered for the wake. Shichinosuke sat without saying a word, huddled in a corner looking dazed and utterly dejected. The sight so moved the neighbors that they agreed among themselves not to trouble him with any of the arrangements for the funeral but to take care of everything themselves. When they told him this, he falteringly uttered his thanks.

"Cheer up!" Sankichi bawled blithely. "Look how nice everyone's being! Anyway, you'll probably be better off without your old lady — what was it they called her? — 'the Cat Lady'? You're on your own now. So work hard and save your money, and with everyone's help you'll find yourself a good wife!"

The hapless Omaki had so lost the sympathy of her neighbors that no one rebuked Sankichi for talking like this in the presence of the deceased. None of them had the courage to come straight out and say what Sankichi had, but in the back of their minds they all harbored exactly the same thoughts. Still, even the hated Cat Lady had been human, and they could hardly commit her to the same cruel, watery grave as her feline pets. Therefore, the next evening the residents of the rowhouses carried her body in its makeshift coffin to a small temple in Azabu to be laid to rest.

There was a heavy mist, almost a light rain, hanging over the city that evening. As Omaki's casket arrived at the temple, another shabby-looking funeral was just ending, and its mourners were starting to trickle away. Omaki's funeral procession filed into the temple's main hall as the other was leaving. Many of the mourners from the previous ceremony were also from the Shiba area, and the neighbors attending Omaki's funeral saw a number of familiar faces.

"Hello, here for a funeral too, are you?"

"Yes. Nice to see you."

The greetings went back and forth. One man, a tall fellow with large eyes, called out to the carpenter who lived next door to Omaki: "Hey, how're you doing? Whose funeral are you here for?"

"Our local Cat Lady," the young carpenter replied.

"'Cat Lady'... what a funny name. Who was she really?" His head cocked to one side, the man listened attentively to the whole story of Omaki's nickname and the manner of her death. Then he said goodbye to the carpenter and walked out through the temple gate.

To his boss, Hanshichi, the man was known as Bathhouse Bear.

[3]

"Don't you think the Cat Lady's death is suspicious?" That night, Kumazō, owner of the bathhouse, went straight to Mikawachō in Kanda and reported to Hanshichi the story of Omaki that he had heard that day. The detective listened quietly.

"What do you think, boss? Strange, isn't it?"

"Hmm, it is a bit odd. But I'm still wary of anything coming from you, Bathhouse Bear. At the beginning of the year, I got burned on that case of the two samurai in the room over your bathhouse. I can't afford to slip up again. Anyway, when you find out more, come back and let me know. Don't forget, this 'Cat Lady' was only human after all. People do drop dead all time, you know."

"Sure thing. I'll do a good job this time to make up for what happened at New Year's."

"I'll believe it when I see it."

After seeing Kumazō off, Hanshichi pondered the case. He couldn't just dismiss what Kumazō had told him: Omaki's cats, whom she loved more than her own children, were unfairly snatched from her through the machinations of the landlord and her neighbors, and drowned in the waters of Edo Bay. Then, exactly seven days later, she died all of a sudden. Call it karma or retribution if you like, but one couldn't deny it was just a bit suspicious. Hanshichi decided that it wouldn't do to leave everything to the bungling Kumazō. First thing the next morning, he headed for Kumazō's house in Atagoshita.

As the reader will already be aware, Kumazō's home was attached to the bathhouse that he ran. It was still early when Hanshichi arrived, and there were no customers on the second floor yet. Without saying anything, Kumazō led Hanshichi upstairs.

"It sure is early. What was it you wanted to discuss?" Kumazō asked in a quiet voice.

"It's about that case you mentioned last night. The more I think about it, the stranger it seems."

"I was right, wasn't I?"

"So, have you found any clues?"

"I haven't gotten that far yet. I mean, I only heard about it last night," Kumazō replied, scratching his head in embarrassment.

"If the Cat Lady really died of a stroke, then that's that. But if there's some other explanation as to how she got that graze on her head, then who do you suppose did it?"

"One of the neighbors, I guess."

"I wonder . . . ," Hanshichi replied pensively. "Don't you think that son of hers acted rather strangely?"

"But he has a reputation in the neighborhood for being devoted to his mother."

Hanshichi was perplexed. It did seem incredible that a son so devoted to his mother would commit the grave offense of matricide. But then, once Omaki had yielded and given up her cats, what incentive would any of the neighbors have had for killing her? So if it wasn't the son and it wasn't one of the neighbors, the only explanation was that she had died of a stroke as the doctor said. Still, Hanshichi wasn't convinced. Shichinosuke's odd behavior had been attributed to his youth, but in fact the boy was already twenty years old. Hanshichi couldn't fathom why he would have run to a friend's house a block away without telling any of his own neighbors about his mother's death. That said, neither could he think of a reason why a son well known to be devoted to his mother would kill her in cold blood.

"Well, as I said yesterday, find out what you can," said Hanshichi. "I'll be back in five or six days to see how you're coming along," he added just to be sure, and went home. It was the end of the ninth month, and it rained day after day.

Some five days later, Kumazō showed up at Hanshichi's house.

"Can you believe this rain?" he groused. "Anyhow, to get straight to the point, I haven't had much luck with that Cat Lady case. Her son's been going about his business as usual. Apparently he even stops work early every day so he can call in at the temple on the way home and visit his mother's grave. His neighbors have nothing but praise for him, and they all think the Cat Lady got what she deserved. I didn't have to pry information out of any of them — even the landlord and the watchman made no bones about their feelings. So things being how they are, I don't have any leads yet."

Hanshichi tutted impatiently.

"Do you call that doing your job? I can't leave you alone for a minute! I'm going over there myself tomorrow, and I want you to show me the way."

The next day was a typical gloomy, drizzly autumn day. Kumazō arrived at the appointed hour. The edges of their umbrellas bumped against one another as the two men set out for the street that ran alongside the shrine.

Omaki's neighborhood was bigger than Hanshichi had expected. On the lefthand side as one entered the gate there was a large well. The rowhouses stretched away to the left at right angles to it. They occupied only the right side of the street; on the other side was a vacant lot that appeared to be used by a dyer's shop for hanging out textiles. Here and there were low patches of autumn grasses wet from the rain. A stray dog, looking cold, scrounged around for something to eat.

"This is it," Kumazō said in a low voice. It seemed that the house adjacent to Omaki's on the south side was still vacant. The two men went instead to the carpenter's house on the north side. The carpenter was an acquaintance of Kumazō's.

"Hello!" Kumazō called out from the doorway. "Nasty weather today, isn't it?"

Hearing his voice, Ohatsu, the carpenter's young wife, appeared from inside. Sitting himself down on the doorframe, Kumazō greeted her, saying that he had been passing by on business and wanted to introduce Hanshichi as a newcomer to the neighborhood. Hanshichi's house needed quite a bit of fixing up, he explained, and he wanted her husband to do the work. Following Kumazō's lead, Hanshichi politely added, "Since I'm new to your neighborhood, I don't know any of the local carpenters, and my friend Kuma here kindly offered to bring me by to ask for your help."

"Is that so? Well, I hope my husband can be of service to you."

Thinking she had just found her husband a new customer, Ohatsu put on a smile and greeted Hanshichi warmly. She insisted on inviting the two men inside and brought out a smoking set and some tea. The rain was still falling outside. From time to time they heard a mouse scurrying about in the kitchen, which was dark even at that time of day.

"You have mice, too, I can tell," Hanshichi commented casually.

"As you can see, it's an old house and the mice have practically taken over," Ohatsu said, glancing toward the kitchen.

"You could keep a cat."

"Yes . . . ," Ohatsu replied vaguely, her face clouding over.

"Speaking of cats, how's everything next door?" Kumazō chimed in. "Is Omaki's son as hard at work as ever?"

"Yes, that fellow's a model of diligence."

"Well, this mustn't go outside this room," Kumazō said, lowering his voice, "but I hear some disturbing rumors are being spread outside the neighborhood."

"Is that so?"

Ohatsu turned pale.

"Word is that her son struck and killed her with his carrying pole."

"Oh, my!"

Ohatsu's eyes seemed to glaze over, darting back and forth between Hanshichi and Kumazō as though comparing their faces.

"Hey, wait a minute! You can't go around making reckless accusations like that," Hanshichi said to Kumazō with feigned outrage. "You're talking about matricide, you know, not just any old crime. When the murderer's caught, he and anyone else involved will suffer capital punishment. So be careful what you say."

Hanshichi shot him a meaningful look and Kumazō hastily clammed up. Ohatsu, too, fell silent, and a pall descended on the room. Hanshichi took the opportunity to rise as though to leave.

"I'm sorry to have disturbed you. I just thought a carpenter might be home on a wet day like today. I'll come again later."

Ohatsu asked Hanshichi where he lived, saying she would send her husband around to see him as soon as he returned. But he declined the offer, promising to return the next day. With that, he and Kumazō left.

"She was the one who discovered Omaki's body?" Hanshichi asked Kumazō once they were outside.

"That's right. Did you see the strange look on her face when we started talking about the Cat Lady?"

"Yes. I think I've got a good idea what's going on. You can go home now, Kumazō. I'll take over from here. I can manage on my own."

After saying goodbye to Kumazō, Hanshichi went off to deal with another case. Then, just before four in the afternoon, he returned again to the street of rowhouses. Carrying an umbrella and with a scarf wrapped around his face—fortunately, the rain was coming down even harder than before—Hanshichi crept into the vacant house next door to Omaki's. Quietly shutting the front door behind him, he sat down cross-legged on the damp tatami mats. He could hear the occasional raindrop dripping through the roof into the space above the ceiling. A cricket chirped from beneath a crumbling bit of wall. The empty, unheated house felt terribly cold.

Out in the street, he heard the sound of rain falling on someone's umbrella—it seemed that the carpenter's wife had returned.

[4]

After what seemed about half an hour, Hanshichi heard a pair of wet straw sandals pass by outside in the street and come to a halt in front of the house next door. Omaki's son must have come home, he thought. Just then, he heard the sound of the fishmonger's tub and basket being lowered to the ground.

"Shichi, is that you?"

It would appear that Ohatsu had slipped out of her house and gone next door. Hanshichi heard her whispering something to Shichinosuke as the two stood in the dirt-floored entrance hall of Omaki's house. Shichinosuke whispered something in reply, but Hanshichi could make out nothing of what was being said. Straining his ears, he just managed to catch the sound of Shichinosuke crying and sniveling on the other side of the wall.

"Don't be such a coward. Go talk things over with Sankichi right now. . . . No, I've gone through everything with him once already." Ohatsu spoke quietly but firmly; it seemed she was trying to urge the fishmonger into taking some course of action.

"C'mon, get over there right away. What an impossible person you are!" she said, taking the reluctant Shichinosuke by the hand and pulling him outside into the street.

Shichinosuke complied meekly, and soon Hanshichi heard the plodding of the young man's sandals receding down the street. Ohatsu watched him go and was about to go back inside when Hanshichi suddenly called to her from inside the vacant house.

"Ma'am!"

Ohatsu gave a start and froze. Seeing Hanshichi's face as he opened the front door and slipped outside, her face turned ashen.

"We can't talk out here. Would you mind stepping inside for a moment?" he said. He opened the door to Omaki's house and she followed him inside.

"Do you know who I am, ma'am?" Hanshichi asked her.

"No," she mumbled.

"Well, even if you don't, surely you're aware that Bathhouse Bear has another job on the side. C'mon, you must have heard — Kuma and your husband are very close, aren't they? Well, leaving that aside for now, what were you and the fishmonger whispering about just now?"

Ohatsu stared down at her feet.

"You don't need to tell me — I know. You passed some information on to him and told him to go talk it over with Sankichi.

Kumazō was right earlier when he said Shichinosuke killed his mother with his pole that night. You knew all along what had happened, but you covered up for him while he rushed off to Sankichi's house. Then he and Sankichi showed up, rambling on and acting the innocents. Well, how about it? If I've read your fortune incorrectly, you can have your money back. Your story might have been good enough to fool the neighbors, but I'm not buying it that easily. You and Sankichi went along with the act, so you're both just as guilty as Shichinosuke. Don't worry, I've got enough rope with me to string all three of you together like prayer beads and haul you off to jail!"

Threatened in this bullying manner, Ohatsu burst into tears. She sank down on the earthen floor and begged Hanshichi not to arrest her.

"Depending on the circumstances, there's a chance I won't arrest you, but if it's mercy you want you'd better come clean right now. How about it? I guessed right, didn't I? You and Sankichi conspired to hide Shichinosuke's crime!"

"I'm sorry!" Ohatsu cried, placing trembling hands on the floor and bowing her head down.

"If you're sorry, then tell me what happened," Hanshichi said, his voice softening. "Why did Shichinosuke kill his own mother? I don't suppose he planned to do it, seeing how devoted to her he was. Did they have a quarrel?"

"No . . . his mother turned into a cat," she replied, shuddering as though the mere thought filled her with terror.

Hanshichi's brow furrowed. At the same time, a smile rose to his lips.

"Hmm. So the Cat Lady turned into a cat, huh? I think you're confusing this with the plot of some play."

"No. It's absolutely true. I'm not making it up, I swear. Omaki, the woman who lived here in this house, turned into a cat. I saw it with my own eyes — it was terrifying!"

With his years of experience, Hanshichi could tell from her frightened, quavering voice and the expression on her face that she was telling the truth. Suddenly he was intrigued, and his tone became grave.

"Let me get this straight—you saw the old lady change into a cat?"

Ohatsu swore that she did indeed.

"This is what happened. Back when Omaki still had all her cats, Shichinosuke would bring home a few leftover fish for them to eat every day," she explained. "But even after they'd been drowned at Shibaura and there wasn't a single cat left in the house, Omaki still wanted him to bring home the fish just as before. Shichinosuke is so obedient that he did exactly as he was told without protesting, but when my husband found out about it, he said he'd never heard anything so ridiculous. 'There's no point in wasting expensive fish when there are no cats in the house—you should stop doing it,' he advised Shichinosuke."

"What was Omaki doing with all those fish?"

"Apparently not even Shichinosuke had any clue. He'd leave them in the kitchen cupboard at night, and by the next morning they'd all be gone. He didn't know where they went, he said—it was all a big mystery. Well, one day my husband suggested, 'Don't bring any fish home and see what your mother does. You won't know unless you try.' Well, at some stage Shichinosuke himself must have come around to feeling the same way. One evening—it was the day after the festival ended at the Shinmei Shrine—he deliberately returned without any fish. I'd gone shopping and was on my way home when I happened to run into him on the corner of our street, and we walked back together. I should have left him and gone into my house, but I was curious to see how his mother would react when she discovered his buckets were empty, so I stood near the doorway and watched unobtrusively. Shichinosuke went inside and put his buckets down on the earthen floor. Then his mother appeared from inside the house. She went straight over to the buckets and peered inside. 'What? You didn't bring anything back today?' she exclaimed. As she spoke . . . oh, her face! Her ears got bigger, her eyes flashed, her mouth stretched from ear to ear. Just like a cat!"

Ohatsu peered into the darkness of the house and drew in her breath as though seeing Omaki's horrible catlike face all over again. Even Hanshichi was taken aback.

"How strange! Then what happened?"

"I gave a start, and the next thing I knew, Shichinosuke had raised his pole and brought it down on top of his mother's head. It must have killed her outright, because she crumpled to the floor without a sound. I was shocked when I realized she was dead. Shichinosuke stood there for a while with a terrible look on his face, just gazing at his mother's body. Then he suddenly panicked, and ran and grabbed a carving knife from the kitchen. He was going to cut his own throat. I couldn't let him do it, so I rushed in and stopped him. When I asked why he'd done it, he said he'd seen his mother's face turn into a cat's — just as I had! He assumed the cats must have devoured his mother, and that one of them had changed into her. He had struck with the idea of avenging her death like a good son. But right away he saw that she didn't turn back into a cat — no fur, no tail — it really had been his mother after all! He knew he would be executed for his crime, so he decided to take his own life."

"Did the old lady's face really turn into a cat's?" Again Hanshichi asked, not yet convinced.

Both she and Shichinosuke had seen the same thing, Ohatsu insisted vehemently. Why otherwise, she asked, would a devoted son like Shichinosuke raise a hand against his own mother?

"Even after killing her, he kept staring at his mother's body expecting to see the creature's true form revealed. He waited and waited, but all he saw was his mother's face, not a cat's. I still can't explain why Omaki's face took on that terrible catlike appearance. Perhaps she was possessed by the ghosts of her dead cats? Anyway, it didn't seem fair that Shichinosuke should be punished for killing his mother. After all, it was my husband who'd put him up to doing what he did in the first place. I tried my best to calm him down, then I took him over to see his friend Sankichi. The house on the other side of Omaki's was still vacant, and by a stroke of luck no one saw us returning or leaving.

Sankichi came up with a good plan — I was to return home on my own and pretend to discover the body, screaming for all I was worth."

"It all makes perfect sense now," said Hanshichi. "So when Kumazō and I came by earlier today, you sensed something was up and went out to talk things over with Sankichi. Then you waited for Shichinosuke to come home, and sent him over to Sankichi's place. That's right, isn't it? So what did you all decide to do? Are you going to help him run away? But why am I asking you? I better get over to Sankichi's!"

Hanshichi hurried off through the rain to the next neighborhood, but Sankichi claimed not to have seen Shichinosuke since the morning. At first Hanshichi suspected he was lying, but suddenly he had a thought. Leaving Sankichi's, he rushed over to the temple in Azabu. A new wooden mortuary tablet, showing a few drops of rain, had recently been placed in front of Omaki's grave, but there was no sign of anyone around.

The next morning, Shichinosuke's corpse was found floating in the waters of Edo Bay near the spot in Shibaura where the neighbors had drowned Omaki's cats.

Instead of going to Sankichi's house, Shichinosuke had probably immediately set about looking for a place to kill himself. Even if Ohatsu had testified on his behalf, their bizarre story about his mother's face changing into a cat's would not have spared him from the punishment for matricide. Hanshichi decided that Shichinosuke was better off taking his own life than waiting to be crucified; and he concluded, too, that he himself was glad he was not in the position of having to arrest Omaki's dutiful, hapless son.

"WELL, THAT'S ABOUT ALL there is to the story," old Hanshichi said, pausing for breath. "I made some more inquiries later, and it turned out that Shichinosuke was indeed so devoted to his mother that he couldn't possibly have killed her if he'd been in his right mind. So I suppose that Omaki's face really did turn into a cat's, as the two of them claimed. I don't know whether she was possessed or what, but stranger things have happened. Later, when I searched Omaki's house, I found a huge pile of fish bones under the veranda. I guess she kept throwing them down there long after her cats were gone. I heard the landlord eventually had the house torn down — it must have been too creepy, even for him."

Benten's Daughter

BENTEN MUSUME

[1]

It was the eighteenth day of the third month of 1854, the first year of the new Ansei era. Hanshichi was just thinking about having some lunch before popping out to see the Sanja Festival at the Asakusa Shrine,[1] when a man of thirty-five or -six came calling. He was a clerk named Rihei who worked at the Yamashiroya, a pawnbroker's on the street below Kanda's Myōjin Shrine. Hanshichi knew him to be one of his master's most trusted employees.

"I wish the weather would clear up," Rihei said. "Trust it to go and rain yesterday, on the opening night of the shrine festival! I wonder if today will be any better?"

"Yes, that was a shame, wasn't it? But they say they're going to hold the festival come rain or shine, so I was thinking of heading over and having a look myself in a little while. The sun's started to show through the clouds, so I figure it'll probably have cleared up by this afternoon. Anyhow, the weather's always unpredictable at this time of year, when the cherry's in bloom."

Hanshichi looked up at the slowly brightening sky through the half-open window, whereupon Rihei started to fidget slightly.

"Oh, so you're on your way out to Asakusa now, then?" he asked.

---

1. A festival in honor of three men (the two Hinokuma brothers, Hamanari and Takenari, and Haji Matsuchi) who, according to legend, miraculously pulled a statue of Kannon from the Sumida River with their fishing net in 628. It is this statue that is enshrined at Asakusa's Sensō Temple. Today the festival is held on the third Sunday in May.

"Well, I hear it's going to be a grand affair this year, and someone I know there has invited me to come by, so I thought I should put in a brief appearance at least," Hanshichi said with a smile.

"Ah, I see."

Rihei puffed nervously at his pipe. Something, for certain, was on his mind. It was Hanshichi who eventually broke the ice.

"Rihei, is there something you wanted to talk to me about?"

"Yes . . . ," he faltered. "The fact is, I came here to ask you a favor, but you're about to go out, so I won't keep you any longer. Why don't I come back again tonight or in the morning and talk things over with you then?"

"Don't be silly. It's only a festival, after all. It's not as though it's anything very urgent. So please ask whatever you've come to ask. I know you're busy too — you don't want to have to come back again and again. Just go ahead."

"Are you sure I'm not imposing on you?"

"Not at all. Go on." Hanshichi prompted. "What's it all about? Something related to your work, is it?"

It was a time-honored fact of life that the pawnbroker's trade was inextricably linked to various kinds of criminal activity. The expression on Rihei's face suggested matters as yet unspoken, and Hanshichi sensed that the clerk had somehow gotten mixed up in some shady business. But Rihei still hesitated, unable to give voice to what was on his mind.

"Rihei, I suspect this is a rather delicate matter," Hanshichi said half-jokingly, with a smile. "A love affair, is it? If that's the case, I think you've come to the wrong place, but don't let that stop you. Go ahead and tell me — I'm all ears."

"You give me too much credit," Rihei smiled wryly, with a bow of his head. "I only wish it were something scandalous like that. But as you know, I lead a very dull life. No, Inspector, it's really a very trivial matter, but even so, I wondered if I might have the benefit of your wisdom. I know you're a very busy man, and I really do apologize for imposing on you like this, but I've racked my brains again and again, and still . . ."

Hanshichi was growing impatient during this long-winded preamble. He turned and gazed out the window, making a show of banging his pipe against the side of the charcoal brazier to knock the ashes loose. The noise made Rihei jump.

"Inspector, I'm not good with words," he said, changing his tone. "Anyway, please listen to what I have to say. Actually, it doesn't concern me personally. You see, my master's shop has a problem on its hands."

"Hmm. What's happened then?"

"Well, you may not know, but there was an assistant by the name of Tokujirō employed there. He was sixteen years old and would soon have had his coming-of-age ceremony — shaving his forelocks, that is. Well, Tokujirō died yesterday of a mysterious ailment."

"My, my, what a pity. I can't say I remember him all that well, but it's sad when a young person like that dies. How did it happen?"

"About a fortnight ago, the inside of Tokujirō's mouth suddenly started swelling up, till he was unable to talk. They called a doctor, but Tokujirō only got worse, and eventually the master had no choice but to put him in a palanquin and send him home. The boy's home was a fishmonger's shop in Aioichō, in Honjo, run by a very decent, honest man named Tokuzō. Anyway, Tokujirō took a turn for the worse after returning home, and we got word that he passed away at about two o'clock yesterday afternoon. It was most unfortunate, but I'm afraid life is like that. As the end was drawing near, however, it seems he managed to say a few words. . . ." Rihei hesitated again.

"What did he say?" Hanshichi pressed.

"Well, sir, with his dying breath, Tokujirō accused Miss Okono of murdering him," Rihei replied in a hushed voice.

Okono was the Yamashiros' only daughter and was well known in the neighborhood for being quite a beauty, but for some reason she had never married. Now twenty-six or -seven years old, she remained the innocent virgin. For that reason, malicious rumors had spread about her, and Okono had been saddled with the nickname "Benten's Daughter."[2] Moreover, the sobriquet was not meant in the usual, positive sense, a fact that apparently distressed her parents a great deal. Hanshichi knew all this already, yet he could think of no reason why Okono might have killed the shop assistant. Peering into Hanshichi's eyes as though trying to discern what he was thinking, Rihei continued his story.

"It was on the night of the Dolls' Festival that Tokujirō fell ill.[3] According to one of the other employees, he had complained in the early evening that his mouth hurt, and that night at dinner he was unable to eat anything. Around dawn the next morning, his condition worsened such that by mid-morning his mouth was swollen shut. He was unable to swallow a thing — not hot water, rice gruel, or even medicine — let alone speak. Eventually his entire face got all red and puffy, making him look like some sort of monster. He was feverish, and he moaned and writhed in agony, but there was nothing the doctor could do for him. We were all terribly worried, especially the master, who finally decided to send Tokujirō home to his family. During his illness, we frequently asked him if he had any idea what might have caused it, but in reply all he could do was moan. So it seemed a bit odd that he should have said what he did after returning home. I mean, why on earth would Miss Okono have wanted to kill him? It's ridiculous. And now, just this morning, Tokuzō came round and stirred up trouble with a lot of talk about what he called 'the deceased's last words.'"

"Is this Tokuzō the boy's father?"

"No, he's Tokujirō's older brother. Both their parents died long ago, so Tokuzō was all he had in the way of family. He's twenty-

2. Sarasvati, an Indian goddess, renowned for her beauty, who represents the gifts of oratory, scholarship, and intuition, and is a patron of the arts, especially music. In Japan, she is also known as Benzaiten and is associated with wealth and young lovers. "Benten's daughter" is commonly used to refer to any beautiful young woman.

3. Held on the third day of the third month.

five, I believe. He's in charge of the fish shop, a very decent fellow usually, but today he behaved like a completely different person. 'I don't care if she is the master's daughter, she won't get away with killing one of the employees,' he said with a terrible look on his face. Even the master couldn't handle him. As I said, when Tokujirō was still at the Yamashiroya, he was too sick to utter a word, so how could he say what he was supposed to have said after returning home? It all seemed rather odd. And yet Tokuzō was adamant about what his brother had said. There was no reasoning with him. For our part, we stuck to our story that we knew nothing about the matter, and . . . well, that's pretty much all there is to tell. We're very worried about what might happen to the family's reputation."

"I understand how you feel," Hanshichi nodded. "Something like that would be most regrettable."

"Naturally, we intended to pay Tokuzō a generous sum to cover his brother's funeral expenses, but then he suddenly made an outrageous demand: if we don't give him 300 *ryō*, he says he'll go to the authorities and accuse Miss Okono of murder. Now, if Miss Okono had really killed Tokujirō, we would willingly pay Tokuzō whatever he asked — a hundred *ryō*, or even a thousand. But as I've already said, Tokuzō wouldn't listen to reason. When we raised doubts about his allegations — blackmail, slander, call it what you will — the master asked me to try to negotiate with him. I offered him fifteen or twenty *ryō* to drop the whole thing, but he flatly refused. In the end, he agreed to accept three *ryō* for the time being, just to cover the funeral expenses. He left saying he'd be back to talk it over again as soon as the funeral was out of the way. So, Inspector — what do you think of it all?"

The Yamashiros had a sizable fortune, but even for them 300 *ryō* was a large sum. Moreover, they must have felt chagrined at the prospect of being bilked out of that much money on a trumped-up charge. Hanshichi quickly discerned that Rihei had an ulterior motive in coming to him for advice: he was trying to make use of the detective's authority to induce Tokuzō to back off. More than anything, Hanshichi hated it when people tried to

cloak themselves in his official mantle in order to gain leverage
in their own financial dealings. If that had been all, he would
have found some pretext to refuse Rihei's request. But he felt a
strong urge to seek the answers to some perplexing questions.
Was there any truth in the dying words of the shop assistant
Tokujirō? Was someone manipulating his older brother Tokuzō
from behind the scenes? He thought for a few moments, then
said: "Listen, Rihei. How come Okono is still unmarried? She's a
very attractive girl, though a bit past her prime, I'm afraid."

"You're right," replied Rihei, frowning.

[2]

According to Rihei, the rumors circulating about Okono were
all entirely groundless. The daughter of the Yamashiroya was
simply unlucky.

Okono was an only child, and ever since her youth her parents had been planning to marry her someday to the son of one
of their relatives. But one summer the boy had drowned while
swimming in the Sumida River. He'd been fourteen at the time,
and Okono eleven. Afterward, she'd been engaged several times,
but in each case, her betrothed had met an untimely death before the knot could be tied. There had been four in all, including the first. The last, a youth of nineteen, had gone mad and
hanged himself in a storeroom in his own house. Such strange
twists of fate were what had kept Okono from marrying all these
years — there was no other reason. But idle tongues will wag;
those who knew the facts said that Okono was under some sort
of curse, while those who remained ignorant spread rumors that
she drank lamp oil, or that she was a monster whose head flew
around on its own at night.[4] Eventually, she was written off as
an old maid.

Of the various rumors, the one most widely believed was that

---

4. *Rokuro-kubi,* legends of which originated in ancient Chinese books pur-
porting to describe strange peoples of foreign lands.

Okono had been born by the grace of the goddess Benten — which was how she'd gotten the nickname "Benten's Daughter." The Yamashiros, it was said, had long lamented the fact that they were childless. Finally, her mother had gone to the Benten Shrine at nearby Shinobazu Pond and prayed every day for twenty-one days. Okono had been the result. Being a gift from Benten, it followed that, like the goddess herself, she would have to remain single all her life. By trying to find herself a man, she had aroused the goddess's ire, and Benten had jealously struck down each of her prospective husbands in turn. Thus her nickname, one that normally evoked images of beauty, in Okono's case had the ring of a terrible curse.

Even those who might try to quash such idle rumors could not deny the fact that Okono's parents had prayed to Benten to give them a child. Rihei himself acknowledged that his master's wife had become pregnant after beginning her daily visits to the shrine, and had later given birth to Okono.

"Anyway, it's a very unfortunate situation," Rihei said, sighing as he concluded his story. "Miss Okono has studied incense, flower arrangement, tea ceremony — she can even play the koto and the samisen, plus she's attractive and well-mannered. There's not a thing wrong with her, but as for getting married, she has few prospects. She'll be twenty-seven next year. She's an only child and her parents feel very sorry for her because of what's happened — you should see how they lavish affection on her! Even so, she dislikes being around the shop with people coming and going all the time, and recently she's retreated to the house behind the Yamashiroya where the master's eighty-one-year-old mother lives."

"Does anyone live there besides Okono and her grandmother?" asked Hanshichi.

"A servant named Okuma lives with them. But she's completely useless — a real country bumpkin. Meals are taken over three times a day from the main house."

"Eighty-one years old, eh? Quite remarkable!"

"Yes, the master's mother is a fortunate lady. But the years are taking their toll; her eyes and ears have started to fail her lately. In fact, she's stone-deaf."

"Is that so?"

A useless servant, a deaf and blind granny, and a beautiful young spinster — there was something about the combination that gave Hanshichi food for thought. At last, he said quietly: "Well, I can tell you're in a difficult position. I'd better see what I can do to straighten things out. Okono knows what's going on, I assume?"

"She knows about Tokujirō's death, but she hasn't been told about his brother's visit or our discussions with him. We felt it wouldn't be good for her to hear she's been accused of murder, even if it *is* all just a lie, so we decided not to say anything for the time being."

"I understand. Well, let's keep it that way then. But listen, Rihei. I think it'd be a good idea to have someone else who has their wits about them staying at the grandmother's house."

"You think so?"

"Just to be safe."

"I see." Rihei nodded, but looked unconvinced. "Well, thank you for offering to help."

"What we need to find out is whether or not Okono really killed the shop assistant. Once you're sure of that, you'll be able to break the impasse with Tokuzō — make a clean breast of all the facts and reach some appropriate financial settlement with him."

"Yes, you're quite right. I'm certainly glad I came to talk things over with you. Well, thank you so much again for your help."

Effusively thanking Hanshichi, the relentlessly formal Rihei withdrew. It seemed that the Sanja Festival would have to wait after all. First, Hanshichi needed to look into the situation at the Yamashiroya. Had Tokujirō really been killed by the pawnbroker's daughter? Or had someone else put Tokuzō up to making a groundless accusation against the family? Hanshichi pondered these questions as he ate his lunch.

"Is the Yamashiroya in some sort of trouble?" his wife, Osen, asked as she was clearing away the dishes.

"Yeah, but it shouldn't be too difficult to get to the bottom of it. Would you get my kimono out for me? I'm going over to see Gen'an."

As soon as he'd put down his chopsticks, Hanshichi changed his clothes and went out carrying an umbrella. Rain like teardrops was falling fitfully, but a pale sunshine was slowly beginning to filter gently through gaps in the clouds. Sparrows were already twittering on the rooftops of nearby houses.

Gen'an was a neighborhood doctor with whom Hanshichi was on good terms, and he had decided to seek his expert opinion about the nature and treatment of various diseases of the mouth. When he had finished questioning Gen'an closely, he left and headed for Aioichō to pay a visit to Tokuzō. As he reached the riverbank at Yanagiwara, the sky cleared completely. The rainwater dripped off the wet branches of the willow trees, gleaming in the sunlight with an effect as though spring had really arrived.

Crossing Ryōgoku Bridge and entering the Honjo district, Hanshichi found Tokuzō's house in the second block of Aioichō. It was a narrow building with a fish shop in front, which was closed as a sign that the family was in mourning. Inquiring at the local household-goods shop, Hanshichi learned that Tokuzō lived with his wife, Otome, who minded the shop while her husband made his rounds carrying his buckets of fish. Tokuzō did quite well for himself. His wife, too, was a hard worker, and it seemed the couple were managing to put some money aside. "I bet they'll have quite a nice little nest egg before long," the woman at the household-goods shop said enviously.

Tokuzō's wife had once worked at a cheap brothel on the outskirts of the Yoshiwara, and when her contract expired she had installed herself at Tokuzō's place. She was twenty-nine, four years older than her husband. She was unusually industrious for a woman of her former profession, working from dawn till dusk without a care for her personal appearance. The neighbors, it seemed, envied Tokuzō his luck in finding himself such a good wife.

Hanshichi left the household-goods shop and stopped in at a few more houses in the neighborhood, where he got exactly the same story: no one had a single bad word to say about the couple who ran the fish shop. It seemed unlikely to Hanshichi that someone with as sound a reputation as Tokuzō would go barging into the house of his brother's employer and make groundless accusations, much less try to extort 300 *ryō* from him. Of course, there was no accounting for human nature, but Hanshichi had trouble swallowing the idea that an honest man like Tokuzō would blackmail someone for that kind of money on his own initiative.

The only thing left to do now, Hanshichi reasoned, was to drop in on the fishmonger unannounced. He stopped in at a stationery shop and bought some black paper and black string, which he used to wrap up a small sum of money as a condolence gift. Tucking it into the breast of his kimono, he headed over to the fish shop. Five or six people, apparently from the neighborhood, were crowded into the tiny house, which was filled with the smell of incense.

"Excuse me!"

Hearing Hanshichi call out from the doorway, a woman seated inside got up. She looked about thirty, with a fair complexion, and was rather scrawny. Hanshichi guessed immediately that it was the fishmonger's wife, Otome.

"Is this Tokuzō's house?"

"Yes it is," the woman answered politely.

"Is the master at home?"

"He's out at the moment, I'm afraid."

"I see," Hanshichi said hesitantly. "The fact is, I live near the Yamashiroya in Kanda, and I heard about what happened to poor Tokujirō. Since I live in the neighborhood, I was on quite good terms with him, and I just stopped by to offer up some incense."

"Oh, really, that's very kind of you. I'm sorry the house is such a mess, but won't you please come in?"

The woman wiped her eyes and led Hanshichi into the house. Tokujirō's body had been laid out on the floor, his head pointing north. An attractive folding screen, probably borrowed from somewhere, had been placed around his pillow. In the usual manner, Hanshichi lit some incense and placed his condolence gift on the Buddhist altar, then he crawled over and sat by Tokujirō's pillow. He pulled back the handkerchief covering Tokujirō's face and took a quick look at the deceased before retreating to a corner of the room. Otome brought him some tea and bowed politely to him again.

"It was very kind of you to come and say goodbye to your friend. I'm sure the deceased would have been very pleased."

"Excuse me for asking, but are you the lady of the house?"

"Yes. I'm Tokujirō's sister-in-law," she said, batting her eyelids. "Tokujirō was all we had in the way of family, and he was so dear to us."

"I'm terribly sorry for your loss."

Reiterating his condolences, Hanshichi, little by little, extracted the following information from Otome: Tokujirō had been apprenticed to the pawnbroker's at the age of nine, exactly eight years ago; he was smart for his age and good-natured. When he'd come home for the servants' holiday on New Year's Day this year, the wife of the *tabi* maker next door had seen him and declared, "Why, Toku is the spitting image of Hisamatsu!"[5] Tokujirō had turned bright red. "Such memories are very painful to me," Otome confided in Hanshichi.

---

5. A young apprentice to an Osaka lamp-oil dealer who fell in love with Osome, his master's daughter, with whom he eventually committed suicide. Their story inspired numerous stage adaptations.

As several other people were seated in the room, Hanshichi felt he could not probe any further. He asked when the funeral was to be held. They would be taking Tokujirō's body to a temple in Fukagawa at four that afternoon, Otome told him. It was nearly four o'clock already; Hanshichi decided that if he waited a bit longer, Tokuzō would be home. What was more, if he tagged along with them to the temple, he might stumble upon some sort of clue. He told Otome that he wished to accompany the body, then sat back and waited. Soon, a young man entered the house. He was short and stocky, and it was clear from the way Otome and the other guests greeted him that this was Tokuzō. Entering behind him were the Yamashiroya's clerk, Rihei, and one of the shop assistants.

Rihei announced that he had come as his master's representative to accompany the body to the temple, and Otokichi, the shop assistant, said that he was representing the other employees of the Yamashiroya. Otome brought Hanshichi over and introduced him to Tokuzō. Rihei seemed in doubt as to what to say, so Hanshichi took the initiative and greeted him as though they were only casual acquaintances. The hour of the funeral was rapidly approaching, and with the addition of seven or eight more neighbors, the tiny house became so crowded that the mourners were all jostling one another.

Amid all the confusion, Tokuzō and Otome disappeared.

[3]

Hanshichi got up slowly, crept over to the doorway of the kitchen and peered inside. The fishmonger and his wife were standing out back by the side of the well. The vacant lot behind the house was surprisingly spacious. Next to the well stood a Chinese parasol tree, presumably planted to provide shade in the summertime but now forming a large canopy of bare branches. Otome stood with her back to the tree, talking to her husband in a hushed voice. From her agitated manner, it did not appear to be an ordinary discussion. Hidden behind the half-closed shoji, Hanshichi observed the two for a while. The couple's voices grew louder.

"You're just being a coward!" she said scornfully. "This is a once in a lifetime opportunity."

"Ssh, not so loud."

"But you're being absolutely impossible. If I'd known this would happen, I'd have gone myself."

"Stop it. People will hear you."

As he tried to pacify his wife, Tokuzō instinctively glanced over his shoulder, and his eyes happened to meet Hanshichi's. Accustomed to such situations, Hanshichi pretended he was merely scooping water from a bucket that had been placed nearby, and once he'd taken a sip from the ladle, quickly retreated to his original seat. The couple returned shortly, but Otome's face was paler than before. Hanshichi noted the occasional fierce glances filled with disgust that she shot at Rihei.

When the time arrived for the funeral procession to leave, some thirty mourners followed the simple wooden casket out. The weather was glorious — "Toku must be smiling in the after-life," someone remarked. Tokuzō tagged along with them trying, somewhat begrudgingly, although it was his own brother's funeral, to make himself useful. Otome remained behind at home, seeing the procession off only as far as the gate.

Although the skies had cleared, the road in Honjo was extremely bad. Picking his way through the mud, Hanshichi deliberately fell back until he was keeping pace alongside Rihei.

"Has Tokuzō been back to the Yamashiroya?" he asked as they walked.

"Yes, he barged in and created another scene."

After receiving the three ryō for funeral expenses, Tokuzō had initially gone home, but he had returned again in the afternoon and urged the pawnbroker to settle the matter once and for all before the funeral was held. The sect of Buddhism to which his family belonged practiced cremation, and after the body was destroyed, he pointed out, there would no longer be any proof of what had happened. He had insisted that the Yamashiroya reach a decision before the wake was over. The pawnbroker had not known what to do, so a messenger was dispatched to Hanshichi's house, but unfortunately he had already gone out by then. They argued over the matter, Tokuzō becoming more and more vociferous, until the pawnbroker had finally given in and offered him one-third of what he was demanding, 100 *ryō*. Tokuzō was told in no uncertain terms that he wouldn't get any more out of them — he must like it or lump it. Tokuzō finally yielded and accepted their offer. In exchange for the money, they had made him sign a statement to the effect that he held no further grievances against the Yamashiroya in regard to his brother's death.

When Hanshichi had heard the story he nodded.

"Hmm, I see. Well, if everything's been safely settled, that's fine, isn't it? I mean, what happened was a great misfortune for both families."

"So I guess there's nothing we can do?" Rihei said, apparently not yet willing to give up.

"Forgive me for being intrusive, but does Okono sew?"

"Why, yes, she's very good at needlework. Since she doesn't have any other responsibilities, she spends all her time at her grandmother's house sewing."

Looking thoughtful, Hanshichi said, "Tell me, is her grandmother's house very large?"

"Not particularly. There are six rooms, I suppose, including the maid's. The old lady spends most of her time in a four-and-a-half mat room at the back of the house."

"I suppose Okono needs a well-lit room for doing needlework?"

"She has a six-mat room facing south that looks out onto the garden. It's very sunny, and that's where she always works."

"Is there an entrance to the garden from the pawnbroker's shop?"

"There's a small gate through which one can enter the garden from the Yamashiroya, yes."

"I see," Hanshichi said, unable to suppress a smile. "Now, this

room of Okono's in her grandmother's house — I don't suppose
the shoji there had to be mended recently?"

"Well, now . . ." Rihei thought for a moment. "I don't know
much about what goes on at the old lady's house, but now that
you mention it, earlier this month one of the shop assistants said
that a cat had torn the shoji and he was going over to repair it.
But whether that was in Miss Okono's room or not, I couldn't
say. . . . Hey, Otokichi!"

Rihei called out to the shop assistant who was walking four or
five yards ahead of them.

"Otokichi, was it you who went over to the master's mother's
house to patch the shoji the other day?"

"Yes," the boy replied. "In the six-mat room where Miss Okono
works. She said the cat had been up to no good — one of the pan-
els three or four rows from the bottom had been torn."

"Do you remember exactly what day it was?" Hanshichi asked.

"Yes, I do. It was the day of the Dolls' Festival."

Again Hanshichi smiled to himself. The three of them fell silent as they continued walking.

They soon reached the temple in Fukagawa, where it was obvious that the funeral was going to be an exceedingly simple affair.
Hanshichi found it reprehensible to do things in such a slapdash
manner, given that Tokuzō had received three *ryō* from Rihei
expressly for the purpose. Before the funeral procession reached
the temple, two or three of the local men came out to meet them
and assist Tokuzō. One of the men recognized Hanshichi and
greeted him politely.

"Oh, Inspector! I didn't expect to find you honoring us with
your presence. I'm afraid it must have been rough going on these
roads."

His name was Densuke. A small man of thirty-two or -three,
he lived in Asakusa. Ostensibly, his trade was peddling cut-leaf
tobacco, which he hauled around to the servants' quarters in
the great samurai mansions and to all the temples in Edo. But
Hanshichi knew that his trade was just for show — in reality

he was a good-for-nothing, two-bit gambler. He undoubtedly felt guilty about this facade of respectability, for when he saw Hanshichi he bowed especially low and greeted him with exaggerated affability. "What bad luck running into this fellow," Hanshichi thought to himself. Outwardly, however, he maintained an air of civility. Densuke brought him a cup of tea and asked him quietly, "Are you a friend of the family, sir?"

"Not exactly. I'd never met Tokuzō before today, but I knew his younger brother from the Yamashiroya — that's why I've come to the funeral. It's very sad . . . he was so young, wasn't he?"

"Yes, indeed," Densuke replied, but his expression suggested that something was bothering him.

"From the way he's put you to work here, I'd guess you must be pretty chummy with Tokuzō."

"Yeah. I like to drop by his place now and then," Densuke replied vaguely.

By the time the funeral was over and Hanshichi was getting ready to leave the temple, the spring day was drawing to a close. On their way out, each of the mourners received the usual gift of sweets. Hanshichi could not be bothered to take his home, so he gave it to the shop assistant from the Yamashiroya. Then he whispered to Rihei, who was standing beside him: "Excuse me, Rihei. I'd like a word with you. Would you send Otokichi on ahead and come with me for a moment?"

"Yes, of course."

As Hanshichi had requested, Rihei sent the shop assistant back to the Yamashiroya and obediently followed the detective into an eel restaurant across from the Tomioka Hachiman Shrine. Hanshichi's face was familiar there, and the two were courteously ushered to a private room at the back of the restaurant. Neither Hanshichi nor Rihei was a heavy drinker, but nonetheless, they decided to start things off with a small drink. After exchanging two or three toasts of saké, Hanshichi sent away the waitress who was filling their cups. Then, in a low voice, he came to the point.

"You're lucky to have settled that matter of Tokujirō's death so discreetly for 100 *ryō*."

"You think so?"

"You have Tokuzō's promise in writing not to bring any more complaints in future, and once the body is cremated tonight he won't be able to cause trouble. In a way, I think you've pulled off a real feat. Make sure you tell your master I said so. Now — excuse me for being pushy, but you really ought to install someone at the old lady's house to keep an eye open and make sure nothing untoward happens to the girl."

"What do you think might . . . ?" Rihei asked, furrowing his brow. "You think Miss Okono is somehow mixed up in this after all?"

"So it seems," Hanshichi said gravely. "But there's nothing left for me to investigate. After all, I can't very well take the girl aside and interrogate her, now can I?"

There was much that was still unclear about the case to Hanshichi. But so far, his appraisal of the facts was as follows.

It was a mystery how Tokujirō, on his deathbed, had at long last found the ability to speak, but nonetheless, his claim of Okono's responsibility had the ring of truth to it. No doubt the relationship between the beautiful but lonely twenty-six-year-old spinster and the shop assistant with his theatrical good looks had gone beyond that of mistress and servant. Hanshichi surmised that an innocent prank had gone awry and touched off the events leading to his horrible, tragic death. Given that the room where Okono sewed faced onto a garden providing access to the shop by way of a gate, it was not hard to imagine that Tokujirō had often secretly paid her visits. The master's eighty-one-year-old mother was hard of hearing and the maid never lifted a finger, so no one would have gotten wind of their little secret. Then the fateful night of the Dolls' Festival had arrived.

That day, Okono had been in her six-mat room sewing (as usual) when Tokujirō had come to see her (again, as usual), taking advantage of a lull at the shop — or perhaps he had left pretending he was going out on an errand. He had tiptoed into the garden, crept up to the veranda, and then, probably, coughed as a signal to let her know he was there. Although the shoji were tightly shut, he could tell that she was seated inside. Teasingly, she had not answered him. So, clambering onto the veranda, he had used his tongue to poke a small hole in a panel of the paper screen, intending to peek into the room — a common, childish prank: after all, Tokujirō was just sixteen, though he looked older than his age. On the inside, Okono, seeing his little bit of mischief and feeling mischievous herself, took her needle and pricked Tokujirō's tongue. Of course, she'd only meant to prick it gently, but in the excitement of the moment, the needle went in deeper than expected. There was surprise on both sides of the screen, but Tokujirō stifled any cry in case he should give away their secret rendezvous.

Yet it was only a pinprick — painful as it might be for a little while, neither the wounded Tokujirō nor Okono had any idea what a terrible turn it would take. They applied medicine to the tongue to stop the bleeding and thought the matter finished. Unfortunately, the needle must have carried some unknown but virulent poison; after his return to the shop, the pain in the tip of Tokujirō's tongue was suddenly exacerbated, eventually leading to the beautiful youth's tragic demise.

This was the conclusion that Hanshichi had reached, based upon the knowledge imparted to him by the doctor, Gen'an, and supplemented by his own guesswork. It was probably not the case that Tokujirō's suffering had rendered him entirely unable to speak — rather, he had purposely kept quiet in order to protect his and Okono's secret. Once he returned home, however, and it dawned on him that the end was near, he probably divulged the secret under repeated questioning by his brother and his sister-in-law. His statement that Okono had killed him was, so far as he knew, an honest confession.

Hanshichi's theory was corroborated by the fact that the shoji in Okono's room had been mended. The position of the damaged panel — three or four rows above the floor — was precisely the height at which Tokujirō would have held his head as he knelt on the veranda. The next day, Okono had ordered the screen mended, claiming that a cat had done it. A cat indeed — yes, a big cat named Tokujirō! It would not have taken much imagination for the twenty-eight-year-old Okono to think of enlarging the hole made by Tokujirō's tongue in order to pin the responsibility on a cat.

What all this boiled down to was that Tokujirō's brother had not been wrong to come bursting into the Yamashiroya seeking compensation. Of course, Tokujirō had been a mere servant, and his death simply an accident resulting from a foolish prank. Thus Hanshichi knew that, even if the matter had become public, the young mistress of the Yamashiroya would not have been severely punished. But it would probably have led to her secret liaison with Tokujirō coming to light, which, added to the other rumors already circulating about her, would have left her reputation irreparably tarnished. It was not impossible that the Yamashiroya's business would suffer as well. Out of common decency, it was only right that the Yamashiros should make restitution to the deceased's family. Such was Hanshichi's opinion.

Rihei listened, riveted, to Hanshichi's explanation. When the detective had finished, Rihei gave a deep sigh and said: "I'm much obliged to you, Inspector. Listening to your story has given me a sudden realization. . . ."

[4]

"What is it?" Hanshichi asked, noting the gloomy expression on Rihei's face. Now it was his turn to listen.

"It happened this past winter. The master's mother was sick in bed with a cold for about a fortnight. They needed help in looking after her, so they asked us to send over someone from the shop. I sent Otokichi, but the next day they sent him back, saying he was too lazy. This time I sent Tokujirō, and Miss Okono was so pleased with him that he stayed there until the old lady had recovered. After that, whenever they needed any help over at the other house, they asked for Tokujirō. I didn't think anything of it at the time. But it seems that Miss Okono gave him some extra pocket money for the servants' holiday at New Year's. Then, at the beginning of the second month, the maid, Okuma, came to me in a fright, saying that several nights in a row she'd heard the rain shutters rattling on the side of the house facing the garden. We were concerned about it in the shop, but when I asked Miss Okono she flatly denied hearing anything: Okuma must have been dreaming, she said. Well, that set my mind at rest, but looking back on it now and putting two and two together, I see that your appraisal of the situation must be absolutely correct. It's really embarrassing that this was going on right under our noses, but we were too caught up in our work to notice. Inspector, I suppose I ought to tell the master about this in the strictest confidence?"

"I think it would be best if he knew. After all, the matter might come up again in the future."

"You're absolutely right. Thank you again for all your help."

Rihei tried to pay the bill but Hanshichi wouldn't let him. He led the way outside, where a warm mist hung in the night air after a spring shower. The very small amount of saké Hanshichi had drunk had left him feeling extremely sleepy, and though he no longer had any desire to go to the festival in Asakusa, he felt duty-bound to put in an appearance. Deciding that late though it was he would just go for a quick look, he wished Rihei goodnight and headed off.

He dropped in at an acquaintance's house in Asakusa's Namikichō neighborhood, then at another on the main thoroughfare.[6] At both stops, his hosts plied him with festival saké. Before

---

6. Hirokōji (now called Kaminarimon Avenue), the main street running past Kaminarimon, the large crimson gateway leading to Sensō Temple. Namikichō was directly opposite Kaminarimon.

long Hanshichi, never known for holding his liquor, was dead drunk, and had to have a palanquin called to take him home. He arrived back at his house in Kanda sometime after ten o'clock, collapsed into bed immediately, and slept like a log until morning.

When he opened his eyes again it was eight o'clock, and the morning sun was peeking cheerfully through the window. Squinting in the bright light, he rubbed his eyes and reached out for the smoking box that he kept by his pillow, pulling it toward him. He was puffing on his pipe when Zenpachi, one of his deputies, came bursting in as though making a dawn raid.

"Boss! Have you heard? Er, well . . . from the look of things I guess you haven't. There was a murder in Honjo last night."

"Where in Honjo? Don't tell me it was at Lord Kira's mansion."[7]

"This is no time for jokes. It was a fishmonger in Aioichō."

"Fishmonger . . . you don't mean Tokuzō?"

"Wow! How did you know that?" Zenpachi exclaimed, wide-eyed with astonishment. "Did you dream it?"

"Yeah. I went to the festival in Asakusa last night and prayed, so the god of the shrine came and told me in a dream. Do they know who the murderer is yet? What happened to Tokuzō's wife?"

"She's safe. Last night, after they returned from the brother's funeral and went to bed, someone broke in and tried to make off with all the condolence gifts. Tokuzō woke up and attempted to nab the thief, but the guy grabbed a fish knife from the shop, stabbed him in the forehead and the chest, and made off. The neighbors came when they heard the wife's screams, but it was too late. The murderer got away, Tokuzō is dead, and the whole neighborhood's in an uproar — I thought I'd better get over here and tell you right away."

---

7. A reference to the predawn attack made by forty-seven *rōnin* on Kira Yoshinaka in 1703 as revenge for the death of their former lord, Asano Naganori — the basis for the kabuki play *A Treasury of Loyal Retainers*.

"I see. I suppose someone's already inspected the crime scene? Do they have any idea who the assailant was?"

"Not yet, it seems," Zenpachi replied. "The wife's sobbing like a madwoman, too distraught for them to get anything out of."

"I'm sure she's had a lot of practice at sobbing — she's a former prostitute after all," Hanshichi said sarcastically. "Incidentally, Zenpa, get over to Torigoe and find out what Densuke, that tobacco peddler, is up to."

"Is he under investigation for some reason?"

"Just go and casually check him out. But don't let him see you."

"Got it. I'll be right back."

"I'm counting on you."

When Zenpachi had gone, Hanshichi left for Honjo. The neighborhood was in commotion. Outside the fish shop, a large crowd had gathered and people were peering inside, disbelief written on their faces. It was only yesterday that the neighbors had buried the younger brother; now the older one's corpse was lying stretched out inside. Hanshichi pushed his way through the melee and entered the shop. Otome had been called out to the watchpost and had not returned yet. He recognized a number of the neighbors from the funeral and started asking questions, hoping to glean some clues from them about Tokuzō's death. But they were all too flabbergasted to make any real sense of the situation.

The first person to get wind of the disturbance had been the *tabi* maker who lived next door. Startled awake by the sound of someone banging around inside the fishmonger's house, he had rushed outside in his nightclothes. When he opened the front door of the fish shop, Tokuzō's wife was shouting "Thief! Thief!" Alarmed, the *tabi* maker had joined in, shouting "Thief! Thief!" out in the street. The clamor brought neighbors running from all directions, but the bandit, having murdered Tokuzō, had already escaped out the back door. Since the fishmonger was not the sort of man to have enemies, the *tabi* maker told Hanshichi, he supposed that the burglar had only been after the condolence money but that things had gotten out of hand when Tokuzō confronted him. The others present more or less concurred with this view.

Hanshichi sat himself down at the entrance to the shop and waited, but still Otome did not return. While he was waiting, he took the opportunity to have a good look around him. The shop had been closed since the previous day, so the sinks were completely dry. Tokuzō's buckets were neatly piled in a corner. He noticed several large conches and clamshells lying scattered on the floor behind the buckets. Surprised at their size, he went over and picked up one or two of them; they were indeed just empty shells. But when he grabbed the tip of the biggest conch and tried to lift it, he found it was extremely heavy. Rolling it over on its side, he peered into it and saw that a paper packet was stuffed inside. He quickly pulled it out and inspected it — it contained 100 *ryō* in gold coins. Moreover, on the outside of the paper there was a bloody fingerprint.

Checking to see that no one was watching, Hanshichi stealthily slipped the coins into the breast of his kimono. He was looking around for any further discoveries when Densuke came strolling in through the front door, carrying his bundles of tobacco as though in the midst of making his rounds. Looking first at Hanshichi, then into the house, he hesitated for a moment, then said to Hanshichi: "Morning! Good to see you at the funeral yesterday. More trouble here today?"

"Yeah. Big trouble. Tokuzō was killed last night."

"Huh?" Densuke stood frozen, his mouth gaping.

"Oh, by the way, I wanted to ask you something. Would you step out back with me for a moment?"

Densuke followed Hanshichi obediently down the alley at the side of the house and around to the well at the back.

"WELL," OLD HANSHICHI said to me, "by now I suppose you've already figured out what had happened. Densuke and Otome had been lovers since her days in the Yoshiwara, but when her contract expired, he didn't have the resources to take her in himself, so together they agreed to install her at Tokuzō's place instead. Densuke was a regular visitor to the fish shop and the two of them skillfully arranged their trysts so that neither husband nor neighbors were any the wiser. The strange thing was that Otome proved to be incredibly industrious for a former prostitute and worked so hard that no one would have suspected that she led a double life. She was much too good for that ne'er-do-well Densuke. And she wasn't just putting on an act to fool people either; she really didn't have a vain bone in her body. She scrimped and saved, but it turned out that she didn't give her lover Densuke a penny. In other words, she was a born miser!"

"Do you mean that blackmailing the Yamashiroya was all her idea?"

"Of course. She put her husband up to demanding 300 *ryō*, and when Tokuzō caved in and returned with only a hundred, she heaped abuse on him; but there was nothing she could do about it. In the end, she had to grin and bear it and go ahead with Tokujirō's funeral."

"So her intention was to kill her husband, take the 100 *ryō*, and marry Densuke, eh?"

"That's what one would be inclined to think," Hanshichi smiled. "I thought so too, at first, but the confession I managed to extract from Densuke told a slightly different story. Densuke and Otome certainly were carrying on an affair, but as I said, she never gave him any money. Quite the contrary — she'd come up with any number of pretexts to wheedle the odd bit of loose change out of him. That's just the way she was, and Tokuzō's murder had nothing to do with Densuke — it was all Otome's doing."

"I see. I must say I'm surprised."

"I was surprised, too. As to why Otome killed her husband, it was simply because she wanted the 100 *ryō*. Most people think that what belongs to a man belongs to his wife — that it's not a question of ownership. But that's what made Otome differ-

ent; she wanted that money all for herself. Even so, at first she
didn't simply decide to murder Tokuzō. Her plan was to wait
until she was sure her husband was asleep, steal the money, hide
it under the floor in the kitchen, and make it look like a burglar
had broken in. But Tokuzō caught her. Even then, if she'd simply
apologized, that would probably have been the end of it. But for
some reason, she just didn't want to let go of the money she was
clutching in her hand. Suddenly, in a kind of daze, she reached
for a carving knife and stabbed her husband twice. No — she was
a nasty bit of work, that Otome. You wouldn't want to run across
a woman like her."

"But did she make a full confession?"

"I questioned her as soon as she got back from the watchpost.
Of course, she feigned ignorance at first. Then I shoved the bundle of gold coins in her face, and her composure crumbled. If
it had been a burglar, I asked her, why hadn't he made off with
the money? Why had he gone and hidden it inside the conch?
On top of that, the bloody fingerprint was a perfect match, so
she was trapped. According to her confession, when her struggle
with her husband roused the *tabi* maker, she looked around for
somewhere to stash the money, and hurriedly stuffed it into one
of the shells lying on the floor. That's when her luck ran out.
Later, she admitted that even after killing Tokuzō she still had
no intention of marrying Densuke. She planned to take the gold,
plus about six or seven *ryō* she'd saved up, return to her home-
town of Nagoya, and set herself up as a moneylender, leaving her
lover Densuke behind in Edo. He'd have resented being jilted,
but he'd also probably consider himself lucky to have escaped
with his life. Given the magnitude of Otome's offense, it goes
without saying that she was paraded through the streets before
being crucified at Senju."

This resolved the question of the fishmonger's murder, but something still troubled me about the case of the Yamashiros' daughter. Given that the 100 *ryō* in gold coin had been the cause of such
a horrendous crime, there would certainly have been an investi-

gation into the source of that money. So hadn't the Yamashiroya's secret come to light after all? When I pressed old Hanshichi for an explanation, he replied: "Yes, in fact the Yamashiroya was most unfortunate. After all the pains they'd taken to hush up the whole affair, the furor caused by Tokuzō's murder brought everything out into the open. Of course, Okono had to be interrogated, and it turned out that the death of Tokujirō had happened exactly as I'd surmised. Fortunately, she escaped punishment, but her marriage prospects became so remote that her parents finally stopped looking for a husband for her and instead tried to persuade Rihei to marry her himself and take over the business. He refused a number of times before his master came to me for help. He took Rihei and me out to a restaurant, where he again begged the clerk to accept their offer. I put my word in too, and between the two of us we somehow won Rihei's consent. Surprisingly, Okono also agreed to the idea. The wedding went off without a hitch, and the couple seemed extremely happy. Mr. Yamashiro breathed a big sigh of relief, and even I was secretly pleased. Then, a year later, Okono died."

"Of illness?" I shot back.

"No. I think it happened around the sixth month. . . . One night, she stole out of the house and threw herself into Shinobazu Pond. It was rumored that they never recovered her body, but I know for a fact that it was found floating among the lotuses and brought back to the Yamashiroya. You would think that if she'd wanted to die, she would have killed herself before getting married. But who knows why she did it? Anyway, the word on the street was, 'What Benten giveth, Benten taketh away.' Later, it was said that someone had seen Okono's ghost hovering over Shinobazu Pond on the night of one of the goddess's prayer days,[8] but whether that was true or not, I can't say."

---

8. *Ennichi,* a day (of which there are two or three each month) sacred to a particular deity.

The Mountain Party

YAMA IWAI NO YO

[1]

Hakone was an entirely different place in those days."

Old Hanshichi opened a small volume from the 1830s entitled *The Traveler's Illustrated Pocket Treasure* and showed it to me.

"Here, take a look—nothing but thatched houses in these pictures of Yumoto and Miyanoshita, is there? That gives you an idea of how much things have changed. In those days, going to take the waters at Hakone was a big deal—a once-in-a-lifetime event. No matter how rich you were, it was a difficult journey. You'd usually set out from Shinagawa in the morning and spend the first night in Hodogaya or Totsuka. The next day you continued on, stopping for the night in Odawara, but it could take three days to get there if you were traveling with people who walked slowly, like women or old folks. Leaving Odawara, you started the ascent to Hakone. Even getting to Yumoto, the real start of the climb, wasn't easy.

"The second time I went to Hakone was in the fifth month of 1862. I was accompanied by a young deputy named Takichi. We set off from Edo the day after I'd taken down the irises with which we'd decorated the eaves for the annual Boys' Festival on the fifth. Our first night on the road, we made the usual stop in Totsuka, then the following day we arrived at the post town of Odawara. The long summer days made the trip easier, but I wilted in the heat—under the lunar calendar, the weather was already quite hot by the fifth month.[1]

---

1. Mid-June by current reckoning.

"Anyway, I wasn't going to Hakone to soak in a hot spring or anything like that. My boss's wife had been suffering from nerves since giving birth the previous month, and she'd gone to Yumoto to recuperate. Somehow I got stuck with the job of going to check on how she was doing. So as soon as there was a lull in my work, I set off on the journey, armed with the miserly travel allowance I was given. Even so, once we were out on the road I felt a sense of release, and walked happily along beside my young traveling companion. On the evening of the second day, we crossed the Sakawa River and, as I've already said, reached the castle town of Odawara, where we halted at an inn called the Matsuya and rested our weary legs. That night, a rather strange thing happened. . . ."

IN THOSE DAYS, the post towns of Odawara and Mishima were by far the most prosperous of all the fifty-three stages along the Tōkaidō. The government checkpoint at Hakone was located between these two towns, and it was customary for travelers from the east to spend the night in Odawara, and those from the west in Mishima, before starting along the thirty-kilometer road through the mountains the next day. The result was that those who had left from Odawara stayed overnight in Mishima, while those who had set off from Mishima put up in Odawara. In this way, everyone traveling by foot along the Tōkaidō had to pay for food and lodging in both these towns, whether they liked it or not. Although Hanshichi was not traveling as far as the checkpoint, he had decided to stay the night at Odawara before continuing on to the spa in Yumoto where his boss's wife was staying.

The two men had walked at a leisurely pace, stopping here and there along the way, so it was already nearly seven in the evening when they reached the Matsuya. As soon as they'd had their baths, a maid arrived in their room carrying dinner trays. Hanshichi himself was not much of a drinker, but Takichi had seen to it that a flask of saké was included with their meals, and

Hanshichi joined his companion in downing two or three cups. Soon his face was bright red, and by the time the maid returned to remove the trays, he was sprawled out on the floor.

"Hey, boss. You look beat," Takichi said, waving one of the Matsuya's red fans around his knees to keep away the mosquitoes.

"Yeah. All those detours we made along the way wore me out. I'm exhausted. I don't have the energy I had when I climbed Ōyama[2] the year before last!" He laughed and stretched out on the floor.

"By the way, boss — on my way to the bath just now I ran into someone rather suspicious."

"Who?"

"I don't know his name, but he's a shady-looking character," said Takichi. "Somehow I think I've seen him before, but I can't remember where. Anyhow, when he saw me in the hallway, he quickly looked away and kept on walking, so I'm sure he recognized me. We should be on our guard with someone like him staying here," he added in an ominous whisper.

"C'mon now — that doesn't make him a thief," Hanshichi laughed. "If he's some two-bit gambler he probably hasn't come here to cause trouble. In fact, these playboys are usually very well-behaved."

Finding his audience unreceptive, Takichi fell silent. At about ten o'clock, they had the maid come in and lay out their futons, and the two men turned in for the night, their pillows lined up side by side in the six-mat room. In the middle of the night, Hanshichi suddenly opened his eyes.

"Hey, Takichi. Wake up! Wake up!"

After Hanshichi had called his name two or three times, Takichi finally sat up and rubbed his eyes sleepily.

"Boss. What is it?"

---

2. A mountain in present-day Kanagawa Prefecture that attracted many pilgrims during the Edo period.

"There's some sort of commotion going on downstairs. Maybe it's a fire or a burglar. Get up and take a look."

Still in his nightclothes, Takichi crawled out from under the mosquito netting and headed downstairs. A few minutes later he came back in a fever of excitement.

"Boss! It's worse than we thought — there's been a murder!"

Hanshichi sat up in bed. Takichi promptly informed him that two merchants from Sumpu[3] had been murdered in their beds and their money belts stolen. One of them had had his throat cut while he slept. His companion had apparently awoken as the murderer was trying to pull the dead man's money belt out from under his futon, and he'd been cut down in his turn. His body was found half out of bed with a diagonal slash across the nape of his neck.

"The local officials are here and they've already examined the crime scene. They seem to think it was an inside job, so they'll probably be coming up here to question us pretty soon," Takichi said.

"What a nasty business," Hanshichi said, shaking his head. "Well, we'd better not leave our room until they come. Let's just stay put."

"Right."

The two men sat on their beds and waited. Soon they heard hurried footsteps approach along the corridor and stop in front of their room. Abruptly, the door was flung open and a man came in. They heard him calling through the mosquito netting: "Takichi! Hey, Takichi. You gotta help me!"

"Who is it?" Takichi responded, peering out. In the dim light cast by the oil lamp, he made out the man he had seen in the corridor earlier, a swarthy, well-built fellow of about twenty-eight or -nine. His heavy breathing suggested that he was very agitated.

"It's Shichizō, from Komori's place — I'm sorry I pretended not

---

3. The domain of the ruling Tokugawa clan (present-day Shizuoka Prefecture).

to recognize you earlier," he said, "but I thought there might still be some bad feelings on your part. Please, I need your help!"

Hearing the man's name, Takichi finally remembered: Shichizō, a mid-level retainer in service to a samurai named Komori in Shitaya, was an unsavory character. He seemed to spend all his time gambling with other retainers from the big houses of Edo. Toward the end of the previous year, Takichi had encountered him walking around outside in the cold with next to nothing on, having wagered everything he owned, and lost. Takichi had taken pity on him and loaned him a few pieces of silver. Shichizō, overjoyed, had sworn he would repay the money without fail by New Year's Eve. Since then until this day, Takichi had seen neither hide nor hair of him.

"No kidding? Shichizō from Komori's place, eh? You ungrateful wretch!"

"But I'm apologizing, aren't I? Takichi, I'm begging you to help me, please!"

"You can beg all you want. No way! Forget it!"

Finding Takichi's rebuff a bit harsh, Hanshichi broke in.

"There now, don't be so coldhearted, Takichi. Shichizō here has come asking for help." Then he added to Shichizō, "I'm from Kanda, by the way — Hanshichi's the name."

"Oh, pleased to meet you." Shichizō bowed politely. "Inspector, please, won't you help me?"

"What can I do for you?"

"My master says he's going to kill me and then take his own life."

"What?"

The announcement took even Hanshichi by surprise. It wasn't every day that a samurai decided to execute one of his own retainers before committing seppuku himself. He wondered what the reason could be. Takichi, too, was taken aback. Sitting up on his futon, he said to Shichizō: "Well, come in here under the net. Now, tell me what this is all about."

[2]

Shichizō's master was a twenty-year-old samurai named Komori Ichinosuke. At the beginning of the previous month, he
had traveled to Sumpu on official business. Last night, on his
way back to Edo, he had spent the night in Mishima at the government-designated inn there. Always the profligate, Shichizō
had gone out, telling his master he wanted to take in some of the
local sights, and had started looking around for a brothel, when
he was approached by a man of about thirty-five or -six, well-
dressed and with the appearance of a merchant. He carried a
sedge hat in his hand and had a pair of bundles slung across his
shoulders. Spotting Shichizō — whom he immediately identified
as the retainer of a samurai — in the street, he called out to him.

In a most ingratiating tone, he inquired of Shichizō whether
he happened to know of a good inn in the town. It was not long
before he had invited Shichizō to join him for a drink. Man of
the world that he was, Shichizō quickly guessed the real meaning behind the words and immediately agreed to accompany
the man to a nearby restaurant. His new friend ordered saké for
them, and Shichizō gulped it down like a fish, with no qualms
whatsoever. Soon he was good and drunk, whereupon the traveler leaned over toward him and whispered: "By the way, friend.
I have a favor to ask you. Would you permit me to accompany
you and your lord on your journey tomorrow?"

It turned out that the man did not have the necessary papers to
pass through the Hakone checkpoint. He was one of those travelers who roamed the streets of Odawara and Mishima, waiting for
some retainer to happen along whom he could bribe into helping
him slip through the checkpoint. Of course, the passport of a
samurai such as Ichinosuke had to stipulate the number of men
in his entourage, but if the retainer — in this case Shichizō — told
the checkpoint guards that he had needed to hire a porter along
the way to help carry extra luggage, the guards would generally

allow them to pass through unquestioned. In particular, they rarely made any trouble for those traveling on official government business. Knowing all this, the man asked Shichizō if he might join the latter's retinue the following day.

From the very beginning, Shichizō had guessed that this was what the man wanted. He accepted three coppers from him, then quickly drank up and left, telling the man to be at their lodgings by six o'clock the following morning. This sort of practice was considered one of the perquisites of being a retainer, and all but the strictest of masters tended to overlook it. Shichizō's master, Ichinosuke, being very young, was especially inclined not to interfere in his retainers' business.

The next morning, the man appeared at the inn as promised and presented himself to Ichinosuke:

"My name is Kisaburō. Pleased to make your lordship's acquaintance."

Then, purely as a matter of form, he picked up a bundle of something or other and fell into step behind Ichinosuke and Shichizō. When it came to travel, he appeared to be an old hand, for as they made their ascent to the Hakone Pass, he helped them forget their fatigue by prattling on about various adventures he had had on the road. Even Ichinosuke had to admit that he was an amusing fellow.

They passed through the barrier without incident. As they reached Odawara, Kisaburō asked that he be allowed to stay the night with them. The men had stopped at a rest area by the side of the road just outside of town, and Kisaburō left them and hurried on ahead. He returned a short while later saying that two daimyo retinues were already staying at the primary government-designated inn, and a third party was booked into the secondary one. Anyway, he told them, an ordinary hostel would be quieter and nicer than crowded places like those, and offered to take them to one that he knew called the Matsuya.

It was true that they were on official business, but it was constraining to have to stay at the government inns. One couldn't send for women to come and provide entertainment. One couldn't drink and raise hell. Having crossed the mountains, they were now technically in Edo, but for Shichizō that didn't mean they must cram themselves into some stuffy old government inn rather than staying at a nice, clean hostel where they could stretch their legs and enjoy a good cup of saké. With such enticements, Shichizō was able to persuade his reluctant master, Ichinosuke, to agree to stay at the inn Kisaburō had recommended. Together, the three went and checked into the Matsuya.

"Excuse my impertinence, but I would like to throw a 'mountain party' for you tonight," Kisaburō said.

In those days, it was customary for travelers to celebrate their safe passage through the mountains by holding a party upon reaching their inn. In principle, Ichinosuke, as the lord, was expected to tip his men 300 coppers each and stand them drinks as well. Ichinosuke took out the money and handed both men's shares to Shichizō, who took it and shoved it into the breast of his kimono. He then turned to Kisaburō and ordered him to buy the saké for their mountain party. Kisaburō readily agreed.

Ichinosuke, showing his true samurai spirit, protested, saying that even if Kisaburō *was* a member of his retinue in name only, he could not allow him to pay for their drinks. But Shichizō overrode Ichinosuke's objections, assuring him that he would take care of everything; for Shichizō knew that he couldn't very well let out all the stops if he was drinking at his master's expense, so his plan was to get Kisaburō to foot the bill. Kisaburō cheerfully accepted this responsibility, arranging for a great quantity of food and drink to be brought to their suite.

"Well, here's to a successful journey," Ichinosuke said.

"Hear, hear!" the two men responded, bowing their heads.

Ichinosuke was persuaded to drink a small amount of saké. Predictably, Shichizō drank like a fish. At an opportune moment, Kisaburō took the now drunk and senseless Shichizō in his arms and helped him from the room. Ichinosuke retired to the six-mat room in back, while the two other men shared a four-and-a-half-mat room next door. In the middle of the night, Kisaburō sneaked upstairs, killed the two merchants from Sumpu, and made off.

"So he was a bandit, then?" Ichinosuke had said, startled.

But no one was more stunned than Shichizō. He paled as he realized that he had allowed himself to be seduced by money and drink into bringing this scoundrel into their midst.

As already noted, it was commonplace in those days to pass a stranger off as a traveling companion in order to help him through the Hakone checkpoint. Even so, if it came to an official inquiry, the matter would be treated very seriously. When one got right down to it, it was tantamount to smuggling. Although nothing usually came of such incidents, this case was different because of what had transpired at the Matsuya. There was no question of hiding what Shichizō had done; but it was Ichinosuke, of course, who would be held to account. Not only had the men stayed at an ordinary hostel while on official business rather than going to one of the government-designated inns, but the murders at the Matsuya were essentially their fault. Should Ichinosuke be accused of conduct outrageous in a samurai, he would have no choice but to plead guilty.

That was why the youthful Ichinosuke had resolved to kill Shichizō, the instigator of the misconduct, then slit his own belly. Shichizo's drunken stupor from the previous evening having worn off, he was now scared out of his wits.

"Please, let's not be hasty, milord. Patience—that's the thing!"

While he was desperately trying to calm his master down, Shichizō recalled having passed Takichi in the corridor the previous night. If he could get Takichi to capture Kisaburō, there might still be some hope of saving himself. He rushed straightaway to the room where Hanshichi and Takichi were staying.

When they had heard Shichizō's story, Hanshichi and Takichi looked at one another.

"My, your master's resolve is admirable!" exclaimed Hanshichi. "I suppose he really has no other option. How about doing the proper thing and resigning yourself to your fate?"

"Don't say that! Please, I'm begging you to help me! Here, look!" Facing Hanshichi, Shichizō placed his hands together in prayer. Deep down, Shichizō's villainy was not as unshakable as it might seem. At that moment, his face had the ashen hue of death.

"If your life is that dear to you, I suppose I've no choice," said Hanshichi. "You'd better clear out of here quickly."

"You mean it's okay if I cut and run?"

"I can figure out a way to save your master without you around. Go on — get going. Here's something for the road."

Hanshichi reached under his futon for his purse. He took out half a ryō and tossed it to Shichizō, telling him not to return to his room but to waste no time in making himself scarce. Clutching the money, Shichizō hurried out.

Hanshichi changed into his kimono and headed downstairs, intending to visit Ichinosuke's room. At the bottom of the stairs he encountered the maid pacing to and fro.

"Hey. Have those officials left?"

"No," the maid whispered, trembling. "Everyone is still in the proprietor's office."

"I see. I understand there's a samurai staying here with a couple of his men. Which room is theirs?"

"Er, well . . ." the maid hesitated.

Judging from her reaction, Hanshichi guessed what had happened: Ichinosuke had attracted the local officials' attention, but they were proceeding with caution because he was a samurai. The maid had some inkling of what was going on and was reluctant to show Hanshichi where Ichinosuke was. But Hanshichi was in a hurry and pressed her for an answer.

"C'mon, tell me quickly. Which room is it?"

The maid gave in and pointed the way to the samurai's room. "Go straight along the veranda here," she said, "then turn left and you'll see the entrance to the bath. Pass it and go all the way till you get to a small courtyard. Beyond it, there's a suite of two rooms. That's it."

"All right, thanks."

Hanshichi headed along the veranda as he had been told, and was soon standing at the entrance to Ichinosuke's room.

"Excuse me, anyone there?" he called from his side of the shoji.

Receiving no reply, he carefully slid the screen open a fraction and peeked inside. Two of the four straps that held up the mosquito netting were broken and half of it had fallen to the floor. Beneath it, a man lay covered in blood.

"I'm too late — he's already committed seppuku!"

Casting reserve aside, Hanshichi flung open the shoji and entered the room. The light of an oil lamp, which had been pushed toward the wall, fell on the folds of the mosquito netting. Beneath those folds lay the body of Shichizō. It appeared that the retainer had not fled quickly enough and had suffered by his master's sword. But what had become of Ichinosuke himself? The samurai was nowhere to be seen. Had he made off after dispensing Shichizō's punishment? For a moment, Hanshichi stood undecided about what to do.

Just then, his keen ears detected the sound of someone outside on the veranda. Whipping round, he peered into the darkness beyond the shoji. The maid who had directed him to the room was kneeling there, watching. Without hesitation, he rushed out of the room and grabbed her by the arm, dragging her back inside. She was about twenty years old and had a round face and fair skin.

"All right, so what're you doing here? You'd better tell me the truth, for your own sake. You knew one of the guests who was staying in this room, didn't you? All the other maids have scurried off and hidden somewhere, but you've been lurking here for a reason, right? Do you know this man?" Hanshichi pointed to Shichizō's body.

Shrinking away, the maid shook her head.

"Well, did you know the man he was with?"

Another denial. Terrified, she kept her gaze fixed on the floor, but Hanshichi noticed that she occasionally cast nervous glances in the direction of the closet next to the alcove in the corner of the room. In those days, rooms in hostels of that type normally had nothing in the way of closets, but this one appeared to be special: in addition to the ornamental alcove, there was a closet about six feet wide.

Glancing at it out of the corner of his eye. Hanshichi nodded knowingly to himself.

[3]

"All right, miss, out with it. Of the three men staying in this room, you were mixed up with one of them. You'd better come clean, or I'll turn you over to those officials. If that happens, you won't be the only one inconvenienced, I imagine. On the other hand, if you confess, I'll see to it that no one else gets into trouble. Haven't you figured it out yet? I'm an inspector from Edo, and I just happened to be staying here tonight. I'll see that no harm comes to you, so tell me everything."

The young woman was all the more intimidated when she learned Hanshichi's identity, but by threatening and cajoling her some more, he finally got her to confess. Her name was Oseki and she had come to work at the hostel the year before. The previous evening, when the three men had held their "mountain party," Oseki had waited on them and poured their drinks. Shichizō and Kisaburō paled into insignificance in comparison to their master — so handsome and dignified was the young samurai that the maid found herself unable to take her eyes off him. The other two men noticed what was happening and began teasing her. If she wished, they whispered, they would be happy to arrange a tryst between her and their master.

This went beyond a mere joke when Oseki, showing Shichizō the way to the restroom, discreetly asked him in the corridor to arrange a rendezvous for her with Ichinosuke. The intoxicated Shichizō had breezily agreed to make the arrangements: "Not to worry, I'll put in a good word for you. As soon as everyone's gone to bed and the house is quiet, sneak into his room." Oseki had taken Shichizō at his word. In the middle of the night, she had crept out of bed and gone to the door of the samurai's suite, but once there she had hesitated. Her hand poised on the door, she was suddenly overcome by shyness. She decided that first she had better wake up her go-between and confirm things with him, so she went to the next room and pushed open the shoji. Shichizō was lying passed out on his futon with one leg sticking out from under the mosquito netting, snoring away like a hippopotamus. The futon that had been laid out for Kisaburō next to his was empty.

No matter how hard she shook him, Shichizō would not wake up. Oseki was at a loss. At that point, Kisaburō, returning from somewhere or other, slipped back into the room. He gave a start when he saw Oseki and stood staring at her for a while. Feeling even more uncomfortable, she mumbled something about having come to fill the oil lamp and hurriedly left the room.

Even then, Oseki did not want to give up on Ichinosuke, and she lingered surreptitiously on the veranda instead of returning to her room. It sounded to her as though Shichizō had woken up. She could hear the two men exchanging whispers. After a few moments, the shoji opened quietly and someone emerged, but Oseki fled back to her room in a panic without getting a good look at the person. It was about half an hour later that the man whose job it really was to fill the oil lamps had discovered the double murder in the back room on the second floor.

Afraid of getting involved, Oseki had kept her mouth shut when questioned by the local officials. But upon reflecting on what had happened, she realized that Kisaburō must have been returning from committing the murders when she'd run into him in Shichizō's room. Then, after the two men had talked things over, it would have been Kisaburō who left again, probably escaping over the fence in the garden. Of course, Oseki herself was not mixed up in the murder. It was merely anxiety at having been in the wrong place at the wrong time, plus her concern for Ichinosuke's safety, that had caused her to loiter outside the samurai's room while Hanshichi was inside it.

"Is that so? Now I understand," said Hanshichi, nodding as Oseki finished her story. "Now, what's become of that samurai?"

"He was here a moment ago . . ."

"Don't hide anything. Is he in there?" Hanshichi motioned toward the closet with his chin.

He had spoken softly, but the person hiding inside the closet must have understood his meaning immediately. Before Oseki could get out an answer, the closet door slid open and the young samurai, looking extremely pale, poked his head out. He was holding a sword in one hand.

"I am Komori Ichinosuke. I put my retainer to death and was about to slit my own belly when I heard footsteps outside. Thinking it would be shameful to be captured, I decided to hide in the closet for the time being. Unfortunately, you've discovered me. Please be kind enough to allow me to kill myself in peace."

As he readied his sword, Hanshichi hurriedly reached out and grabbed him by the elbow.

"Just a moment . . . let's not be hasty, now. How is it that Shichizō came to be here in your room?"

"Having resolved to take my life, I went to the bath to purify my flesh. When I returned, I found the scoundrel with his hand underneath my bed in the process of stealing my money belt. I promptly cut him down with my sword."

Sure enough, Shichizō's hand was gripping a money belt. Hanshichi lifted him up into a sitting position. He was still breathing. Hanshichi took out a restorative that he always kept with him and placed it in Shichizō's mouth. Ordering Oseki to bring some cold water, he made Shichizō drink. As a result of these attentions, Shichizō temporarily regained consciousness.

"C'mon, pull yourself together," Hanshichi said, putting his mouth next to Shichizō's ear. "So, you rascal — you thought you'd pull a fast one on us too, eh? How much did that Kisaburō give you?"

"Nothing," Shichizō replied faintly.

"Liar! Kisaburō cut you a share of his loot in exchange for helping him get away. This maid here is a witness. How about it? Do you still deny it?"

Shichizō made no reply and his head slumped onto his chest.

"WELL, THAT'S THE END of the story," old Hanshichi said. "Shichizō wasn't in cahoots with Kisaburō from the beginning, but thanks to Oseki, he had woken up just as Kisaburō was returning from finishing his business. Kisaburō knew he had been caught in a compromising situation and gave Shichizō fifteen *ryō* to keep his mouth shut and let him go. Shichizō had meant to keep quiet about it, but then things took an unexpected turn and Ichinosuke announced his intention to kill Shichizō and commit seppuku. That gave Shichizō a nasty shock and he came running to us. He'd have been okay if he'd had the sense to leave right away, but instead he went back to his room to collect his things. Then, his master not being around, he suddenly got itchy fingers again and thought he might as well take the opportunity to help himself to his master's money belt — that's when his luck ran out. You know what happened next. I managed to resuscitate him briefly, but his wounds were very severe. He died at dawn the next morning."

"And what happened to his master?" I asked.

"I had an idea for making it look as though everything had been Shichizō's fault. He'd been a scoundrel through and through, so I didn't feel bad about it. In short, I fabricated a story about how Ichinosuke had engaged Kisaburō temporarily as a porter believing he was Shichizō's relative. Well, that seemed to lay the matter to rest. Even so, at any other time, Ichinosuke would have received a stern reprimand from the authorities. But this was toward the end of the Tokugawa era, and the government in Edo was going out of its way to look after direct vassals of the shogun like Ichinosuke. So all the blame ended up on the hapless Shichizō's shoulders, and Ichinosuke got off scot-free."

"But didn't you manage to track down Kisaburō?" I asked.

"Ah, as a matter of fact, by a strange twist of fate, he fell right into my hands. After we'd settled everything in Odawara, Takichi and I continued on to Hakone. While we were there, Takichi came and told me about a suspicious character staying at the hot-spring inn next to ours. Well, I did some poking around and found that the fellow in question had a sprained left foot. To be on the safe side, I sent for the Odawara innkeeper and got him to take a peek at the man. He confirmed that it was the same person who had stayed at his hostel that night, so I raced in and arrested him on the spot. It turned out that Kisaburō had fallen and twisted his ankle as he was climbing over the fence to escape. He hadn't been able to get very far in that condition, so he'd decided to lie low in Yumoto, hoping that soaking in the hot springs would cure the sprain. It was far from being a brilliant achievement on my part — just dumb luck, really.

"After we returned to Edo, I had a visit from that young samurai. He came by to thank me for my help, and was thrilled to hear my story about capturing Kisaburō. Incidentally, later I heard that during the Meiji Restoration Komori Ichinosuke was killed in battle up near Shirakawa[4] in Ōshū. Still, I suppose that living a few extra years and dying an honorable death like that was far better than plunging a cold sword into his belly at a cheap hostel in Odawara."

---

4. A city in present-day Fukushima Prefecture that was once a strategic point between northern Japan and the Kanto region.

Ian MacDonald received a Ph.D. in Japanese literature from Stanford University, where he minored in Japanese art history. He spent five years living in Japan and has worked as a freelance translator for ten years. He has also taught translation theory and served as a curatorial assistant in Asian Art at Stanford. MacDonald has translated stories by Mishima Yukio, Kurahashi Yumiko, and Izumi Kyōka, among others, and was awarded first prize in the Shizuoka International Translation Competition in 1997. He is currently working on a second translation of stories set in the Edo period by Kitahara Aiko for the Japanese Literature Publishing Project.

Production Notes for MacDonald | THE CURIOUS CASEBOOK OF INSPECTOR HANSHICHI
Cover and Interior designs by April Leidig-Higgins
Text in Minion and display type in Champion and Tai Chi
Printing and binding by The Maple-Vail Book Manufacturing Group
Printed on 55# Sebago Antique, 360 ppi

COVER ART
Utagawa Hiroshige I, Japanese, 1797–1858
Publisher: Uoya Eikichi, Japanese
Fukawaga Susaki and Jūmantsubo (Fukagawa Susaki Jūmantsubo), from
    the series "One Hundred Famous Views of Edo" *(Meisho Edo hyakkei)*
Japanese, Edo period, 1857 (Ansei 4), intercalary 5th month
Woodblock print (nishiki-e); ink and color on paper
Vertical ōban; 34.8 × 24.5 cm (13 11/16 × 9 5/8 in.)
Museum of Fine Arts, Boston
William S. and John T. Spaulding Collection
21 9508